ISBN-13: 978-1-335-21279-5

The Witch King

Inkyard Press
22 Adelaide St. West, 40th Floor
Toronto, Ontario M5H 4E3, Canada
www.InkyardPress.com

Printed in Italy by Grafica Veneta

For every trans kid scared to embrace their magic.
A new world is waiting. We need you in it.

A NOTE FROM THE AUTHOR

DEAR READER,

My debut novel, THE WITCH KING, is not the first book I ever wrote. For years before sitting down with this story, I fretted away at other manuscripts. I'd always known I wanted to be a writer. It was obvious, from a very young age, tromping through southern swamplands and talking to the creatures my imagination concocted, I only ever half-existed in this world. The rest of me was elsewhere, in places of my own creation, and writing allowed me to craft a doorway through which others could join me.

The problem was fear. I was terrified. See, the stories I wrote before this were not bad. They were interesting and heartfelt and each one made me a little better at what I do. But they were not honest. I wanted so desperately to share my inner world with other people, but I didn't believe I could show the truth of it. For as far back as I can remember, there have been parts of me I've been made to feel ashamed of. And I truly believed, if I put all of those parts onto paper, no one would ever want to read about them. How could I expect *you*, Reader, to embrace the pieces of me I was struggling to come to terms with myself?

THE WITCH KING is what happened when I finally confronted that fear head-on. Wyatt Croft is the closest thing to a piece of my own heart I've ever written. Into him, I poured so much of myself. All the parts of me I'd been taught to hide, I handed him. His transness, his gayness, his trauma and anger—all of them he inherited from me. And as such, he also inherited my shame. But as I finally allowed myself to deal with these things on paper, coming to terms with them in the real world became easier and easier. If I could love Wyatt, if I could recognize he was just a boy doing his best to handle impossible situations, if I could accept he was flawed but no less deserving of a happy ending, I could extend myself the same compassion.

And in that way, this book became about embracing ourselves for precisely who we are. Wyatt's struggles as a witch mirror many of the struggles queer people, especially trans people, face in the real world. He deals with losing those who are supposed to love him and the guilt of that loss. He's treated like a pariah by a regime that does not want to understand him. And he feels as if his future is not his own, being forced to simply play a role he knows he doesn't actually belong in.

Unfortunately, because of the exploration of trauma I finally allowed myself to write, there is content in these pages that has the potential to trigger you. Specifically, I would like to issue warnings for: violence, child abuse, childhood sexual harassment and assault, allusions to pedophilia, suicidal ideation and mentions of suicide, misgendering, drug use, and mentions of infertility and miscarriage. I want you to go into this book prepared for what you may find.

But I also want to be clear that this is not a queer pain narrative. It is a story about queer hope. Because Wyatt is also capable of incredible humor in the face of terror. He's powerful in ways he doesn't even realize yet. He's wanted. And he is so loved. For every person he's lost because of who he is, there is someone who truly loves the most authentic version of him. This, too, mirrors the experiences of our community. We are not defined only by the worst things that happen to us.

Writing this book was a healing experience for me. And I'll admit, I'm still a little afraid. It is a vulnerable act to take a piece of my heart and hand it off to a stranger. But I'm also hopeful. I'm hopeful this story will land in the hands of those who need it most. Hopeful Wyatt's journey will resonate with you, and maybe offer you a bit of the same healing it gave me.

Now, come on. Let's step through the doorway together.

—H.E. EDGMON

CHAPTER ONE

DEATH, REVERSED

I open the back door to let the dogs out, and Nadua's got her gardening shears buried like a knife in one of my fiancé's wings.

Today turning out to be a shitshow isn't a huge surprise. Every morning, I pull a card from my tarot deck to get an idea of what the day stretched out in front of me might hold. It's the one piece of magic I let myself dabble in, the one reminder of my old life, besides the scars. This morning, I pulled Death, reversed.

Resistance to change. Refusal to let go. Bitterness. Transformation.

I'd known right then and there something unfortunate was about to go down, but I hadn't expected *him*.

Emyr North. Prince of the North American fae.

The first sight of him in years doesn't put me on my ass the way I always worried it might, though the feral animal of my heart threatens to claw its way out of my rib cage.

Down, boy.

He looks like he did three years ago, but also not. Every part of him is bigger than the lanky pubescent boy I remember. His body has stretched from boyhood to manhood, gangly limbs giving way to chiseled muscle and a frame that has to be a foot taller than my own. All the pieces might be bigger than they used to be, but it doesn't matter. I would know the pieces of him anywhere.

Massive brown wings—thin, veined, and leathery—stretch out on either side of him, tipped with golden claws. His horns have curled into two spirals of soft brown atop his forehead, glinting gold in the light of the afternoon Texas sun. His fangs, long and lethal, peek over his lower lip.

The last time I saw him, he was just a boy. Now he's a monster.

The fae are all monsters.

But so am I.

He's more put-together than I remember, too. No more dirt stains on his knees or leaves tangled in his hair from romping around in the woods. His nearly obsidian skin is flawless, the sides of his head shaved to expose the dramatic points of his ears but left long down the center of his skull.

He's dressed in a pink suit so dark it could be red, patterned with gold flowers, subtle enough that they almost blend into the pink fabric. A chain is hooked into his septum ring and stretches up to connect to a gold cuff on the tip of his ear, and an assortment of bejeweled rings decorate his long fingers, necklaces dangling around his neck. His lids are painted with black eyeliner and a shimmery golden powder.

The softness I remember from our youth has been carved away to reveal the regal warrior underneath. Even with blood spilling from the wound in his wing, he looks like he's the one in control.

One thing hasn't changed. The golden glow of his energy sweeps around him like a halo, framing the sharp angles of his face, draping down over his shoulders. A constant emanation of light, like he's some kind of wicked angel.

Of course he's beautiful. But he was beautiful the last time I saw him. It doesn't change anything.

I still don't want him here. I never wanted him to find me.

The dogs rush him, losing their ever-loving minds, barking like they do whenever a rabbit hangs out just past the fence line. He doesn't seem to notice them. Some of those mutts are near a hundred pounds, and he's got six of them banging up against his legs, but he doesn't sway an inch. Neither do Nadua's fingers around the shears.

There are three types of fae magic: Feeling, Influencing, and Healing. Emyr is a Healer, able to use his magic like medicine on wounds. Not just the kind that come from weapons, either. Healers have been known to transform barren fields to lush gardens. Some, the most powerful of their kind, can even raise the dead.

I don't know how powerful Emyr is these days, but a stab wound wouldn't be much for even the most mediocre of their kind. Still, it's gotta hurt.

Emyr's dark eyes find my face and I think, for the splittest of seconds, I see his confidence waver.

I am not beautiful. I might've been, the last time he saw me, but I'm not now. The person he's been looking for all this time doesn't exist anymore.

But whatever look I thought I saw is gone, replaced by a calm, guarded expression. And then he opens his mouth and says a name. It's not *my* name, though he's clearly addressing me. I don't have it in me to react to my deadname, 'cause the sound of his voice threatens to take a baseball bat to my knee-caps. It's deeper than I remember it, a rolling baritone, crisp on the consonants and honeyed on the vowels.

I would like to die.

He found me. Three years trying to escape where I came from, finding a new family, finding a new self, pushing my magic away and blending into the human world until I was practically a ghost, and somehow he still found me. I don't know why I ever thought I could be free of the fae. I don't know why I let myself get comfortable.

"Wyatt," Nadua drawls, voice raspy from thirty years of smoking and barking orders. "This a friend of yours?"

I guess there goes any plan I might've concocted about feigning ignorance.

That she seems relatively calm despite the presence of a be-horned creature of unknown origin in her backyard should probably concern me more than it does. She doesn't know anything about what I am. The only one in the world who does is her daughter, my best and only friend, Briar. Nadua should be freaking out more than this. But in the two years

THE WITCH KING 15

I've known her, I've never actually known Nadua to *freak out* about anything.

Still, if there were ever an appropriate time, this would be it.

"Uh." Oh, as it turns out, I can still speak. Kinda.

Emyr asks, "Wyatt?"

I'm not sure if he's looking for clarification on the name or asking me to tell her he is, in fact, my friend, but I can't seem to do either. I open my mouth a couple times. Close it just as many. Finally, I throw my hands up and what comes tumbling out of me is, "Briar and Sunny are making a huge mess in the kitchen."

Sunny is Nadua's husband, Briar's dad. As I passed the two of them on the way to let the dogs out, they were in the middle of carving up the deer carcass Sunny brought back in the bed of his pickup the night before. Playing with roadkill isn't unheard of in the Begay-Brown household, but Sunny and Briar never properly mop up the blood.

Nadua turns her head just enough to meet my stare and hold it, brown gaze splitting me open like the buck knife her husband is using right now on the dead animal inside. She has this way about her, this inexplicable *knowing* that makes me feel uncomfortably seen. It's been this way since she found me, fifteen and alone, hungry and anxious and hiding in the back of the San Antonio library just before close, hoping not to be discovered and thrown out before morning. She picked me up, draped her cardigan over my shoulders, and clucked her tongue, then took me home to Laredo like a stray collected from the side of the road. I've belonged to this family ever since.

Whatever she sees, she must come to some decision. She yanks the shears free from Emyr's wing and, with one last withering look, turns her back on him and stalks away. Her energy, deep red like the clay dirt she comes from, lingers near him until it can't any longer, until it snaps back to her spine like a rubber band. She pauses at my side, thick dark eyebrows tight over a tense expression.

I don't know what I expect her to say. But it is definitely not what she actually says, which is, "Take him behind the shed before Doli sees."

Doli, Briar's eight-year-old sister, was inside watching PBS in her grandmother's lap the last time I saw her. But, uh, yeah. No. Nadua might be uncomfortably calm, but Emyr would probably be nightmare fodder for that kid. She doesn't even trust Santa Claus. Sunny had to explain he wasn't real after Doli spent last holiday season wailing about not wanting some strange old apparently omnipotent man to break into her house.

Silence hangs between us. Emyr raises his hand to his still-bleeding wound and, with a pulse of golden light, it disappears. The fae can't actually fly—not anymore, anyway, though I've heard they could once, in Faery—so it's not like the injury would've hindered that. Still, it's probably best he doesn't keep bleeding all over the backyard.

Not once does he move his gaze from my face.

I wish I could read his mind. I've never been particularly good at understanding other people, though there was a time when reading Emyr was as easy as breathing for me. That time is long past.

It's a cool day for mid-May in this part of Texas, hovering

somewhere in the eighties, but the direct sunlight beating down makes it feel hotter. Or else it's the fault of the black hoodie I've got on. Or maybe I'm sweating for an entirely unrelated reason.

"You couldn't put a glamour on before you showed up?" I finally demand, flicking my wrist at him demonstratively. Seriously. Fae travel all the time, in and out of their hidden kingdoms. They usually put the wings away before they do.

He frowns, glancing down at himself as if only just now realizing what he looks like. "The glamour wore off...but I was so close to finding you, I didn't realize until it was too late."

The idea of him so wrapped up in a desperate attempt to get to me that he couldn't pay attention to anything else... definitely does not make me feel anything. Nope. Not at all.

Emyr shrugs one shoulder, nonchalant. "It doesn't matter. No one but the woman saw me. The Guard will send someone to deal with her memories."

The Guard are the officers in Asalin, the fae kingdom over which Emyr's parents rule.

"I think the fuck they won't," I snap back, flashing fang. "Keep your pigs away from here."

Emyr's gaze settles on my mouth. Witches' fangs are smaller than those of the fae. They're usually indiscernible from human canine teeth. But three years ago, in a gas station bathroom in the middle of nowhere Midwest, I took a nail file to mine. I carved them from useless accessories into weapons. I wonder if that's what he's looking at now.

The girl you used to love is dead, Emyr.

A shadow moves in my periphery, in the window of the house, and I remember Nadua's warning to hide. With a quiet growl, I shove my hands in the front pocket of my hoodie and stomp toward the shed. Emyr follows at a distance.

Most of the dogs have lost interest in him, all except Bella, a pit mix of questionable origin. She trots alongside us, fat brindle body swaying, tongue lolling around in the heat. When we finally settle behind the shed, I turn to face Emyr again. Bella sniffs his hand, and he cocks his head at her before turning his fingers over and offering her his upturned talons. Bella gives his palm a considerate lick before dropping down into the shade of the shed and closing her eyes at his feet.

Emyr looks at me again.

We're closer now than we were a moment ago. From this distance, I can actually smell him, musk and smoke and just a hint of something feminine, floral and sweet like candied rose petals. He smells like Asalin. Or maybe it's not that exactly. Maybe it's that he smells like home.

I'm not doing this right now.

His golden energy bobs in the air near mine, as if testing the limits. But the blackness that surrounds me, the ever-present darkness that clings to my skin, practically snaps its jaws at him. Emyr's energy slinks back around his shoulders, rejected.

Everyone has this energy—fae, witches, humans. The humans can't see it, but even they *feel* it sometimes. They call it different things than we do. Like an aura. And everyone's color is different.

I used to think Emyr was golden like the sun, and my blackness was like the shadow he cast. I still think that's true, but it holds a different meaning now.

"Wyatt?" Emyr asks again, quieter this time.

He's staring at me with a look I can't quite place. Some

hybrid creature bred from concern and confusion and something else, something I've never been able to name, something that sometimes crosses the faces of the fae when they look at their mates.

Mates. It's been a long time since I've considered myself anyone's mate. I used to wear the title with a bit of smug pride. One of the rare few witches ever to be mated to a fae, and certainly the first ever to belong to their *prince.* Always under the protection of the Throne. Un-fuck-with-able. Now I think the term reeks of some weird bio-essentialism I want nothing to do with.

That look, though. One part concern, one part confusion, one part something that makes my fingers clench.

I wonder what he's seeing as he looks at me. I mean, I know what he's seeing, technically. Like, I own a mirror. That growth spurt I kept hoping might hit one day never did; I still barely hit the five-two mark. I've put on a little weight since moving off the streets and into this house, because Sunny's cooking *and* fast food are too good to not eat too much of. I shaved my head last year and have kept it that way since. My black hoodie covers the scars and any hints at cleavage my binder doesn't properly squash down.

So, I know what he's seeing, yeah. But I wonder what he makes of it.

"Wyatt," I repeat, defiance jutting out my chin, practically daring him to say some shit I don't want to hear.

Instead, he asks, "Pronouns?"

The question takes me so off guard I almost think I must've heard him wrong.

It's been a year since I came out to my little surrogate family. They handled it better than I ever would have expected, but maybe that's because they knew it was coming. I'd spent almost the whole year before that watching way too many YouTube videos from trans guys vlogging their transitions, convincing myself I was just a really supportive ally. By the time I finally admitted to Briar I was trans, she just squeezed my hand and told me she was proud of me, in a tone completely lacking any surprise.

There are trans people in the fae world, technically. I'd heard of the concept before living around humans. But they aren't nearly as visible. And *me* being trans never would've been allowed in that world. Because as far as the fae are concerned, I've only ever had one purpose. From the moment Emyr met me, when we were just two naive children running aimlessly around Asalin's palace, my only value became what I could do for the Throne. Namely, produce heirs. That's the whole point of the bond—finding the person a fae is most *genetically compatible* with, to beget the most perfect children.

At least, that's the story they preach.

Growing up being viewed as nothing but a baby-making factory, I was told to be grateful for that much. Because they could've simply *done away with me*. To hide the shame of the prince being bound to a witch.

My being a man probably isn't what the fae had in mind as a show of gratitude.

"He, him," I answer, anyway, leveling Emyr with a skeptical look.

At his sides, his fists clench and unclench. The clawed tips of his wings flex, dipping down over his shoulders. After a moment, he asks, "And these people, who are they?"

"They're my family." I don't hesitate to supply the answer. It's the truth.

Though a pang of guilt does resonate deep in my gut. Because all I've ever wanted was to keep them safe. Especially Briar. And now what have I done? I've brought an inhuman danger right to their doorstep.

Or maybe there's another reason for the guilt. They aren't the first family I've ever had. And I know what happened to the first one, because of me.

I bite at the inside of my cheek until I taste blood. When the flash of iron hits my tongue, I spit a stream of red onto the ground at my feet.

"What do they know of our kind?"

"Nothing." A lie, at least in part. Briar knows everything.

I think he knows I'm lying. Sensing emotions, reading minds, that kind of power lies with the Feelers, and Emyr isn't one of them. But he stares at me for a long moment before huffing, nostrils flaring with agitation. He curls his fingers around his hips and shrugs his broad shoulders. "Fine. It doesn't matter. You're leaving here, tonight."

"Like hell I am," I snap back. "The Guard will have me killed. You know that."

"You will face the consequences of what you've done," Emyr agrees, and that doesn't instill any hope in me. "But I will not allow them to sentence you to death. I cannot imagine you ever intended to hurt anyone."

"What if I told you I did?" The question escapes me before I can stop it. I swallow back a lump in my throat, burning eyes meeting Emyr's. "What if I told you I meant everything I did that night?"

Again, the briefest look crosses his face before it's gone, his expression schooled into a mask of control. This time, beneath the surface, I see his horror.

"It doesn't matter," he finally says. "I need you. We will keep your magic under control, if need be."

A chill creeps up the back of my neck. What would that look like? Being kept *under control* by the fae?

"I know you got a shitty deal here, being stuck with me and all, but you're barking up the wrong tree. It'd be better for both of us if you pretended you never found me."

How *did* he find me, anyway?

"Unfortunately," Emyr drawls, "our biology has decreed you're the only tree I have to bark up."

Biology. I can feel a heat start to sizzle inside my veins, pumping through my bloodstream, threatening to spread to the palms of my hands. I squash it down, the way I always do.

Anyway, that's not entirely true. Bonded fae are *compelled* to be with their mates, or so I'm told, but they aren't forced. He could have anyone of his choosing, biological matchmaking be damned. All this time, I'd hoped that was exactly what he'd do.

Hoping for anything has never done me any good.

"The Throne needs us. Both of us. It can't wait any longer."

"Unfortunately," I retort, words sharp as my tongue flicks against my teeth, *"my* biology has decreed that the Throne can kiss my ass."

Emyr glares at me. His wings twitch again, and this time the sharp tips of his horns tighten as I watch with morbid fascination. "You have somehow become even worse with people than I remember you being, do you know that?"

I raise my brows in a *You don't say* kinda way, but don't bother with a retort.

The backyard falls silent again, except for Bella's snoring and the far-off sounds of the other dogs romping through the dirt. Emyr's fangs worry his lower lip. His hands twist in front of him, long claws scraping the backs of his palms. After a moment, he reaches up to tug at one of the earrings dangling by his throat. I consider asking him if my good looks have rendered him speechless, but instead I just keep watching him.

Finally, he asks, "Do you remember my cousin Derek?"

Derek. Unbidden, my stomach lurches. The back of my neck heats. Of course I remember Derek Pierce.

My truly good memories of Asalin are spotty. Most of them are vague flashes of woods and smoke and Emyr's fingers twisted in mine—childhood games of make-believe, stumbling over magic like shoes too big for my feet, and my heart lit up in a way it's since gone dark.

It was only as I got older and less naive that things started getting bad. I began seeing the fae for what they were and doubting the life that was planned for me. Emyr and I started fighting, the childhood friendship and blooming *something* between us warping as I began to question my place in his future. As I started to realize he saw me the way all the fae saw me. Not for who I was, but for what he could do with me.

The bad memories are the ones sitting at the forefront of my mind when I think of Asalin. But it would take a lot more than that to make me forget about Derek. My childhood infatuation with him was inappropriate for about a dozen reasons, starting with him being a good decade older than me and ending with the fact that I was betrothed to his cousin.

Still. I'm pretty sure the first time I saw him shirtless in the lake something in me woke up.

"Vaguely," I tell Emyr.

"He's become the head of the Guard. He's amassed a certain amount of power and influence for himself. And now, he's decided to make a bid for the Throne."

I blink. His tone is ominous, as if he believes he's just dropped some very worrying news on me. But I don't actually care.

"All right?"

Emyr visibly balks, eyes widening as if he was expecting a very different answer. Then he grumbles, shaking his head. "No. Not all right. Not all right at all. He wants to displace me and take the kingdom for himself. He's called my legitimacy as heir into question."

I raise one eyebrow. "Because you're adopted?"

The whole thing is scandalous, and always has been in fae circles. Kadri and Leonidas, Emyr's parents, are fated mates. Yet somehow, despite all claims that *biology* and *perfect reproduction* are what make a fated pair destined for one another, Kadri was never able to produce an heir for the royal line. Infertility among the fae isn't unheard of. But, just like transness and witch mates, it's rare.

Hearing about Derek's bid isn't what I expected, but it also doesn't surprise me that Emyr's claim is being called into question.

Emyr nods. "There's never been, as far back as we've studied, a situation like mine. Thrones are *always* passed down through the bloodline. He believes we're abandoning our ways. And he isn't the only one who thinks this way. He's got a whole gang of followers supporting him. There are protests, petitions being presented to the Court on his behalf—we're on the verge of civil war because of him." His tone roughens as Emyr whispers, "I barely know who I can trust anymore."

"Huh. That sucks."

His palm connects with his face, claws scraping from his forehead and down his cheeks, and he groans. "You are insufferable."

"I've been told. I imagine being married to me would really suck."

"Actually…" Emyr lowers his hand, shaking his head. "I disagree. Derek's lackeys have convinced the population you are gone from Asalin forever. He warns of a future in which I rule alone. Where the royal line ends with me, regardless."

"And?" I ask.

"And I intend to prove him wrong!" Emyr throws his hands up, exasperated. "I need you with me to present a united front to the dissenters. With you at my side, I'll be able to quell the nerves of some who are uncertain about the Throne's future."

"I don't think a wanted criminal is the ruler your people are looking for."

Emyr considers that, eyeing me, before he shrugs. "I promised I would protect you, didn't I? Besides, everyone loves an underdog. They'll see someone who came from nothing and rose to sit at the side of the king. It'll be inspirational."

"You want me as your show dog." And therein lies the problem. I've never been a whole person to the people trying to shape my future. I've always been a chess piece, a move to play to get where they intend to go.

Somehow, it stings a little extra coming from him. Maybe

some naive part of me—a secret, hidden part I would never admit to out loud—hoped he would understand. Hoped that when Emyr realized how desperately I didn't want to marry him, he would let me go.

I loved him once, and he loved me, too, in his own way. Apparently, neither matters anymore.

"No, I want you as my husband." He raises his eyebrows. "Some would say we have quite the love story."

Husband. The word yanks at my insides. I'm going to throw up.

"We do not have any kind of love story," I counter, but Emyr doesn't seem to hear me.

He's begun pacing, rubbing his fingers along one of his pendants. "And once we are expecting our first child—"

"Our first what exactly?"

"Child." Emyr pauses long enough to narrow his eyes at me before he starts pacing again. "We'll need to secure heirs for the Throne. Once we do that, Derek's bid for king will crumble. The only thing people love more than underdogs and love stories are royal babies."

This is why my resentment toward this engagement started growing in the first place. I'm expected to trade my life, my freedom, my *personhood*, for some political game I don't care anything about. I'm supposed to smile and wave and perch some sticky, crying child on my hip so Emyr can keep his precious Throne.

The idea makes me want to screech. Or set something on fire. Or both, maybe.

I'm seventeen years old. I just want to *live* for a while. Even in some alternate universe where I'm in love with Emyr, where I want to marry him, I'm not ready for a kid. He's out of his mind.

I suddenly hope Derek Pierce gets everything he wants.

"And how do you suppose we'll go about doing that? Securing these heirs?"

He rolls his eyes. Rolls his *fucking* eyes. I want to rip them out of their sockets. "Couples like us have children every day, I presume. We will figure it out."

"We are not a couple."

He crosses his arms. "We're engaged to be married. What would you consider us?"

I don't have an answer for that. "What about your parents? They're still king and queen, aren't they? Shouldn't this be their problem?"

The corners of his mouth tug down. Again, an unsettled expression whispers across his face. "Mother and Father need their rest. They should have stepped down already, but with Derek and his supporters making their intentions clear, they're worried what might happen if they do." His jaw tightens, his frown disappearing into a scowl. "This is why we have to get married now. Once we've established ourselves, they can retire and we can ascend to the Throne." He shrugs. "Besides, this is what we agreed on. You're seventeen now. By the laws of Faery, you're an adult. It's time for us to make good on our oath."

"We don't live in Faery! No one has lived in Faery since our ancestors crawled through the door to Earth in the 1500s! And *we* didn't agree to anything," I snap back. "These plans were made *for* us."

Emyr gives a small shake of his head, that stoic resignation returning to his features. "Be that as it may, they were made just the same."

Something heavy and unspoken settles over us as we stare at one another.

I don't have anything to combat what he's saying, not really. I need him to understand why this is as messed up as it is, but I think it might be a lost cause. He's convinced himself he needs me to keep the kingdom from going to war. What am I supposed to say that could persuade him otherwise?

Please don't make me marry you. I don't want to be king of the fae. All I was ever meant to be was nothing. Why can't you just let me be nothing?

Finally, after we've stared at one another long enough for the sun to move infinitesimally in the sky, Emyr sighs. "There is a flight leaving Laredo Airport tomorrow at four in the afternoon for Rochester. I expect you to meet me there no later than two."

"Please." The word feels acidic on my tongue. I hate begging like some kind of kicked dog. But I don't know what else to do here. "If you want to convince me this could actually work between us, I'm gonna need a little time. I can't just get on a plane tomorrow. Stay here. Let's talk about this some more."

I watch with a sort of guilty fascination as the sharp point of one fang presses into Emyr's plush lip. Finally, he shakes his head. "Time is not something we have."

So much for begging. "I could run again."

"And I would find you again." His wings flutter behind him. "Do you want to be a fugitive for the rest of your life?"

Does he expect me to believe he cares what I want?

"Fuck you," I say, because I don't know what else I can offer.

What happens next happens very quickly. So quickly I don't have time to process until it's over, so quickly I couldn't have stopped it even if I wanted to.

Emyr reaches for me. His fingers curl around my wrist, and his thumb claw presses gently into my skin. Not tight. Not enough to hurt. But that doesn't matter.

I don't like to be touched. I really don't like to be touched by the fae.

My magic, dusty from years of disuse, surges. Blackness, that same inky blackness that bobs around my body, slicks up my hands. Flames rise, unbidden, the tips of all ten of my fingers flicking to life like ten freshly struck matches. My free hand shoots out to shove at his chest, hard, and Emyr reels back, releasing me from his grip, his eyes shooting wide.

His own magic responds to the threat, gold painting across his hands and up to his elbows, his eyes glowing that same gold, horns twisting tighter on the top of his head.

But there is no threat. Not anymore. As quickly as it started, it disappears. The flames go out, leaving only smoke. My hands return to white.

In the aftermath, I can hardly think through the rush of adrenaline. Through the sound of my own too-frantic heartbeat.

Emyr's silk shirt is singed to hell and back. He's staring at me like he's afraid.

He should be, I think. He should be afraid of me. I'm a little afraid of me.

I never wanted to feel the fire again.

Emyr's body, too, returns to normal. He's still looking at me like he isn't sure what to do with me.

I want to take some pride in that. I want to make him afraid.

But I can't make myself feel anything but ugly.

"I will see you tomorrow, firestarter," is all he says before he slips away.

CHAPTER TWO

DON'T YOU WANT TO BE SOMETHING SPECIAL?

"What if I don't want to marry him?"

I'm fourteen years old and my resentment toward the fae has been growing for more than a year now. I don't know it yet, but it's only hours before the worst night of my life.

When I ask the question at the dinner table, everything goes silent. No more forks scraping against glass. No more persnickety sipping of blackberry wine, glasses held daintily between perfectly poised fingers.

My father shakes his head, looking down at his plate with exasperation. My mother stares at me, lips parted in surprise. The glare on my sister's too-familiar face is what rattles me most. I think, and not for the first time, Tessa would kill me if she had the chance.

"I'm just asking. Maybe it's not what I want for my future."

"Of course not. Because being queen of the fae is just too mundane for you," Tessa spits, batting one hank of dirty blond hair over her shoulder.

I bristle. I know if I acknowledge her, it's going to make this fight worse than it needs to be. But I'd like to smack the hateful look right off her face.

My mother sighs. *"Sweetheart, I know you must be anxious. A lot is going to change over the next few years. I can only imagine how that must feel."*

She reaches across the table to rest her warm, soft hand over top my own. I wish I could find some comfort in the touch. I wish it could make me feel anything other than trapped.

"But this is going to be such a good thing for you. The first witch to ever marry into a royal family? We're talking about making history."

I don't care about making history.

"Revolutionaries usually end up getting killed by the masses," I remind her. *"No one wants me to rule. Aren't you a little worried they'll revolt against a witch wearing their crown?"*

My mother sniffs. *"People will adjust."*

"But—"

"This conversation is pointless," my father interjects, tone firm. *"There is a contract in place. You will marry Emyr North or you will die."*

When my black energy sweeps out around me, it brushes up against the energies of my family. My father's biting ice blue. My mother's, the same shade as her favorite red lipstick. My sister's, a perfect mix of the two—a field of lavender.

My darkness and I don't belong here. We never have.

My mother snatches her hand back as if I've burned her. If I did, it was a happy accident.

"Contracts can be dissolved," I insist through clenched teeth. "You can ask the king and queen to talk to the Court, tell them—"

"We will tell them nothing." My father isn't even looking at me. "What's done is done."

"You should be so proud," my mother insists, shaking her head. "Most of your kind would be thrilled to take your place."

"Then let one of them," I snap back, fists clenching until my nails dig puncture wounds into my palms.

"For crying out loud," Tessa scoffs, rolling her eyes. "You're a witch. And you want to run away from the one thing that might make your life worth something? Are you seriously dumber than you look?"

I do not point out that we look eerily similar.

"Tessa. Please." My mother sighs at her before she turns her attention back to me. "When we were made aware of Emyr's bond, we were so excited for you. So proud. And we demanded the contract be put in place to protect you. To protect your future here. Don't you understand why?"

Of course I do, but I wonder if my mother does. I know it's because she's like a hellhound on a scent, catching the whiff of power from a hundred miles away. Why does she think she did it? Does she actually think she's the good guy here?

I shrug.

"When you were born, when we learned you were a witch, we were terrified of what your life might look like. We were so scared of who you would grow to be."

"Should've dumped you in the human world and left you for dead," Tessa interjects, and my mother silences her with a glare.

I've grown up hearing that line my entire life. How lucky I am that my parents chose to keep me, their broken little daughter, when *so many of the fae abandon their witchling offspring outside the gates of Asalin. To starve to death or be eaten by wild animals, whichever should come first.*

How lucky *I am that my mom and dad were willing to take on the burden of keeping me around.*

"Sweetheart, marrying the prince is the only thing that will save you from being like the rest of them. You don't want to be like the other witches, do you? Don't you want to be something special?"

As I look between their faces, I know I have my answer. Nothing I can say or do will sway them. My parents will never take my side, because they believe the way the rest of their kind believe. That the only value my life has is what I can do for the fae around me.

The terms of my engagement are clear, signed with Emyr's and my mingled blood when we were barely old enough to spell our own names. We will *be married. It's only a matter of when. One day, the contract will finally be called in. If I'm not there to meet him at the end of the aisle, he can trigger the clause that forces my own blood to wreak havoc on me. The magic in my system will eat away at my insides until there's nothing left, until I'm nothing more than an unanchored energy that can never move on, never find peace. The same would happen to him, if he were to break our pact.*

It sounds like a terrible way to go.

But so does putting on a white gown and a fake smile and living the rest of my life as a placeholder in someone else's fantasy. Being forced to produce heirs for the Throne. And what would they do to those children if they were born witches, like me? Would I be forced to keep having baby after baby until I gave them a fae? What if I never did? Would they ever let them rule? Or would the fae mob finally bubble over and do what they've wanted to do for a long time?

Dying because I broke the contract would suck. But there's a good chance I'm going to end up dead because of this engagement either way.

The memory eats at me as I make my way back inside. It comes to my mind often, the last conversation I ever had with my parents. The fire happened the next night.

I can't tell Emyr no unless I'm willing to die—or kill him, I guess. He has the ability to call in the blood contract whenever he wants, but so do I. We have the power to destroy each other, have since we were children. And it isn't like the idea has never crossed my mind. Triggering his clause instead of mine. After all, whether he'll say it out loud or not, that's the very thing he's holding over my head.

But even entertaining the passing thought makes me feel sick.

The Begay-Brown home is a little small, a little run-down. There are brown watermarks at odd intervals on the ceiling, and in a few places where the rot's gotten very bad they've nailed down pieces of wood to keep the elements out.

But there's something in the air here. The furniture, worn out and covered in dog fur, looks lived in, the living room the kind of place that's seen thousands of family movie nights. The walls are covered in political posters and family pictures, alongside tapestries and beadwork made by members of Nadua's and Sunny's Nations. There's a feeling of community, of *unity*, that I've never quite known how to put into words.

And even though the house could use a few repairs here and there, it's incredibly clean. Everything is organized, every odd and end has a place. After two years of living here, I've begun to see the patterns in the chaos.

I expect some added chaos when I walk in, but instead I'm greeted by things seeming far too normal.

Doli and her grandmother are still sitting on the couch watching a game show. Sunny's whistling a tune in the kitchen. He smiles at me when he catches me staring at him. He doesn't look at all like his wife just told him she stabbed a mythic creature in her backyard.

He's a mountain of a man, built like a bear. Well over six feet tall, easily more than three hundred pounds. He has warm eyes and the kind of smile that makes people smile back at him. His swirling energy reminds me of tangerines, bright and fresh. The prison tattoos covering his big body don't take anything away from how good it is just to be in his presence.

He's standing over a pot of something simmering on the stove and motions me forward with a big wave of his arm. "Wyatt! Come here, taste this!"

Stepping over, I blink down at what appears to be soup. It doesn't *look* great. Bits of hacked-up meat and mushy vegetables float in a brown broth decorated with leaves and spices. (I think there's a good chance the unidentified meat is from the deer carcass he and Briar were hacking up when I went outside.) But the *smell*. Holy shit, it smells so good I almost start to drool.

Sunny holds out a spoon to me and I take a bite. *Oh.* My eyes nearly roll back in my head. He seems to gather from my reaction that I'm enjoying it and he laughs, a big, barking sound that dances around the room.

"Go tell Briar and Nadua lunch's ready," he demands, swatting the soup ladle at me. "Think they're back in your room."

The bedroom at the back of the house that Briar and I share is tiny, and it feels even smaller because of all the *stuff.*

We swapped out her bed for bunk beds a while after I moved in and, officially, I'm supposed to sleep on the top bunk. Unofficially, we both sleep on the bottom, and the entire upper bed is covered in sketchpads, books, weird cool shit we found outside, and empty food containers we should've thrown away forever ago.

A little white table is shoved in the corner, every inch covered in beads and string and other crafting supplies. There are clothes everywhere, a folded pile at the foot of the bottom bunk, a wadded-up bundle under the nightstand, a collection of mismatched socks spread out by the little window. Unlike the rest of the house, there is no method to this madness, no secret organization. Or if there is, it's one only Briar understands.

Every inch of the walls are covered in posters, or pictures of the two of us, or more pieces of clothing hanging from anything they can hook themselves onto. The floor-length mirror is decorated with stickers reading things like There Is NO Planet B! and The Government Doesn't Care About You. Briar's denim jacket, smothered in pins and patches—BI FURIOUS with a double-headed battle ax is my favorite— hangs limply from the corner of the window frame. The trans and ace flags hang side by side on the ceiling.

I know they've been talking about me as soon as I walk in and the room goes uncomfortably quiet. Briar is sitting on the bottom bunk with her arms crossed over her ample chest while Nadua stands in front of her, a stern expression on her face.

After a beat, Nadua sighs. "Think about what I said." She brushes past me as she leaves the room, taking her red clay energy and a faint smell of smoke with her.

When she's gone, I ask, "What did she say?"

Briar stares up at me, lips parted.

I'm gay as all hell, but Briar is the most beautiful woman I've ever seen. Her skin is deep, warm brown, her curves generous. Her broad nose sits over a thin upper lip, and her white front teeth have a slight gap between them. There are flowers braided into her long black-and-teal hair today, purple coneflowers that match the T-shirt under her overalls.

Her energy is so bright I can feel it from across the room. Could practically feel it from the other side of the house. It's yellow like sunflowers and bumble bees and lemonade. Everything about her reminds me of spring. New life.

Fitting, since it's Briar who brought me back to life once. When Nadua brought me here, a shell of a person, hollowed out from the inside, Briar's the one who helped me relearn how to exist. I'm never going to be able to pay her back for that.

After a beat, she asks, "Was one of them really here? In the yard?"

I sigh, moving over to our bed and dropping down next to her. She wiggles out of the way until I can throw myself sidelong against the far wall, dragging a pillow underneath my head. "Not just one of them. Him. Emyr."

"Shit."

"I know."

We aren't supposed to tell humans about us. Like, the number one rule of magic club is that you don't talk about magic club, or whatever. Humans aren't supposed to be involved in our affairs unless *absolutely necessary*, and even then we're supposed to get permission from the Throne.

Personally, I think that's bullshit. I mean, I'm a wanted criminal, I guess, so it's not like I asked anyone for permission to tell Briar my life story. But even if my record was squeaky clean, even if I was just some random witch living in the human world, I don't see why I would have to play by the rules of the fae.

Technically, all fae and witches living in North America are under the rule of the king and queen of Asalin, Emyr's parents. There are other fae kingdoms around the world, and every fae and witch within each territory answers to their monarchs. And for the fae, sure. I get it. But what about the witches? Why should we have to answer to the rulers if we leave their kingdoms? After all, they've made it plenty clear we aren't their equals.

Witches are born to fae, but we *aren't* fae. We don't have their wings, or their horns. We don't access our magic the same way.

There are three types of fae, each with a different sort of magic at their disposal. Feelers can read things, like the emotions in the room or psychic visions of the future. Influencers can manipulate things, like the elements or even the thoughts in people's heads. And Healers...well, they heal.

Witches, on the other hand, can access whatever magic they want. The difference is that, while the fae's power comes naturally to them, witches require practice, and training, and the proper conduits. In order to be any good at what we do, we have to learn from each other. And without the ability to do that, really bad things can happen.

Like the fire.

No one is totally sure *why* witches are the way they are. No one could tell me why I was born to two powerful fae, with a perfect fae sister, and I came out like *this*.

It just happens sometimes. Rarely, maybe one in a hundred. And of those, probably only half actually make it to adulthood. That's my best guess, anyway. It's not like there's anyone doing studies on this shit.

I am one of the fae, officially. Their blood runs through my body. Their magic is mine, even if it's twisted and ugly and I don't want any part of it. But I'm *not* one of them. I am an entirely different creature, born into a world that's never known how to handle me or anyone like me.

"He expects me to go back to Asalin with him tomorrow."

Briar lies down so she can join me properly, the mattress dipping with her added weight as she curls up against my side and rests her head on my shoulder. Her skin smells like cocoa butter. "What are we going to do?"

Always *we* and never *you*. Briar has this thing where she's always adopting other people's problems as her own. Mine in particular.

I nose against her shoulder. "I love you," I tell her, because I do, and because sometimes I need to say it to remind myself I'm capable of feeling it in the first place.

She doesn't say it back, but she kisses my cheek and that's just as good.

After a moment, I sigh. "I don't think I have much of a choice."

"But...but what about the fire? Won't you get in trouble?"
I shrug. "He says he'll protect me."

I don't know if I believe him, but I guess that doesn't matter.

Briar worries her lower lip between her teeth, one hand resting against my chest, over the fabric of my hoodie. She tugs aimlessly at the drawstrings for a moment before finally sighing and asking, "Can't you just...ask him to let you go? I mean, he has to understand how bad it would be for you to go back to Asalin. Doesn't he care? You said you were best friends once."

We were. Best friends. More than best friends. Once.

My mother worked at the palace when I was young. She was an Influencer, and she specialized in making unique garments for fae high society, woven with spellwork to make them impenetrable to outside magic. I wasn't welcome at the school for fae children and my parents didn't want me socializing with other witches, so she kept me with her. I would toddle around underfoot and try to stay quiet.

And then, one day, Emyr saw me.

I don't know what it feels like when a fae lays eyes on their mate for the first time. I don't know how he knew what I was to him. But he knew. Suddenly, he wanted to be around me all the time. And I, having spent my life up to that moment feeling completely on my own, was just happy to feel like someone actually wanted me around. We were, for a time after, inseparable.

Most of my earliest memories feature Emyr front and center. The two of us running through the halls of the castle together, chasing the feral cats or wild chimera kittens who would sometimes wander in from outside. The two of us hiding behind boulders and hills to watch the pixie and goblin communities from a safe distance. The two of us in the woods building forts from sticks and brambles, coercing perytons to eat from the palms of our hands, making up stories about the human world beyond our home and what it would be like to live there. Playing make-believe as if we were the humans, just two human kids living human lives, away from Asalin and the Throne and all of the responsibilities waiting in our futures.

Certain nights stick out more than others. The first time Emyr's father, the king, took us flying on dragonback, the three of us thousands of feet aboveground and me feeling like I never wanted to come down. My sixth birthday, when Emyr and I found Boom, a sickly, pint-size hellhound puppy on the verge of death. We snuck him into the castle, and Emyr poured his Healing into him. He was our dog after that. We joked we were his parents.

My heart gives an uncomfortable twist, my throat tightening.

There are a lot of good memories, but there are a lot of bad, too. And whatever Emyr and I used to be to each other, we aren't anymore. He's made that perfectly clear, showing up here to drag me back to Asalin against my will.

"I tried," I finally answer Briar, blinking away whatever burning emotion might've bubbled up because of my childish nostalgia. "Apparently, that's not an option. He *needs* me."

"Needs?"

"His cousin Derek is vying for the Throne."

I don't know what I expect her to say to that, but it definitely is not what she actually says, which is, "Derek? What kind of name is *Derek* for a *fae*?"

I frown, looking at her bewildered expression. She isn't wrong. I've been in the human world long enough now to know that Derek is hardly the kind of name that inspires fear in the hearts of the masses.

"Fae started adopting human names after they got here from Faery. Makes it easier for them to travel in and out of Asalin, like when they need to travel to the other kingdoms. His parents probably just heard the name somewhere."

Honestly, I don't know how much the fae have changed since they dropped here from Faery. I don't know how much the human world has influenced them, how different things might have been if I'd been born in that world instead of this one.

Oh, right. See, fae are *not* of this world. They never have been. But five hundred years ago, their homeworld, Faery, was on the verge of collapse. Fae magic sucks its power from the natural world around it. Because of their magic, their world was dying, turning into a barren wasteland that could no longer sustain life. The Court convened and made the decision to flee.

The most important, most powerful, and wealthiest fae across Faery gathered together and opened a door to another plane, not knowing what would greet them on the other side. That door led them here, to Earth, to what the humans know now as Upstate New York.

Emyr's adopted ancestors built their kingdom there, swearing to watch over the door generation after generation. The other four monarchies spread around the globe, each building a hidden kingdom of their own in a separate corner of the world. Right under the noses of the oblivious humans.

"I mean, I guess." Briar frowns. "It's just, you know, you hear fae, you think names like…Twinklepumpkin."

I blink. "Twinklepumpkin?"

"You know, I knew as it came out of my mouth that it wasn't good, but I couldn't stop it."

She flushes and I chuckle, and then the room goes silent and heavy again. I curl one hand around her upper arm, stroking my fingers back and forth against her skin.

I remember what it felt like, standing outside, to wield that fire in my hand. The warmth. The surge of power. I hate how much I want to feel it again.

Finally, Briar announces, "Well, I guess we're just going to have to go to Asalin to sort this all out."

I blink at her.

Really, it's great that Briar wants us to be in this together, but that's taking it a step too far.

"You cannot go to Asalin."

"Why? It's not like I'll be missing anything here."

Briar's parents homeschool her, though their approach to learning is more about throwing their kids outside and letting them experience the world around them than it is curriculum-based. My mother never showed much of an interest in teaching me anything. It was only after I met Emyr that I started picking things up from him, sitting in on lessons with his tutors and absorbing a secondhand education that way. Briar and her family have mostly filled in the gaps for me in the years since, offering lessons on anything I've shown interest in from human history to how to use a laptop, but there are still plenty of things that don't make any sense.

It's a good thing I'm gay, so no one expects me to be good at math.

"It's against the rules."

"Oh, you're right." She rolls her eyes at me. "I forgot about your lifelong dedication to rule following."

I narrow my eyes and scoff. "Okay, fuck off. I just don't know how you plan on me sneaking you into Asalin. I'm not sure you'll fit in my duffel bag."

She gives a considering glance toward the closet where the bag is stashed, then shrugs. "We'll tell him that where you go, I go. And if he won't allow it, we tell him he can shove his contract up his ass. And...if he tries to call our bluff, then we go from there."

"And what about your parents? You know, the adults responsible for making sure their seventeen-year-old child doesn't get into trouble? Flying to New York to invade a fae kingdom seems like a great way to get into a lot of trouble."

She crinkles her nose at me again. "I'll talk to them."

"I'm sure that conversation's going to go swell."

She rolls her eyes at me, sits up, and punches me gently in the arm. "Shut up. My parents are *very* antiestablishment. I just have to explain to them that a great injustice is being done and I have to help stop it."

"I think you're overestimating your own charm."

"Oh, I think you're very wrong about that." Briar smiles, fluttering her eyelashes at me. "So, what time are we leaving?"

CHAPTER THREE

MONSTERS AREN'T SUPPOSED TO BE BEAUTIFUL

Apparently, Briar is very aware of exactly how charming she is. At two in the afternoon the next day, the two of us are strolling up to the main lobby of the Laredo airport, bags in tow. Though I wasn't privy to the conversation she had with her parents and grandmother, I'm told it went something along the lines of this.

"Everyone, I want you to know I'm going away for a while with Wyatt."

WHAT?

"As you know, his life before he came here was a bit of a

shitshow. Now, he's embroiled in some legal mess he's got to get himself out of."

GASP.

"He needs moral support while he works through this. I'll call and text every day and let you guys know if there's any way you can help. But I can't just sit back and watch my friend suffer alone."

TEARS. APPLAUSE.

Honestly, if she didn't hate everything about American politics so much, I'd suggest she run for president—assuming that's actually how the conversation went. There is a chance she's skirting the truth, so I don't feel bad for whatever lies she had to spin to convince her family to let her get on a plane.

Of course, even though Briar is here with me, that doesn't mean she's actually going to come to Asalin. We still have to talk Emyr into it.

When we get there, he's waiting for us, just inside the entrance. Well, waiting for me. The first thing I notice—his horns and wings are gone. He's got a glamour in place now.

Would have done you some good yesterday, before Nadua ripped a hole in you, huh?

But where did he get the glamour? He appears to be totally alone. And as glamours are Influencer magic, there's no way he could've done this as a Healer.

When he spots us moving toward him, he narrows his eyes. As soon as we're within earshot, he snaps, "Who is this?"

Briar doesn't give me a chance to respond. "My name is Briar. And I'm coming with him."

Emyr looks surprised that she addressed him directly. He

clears his throat, standing up straighter. "You absolutely are not. Asalin is no place for a little human."

"I'm hardly little, my guy."

He slides a shrewd gaze toward me. "This girl. She's yours?"

Mine? Like— Oh. Like, *mine.* I think he's asking if Briar's my girlfriend. And, like, no. She isn't. I mean, there was a time when *yeah*, kinda, but then I realized I was a huge homo, and anyway, we work better as friends, but— No.

And also, it isn't any of his business.

I don't answer the question. Instead, I say, "If she can't come, I'm not going. I might not be able to run forever, but I can definitely make this as inconvenient as possible for everyone involved."

Emyr glances around, gnashing his teeth. His gaze flicks across the dozens of humans moving this way and that, filing through the airport around us. Wondering if he could throw me over his shoulder and carry me past the TSA agents without causing an incident?

At length, he seems to come to a decision. "Fine. But I'm going to have a hell of a time explaining this to my parents."

That seems odd, coming from his mouth. Big and muscled and princely as he is, it's weird he's concerned with answering to anyone, even the king and queen.

He *looks* weird, too, without the wings and horns. And his *ears.* They're all rounded and short, perfectly human instead of pointy and fae-like. It reminds me of those baby dolls that look almost real, almost human, and that creeping feeling of discomfort they cause. An uncanny valley.

He isn't dressed like himself, either, the pink suit and excessive jewelry gone and replaced with a pair of gray track pants and a powder-blue T-shirt with a V-neck so deep I can almost spot his nipples. (That part, at least, reeking of over-the-top indulgence, seems on brand for him.) He has a single bag in one hand, a black leather backpack. The whole thing seems kind of *off*. He's smaller, maybe, in more ways than just how much space his body takes up.

But I guess the wings and horns are still there; we just can't see them. Because when he turns to get into line at the ticket counter and I step in behind him, I ram right up against them—invisible but as solid as ever.

In the few seconds between running into him and jerking away, my mind has just enough time to process a few things. His wings are as soft as I remember them being, like velvet to the touch even though they look like leather. And they're thin. I can feel the threads of bone underneath the supple skin—and, as I jerk back, a hint of the razor-sharp barbs that shoot out of them when we touch, a weaponized reflex to the unexpected brush of my body on his.

My heart thunders as I backpedal away and collide with Briar, who steadies me with a hand in the crook of my elbow. Close call. Any slower to pull away and I could have nicked myself on those things. The mental image of my skin flayed and my blood leaking all over the floor is enough to make my veins itch.

I guess Emyr would have just healed me. But *still*. Talk about an incident.

Emyr looks over his shoulder to blink down at me. Shit, he's tall. I mean, I'm short, I know I'm short, but he'd be tall compared to anyone.

"Are you all right?"

Even though nerves are shaking their way through my body and making my tongue feel like lead, I snap, "I'm fine."

He narrows his eyes and huffs, turning around.

Briar and I exchange a silent look.

She shakes her head to say, *This is going to be a disaster, isn't it?*

I roll my eyes. *Pick up on that, did you?*

The plane ride isn't so bad, really. Emyr gets us three first-class tickets on a nonstop flight, because of course he does. Our seats are side by side, technically, with Briar's in front of us. That goes about as well as he should have expected. I drag Briar down into the seat meant for him and glower until he sits alone in the row ahead. I spend the first half of the flight bouncing the soles of my boots against the back of his chair just to annoy him and the second half writing profanities on my jeans with a Sharpie and watching Briar sleep.

How she can take a freaking nap with all of this going on is beyond me. She questioned me for hours last night about what Asalin would be like, what she would see when we got there. She was delighted at any mention of the creatures there—creatures she would never get the chance to see outside of a fae village. She's excited about this whole thing, like we're going on a vacation. I sort of get why. She's endlessly optimistic everything's going to work out in the end.

I don't share that same positivity.

I catch Emyr's gaze on me, his head twisted over his shoulder to watch me—probably through an invisible wing—and raise my eyebrows. "What?"

"You're very beautiful."

Oh, we are absolutely not doing that. "Shut up."

He balks before he *growls* at me, the reverberating noise making my hair stand on end and my fingers flex. "Why would you say that?"

"I am not beautiful."

He opens his mouth as if to argue before stopping short. Frowning, he hesitates before he informs me in a clipped tone, "Beauty is not specific to women."

Ugh. I don't want to have this conversation. "I know that, loser."

And I *do* know that. I've known plenty of beautiful non-women in my lifetime. I'm sitting here talking to one of them right now.

Not that I'd tell Emyr as much. He doesn't need to get it in his head that just because I can't stop looking at the sharp angles of his face, his full mouth, those dark eyes framed by long lashes, the lean, tightly muscled length of his body...

Where was I going with this?

"Then *why* would you be offended by a compliment?" His irritation is growing more obvious. Good. Let him be irritated. Let it sink in properly that I am not the golden goose. I am more like an actual goose, hissing and honking and attacking small children who just want to give me bread.

Anyway, I want to tell him I'm not offended, that he doesn't have the power to offend me, but that isn't the truth. I stare into his eyes, my mind filing through the other possible responses.

Because I don't want to be beautiful. Because I don't want any sliver of my value to be defined by you or anyone else finding me nice to look at. Because I'm a monster, and monsters aren't supposed to be beautiful.

I'm saved from having this conversation by the light above us dinging on. A too-cheerful voice instructs us to prepare for landing.

Emyr sighs and turns back around. "I hope you're ready to go home, firestarter."

Yeah. Me, too.

A limousine with dark-tinted windows picks us up from the airport. A limo! Like we're headed to the worst prom ever! (Though I suspect most proms are pretty bad. I've never actually been to one, but it seems like a fair assumption based on what I know about both human high school and straight people.) The driver, a witch, flashes a wink and tiny fangs at me when he opens the door to the back seat. As soon as he starts to drive off, Emyr presses the button to close the partition.

"So," he begins, leaning back on his side of the bench, eyeing Briar in a way I don't appreciate. Which is just to say, I'd rather the fae not have their eyes on my best friend at all, ever. "You're human."

Her nose crinkles up. "Well, sure, mostly, last I checked. I mean, I haven't checked in a while, though, so it's possible things may have changed. I once went through a phase when I was five where I thought maybe I was a puppy. I would demand all my meals be from a bowl on the ground and I..."

She trails off, laughing softly as her cheeks turn plum colored. "You know, I thought that would be a funny story, but in hindsight, I think it just makes me look like a weirdo."

Emyr hums, neither confirming nor denying he thinks she's a weirdo. "How did you two meet?"

"My mother found him. She has a problem with turning

our place into a safe house for anyone who needs it. I mean, not that it was so much a problem when she brought home Wyatt. But it can be an issue. She just shows up with feral cats sometimes, you know? Oh, and once she found this backyard dog breeder on Facebook— Do you have Facebook?"

"Of course they don't have Facebook," I say at the exact same moment that Emyr says, "Yes."

I tilt my head, eyes narrowing as I consider him with skepticism. "That's new."

Emyr nods, his thighs parting wider so he can reach into the pocket of his sweats and fish out a cell phone. My tongue involuntarily flicks out at my lower lip. "It's been a pet project of my mother's and mine for the last few years, bringing more human advances to Asalin. Other kingdoms have been doing this for far longer, integrating bit by bit into the human world. And the more advanced they've become, the harder it's been for us to stay connected to them. This is my attempt at changing that."

Huh. Well, I don't know how things work for fae in other parts of the world, but Asalin *has* done a great job of hiding itself away and staying disconnected.

Maybe that's another reason on an already long, long list that I can't imagine being happily married to Emyr. Giving up the human world? Walking away from people like Briar and her family? Never going to Starbucks again? That sounds miserable.

But hey, at least I could still use Twitter.

He continues. "There's been some pushback from the more traditional sects. But we're making progress. My people do enjoy the Netflix."

Briar grins, almost as if in spite of herself.

I nudge her thigh with my knee, hard enough to get her attention. She turns her head toward me and offers an *Are you seeing this guy?* kind of smirk.

I narrow my eyes. *I hate you.*

It's not true, and she knows it. I could never hate her.

When she looks back at Emyr, her eyes widen until they're two black saucers with thin white rims. Her lips part, and she breathes a gasp so soft it's almost indiscernible.

My gaze shoots toward him.

Oh.

The glamour is wearing off.

Emyr's horns have begun to appear, color slowly bleeding from the top of his head to swirl up around them. The same thing is happening to his wings and claws. I can make out a hint of fang between his lips.

It's a strange sight to behold, the way his inhuman appendages come to light. It reminds me a little of the way our energy reacts when magic shoots through us, like someone's taking a paintbrush and swiping it over our bodies. I can't help but stare until every piece of him is visible once more.

My gaze returns to Briar. She's still wide-eyed and slack-jawed.

Emyr's brow furrows. He's watching her, too. "You aren't afraid?"

"A little," she admits quietly, finally pulling her gaze from his wings to look back into his face. "But not because of the way you look. Mostly because I'm pretty sure you're a shitty person. You are forcing my friend to be here, after all."

He shakes his head, audacious enough to actually try and

refute that. "I'm not forcing anyone to do anything. Fate determined where our paths would lead a long time ago."

"Do you really believe that?" she asks. "That your marriage is unavoidable? That this bond means you *have* to be together?"

Of course she knows the story. Briar knows everything.

"I do," Emyr answers quietly. When I look at him, I realize it's me he's staring at and not her. It's that same look I can't name—too fierce, too hungry, too wild. It makes my legs itch with the need to run.

"And you're okay with that?" Briar demands, leaning forward, her gaze intense. "You're fine with signing away your future for this?"

Emyr frowns. "Wyatt may not be what I would have chosen for myself—" *no fucking kidding* "—but this is the way things are. There will be no one else for me."

I don't believe that. I *refuse* to believe that. There is no way in hell that I am Emyr's perfect baby machine.

Briar eyes him like she's not so sure what to make of that, either.

Wanting to talk about anything but this, I ask, "So, how do you do it? The disappearing act there?"

"Hmm? Oh. It's this." Again, Emyr holds up his phone and flashes it toward us.

I frown, looking between him and the device. "I don't get it."

Emyr holds the phone out to me and, after a moment of hesitation, I take it. At first, I think it's just an iPhone. It looks close enough to one. But upon further inspection, I realize it isn't. It's close enough that no one would be able to tell

without holding it in their hand, but it's heavier. The casing
is made from something different than whatever most cell
phones are made from—it looks like gold, and I guess there's a
chance it is. Emyr doesn't have a wallpaper; instead, the touch
screen is plain black with a simple analog clock in the center.

"Still don't get it, dude."

"The phone carries magic."

When I glance up at him, he's grinning. The smile takes
me aback, throwing me off balance. He looks so damn happy.
He has dimples. The corners of his eyes crinkle.

For the briefest, most ridiculous moment I can see something in my mind's eye. Emyr's head turned up to look at the
sun, that perfect dimpled smile etched onto his mouth, our
hands entwined so I can feel his life pulsing in my palm—

I swallow and look back down at the screen. No. I'm not
doing that.

"What the hell are you talking about?"

"Another pet project. A witch friend of mine is working
on it with me. They have one phone, I have the other. The
phones were created using Influencer magic. They're sort of
like…vessels. But it's not all magic. There's some coding involved, too. We have phone numbers, so we can make calls
or send texts. But they can also send me spells."

"*Send you spells?*" That doesn't make any sense. Or maybe
I'm just having trouble keeping up.

Emyr holds out a hand for his phone and I set it in his palm,
careful not to let my skin brush his when I do. He punches in
his pin with his thumb and then shows me the screen again.
He's opened up an app I don't recognize. The coding is sim-
plistic, but I realize what he's talking about right away. There's

a list of spells going down the app, each with buttons next to them to Delete or Download.

"Well, shit." I've never seen anything like this before. It's beyond impressive. But I don't tell him that.

"Like I said, it's not perfect, but we're getting there. It's how I managed to find you actually. They worked up a tracking spell, using the blood from our contract and the GPS system built into the phone." He sounds proud, praising the nameless witch in a way fae are not known to do.

I'm not swayed.

"So, they just send you these spells through the app, and you can access them anywhere in the world?"

"Exactly." He grins again.

"So, you've found a way to keep the witches *literally* in your pocket instead of just figuratively."

Emyr's smile vanishes.

Briar pipes up for the first time during this demonstration. "So, riddle me this—you're more than happy to take things from the human world when it suits your needs. The good stuff. But what about the bad stuff?"

He eyes me with annoyance for a moment longer, before he finally drags his gaze to Briar. "What are you talking about?"

"There are people among you who could snap their fingers and give every city in the world clean water, right? You could save the planet from all the evils currently wrecking this place, but you're only looking out for yourselves. How do you stomach that?"

"Ah." Emyr looks at me, as if seeking help. I smirk at him and wave my hand in her direction. This is Briar.

"If we overextend our magic, it can have negative effects on the environment."

"Our environment is already a disaster. You sure your presence here doesn't have anything to do with that?"

He leans toward her, eyes narrowing. I lean in closer, too, trying to wedge myself between them. I don't want him getting near her. "I suppose I've never considered that. We don't tend to mingle in human affairs unless necessary."

"You share a planet with humans. That feels necessary."

"That is certainly a perspective I hadn't considered." Emyr nods, his gaze lingering on me for a moment too long before he leans back in his seat again. "Perhaps that is something we can discuss as things move forward. Many things are changing in Asalin. I would like to see them continue to do so— to the benefit of us all."

After a moment, as if assessing his sincerity, Briar gives a firm nod. She smiles at me, tender and small, reaching over and taking my hand, giving it a gentle squeeze.

I can feel Emyr's gaze on me the rest of the ride, but I refuse to look at him. I stare down at my knuckles, fingers threaded with Briar's. My hands are all bone, long and sharp. Hers are plush and soft. The tips of my fingers are always freezing, like they're missing the rush of fire they know they can produce. Her grip is warm around mine.

Though I'm not sure *how* I know, I know the minute we pass from human territory into Asalin. Things feel different here, like suddenly my body is extra alive, nerves thrumming, heart beating harder.

Or maybe that's the old trauma, making me hyperaware of my surroundings.

The limo's tires crunch against rocks and twigs underfoot, jostling our bodies back and forth. The forest looming on either side of the winding dirt road is made of a thick cluster of honey locust trees standing nearly a hundred feet tall. When I see a peryton darting through them, I'm *certain* we've arrived. I try and point the animal out to Briar, but it's gone by the time she twists her head to look.

Suddenly, I'm anxious to get out of the car. To look around and see this place again. How much has it changed? How much did *I* change it? The idea that I might feel the shock waves of the night I left, that I might see some visual reminder of the worst thing I've ever done, doesn't escape me. It makes my knees shake.

And still, I want to see it all. To stretch my legs and walk this ground. To feel this kingdom under me, around me, and know I'm home.

Home. It's been so long since I considered Asalin home that the thought strikes me as odd. I was born here. I come from here. But is it *home*? The gnawing sensation in my gut might be a yes. Or it might mean I should have eaten the free lunch they offered on the plane.

After a few minutes, the village itself comes into view. Here, the dirt road turns to rough pavement that shakes the car just as hard, but in a new way. The first thing I notice are the power lines stretching down the street, a new addition in the years since I've been gone. Other than that, things look almost exactly the same.

It's as if I was never here. As if *that night* never happened. Time has all but erased me from this place. If only that were true in more ways than one.

The main road is lined with little log cabins with green tin roofs, pushed back so tightly against the tree line they almost disappear as part of the woods themselves. Some of the houses are private homes, decorated with flower boxes in the windows or ugly figurines on the lawn, and a handful of them have cars parked in rock beds out front. Others are businesses, marked by signs hanging from the front doors.

One building appears closed down, lights off inside, two-by-fours nailed in an X across the front door. A sigil I don't recognize is sprayed over it in red paint, like blood, like a warning. A chill creeps up the back of my neck.

I might not know what it means, but I know what the sign hanging in the window next door is.

To someone who's never seen the Faery flag before, it wouldn't be anything special. A rectangle of white cloth with a red hand in the center, surrounded by a pair of black wings. Along the edges is an inscription in the Old Language. I can't be sure of the word-for-word translation, but I've been told it means something along the lines of *Fae first, Fae forever.*

It's anti-witch dog-whistling, and it isn't new.

On the streets, fae and a few witches cluster in groups of their own kind. But everyone stops to turn and look in our direction, pointing and calling out to one another or whispering behind cupped hands. I can guess what they're saying, and I'm betting it's for the best I can't hear them.

The people here can't possibly have anything good to say about me.

Moot, though. I don't have anything good to say about myself, either.

Eventually, we leave the village behind, and the road becomes dirt again. We make our way up the long winding path toward the castle, my gut aching more and more with each second that passes. Anticipation tightens my lungs until I can hardly breathe. Suddenly, the car is too small. I can't be in this back seat anymore. I'm going to pass out. As soon as we come to a stop, I jump for the door handle, yank it open, and clamber into the open air.

The drive has delivered us directly to the steps of the palace. Made from mountain stone, each cut with precise magic into massive bricks, it looms hundreds upon hundreds of feet tall, the sharp tops of each turret looking like knifepoints. Ivy and moss have grown together from the roots of the palace to wrap around the walls, draping daintily over balcony ledges and obscuring most of the windows. Carved into the stone above the steps is Vorgaine, Faery's ancient deity, her face covered in a hundred eyes, her wings tipped with flame. The New York flora has almost obscured her entirely.

To humans, the castle would probably look like an old, broken-down building cobbled together with rocks. Nothing too impressive. But I'm struggling to catch my breath, and I have no idea why.

Briar brushes up against my side, leaning her cheek against the top of my head.

Emyr moves around from the other side of the car to stand in front of us both, blocking half my view of the castle and forcing me to look at him. That unreadable something or other has returned to his expression again. "Welcome home."

Something inside me shifts in a way I don't appreciate.

I open my mouth to offer a nasty retort—lest things get

too comfortable—but the doors to the castle fling open and cut me off.

Five fae stomp out onto the front steps, their pace quick as they descend. Each wears the red-and-black uniform of the Guard, red pants tucked into black boots, and a thick black jacket that hangs down to midthigh, cinched at the waist with a red rope and emblazoned with red stripes on the chest. Each stripe denotes a different rank in their militia, ranging from one to five. Their hands are covered in black gloves, holes pricked in the tip of each finger to let their claws through.

Iron shackles hang from chains at their waists. The gloves are to make sure they don't have to touch the cuffs directly. Though it wouldn't kill a fae, iron would burn like hell if it touched their skin.

Emyr turns to look as they storm toward Briar and me with those shackles.

One of the Guard grabs me by the back of my neck and yanks me forward while another jerks my arms behind my back and presses my wrists together. Cool metal clicks over my skin, holding my hands in place. It doesn't burn me the same way it would a fae, but it does sting enough to hurt.

"What the fuck?" I demand, struggling to free myself. I throw my body upright, out of the grip on my neck, and press my back into the chest of the Guard behind me, trying to kick the one in front. He grabs my ankles and tosses them toward the ground, putting his hand on my shoulder to hold me in place.

"What are you doing?" Emyr shouts, reaching up to place a hand on the arm of the Guard in front of me. "Release him at once!"

I try to bring my fire to the surface, willfully try to summon my magic for the first time in a long, long time, and it doesn't work. The shackles render my power dormant. I'm even more useless than usual.

Still, when I see them handcuff Briar, my efforts double. If I can't curse them, I can *bite* them. I snap my teeth and turn my head to the side, fangs clamping down on the wrist of the guy touching my shoulder and sinking in as deep as they'll go, until I can taste the wet, coppery rush of blood against my tongue.

He yelps and yanks his hand back. It gets caught on my fangs and tears, a bit of his skin getting stuck between my teeth. With a snarl, the Guard raises his other hand and brings it down hard against the side of my head. Suddenly, the world is swimming.

"Get your hands off him!" Emyr demands. I can't see him through the black spots in my vision, but he sounds panicked. "I was told he would be allowed to turn himself in. My parents assured me he would not be taken into custody."

Finally, a far-off voice responds, one I recognize, though I can't see through the haze to pinpoint where it's coming from. "Your parents are not the head of the Guard, Emyr. *I* am." Derek almost sounds like he's laughing. "And by my order, your mate will be put to death."

CHAPTER FOUR

THE SELF-APPOINTED HEAD GAYS OF ASALIN

I don't have the patience to deal with the fae boys tonight. I've just left Emyr at the palace after yet another fight. I don't understand why we can't stop fighting these days. He hasn't changed. He's as good to me as he's ever been. He loves me so much, and he tells me often.

But there is something ugly in me, I think. Something wicked growing that I can't put a name to. When he whispers to me how I will be queen of Asalin someday soon, this ugliness winds its way up my windpipe until I can't breathe. I find myself lashing out, even when I don't mean to. I blame him for things that aren't his fault, not really. He doesn't understand me anymore. Truthfully, I don't understand me, either.

Now, headed home alone, I just want to nurse my wounded feelings. Instead, I have to listen to these boys.

They're all older than me, some by several years. I've gotten used to their jeering, their lewd taunts, as I walk home each night from the palace. Emyr tells me every time that I should let one of his Guard walk me home. He doesn't understand that the Guard can be just as bad, if not worse.

There are so many things about this kingdom Emyr fails to understand.

Tonight, there are five of them, trailing down the winding path behind me, calling out disgusting questions I fight to ignore.

It's the same disturbing interrogation every night.

Has the prince put it in you, yet? Is that what the two of you do all night up in the castle? Play house? Maybe you could use some extra practice. C'mon, little witch, why don't you practice with me?

They're gross, but they don't scare me. I can handle myself against the boys if I have to. They won't do anything, anyway. They're all scared of Emyr. They don't talk to me like this when we're together.

Someone grabs my arm. I narrow my eyes, turning my head over my shoulder to glare at the boy touching me.

He's their ringleader, a skinny little shit a few years older than me, with orange hair and a single straight horn in the center of his head like a freaking unicorn. As he stares down at me, the others start to circle, their wings spreading out to create a dome, trapping me like a bug under a tipped glass.

I'm still not afraid. I am annoyed, though.

"I'm getting sick of you ignoring us," *Unicorn Boy sneers, his grip on me tight.* "Why are you such a bitch?"

The others crow their agreement.

"Why are you such an ass?" I counter, snatching my arm to try and jostle free from his hold. It doesn't work, and his fingers tighten hard enough that pain shoots across my skin.

"That wasn't very queenly," he sneers, stepping closer to me. His energy, bright white like bleached linoleum, creeps toward my throat. "We should teach you some manners."

The other boys continue to hoot and holler.

The redhead shoves me with his fae strength and speed, the hit so fast my body can't keep up. My belly hits the dirt and knocks the wind out of me, my lungs suddenly sore.

When the fear finally comes, it hits me all at once, a chill that shoots through my body, icy cold and turning my veins brittle. Adrenaline bursts like bullets into my chest cavity and I struggle against them, kicking and scratching and biting to try and break free.

Their hands are too strong. These fae boys are too big, too powerful. I don't know how to fight them. I don't know how to win.

Over the rushing in my ears, I can barely hear their taunts now. But my anger returns. It's a fire that burns through my body, replacing the chill of fear. It winds its way across my bones, flooding every cell that makes up my system, and whispers, "You are not a queen. You are a *witch*. Teach them who should be afraid."

When blackness drips across my arms and eyes, the boys still their advances. When fire buds in my palms and lurches forward like a flamethrower, they give their own cries of panic, scrambling away from me.

I rise. Fury rumbles through me, my familiar anger finally finding a proper target. I will teach the fae who should be afraid.

With a scream, I unfurl a gust of flame from my hands, watching as the tendrils of fire lick across the ground, searching for a safe place to land. They leave scorch marks along the dirt road in their wake.

But that isn't enough. It's not enough! They need to learn! They all need to learn!

I throw my head back and raise my hands above me. Black magic slides up my arms to my throat. Thick, black smoke surrounds me, billowing from the palms of my hands and draping down like a cloak. Fire shoots from my fingers like fireworks, soaring off in every direction, hunting for targets.

All around me, fae begin to scream as houses are caught in the blaze.

Asalin burns.

An hour later, my head is still pounding from the Guard's beating when a Committee member arrives to release us.

There is something familiar about the man, but I can't place him. His wings are *bizarre*. They remind me of a flying squirrel, big droopy tufts of brown fur attached to the sides of his arms. His uniform has been tailored to accommodate them, slits cut into the biceps instead of the spine like typical fae clothing. That's not the only way his uniform is different. Most Committee uniforms are identical to those of the Guard, only with red fabric switched out for green. But his pants seem tighter, better fitted to his body. His boots have a heel the others don't, a subtle glint of metal at the sole. The green rope around his waist isn't rope at all, but silk, maybe, more like a ribbon. A dozen different earrings decorate each ear on either side of his tan white face, and his long blond hair is tugged into a bun at the top of his head. His horns remind me of a moose's antlers, so wide he has to twist his body sideways to fit through the cell door. His energy is a deep, dark green that reminds me of getting lost in the forest.

Maybe he isn't familiar at all. I think it would be hard to forget someone like him.

"Sorry about all this," he says as he moves over to undo my cuffs. His voice sounds like a lumberjack. I don't know why. Just does.

He also doesn't sound particularly apologetic.

As soon as he frees me, my energy snaps back to life, magic settling underneath my skin. It's as comforting as pulling the blanket over your head in bed, stealing a few more minutes of sleep in the darkness. It's weird. For something I've spent so long trying to push away, I don't feel entirely like *me* when it's gone. During the months I spent on my own in the human world, before Nadua rescued me, the flames fought to burst free constantly. Every time someone got too close, every time some human man saw me and thought I was easy prey, the fire was always there, begging me to let loose. But it was too soon, after that night. I was more afraid of myself than I was of anything the humans could do to me.

After I moved in with Briar and her family, ignoring my magic became easier. There were no threats. I was safe. And I got comfortable—too comfortable. I guess that's why seeing Emyr brought everything back to the surface.

I flex my fingers, reaching for the hint of fire underneath the tips, feeling the way it burns just under my skin.

"The Guard can be a little trigger-happy," the Committee member continues.

Briar and I exchange a look as he undoes her shackles next. Fae or not, the Guard is just another branch of the police. Briar's parents have always been deeply entrenched in activism, and they've gotten into more than a handful of altercations with law enforcement because of it. Sunny spent a few years in prison for supposedly resisting arrest at a pipeline protest. Even Briar, the sweetest person I've ever met and not yet eighteen, has had her run-ins with police.

She doesn't trust cops, human or otherwise. And I don't trust anything she doesn't trust. This Committee guy saying the Guard can be trigger-happy just confirms what we already know.

"The Throne has granted permission for you to stay," he informs Briar as her bright yellow energy comes back to life, dancing in the dimly lit spaces of the dungeon like a spinning top. He steps back and motions for us to follow him toward the flight of stairs.

I'm more than happy to escape the dungeon. This place is really just a hole in the ground, a tomb buried underneath the castle. The walls are nothing but packed dirt, damp and crawling with bugs, imbued with a crackling magic to keep prisoners from digging their way out. Each cell is a tiny little room not much bigger than a closet, and the doors are made from wood that seems to grow down from the dirt ceiling, like the roots of a tree. They're always slightly rotted, but protected by the same magic as the walls, impossible to break down. The whole place smells like moist death.

"You, on the other hand," he continues as he shoots me a look over his shoulder, "will be expected to sit trial."

"Trial, huh? Thought I was just going straight to the gallows."

"That is still entirely possible, given the extent of your crimes," the fae drawls.

Oh. Okay. An uncomfortable silence settles over the three

of us as we make our way up from the dungeon and then through a twisting hallway. The overgrown windows make it difficult for much light to pass through from outside, and Emyr's attempts at modernizing Asalin have not, apparently, extended to adding more lighting. Everything feels shadowy and wrong. I shove my hands into the pocket of my hoodie and keep my head down.

I've always been aware returning to Asalin would probably end with my death, but *this* isn't how I saw it playing out. I can't put a finger on the way it makes me feel.

Resolved, I guess. Maybe a little bored. How anticlimactic it would be, coming back here after all this time just to be offed within a few hours. That's not a very good story. But whatever. I was never meant to have a very good story, I guess.

A group of giggling fae children rush past us. My teeth grind together at the sight of them. Happy and innocent. Naive and oblivious. I remember racing through these dark halls. Dancing beneath the high, sloped ceilings. Gazing out the tall windows and leaning over the balconies to observe the world around me, daydreaming about how someday all of Asalin would be mine. What a little fool I was.

The fae drops us at a door, dismissing us with a curt nod and nothing else.

Briar watches him go, her eyebrows furrowed. "So, he wasn't a Guard?"

"No. Committee."

Fae government is separated into three branches—the Throne, which makes up the royal family; the Guard, who are basically cops and judges; and the Committee, the glorified assistants who handle planning and arranging things for the other two. If any *Big Important Shit* goes down, they might be expected to call upon the Court, which is the Thrones from all five kingdoms mashed up into one.

The Court are the only ones with the power to establish and dissolve blood contracts.

The door where we've been deposited leads into a bedroom. A single four-poster bed made from black wood sits in the center of the room, with gauzy green fabric draped over it to make a canopy. One set of doors leads to the moss-enveloped balcony outside, another to the en suite, a third to a closet.

"I think this is bigger than our entire house," Briar says flatly.

"I think this is the smallest room in the castle."

She shakes her head and mumbles something under her breath, moving to the bed and bouncing down on the end of it. "So. Maybe agreeing to come here was a bad idea."

I want to say, *No shit, you think?* but instead just shrug, joining her on the edge of the bed. "It'll be all right."

It probably won't be, but that isn't what Briar needs to hear. What good is it going to do anyone to tell her I think I'm going to be dead by the end of the week?

"I mean, Emyr isn't going to let them execute you, right? He was obviously upset when they put you in handcuffs. He outranks the Guard, doesn't he?"

"Technically? I guess."

"Yeah," Briar whispers, bobbing her head. "Yeah, it'll all be all right."

She's trying to convince herself, and I let her. One of us should remain optimistic about this whole thing, and it sure as hell isn't going to be me.

I've never been to one of Asalin's executions before, but my parents were frequent fliers there. I know enough about them to know what I can expect. A crowd of people gather in a circular arena surrounding the main stage where the pyre sits. The royal family get special box seats at the top. A member of the Guard drags the prisoner onto the stage. The crowd yells their accusations. The fire is lit. Everyone cheers. The guilty is burned alive.

There are plenty of ways they could kill a person that don't involve this level of cruelty. Magic would be faster, cleaner, more effective. But the fae do have a flair for the dramatic, in everything they do. Even murder.

Anyway, I guess fire's as fitting an end for me as anything else.

I'm feeling oddly resigned about my impending execution. It occurs to me, in a sort of detached way, that this is probably not entirely normal.

Someone knocks on the bedroom door, and Briar and I exchange a look. We wait a beat, hoping whoever's out there will turn and walk away when no one responds.

A second knock comes, followed by a familiar voice saying through the wood, "I know you're in there."

With a sigh, I drag myself to my feet and open the door.

Emyr takes that as an invitation, brushing past me to enter the room.

"Gee, come on in," I snap, slamming the door closed behind him.

Briar jumps up, pointing an accusatory finger at Emyr's chest as her yellow energy flares around her. It sort of reminds me of one of those warning signs. But instead of Caution: Wet

Floor, hers would read something like Caution: I'm About to Tell You About Yourself. "Dude, what the hell?"

That's about as close as I've ever seen Briar come to being truly rude, which means she must be apoplectic.

"I apologize," Emyr says with the barest inclination of his head, a fractional sign of respect for her. Even his golden energy submits to hers, backing down instead of confronting hers head-on. "I would have had you both freed sooner, but my parents were on dragonback. It seems they lost track of the time. It took me a while to reach them."

Briar blinks at him. I can practically see the way the anger poofs right out of her, the way all of her sort-of-hateful words die on the tip of her tongue. She stares at him, her lips parting. "Dragonback?"

"Yes. Riding their dragons." At Briar's continued gaping, he adds, "It's one of my mother's favored pastimes."

It's the favored pastime of *most* of the fae, at least those privileged enough to get close to the herd. I'm not sure why the fae would be able to fly on their own in Faery but not on Earth, maybe something about the gravity here being different, or maybe it's a skill they have to learn, old knowledge that was lost a long time ago. I don't know. What I do know is that dragonback's as close as they can get to who they used to be.

"Dragons." Briar says the word like she doesn't know what it means.

Emyr nods, slowly. "You should be able to see the herd from your balcony. They like to come into the southern fields around this time to sunbathe."

Any scrap of indignation gone, she all but trips over her feet as she races to burst through the double doors that lead to the balcony. A moment later, she shouts, "Wyatt! Wyatt, oh my god! Look at this!"

I don't move, though. I've seen dragons before, and I don't trust Emyr enough to take my eyes off him. Instead, I cross my arms, lean back against one of the bedposts, and narrow my eyes. "You promised to protect me."

He's changed clothes since arriving, traded in the human sweats for a pair of low-slung black harem pants and a sheer white shirt. I actually *can* make out his nipples through this one.

Not that I'm looking at them or anything.

It seems like he's had a shower, too. Lucky him. Must have been nice, getting pampered while Briar and I sat in our coffin-like cell, the life force sucked out of us.

"I had you released, didn't I? You aren't dead yet."

"I only needed to be *released* because I was *arrested*."

"Yes, well. Perhaps you should have considered that before setting the village ablaze."

I raise my eyebrows at him. "Fuck you."

His wings twitch behind his shoulder blades, their clawed tips flexing with tension. After a moment, he sighs. "I had no idea Derek was going to do that. I thought I'd taken care of it."

"It sounds like Derek is better at strategizing than you."

"Maybe he is." Emyr shrugs. "I don't believe that means he'd make a better king."

I don't know enough about Derek to have an opinion on that. Back when I was prone to fanboying over him, I was far more interested in his jawline than his skills in diplomacy.

These days, I don't know anything about the guy except that he had me arrested. So, I say nothing.

Emyr's eyes roam away from me to the king-size bed in our suite. Then his gaze flicks toward Briar, still standing on the balcony, her delighted giggles filtering through the open doors. Bed. Briar. Bed. Briar. Then back to me.

"You're both staying in here?"

"This is the room they gave us."

"They should have given you two rooms. I will make a call and have her moved somewhere on her own."

"I'd prefer she stay with me."

"Then I will move you both to a larger suite."

"We're fine here."

"There is only one bed."

"Bravo. You can count to one." I shrug one shoulder. "We usually sleep together."

His eyes flash their inhuman gold. Wet paint dripping across a brown canvas. "I suppose I have my answer, then. She's your girlfriend or something?"

"She's definitely something," is all I offer.

Emyr studies me for a long moment before shrugging and looking away. "It doesn't matter. Kings throughout history have been known to keep concubines. You can sleep with whomever you want. You're still going to marry me."

I barely have time to register my own indignation at him giving me *permission* to sleep around before the bedroom door swings wide open.

"I can't take this anymore," exclaims a pale waif of a girl with a mountain of blond curls and deerlike antlers instead of horns. "Did you seriously just say that to him?"

At her side, the tallest person I've ever seen in my life grins, shaking their head. No wings or horns, so a witch. They toss shaggy black hair from their dark eyes and flash a grin. "Truly, Emyr, you are tragic at flirting."

"Clarke. Jin." He says the names through clenched teeth. "This doesn't concern you."

"Oh, on the contrary," The blonde—Clarke, I think—snickers, gliding deeper into my room and tossing herself on my bed as if she owns the joint. Her feathers rustle behind her, white and poofy and dainty, more like an angelic Halloween costume than anything else. Her sequined corset shows off a stretch of white skin on her stomach and a pierced navel before her low-slung white skirt begins, the soft-looking fabric gathering around her knees where her legs hang off the edge of my mattress. "As the self-appointed Head Gays of Asalin, it is absolutely our responsibility to make sure you don't screw this up beyond repair."

She tilts her chin toward me and winks, bright pink energy snapping around her like a popped bubblegum bubble. "Hey there, dollface."

Something about her tone strikes a memory in me.

Clarke. I remember her now. She's a few years older than me, was about my age now when I ran from Asalin. She's Emyr's cousin—and Derek's sister.

She was already this obnoxious when we were children, though back then she didn't have the time of day to call me dollface. She was too busy terrorizing her maids and throwing tantrums in the village square.

"It's good to finally meet you, Wyatt." Jin grins, reaching up to push a hank of hair away from their dark eyes. They're even louder in appearance than their counterpart. Huge muscles and their giant stature are compounded on by the piercings in their lip, between their eyes, two in one nostril, and each eyebrow. Several colorful tattoos decorate their beige skin. Their leather pants are held together at the sides by ombré rainbow-colored ribbons, and their top is little more than a black sash across their chest. "Being the token trans witch was getting old."

"Oh, please," Clarke chides playfully. "You adore the spotlight."

"I adore *you*."

My face screws up in consideration of them. Relationships between fae and witches are not unheard of, but they aren't exactly common, either. Especially not this close to the Throne, hence the shitshow of opposition that followed my and Emyr's betrothal.

I suppose I could take this as an indication that Asalin is changing for the better, but as I was just released from the *dungeon*, that seems unlikely.

Jin grins at Clarke before looking back down at me. "Really, it's nice not being the only out trans person in Asalin anymore. I'm what you might call a theydy."

It doesn't surprise me that news of my arrival—and transition—has already spread through the palace. Not much happens in a kingdom that's more or less cut off from the rest of the world. Anything remotely exciting tends to move through the grapevine like wildfire.

"Theydy?" I am absolutely sure I would never call anyone that without being prompted.

"Nonbinary lady. They pronouns, very lesbian."

Oh. I've never actually met another trans person before—
not off the internet, and not as far as I know, anyway. I try
not to stare too hard, though there's an obnoxious part of me
that would like to analyze everything about Jin. I find myself standing up a little straighter, tugging at the front of my
hoodie, chin jutting out to pretend I've got a decent jawline.
Don't know what the hell that's about except that maybe, as
much as cis people's opinions don't mean shit, this is different. There's some weird desire to be recognized by someone
like me. To be acknowledged as community.

Ugh, I hate myself.

Anyway, Emyr asking for my pronouns the other night
suddenly makes a lot more sense. This must be the witch in
his pocket, the one who built him his magical little iPhone
knockoff.

Jin inclines their head toward the balcony. "Now, who's
your friend out there? The whole palace has been talking
about you two. *Helloooo?* Human?"

I gnash my teeth until the sores from chewing the insides
of my cheeks threaten to reopen. I have no idea how to interact with these people. A glance in Emyr's direction tells me
he probably feels the same way, upper lip wrapped over his
fangs, eyes narrowed into slits. His fists are curled so tightly
I think his claws are probably drawing blood in his palms.

Briar squeals as she reenters the room. "Dragons!"

"A fan of the sky puppies, are you?" Jin asks, sweeping toward her and giving a too-deep bow. Their energy crackles
around them, a deep purple streaked with white, like the night
sky painted by flashes of lightning. "Jin Ueno. The little red

one with the bad attitude is my girl Auriga. I could take you for a ride sometime."

Briar looks gobsmacked. "Yes. Absolutely."

"Witches aren't allowed dragons," I say, though I suppose it makes me sound like I don't know anything about anything, considering this witch just said they do, in fact, have one. But that's fine, I guess, because witches *aren't* allowed dragons, as far as I know. And also, I *don't* know anything about anything.

Jin smiles at me, shrugging and flicking their wrist in a way that feels like feigned nonchalance. "I'm not most witches. I work with the herd actually. Head handler. That's how your boy and I first became friends."

I'm assuming by *my boy* they're referring to Emyr.

Which... No.

Clarke snickers, rolling onto her belly on my bed and propping her chin in her hand. She flutters her eyelashes at Briar. "I'm Clarke. We *never* get humans in Asalin. You're precious. I love your outfit."

Briar is wearing her favorite ratty, paint-splattered old sweats and a tie-dyed T-shirt, having maximized comfort on the plane. She frowns, considering herself and then the other girl, as if doubting the sincerity of her compliment. Still, she manages a "Thank you."

"Clarke. Jin." Emyr forces the words out. When his hands unclench, I can see there *is* blood trickling over his fingers. "My fiancé and I were in the middle of a private conversation. If you would like to get acquainted with Briar, perhaps you should—"

"Briar? Oh, that's such a pretty name." Clarke sighs dreamily, her fingers brushing against her chin.

"Pronouns?" Jin asks.

"She/her are fine." Briar flushes under the attention.

"How are you enjoying Asalin so far?" Clarke asks. "Well, I suppose you haven't seen much outside of the dungeon, but—"

"Clarke!"

Clarke huffs, finally turning away from Briar to glare at Emyr. "We heard your private conversation with Wyatt. You told him you didn't care if he had a side piece so long as he stayed with you for the Throne. It was the least romantic thing I've ever heard. Frankly, I don't trust you to be alone with him ever again."

"Perhaps you should allow all communication between the two of you to go through us first. We're great at romance." Jin hoists their very large body onto the footboard of my bed, before brushing back some of their thick, ear-length black hair.

Emyr stares at them before meeting my eyes. "I don't think he cares about romance."

Oh, screw you.

He has no right to sound as disappointed as he does. I was fourteen, acne-riddled, and pissed at the whole world the last time he saw me. Hell, I was barely bigger than a freaking toddler when my mother pricked my finger to sign me away in our contract! Regardless of his opinion on the matter, I don't see the makings of an epic love story here.

"That's not at all true." I shrug. "I just don't care about romance coming from you."

"Oooh. Sick burn." Jin reaches over to clasp Emyr's shoulder, giving it a gentle squeeze. "That's gotta hurt, huh, buddy?"

Emyr just glares at me.

I offer him my most peachy-sweet smile in return.

"So, you're still planning to marry him?" Briar asks, as if she's only just remembered what's going on here. "I suppose that means you don't think he's going to be...you know."

"Charred to a crisp?" Jin suggests. "Ugly business, that. Wouldn't recommend it."

Emyr rubs his thumb against the bridge of his nose, taking a deep breath and letting it out slowly. "I've spoken to my parents and they've met with Derek. Wyatt will sit before the Guard the day after tomorrow to offer his side of the story. I cannot imagine them actually executing him for an accident when he was a child."

"It wasn't exactly an accident," I say, but no one is listening.

"I mean, they might." Clarke gives a considerate wiggle of her wrist. "People did, like, die."

The room goes very, very quiet. Emyr glares at Clarke.

In her defense, Clarke looks pretty ashamed of herself. "I'm so sorry. I have such a big mouth."

Jin offers me an apologetic look.

I don't let myself react at all.

"*Regardless,*" Briar pushes forward, and I have no doubt it's because she knows better than anyone not to bring this topic up. She does put her hand in mine and squeeze my fingers. "Emyr, *you* think it'll be okay?"

"Because it was *clearly an accident*—" Emyr may be trying to convince himself of that "—the Guard will never be able to justify an execution, much as they might like to. I anticipate the most they'll expect from him will be reparations for the destruction that was done." He shrugs. "As I suspect he is destitute, my family will pay them."

Briar smiles at me as if this is good news. As if I should be happy.

This is going to be a disaster.

CHAPTER FIVE

A LOADED QUESTION WITH MANY ANSWERS

Briar and I were in love once.

Or maybe that's not true. Maybe I was never really in love with her. Or maybe I still am. I guess it depends a lot on your definition of being *in* love with someone versus *loving* them. Maybe the difference is too minute to really be able to explain it. She still holds my heart in the palm of her hand like a caretaker tending to a wild animal. I would still rend the spine from the body of anyone bold enough to try and hurt her.

The webs of our lives are too sticky and tangled to ever separate, even if we wanted to. She was the first person to ever love me in a way that felt selfless, to love me even though I couldn't *do* anything for her. She was the first person to look at me and make me feel like she really saw me, and not just what she wanted me to be. At my most vulnerable, my most broken, my most self-hating, she sat with me and never let me stay too long in my own abyss.

I think I'm still in love with her. It just isn't being in love in the way most people understand it.

So, let me start over.

Briar and I used to make out once.

It didn't last long—that time in our lives, not the individual make-out sessions. There was this blip in my timeline, this brief period between realizing I was different and realizing *why* I was different where I landed on "lesbian." And when I tried that word on, tried fitting into yet another box I didn't fit into but didn't realize was improperly shaped yet, I figured, why *not* Briar? Why not the person I loved that much? My best friend, keeper of my heart, the most beautiful girl I'd ever known?

When it ended, I expected the world to be ripped out from under me. Instead, it just got a little torn around the edges. I have Briar's endless grace to thank for that.

As it turns out, my *type* skews more toward lanky dudes with piercings and patches on their jackets, with nimble fingers and sharp tongues and, like, unfortunate nicotine addictions. At least, that is apparently my type, since that describes the only two guys I've dated since I ended things with Briar.

There is a point to all of this. And that is to say that the guy who wakes me up the next morning with a knock at my door may not be my *type*, but he was definitely my gay awakening, even if I didn't realize it at the time.

Derek has velvety black wings and two thin horns shooting straight up from the sides of his head. His blond hair is slicked back, but a single tendril falls over the most irritatingly blue eyes I've ever seen. His jawline is sharp enough that it could probably slit my throat, if the fangs peeking out from behind his full pink lips didn't rip it out first. His dark clothes are perfectly tailored to his muscular frame, his white skin tanned and perfectly unblemished.

He's way too old for me, I'm technically engaged, and also I hate him.

But damn, that face.

"Wyatt?" His voice has a lyrical quality to it, like he's someone used to talking to other people. I can see him standing on a stage somewhere giving speeches, holding an arena at attention.

Something tugs at the back of my mind. The memory of the Guard cuffing Briar as she cried out in fear and pain. Derek's taunts as he told Emyr I would be put to death. This was only yesterday. Why does it feel so long ago? Why can't I seem to summon up the appropriate rage or disgust?

He's just so nice to look at.

"Mmm?" I tell myself it's the early hour and nothing else that's apparently robbed me of my ability to speak.

"Do you know who I am?"

How could I not? That face has rendered me speechless hundreds, if not thousands, of times throughout my life already. I'm pretty sure that face was the star of my very first wet dream. "Derek."

He smiles, flashing those bright white teeth. "I was hoping you might want to take a walk with me."

Douse of cold water. "I don't."

Childhood crush or not, I don't have any interest in play-ing nice with Derek Pierce. He's the one trying to have me *executed*.

He seems undeterred by my dismissal, glancing over my shoulder to peer into the bedroom. Briar is still asleep, stretched out to take up well over half of the bed. I step out of the room, pushing myself closer to him so I can close the door and block her from his sight.

Oh. He smells like expensive cologne, clean and sharp and masculine. That's fine.

The chaotic energy of me entertaining gay thoughts right now is unmatched.

Derek chuckles. "There are things I wanted to discuss with you. I assume you don't want us waking up your friend. Go, get dressed."

"Which part of my *no* confused you?"

"I want to help you, Wyatt." He leans in closer. I dig my nails into my palms and refuse to inhale. "The Throne may be able to still my hand from having you sent to your death. But I can make your stay here as miserable as possible. And that's to say nothing of what I can do to your human."

Immediately, heat flares in my palms again. After years of disuse, the fire in my veins seems determined to make a come-back. I bare my teeth, tilting my head up to meet Derek's gaze, our noses nearly touching.

He raises his perfectly groomed brows. An almost-smile taunts at his lips. "Alternatively, I can help you get everything you want. Are you certain you don't want to take that walk?"

★ ★ ★

Derek's energy is the same shade of blue as his eyes. It bounces around us as we walk through the maze garden on the northern side of the castle, cerulean crests swirling around my own aura like a whirlpool.

"How much do you know of the situation here in Asalin?" he asks, hands clasped behind him as we make our way down paths lined with thick ivy and rows of blossoming flowers. It's peaceful here, in this tangled bouquet of a labyrinth. It feels like a secret, the tall hedges standing between us and the rest of the world.

"I know you want to be king," I offer up.

Derek sighs as if disappointed by that answer. "I don't want to be king. I want someone *qualified* to be king."

"It just so happens you're the only one qualified?"

He pins me with an exasperated sort of look. "I'm next in line, after Emyr. I don't have any grand lust for power, you know. I just care a great deal about this kingdom."

Can't relate, but fair enough. I guess it's admirable to be patriotic or whatever. I've never felt any allegiance to anything bigger than myself—and Briar's family—so I wouldn't know. Of course, I've also never been admirable in any capacity.

Still, it seems doubtful one would plan a coup because of their great love of their kingdom.

"Really?"

Derek considers me at length and finally shrugs one shoulder. "Perhaps I also lust for power. A bit. But don't we all?"

There we go.

"And what makes Emyr so unqualified?"

"That is a loaded question with many answers."

"Why don't you toss me one?" I roll my eyes. I hate diplomats and the roundabout way they talk, the way they try and weasel out of any accountability by being as vague as possible. Yet another reason I would make a terrible political leader. I have no idea how to be coy.

Derek rubs a hand over his stubble, thick black claws gently scraping against his jaw. "You are aware of Kadri North's... interesting history?"

Kadri North is Emyr's mother, queen of Asalin.

But Kadri is notoriously unlike any queen who's sat on Asalin's Throne before her. When she married Leonidas, she didn't accept that her role was to sit back and quietly allow her husband to rule. She expected them to be *equals*. She held meetings. Enforced new rules for the Guard and Committee. Plotted innovations for the kingdom that now belonged to her. Leonidas choosing to take *her* name, rather than passing on the Pierce name the Throne had held for generations, was a scandal of apparently epic proportions. The rest of the family believed she was trying to distance herself, and the Throne, from them. From people like Derek. And in fairness, they might have been right about that.

Of course I know her story. Every fae and witch in the world probably knows her story. I nod.

"Well..." Derek sighs. "As I'm sure you recall, the queen has passed some of her more...questionable eccentricities on to her son."

"Eccentricities?"

"Her values have always been in contrast with the traditions of Asalin. She's raised Emyr to uphold a certain set of ideals that many in our community don't understand. The two of them are so set on pushing our kingdom forward they don't seem to have any concern for what they're leaving behind. The traditions we'll lose as we become more and more like the humans. After all, progress for the sake of progress often does more harm than good." He frowns, reaching up to rub a hand over his mouth. "Which is to say nothing of the fact that Emyr is rather…melancholic."

"Melancholic," I repeat, because I have no idea what he's getting at.

"Emyr is an odd child. He always has been." Derek shakes his head. "I love my cousin, I do. But he's a weird little thing. Always disappearing into the fields, spending all his free time with the animals. And now, with all his…human gadgets. The people here don't understand him."

No one in Asalin has ever embraced change. I remember that well. When news broke about the prince's engagement to a *witch*, people were furious. I was too young to understand at the time, too naive to see the way the fae would sneer in my direction or understand the cruel things they would whisper about my family and me. But I got older. And eventually I realized I would always be seen as *other* to the fae. My bitterness grew from there.

"Do they need to understand him? Plenty of kings are eccentric."

"Emyr was never meant to be our king." Derek snaps the words between his teeth like cracking a whip, and I stop walking. He pauses when I do, reaching up to press his thumb to the collar of his shirt. He composes himself and says, "That may sound harsh, but it's true. He is not a Pierce. Not by name, or by blood." Derek eyes me and shakes his head.

"Wyatt, my family was given this kingdom because of our commitment to protecting faekind. As the other kingdoms change around us, we have always held fast to our most sacred traditions. We are the keepers of the door. We maintain a tether to the ways of Faery."

I'm actually pretty sick of hearing about the ways of Faery. You'd think, after five hundred years, they would have developed some *new* ways. Even Emyr, as worryingly progressive as Derek finds him, threw those words in my face just days ago, reminding me I had no choice but to marry him.

Faery is dead. These people need to let it die.

"And then, of course, there is the issue of the humans," Derek continues. "Already, Emyr has welcomed a human into our midst, and he is not even king yet. Staying hidden is our most *hallowed* law, and he's spit on it. You've lived in the human world, Wyatt. You should know better than any of us what humankind would do to the fae, should they learn of our existence."

He isn't wrong about that. The magic that protects the fae kingdoms keeps humans from accidentally stumbling upon them, but what if they came looking? How would fae magic hold up against human technology if the two were to face off one-on-one? Once upon a time, iron was the worst thing the fae had to fear from humankind, but now they've got weapons of mass destruction at their disposal. And they have a tendency to destroy anything they don't understand—as soon as they find out how to take whatever they want first.

Of course, that is not entirely unlike the fae. They have more in common than they realize.

In fact, the way witches are treated here reminds me distinctly of the way queerphobia manifests in the human world. Witchlings (queer kids) are born to fae (cishet) parents and so often treated as if this huge part of their very existence is a terrible mistake. Of course, it isn't. But those with power have never really needed an explanation for oppressing people other than they *can*.

And it isn't like it's escaped my notice that Kadri and Emyr, who've never had the chance to rule without their every move being questioned, don't look anything like the rulers who've sat on Asalin's Throne before them. Fae and human history are not closely interwoven, and the fae don't have the same racist origin story humans do. The oppression of people of color, especially Black people, people who look like Kadri and Emyr, isn't the entire foundation our civilization is built on, the way it is for humans.

But how much might human influence have changed the way we interact with race ourselves over the last five hundred years? Are there microaggressions I've never noticed, protected by my own whiteness? Is part of Derek's motivation rooted in the color of Emyr's skin? I guess I don't really know, and that's my own fault.

What I do know is that the way humans interact with systemic oppression comes in a different box than the way the fae do. It looks different on the outside, and it operates by a different set of rules. But really, when you get down to it, bigotry is bigotry.

Derek touches a hand to his temple as if to rub away a headache. "I understand this may mean very little to you, but it means a great deal to a lot of people. For all his convictions about change, I don't believe Emyr is strong enough to face the backlash that will inevitably come with his inauguration. He will crumble under the stress of being king when he realizes no one in Asalin supports his new ideas. And should his meddling in human business risk our exposure? I don't believe he is strong enough to defend us."

I'm not sure what to do with that. Emyr seems pretty adamant about being king. Adamant enough to drag me here because he thinks I'm somehow going to help his chances of winning the popular vote. Not that there's an *actual* vote. In this scenario, winning just means avoiding some kind of revolution.

"Even your marriage…" Derek frowns, like he's trying to find a way to say what he needs to say without offending me. "It's very unorthodox. No one understands why the king and queen agreed to this contract in the first place. It has nothing to do with you as a person, Wyatt. I understand Emyr cannot help the bond. But he could have kept you hidden. He could have chosen the crown over his selfish desire."

We were children, I don't say. Children are *meant* to be selfish.

"And now the damage has been done. The fae don't want to see a witch on the Throne. Tell me, do you believe the humans would want a dog for president?"

I want to say something about the fact that he just compared me to a dog, but despite a flare of rage simmering under the surface, I can't summon the will to snap back. Maybe because I get what he's saying. Of course the fae are terrified of a witch taking the Throne. Then they might have to deal with an itty-bitty fraction of what the witches have dealt with since the dawn of time, living under the rule of fae without any say of our own.

"He believes this union will help to bring our two sides together. He refuses to acknowledge that all it has done so far is drive us farther apart." Derek sighs. "Hostility on both sides is growing worse. Of course I believe that witches should have the right to live in peace, but…peace is not the goal of every witch."

What does a peaceful witch look like to the fae? One who's quiet? Subservient? I wonder these things, but don't bother to ask. Derek has already made it clear what he thinks of me and people like me. And we're alone out here. I don't need to push him.

At least not any more than I can't help myself to.

"I've tried talking to him," Derek presses. "Tried reasoning with him. I've held meetings with my uncle, sent messages to the Court. I have attempted every high road I can think of. I don't *want* this to get ugly. I never wanted it to come to this. But I have to put Asalin first. The people of this kingdom deserve a leader who respects what they want, who protects their ability to live as they always have. Even if that means taking the low road."

"Okay." I shrug. "So, what's your plan?"

Derek stops walking and turns to face me. His black wings billow across his back, creating a cavern around us both. My throat tightens as he backs me up against a wall of greenery.

Once again, unseen flames light along the surface of my body, burning just beneath my skin. My black energy snaps out around me, creating a shield between my body and his. I do *not* like to be cornered.

He doesn't seem to notice my bad reaction. Derek inclines his head toward mine, pushing right past the barrier of my magic. It dissipates like smoke. His forehead nearly touches mine. I can feel the heat from his mouth against my own when he speaks. "I want you to help me keep Emyr from ascending to the Throne. Whatever it takes."

My chest tightens. The crisp scent of him is overwhelmed by the smell of flowers all around us. "Are you asking me to off him, my good bitch?"

I'm hoping the words will throw Derek off. Will force him to take a step back. Will make him roll his eyes at me. They don't. Instead, he shakes his head. That one errant blond tendril brushes against my temple.

"Of course not. I want Emyr to live a long and happy life. So long as he's far away from the crown." He reaches down and wraps his hand around one of my wrists. I want to jerk away, but I can't. My body, flooded by heat only moments ago, suddenly feels cold. My bones feel impossibly breakable in his big palm. One claw presses into my pulse point. My throat closes. "Wouldn't you do anything to go back to your life out there? To take your human and return home? Do you really want to stay here in Asalin forever, constantly reminded of the horrific thing you did?"

My lips part but not even a breath escapes them. Derek isn't wrong. After a long moment, I finally manage to ask, "Your plan gets me my life back?"

He smiles again, all teeth this time. "I am the head of the Guard. I will drop the charges against you at your trial tomorrow afternoon. You will spend your time here in Asalin making sure there is not one citizen among us, fae or witch, who wants to see you on the Throne. You will make them *hate* you. The more they turn against you, the more they will turn against Emyr. And when there is no one left who will follow his rule, I will take my rightful place."

My tongue drags against my own little fangs. "Everyone already hates me. Emyr doesn't seem to think that's a problem."

"Some of them hate you. Some of them see what you did as the actions of a misguided child. Emyr intends to use you to sway them toward the latter." Derek chuckles against my cheek. "But I believe you would have more fun becoming the villain."

"Oh?" I manage a sneer. "You think you know me?"

Derek's other hand rises to my cheek. His skin is impossibly warm, his fingers soft from a life that hasn't known a day of work. His claws bite tiny imprints into my face. How is he leaning closer still? "I may have missed the last few years, but I watched you grow up, did I not? And unlike my cousin, my eyes were not clouded by some bond. I saw you for exactly who you have always been." His thumb strokes beneath my eye, sweeping down to press into the space above my upper lip. "I have always had a certain fondness for you, though, in spite of that."

I am not breathing when I manage to say, "Back. The fuck. Up."

With a lingering look into my eyes, Derek finally does, taking a few steps back and letting his hands fall away.

I collapse against the hedge, struggling to calm my racing heart. My gaze drifts to the bushes directly behind him. Shrubbery, ivy, flowers. Desperate for something to concentrate on, I focus in on a single white rose, turned to face the sun, petals still glistening with morning dew. A nest of thorns surrounds its delicate body. This flower won't be plucked unless someone is willing to risk slicing their hand open to grab it. Steal the flower, face the consequences.

Finally, my chest begins to unravel.

"I will do whatever it takes to get the hell out of here."

CHAPTER SIX

I WISH YOU COULD BE MY PET

For the rest of the day, I do my best to balance the hurricane in my head with Briar's excited insistence we explore every corner and crevice Asalin has to offer. I manage to placate her with a long tour of the castle, too anxious to venture anywhere else so soon after our arrest, but not at all strong enough to convince her to hide with me all day.

But that night, when we've returned to our room and she's snoring quietly on the other side of the bed, I start dreaming up ways to make sure everyone in Asalin wants my head on a spike. Luckily for Derek and me, I don't think it's going to be that hard.

Part of me wonders if I should feel guilty about doing this to Emyr. Derek isn't wrong about anything he said. But Emyr isn't wrong, either. We are *supposed* to be together. We did love each other *once*, as friends. Maybe as something more. I'm betraying some part of myself by agreeing to go along with Derek's scheming, I know I am.

But Emyr dragging me here against my will feels like a betrayal, too. How might things have unfolded differently if he'd agreed to stay in Texas, to keep talking, to get to know me again as *me*? We'll never know.

I've got a running list of possible shenanigans to get myself into—I am going to do something chaotic with the dragons, I think—but the fantasies aren't helping to lull me to sleep. And as seconds tick into minutes and the night drags on longer and longer, restlessness finally starts to eat away at me. Quiet as I can be, I slip out of bed, drag my hoodie and sweats on, and let nostalgia carry me back to my favorite place in this castle. One of the few places I didn't take Briar today, a little hideaway I'm not ready to share, even with her.

The north tower is the highest point in the palace, up a long, long staircase that leaves me gasping for air by the time I reach the top. The dome and its many, many embrasures have all been taken over by the ivy outside. It climbs in through the openings and covers parts of the floor and ceiling, nearly concealing the walls all together.

I lean against the base of one opening and gaze at Asalin, spread out beneath me. From here, I can take it all in. The moon hanging low over the village down the hill, most of the lights in the houses turned out except for the last few night owls. The field where the peryton sleep and, on the other side of the village, the base of the mountains where the drag-ons have settled in.

In the forests, hellhounds can be heard baying at the night sky. Treetops rustle with energy as the nocturnal pixies begin to wake, shaking the branches of their homes as they do. Though I can't see the goblins—because they don't like to be seen, sticking to the parts of the woods they've claimed as their territory and theirs alone—I know they're probably stomping through the stream right now, muddying themselves up before bed.

There is beauty here, in this kingdom, if someone knows where to look for it.

"Firestarter?"

I grind my teeth. How did I not hear him coming up the stairs?

I turn and find Emyr standing on the other side of the tower. He's dressed in slouchy azure pants and an oversize white cloak that clips at his throat and hangs down to his knees. There are a pair of strappy white sandals on his feet.

When moonlight illuminates his full mouth and the beautiful, dangerous hint of fangs against his lips, I force myself to breathe like a normal person. My god, I don't know what to do with him. And while my brain would love to suggest several ideas, I refuse to acknowledge any of them.

"How'd you find me?"

He approaches me slowly, before leaning against the wall a few feet away. "No one answered my knock when I went to your room. I thought maybe you were still on your tour. This was the first place I thought to look."

Because this was my favorite place, once. Because he knew a lot about me, once.

"Why were you creeping into my bedroom in the middle of the night?"

"I— You are *insufferable*," he growls, a hand shooting up to snatch at his curls. He gnashes his fangs, other hand fisting at his side.

"Are you suffering, Your Highness?" My voice leaves me in a near-singsong. I can't seem to help myself. "Would you like to cry about it? Is that why you were looking for me?"

"I was looking for you because, for some unthinkable reason, I hoped to apologize."

That isn't the answer I was expecting. I slump against the wall, shoving one hand in the pocket of my pants.

"For what?" There's an abundance of things he should be sorry about.

"For how poorly things have gone since you arrived. For Derek's treatment of you. For my behavior yesterday." He scrubs a hand over his face. "I know you had reservations about coming here at all, and I haven't exactly proven to you that you made the right decision in choosing to show up."

It wasn't my *decision*, either, considering I was basically held at gunpoint. (Spellpoint? Whatever.) But he isn't wrong in that things haven't been a piece of cake.

"I didn't expect to be treated any better than this. Not in Asalin."

It's the truth and nothing but the truth, but I still see the way it hurts Emyr when I say it. He winces, rolling over one shoulder to gaze out at the night in front of us.

His profile isn't horrible to look at. Dark, thick eyebrows sit over the long lashes that frame his brown eyes. His sharp cheeks create hollows on either side of his plush mouth. That golden hoop dangles low from the center of his broad nose. After another long moment of staring at his face, I turn my own head in the direction he's staring.

The pixies are beginning to rise from their trees, a thousand tiny lights swarming into the sky, a quiet buzzing filling the air all around us.

"You didn't really think it would be different, did you?" I ask the night.

Emyr swallows, and in my periphery I think I see him shrug. "This kingdom fails its people in many ways. But I believe we can make change for the better. I'd hoped you would be more excited about the prospect."

Be the change you wish to see in the world? Really? I sigh.

As the pixies begin flying across the sky, a handful bobble up toward the tower. Their glowing wings light the air around us like fireflies, little bodies covered in thick white hair floating in front of us. I can just barely make out their pinched faces. When one smiles in my direction, I can see several tiny rows of razor-sharp teeth.

Pixies are cute, but they will eat you alive if they feel like it. I was once incredibly fond of them. No wonder. That's called projection.

When I turn my head, I catch Emyr staring at me this time. I can't help the way I jolt a little, not expecting to find his gaze boring into me the way it is.

"What?"

"You *did* want to marry me once."

He's not wrong. I look away from his face to twist my fingers together, shoulders rising and falling. "Yeah, well. You wanted to become a poet once."

A beat passes before Emyr laughs, the sound taking me by surprise. It's deep, echoing off the walls. Something about it reminds me of a tree, solid and grounded and filled with life. I look back to find he's moved a little closer to me, propping himself up by the elbows to lean back against the opening in the tower wall. His horns glint in the light of the pixie wings. "It took me way too long to realize those poems were just really, *really* bad."

I don't trust this.

And still, I can't seem to help myself. I grin a little, shaking my head. "Remember the one about the turtle?"

"Oh, the turtle poem." Emyr groans, reaching up to scrub his hand over his mouth, claws scratching gently at his chin as he does. "Please, don't."

"How did that go again?" I raise an eyebrow at him, my voice taunting. "Little turtle, green and wet. I wish you could be my pet—"

"Shh." Emyr reaches up and presses a finger to my mouth. "That's enough of that."

Suddenly, I'm a child again, and we're hiding in his closet to try and escape the attention of his nanny. He's reading me one of his poems and my head is in his lap, his fingers sliding through my still-long hair, his voice soft and even and comforting.

Shit. I blink myself back into the tower. I can't think about that.

Still, I can't seem to right myself. His hand is still touching my lips. All around us, my energy gives one shaking pulse, like a wave of black going out in all directions. My heart thrums too hard. I can hear it trying to climb up my throat.

Time no longer exists. It's simply one moment suspended, the two of us in this tower, our gazes locked. In the darkness of night, Emyr's eyes almost look black, but flecks of pixie light catch them and create a smattering of amber specks across their surface. It reminds me of the sky outside, blackness decorated by stars.

Slowly, as if afraid of scaring me away, Emyr slides his hand to the side of my face, moving his finger from my lips so he can cup my cheek. Derek's grip was firm. Emyr touches me as if he thinks I might crumble. His voice has taken on a quiet rasp when he speaks again. "We both grew up. We both changed. But we can find our footing again."

"What if we can't, though?" I twist my hands in front of my stomach, try to think of how to word this. "I know you think the bond is irrefutable. But I have a hard time believing that just because some weird, old-ass fae magic decided I'd be your perfect baby factory, we don't have any choice but to live happily ever after."

Those thick eyebrows drag together, and he says nothing.

So, I press on. "I mean… I know you say you need me. But you don't *want* me. Especially not anymore. Right? You said yourself you wouldn't have chosen me."

Emyr's gaze is heavy as it ticks away from mine. Down the length of my face, hovering over my mouth. Skimming my throat. Along the folds of the black hoodie, down to my hands peeking out past the sleeves. To my thighs behind the fabric of the sweats. Then back to my face.

We both swallow.

Finally, he answers, in his own roundabout way. "You haven't changed as much as you think you have."

I raise my eyebrows, because that seems untrue.

"You have always been *you*. You just found the language to talk about it." He shrugs.

I huff. "Well, it's not just that, you know. I mean, seriously, ask anyone who's spent time with me recently. I'm a complete asshole."

"I don't know how to tell you this, but you've never been a saint."

"Oh. Gee. Thank you so much."

Emyr grins, flashing those dimples again. After a moment, though, he sighs, his expression growing more serious. "The bond is a compulsion. And you're right. I would not have chosen you. Not because I don't want you, but because our union is complicated."

A *compulsion*. I've always wondered what it felt like to be a mated fae. To feel it from Emyr's side, this connection we supposedly have. Witches, though fae in technicality, don't experience that same *need*. He'd tried to explain it to me in the past, but always fumbled over his words, couldn't seem to get it out right. I still don't really understand what Emyr feels when he looks at me, except that he can't seem to force himself to get rid of me.

Still, what he feels doesn't matter. "Yeah, no shit. You're holding my literal death over my head to force me to marry you. That's not just complicated, my guy, that's right fucked up."

Emyr frowns. After a beat, he lowers his gaze to consider his claws, shrugging. "I suppose we could put off the wedding until you find yourself feeling more enthusiastic. I had hoped to go through with things as quickly as possible, but I can give you a little time, if that's what you need."

"I don't know if all the time in the world could make me *want* this."

"What are you asking me, really?"

What *am I* asking him?

Maybe I'm entertaining some really outlandish fantasies right now. But Emyr does care about me. At least, part of him cares about part of me, even if it's involuntary. And he's clearly feeling wistful about what we used to be. It's possible he doesn't want to hurt me. It's possible he could be swayed.

If I could convince him to let me go, I wouldn't have to wreak any of the havoc Derek is suggesting. I could let my list of shenanigans lie. Things wouldn't have to get ugly.

"I don't—" I hesitate, taking a deep breath. "I can't leave the human world behind. I can't just come back here and go back to living by fae rules. I don't *want* this. I'm *never* going to be happy playing this game. So, knowing how I feel...would you consider going to the Court? Would you be willing to ask them to dissolve the contract?"

Emyr stares at me. I stare back. Waiting. Waiting.

And then his answer comes.

"No."

The wind gets knocked right out of me. I feel like someone's just run me over with a car.

Here I am, convincing myself he might care about what I want. And there he stands, admitting without a hint of remorse that he would let me die by way of a blood oath before allowing me my freedom.

As long as I'm in Asalin, I'm as good as his prisoner.

"Please understand, I want you to be happy," Emyr is say-ing quietly, though I'm not really paying attention to him anymore. "But I can't lose you again. You don't know what it feels like, being away from you. Not knowing if you're safe or taken care of. I *will* find a way to make sure you're happy here."

Derek Pierce is a traitorous creep whose greatest asset seems to be that he smells nice and could fuel another several years' worth of late-night fantasies.

Emyr North is a selfish, spoiled prince, intent on using our history to manipulate me into feeling better about being held here on threat of my own death.

Neither of them deserve my loyalty. But to get what I want, I know what has to be done.

"Good night, Your Highness," I say, shaking my head and brushing past Emyr to escape the tower. I can feel his gaze on my back, but I do not stop.

If he wants to play with fire, he should expect to get burned.

CHAPTER SEVEN

AND THE FIRE DOES NOT OBEY

First thing the next morning, I pull the Justice card from my deck. Seems a bit on the nose.

A servant arrives to lead Briar and me to the tribunal room, where I'm forced to sit trial. I've never been here before, never had any reason to be. It kind of reminds me of a British courtroom, at least from what I've seen on TV. There are rows of pews on all sides, each of them facing my seat in the center of the room, and probably fifty people staring at me.

At the back wall, a raised table seats five members of the Guard, each of them with five red marks to indicate they're the highest possible rank. Derek sits in the middle, their all-powerful leader, the eye of the storm.

I guess it doesn't go as badly as it could. I don't even have to speak. Derek upholds his end of the bargain. "Upon counsel from the Throne, the Guard has decided to abandon the charges levied here today. It is our belief that what occurred that night was a tragic accident and no malice was intended. The weight of Wyatt Croft's own loss shall suffice as punishment enough. That, along with a substantial fine for the property damage done."

To my left, Briar gives an elated cry. I glance over and see Jin's curled their fingers over her mouth to keep her quiet. Both of them are grinning. Clarke flashes me a thumbs-up and a wink. The Committee member from yesterday is sitting next to her, looking as dour as I remember him.

He is not the only one who appears unimpressed with the Guard's ruling. The audience grumbles, sharp whispers and hard stares erupting as they begin to stand and stomp their feet. Another of the Guard members slaps a clawed hand against the wooden tabletop in front of her, demanding that everyone be quiet and get on with their lives. I remain seated, glancing rapidly between the rest of the room and my own twisted fingers, my heart in my throat.

How many of these people would kill me themselves if they had the chance?

Eventually, most of the room clears. I stand and turn toward Briar and the others. Emyr has joined them, the group of five standing in front of the pews and watching me. Has he been here the entire time? I didn't notice him. But then, I'd tried pretty hard not to look at anyone for fear of what I might find looking back at me.

If he's here, are his parents? A quick glance around the room tells me no, not unless they've slipped out with the rest of the crowd. I didn't expect them to be, though.

How shameful it must be for the royal family to be tied to a criminal.

"Good job not dying, kiddo." Jin smiles, slinging an arm around Clarke's shoulders.

Briar steps to my side and folds her elbow with mine. Her denim dress rustles against her thick thighs. "I knew everything was going to work out."

Emyr is looking at me. I know because I can feel his gaze, heavy and insistent, pressing into my throat like fingertips choking me, but I can't force myself to look back.

"Wyatt, do you remember my brother, Wade?" Clarke asks with a smile, placing her hand on the Committee guy's chest.

Oooooh. Wade!

I knew he looked familiar the day he plucked Briar and me from the dungeon, but I couldn't figure out *how* I knew him. That's because, before coming back to Asalin, I'm not sure when the last time I got a good look at Wade was. Most of my memories of him involve only catching glimpses while he snuck around the woods, creeping like some sort of overgrown shadow, not wanting to be seen or to see anyone else. He's a Feeler, and supposedly an incredibly attuned empath. People used to say he hid in the woods to get away from everyone else's feelings. Which, like, fair.

This Wade certainly appears as if he wants to be seen. Not for the first time, I note the slight changes to his uniform to allow for maximum fashion, the dangly earrings, the man bun. And he's joined the Committee now, the branch whose entire purpose is taking care of people. I guess he must've learned to manage those emotions.

Lucky him.

He's looking at me in a way that sets my teeth on edge. Studying me like I'm an insect and he's got a microscope. Suddenly, he asks, "They really missed the mark when they decided you'd grow up to be queen, didn't they?"

Beside me, Briar tenses.

Jin's happy smile doesn't fade, but their eyes shift uncomfortably to Wade and then back to me.

Clarke smacks his chest, hard. "Hey!"

I take it, by all of their reactions, I'm supposed to be offended.

But, uh... "What? He's not wrong."

Clarke frowns at me, opening her mouth as if she's going to argue, then pursing her lips.

"I'm not ever going to be a queen." I shrug. "Like, for starters, I'm a dude?"

Wade flicks his wrist and gives an agreeable half nod.

As everyone takes that in, I finally let myself look at Emyr. He's staring at me, as I'd anticipated, dark gaze intent, sharp features settled into a stony mask. He's wearing what appears to be a Hawaiian shirt under a formfitting blazer, which, *okay, then*. The gold of his aura slithers closer to my own. My black magic snaps at it, hissing out a warning.

Jin and Clarke both eye the unspoken energy exchange with visceral discomfort.

I wonder what Emyr is thinking. Does he regret his decision to bring me here yet? Does he feel bad about what he said to me in the tower? Is there a part of Emyr that wants to go back in time and stop himself from befriending me when we were little, from ever laying eyes on his abominable witch? Maybe not yet. But there's time for him to change his mind.

"Well," Jin says breezily, recovering from the uncomfortable moment. "It's a good thing Emyr's always been a little gay. Otherwise, the discovery that he'd been bonded to a boy all this time could have been very awkward."

"Hmm. *Are* you a little gay, though?" Wade turns to look at Emyr, thick, perfectly sculpted brows rising over those keen eyes.

"What exactly do we mean by being a *little* gay?" Briar asks, tucking her fingers beneath her chin, thoughtful. "Like, I'm bi and ace, but I'm still *extremely* gay. What, is Emyr one of those people who's only gay on Saturdays?"

"Do those people exist?" Wade drawls.

"Why Saturdays?" Jin blinks.

"I guess it's possible Emyr will become gayer after the wedding," Clarke proposes, innuendo thick in her airy tone. "I had no idea how gay I could be until I met Jin."

"The answer, if you're wondering, is *very* gay." Jin wiggles their eyebrows and winks at me, as if we're sharing some kind of secret.

Wade's expression is one of alarm. "That is my sister."

"Right, totally, let's go back to talking about your cousin instead." The way Jin nods manages to look sarcastic.

"Let's not." Emyr rolls his eyes at them.

"Oh, no," Clarke suddenly gasps. "What if *Wyatt* isn't gay?"

"No, no, Wyatt is very gay," Briar assures her quickly. "A huge homosexual in a tiny package."

"I'm so glad we cleared all that up," I offer without inflection.

I'm about to tell Briar I'm beyond ready to go when someone interrupts me from behind.

"You know, I thought you were dead."

A thousand tiny needles prick their way across my body.

My sister's voice has always sounded eerily like my own. On the surface, our similarities run deep. Growing up, I was always told Tessa was who I would have been if I'd been born fae. If I'd been born *right*. But where my throat has learned to twist its words like a snarling dog, she coats her tongue in wind chimes. She forces softness where softness does not exist, delicate beauty to hide the ugly, ugly thing that lurks beneath the surface.

We have always had more in common than she would like the rest of Asalin to believe.

In the past, when Tessa spoke, I would hear half-assed apologies roll from her mouth like rotten fruit dropped into a trash can, as if she was always being forced to apologize for things she wasn't sorry for at all. I heard my deadname, hissed like a curse she was desperately trying to manifest, always a few ingredients short of making magic. When Tessa spoke, I wanted to claw the skin off my body and pick my bones from my muscle and become nothing, because she couldn't hurt me if I was nothing.

There is a part of me that has always loved my sister so much it makes me sick. There is another part of me that has always hated her just as much. They war inside me until neither exists at all, until the only thing I feel as I stand in front of her now is guilt.

I could drown in it.

All eyes have moved over my shoulder by the time I turn to face her. I flinch the moment I see her face. I can't not. It's jarring because it's her, and it's jarring because it's *almost me*. Her upturned button nose. Full pink mouth. Long lashes framing green eyes, one infinitesimally darker than the other. Honeyed hair, though hers is kept long and pulled into a bun at the top of her head, two strands falling down to frame her soft face. We are exactly the same height, two monsters trapped in too-small cages.

But where I make every effort to conceal my skin, Tessa seems to have no problem showing hers. A white lace crop top with a high neck is settled over what appears to be some kind of weird copper metal bra. Her tiny brown leather shorts are tucked beneath a floor-length, sheer white skirt. At the waistband of her pants, by the dip of her pelvis a few inches below her naval, she has had something intentionally scarred into her skin. Scarification is popular among the more traditional fae. Hers spells out something in the Old Language, though I can't read it.

Her wings have always reminded me of a dragonfly's, two sets of the thin, shimmering appendages jutting out from her back. And her lavender energy has draped itself over her body completely, curling up against her skin and settling there like pastel armor.

It never occurred to me that anyone might think I hadn't survived the fire. That my own sister might think I'd died that night. I open my mouth to say something, anything. An apology? A nasty retort? I don't know. At this point, my tongue has a mind of its own.

But again, I can say nothing before she cuts me off.

"I wish you were."

Oh.

Well, maybe I deserve that.

The air around me curdles thick with smoke as Asalin is ravaged by flames. I can't stop them. Couldn't if I wanted to. Do I want to? Is there any part of me that wants to pull back, to relinquish my hold on this place? To stop it from turning to ash at my feet?

Maybe the part of me that still loves Emyr. But that part of me is small and flickering, embers of a fire that have been dying for a long time now. He would never understand. He's one of them. He doesn't see the world the way I do. He doesn't see Asalin for what it really is.

This place is a curse. A prison. This place has been my personal hell. Every single witch in Asalin would be better off if it were torched to the ground. And every single fae might finally learn their lesson.

I am not your punching bag. I am not your charity case. I am not a pawn in your chess game, or a pretty face to look good next to you, or a warm body to put your hands on. I am a whole person. I am a person. I am a person, I AM A PERSON, I AM A PERSON, I AM A—

"WHAT ARE YOU DOING?" My father's voice shakes the earth like a dragon's roar.

I jerk my head toward the sound in time to see his big body lumbering toward me through the clouds of smoke. Icy fear washes over me, replacing some of the heat from the fire. I stumble back, tripping over cobblestones, nearly falling flat on my ass.

He doesn't let me, though. One big hand jerks out and wraps around my neck, yanking me to my feet. His palm presses down hard against my trachea, threatens to crumple my windpipe like paper.

This is not the first time he's put his hands on me for acting beyond his control. But this is the first time I do not sink to some hidden place within myself to hide. The first time I rise instead. More
flame erupts from my skin, jutting from the space beneath my jaw
this time and curling around his wrist as if an actual hand has shaped
itself from the fire.

My father bellows again, only this time in pain and not rage. He
releases me from his grip and I sink to the ground, stones digging
sharply into the backs of my legs. He swats uselessly at the fire as it
crawls up his arms to his face, his torso, engulfing him as his bellows
turn into mewling, helpless screams. And all I do is sit there on the
ground and watch, too afraid to flinch, or blink, or breathe.

"STOP THIS!" comes my mother's voice, and suddenly she appears at his side in a flurry of red energy that nearly matches the red
of the fire itself. "STOP! YOU'RE KILLING HIM!"

I try to raise my hands, but I can't. Try to pull back the fire, but
I can't. It's beyond me now. Outside of my control. It has a mind
of its own. It ravages its way down Asalin's main street, relishing in
the screams of the fae it chases from their homes, as it eats my father
alive, and it feels nothing. All I can do is stare in horror.

My mother seems to realize this at the same moment I do. She
comes for me, raising one clawed hand, and I feel it. Feel her Influencer magic work its way into my chest, snatching the air from my
lungs. I feel it as my ribs begin to tighten, threatening to puncture me
from the inside out.

"I tried so hard to love you." She says the words as if talking to
herself. "I wanted so badly to believe I'd been saddled with a child
like you for a reason. That your life would have a purpose. But I see
now I was an arrogant fool. You should have been left to the woods."

She is going to kill me. To save the rest of Asalin, she is going to rip me limb from limb. This is nothing new. I have always known this.

But today, I am not going to let her.

Around the three of us, the fire suddenly burns hotter. The flames flick from orange and red to blue, brilliant, bright, terrifying blue. They crash over my mother like a wave in an ocean, drag her down against my father's side. Her screams join his own. And in an instant, everything goes black.

I am not going to die. They are.

No! No! What am I doing?

This isn't right! I can't do this! They're my parents! What have I done?

Or is it me at all? My magic is hungry. Disused, left to rot in some deep, secret part of me, it has long been aching to burn out of control. And now it is. I don't know how to stop it, don't know how to pull it back now that it's escaped me, like a wild creature slipping its leash. And now, in the pitch-black around me, I can't even see the extent of its damage.

In the darkness, I reach for my parents, and fire reaches back. Only this time, when it touches my skin, it burns me, too. It crawls its way up my arms, twisting around my wrists, my elbows, trying to drag me down.

Screaming. Choking.

Pain. Endless, never-ending pain.

Somehow, in the midst of it, I manage to find my footing. And I flee.

I don't realize I'm right back in that night until Briar steps up against me and curls one arm around me to press her palm into my belly. She tugs me against her chest and nuzzles her curls to the side of my face. I don't realize I'm choking, sucking in the same smoke that floated off my parents' bones, until my best friend whispers in my ear that I need to breathe.

That night was the last time I performed any magic, until the day Emyr showed up and my flame rose, unbidden, to the surface again. Besides the daily tarot reading, I've done everything I can to excise myself from my power. I don't *want* it. I certainly don't deserve it.

For the most part, magic is cruelty. Mine and the fae's.

Briar pulls me, shaking, back into the present, ripping me away from the flashback with tender touches and soft words and the glow of her yellow energy wrapped around us both like a cocoon.

Her familiar eyes, so dark they could be black, are the first thing I see when I finally blink myself into my body. I have to blink a few more times to be rid of the burning tears gathered at the corners of my own eyes, but finally, I can make out the rest of her face. Her lips twitch and tighten around her teeth, and her eyebrows furrow over the bridge of her nose. She stares down at me and I stare up at her, and for a moment, we both just breathe.

You're okay, she says without saying it. *I've got you.*

My Briar has always had this strange magic of her own.

Or maybe I'm just obsessed with my best friend.

Finally, I find the willpower to turn my head from Briar's face to look back at Tessa. She is unreadable, mask firmly in place, armor unrelenting. She stares back at me without an ounce of discernible emotion.

Wade is the one who speaks, unexpectedly. "Tee, I told you not to come."

Tee? It takes me a moment to realize he's speaking to Tessa. He steps around Briar and me to flutter to my sister's side, reaching out and putting one hand at the small of her back. As if *consoling* her.

"I needed to see this for myself," she says. She does not look away from me, though her purple energy mingles with his green, the two of them swaying back and forth like swooshing fabrics. "A fine for property damages. You murder my parents, and you can just waltz back in here under the protection of the prince, with nothing holding you back but a *fee.*"

Of course she hates me. Of course she needs Wade to console her. I murdered her parents. I lost control and now I can't ever take it back. Nothing I can ever do will make this better.

Bile sloshes against my molars, threatening to choke me. Briar holds me tighter. I don't breathe. I don't deserve to.

"Hey." Wade touches his nose to Tessa's jaw and lowers his voice. "Let's get you home now, hmm?"

"Actually, it's good that you came," Emyr's voice comes from behind me. *Very close* behind me actually, so close that I actually jump a little out of Briar's grip.

I whip my head around to find he's sidled up to her and is looming over me, wings outstretched.

My energy seems to have gotten tangled with his and Briar's, the three of them creating a mess of threads hanging over us.

"My parents have requested Wyatt join us for dinner tonight in their private dining room. They would like his family to attend also."

Tessa's upper lip curls over one beautifully sharp fang. She does not say whatever nasty thing is gurgling on her tongue, whatever hideous comeback springs to mind at Emyr's words.

I am pathetic enough to be grateful for her silence.

CHAPTER EIGHT

A GAME I DON'T HAVE A RULEBOOK FOR

Briar doesn't let go of my hand the entire way to the dining room. She keeps our fingers twisted together as we follow Wade and Tessa to the belly of the palace, the very center of it all where the king and queen live. Every now and then, Wade turns his head to look back at us, as if making sure we're still following. Tessa doesn't look back at all.

I don't blame her for the way she feels. I've had three years to get used to seeing my own reflection in the mirror without wanting to claw my skin off. She's only had thirty minutes.

When we finally reach our destination, Wade deposits us in front of a set of ornate, golden double doors and informs us to go in and wait. He gives Tessa a long, deliberate look, and she offers him a subtle nod in return. Finally, he leaves us.

Past the doors is a dining room. It's smaller than one might expect for the king and queen, just one long table with ten chairs, all carved from beautiful raw wood. There's another door toward the back of the room from which voices and clanging can be heard, presumably the kitchen. One wall is made entirely of stained glass, little shards of color that remind me of a kaleidoscope. I think I can make out the mountains outside through the rainbow.

I suppose if dinner goes really, really poorly, I can throw myself through the window.

Briar squeezes my hand tighter, as if reading my thoughts. When Emyr said the king and queen wanted to have dinner with my family, there was no hesitation on my part that Briar was coming. Emyr seemed less than impressed, but he didn't fight it.

I'd thought Tessa might keep Wade around for the meal. The two of them seem close—I wonder if they're *together* together, though I don't actually know enough about her life now to speculate. We weren't exactly close *before*... Well, we just weren't close, even before.

She came alone, though. She gives Briar and me a wide berth, hands clasped in front of her, gaze sweeping the room to take it all in. Tessa's never been here before. While my parents were dressing me up in gaudy gowns for dinners at the palace—"date nights" with the young prince—my sister was off enjoying her childhood.

No one has spoken a word in a while. I'm fine keeping it that way. I still don't know what I would say. Since I first laid eyes on her in the Tribunal room, I've been trying to figure that out. So far, I don't have shit. My tongue feels like wool.

Briar, though. Briar apparently isn't as comfortable with the silence as I am.

She clears her throat softly and then asks, the question a raspy half whisper blown in Tessa's direction, "What does that mark mean?"

From the corner of my eye, I see Tessa's spine tighten. Lavender threads itself like a brace up her back, worms its way down her arms and across her stomach.

She doesn't answer.

Most people would take that as a cue to let it go. Briar swallows and continues. "The one on your hips. It's writing, isn't it?"

Tessa drapes one arm over her pelvis, effectively covering up the mark, and turns her back to us.

The front doors of the dining room swing open.

"Wyatt!" Leonidas North, king of the North American fae, addresses me by name. "It is so good to see you again."

He extends a hand, mouth split into a dazzling smile. I don't know what to do besides shake it, as I shift from one foot to the other and clear my throat. "You, too."

Leonidas laughs, a too-loud sound that booms and echoes around us like thunder, if thunder was feeling celebratory. It matches his energy, a ridiculous neon green that bounces around the room, taking up too much space.

There are stories about Leonidas North that paint him like a god. In his youth, when his own parents were still sitting on the Throne, Leonidas formed an insurgent group of fae to travel through the door to Faery. It was an unheard-of feat that had not been attempted in all the generations since the fae left their homeworld for this one. The door, kept sealed shut with magic for so long, was left open long enough to let Leonidas and his crew slink through. Their mission was to assess the state of the world, to determine if the fae could return.

A return was deemed impossible. In fact, Faery's climate had become so hostile that many of the fae in Leonidas's group died before they were able to make their way back to Earth. They slammed the door closed behind them once more, resealing it and declaring it would never be opened again.

The only good that came from it was Leonidas securing his spot as some kind of fabled badass.

Supposedly, he was also a big ladies' man back in the day. Partly because of his reputation and partly because he was beautiful. And though his tanned white skin has begun to wrinkle, he's still beautiful in a distinguished kind of way. His baby-blue eyes and blond curls, turning smoky with age, remind me of his niece and nephews. He has a row of horns stretched across his forehead, almost concealed under his hair, like their own sort of crown. His wings are as brightly colored as his magic, like a parrot's.

I glance back to the door just as Emyr and his mother sweep into the room.

There are stories about Kadri North, too.

When Leonidas met her while on a trip to Oflewyn, the fae kingdom in Eurasia, their bond was immediate. Within months, she moved to Asalin and they were married.

And everyone here hated her, because she was strong-willed and defiant and *different*. Asalin has always hated things that are different.

Regardless, Kadri had only one real responsibility. People were willing to set aside their distaste for such an outspoken and modern queen because she was going to give them the one thing the fae have always valued above all else. Babies. Precious, perfect little fae children to carry on the royal line.

And then more than twenty years passed without any living children.

Healers attempted to fix what was broken within her that meant she could not carry heirs. Influencers forced her blood to pump faster, her heart to beat harder, changed her hormone levels and her moods. Feelers laid hands on her stomach and tried to sense the distress of each child she lost, tried to see it coming soon enough to stop it. Even witches brewed potions, read cards, threw dice, painted her body in sigils, consulted the stars. Nothing worked.

The whispers about her grew louder and louder and crueler and crueler until the proud queen began to fold into herself. People began to whisper of a false bond. She must have bewitched him. She must have convinced him he felt something for her that he did not, that she was faking her own bond just to steal Asalin's Throne. Why would fate saddle their king with a queen who could not do the one thing she was meant to?

It was a desperate hope. If she was not his true mate, another could still be found. It was not too late for Leonidas to have children. The fate of Asalin's Throne could still be sealed.

The incident happened sometime after the rumors began. One night, Kadri plummeted from the north tower to the ground below, her body crashing and breaking on impact. Some believe she jumped. Others say she was pushed.

She was discovered, but not quickly enough. Leonidas called for the most powerful Healers in the village to come to her aid. Working in tandem, they managed to revive her, but she awoke with no memory of her fall or how it happened.

I consider her as she and Emyr move toward us.

Her shock-white hair in thin braids down her back. Her umber skin covered in pink scars. One silver horn halved on her head, the other with a crack down the center. Both white wings limp, dragging over the floor behind her like the train of a dress. The long claws on one of her hands clutch the head of her cane, black marble shaped to look like the heads of a chimera. Her other hand rests in the crook of her son's elbow.

Her energy is a soft, quiet gray, hovering around her shoulders. Clouds just before the rain comes.

When she catches me staring, I turn my head away.

After the incident, the couple stopped trying to have children. Kadri's fire returned, and she no longer allowed herself to tolerate the whispers, or the prodding, or the blame that Asalin's citizens had spent so long throwing her way.

A few years later, she and Leonidas received word that one of her relatives in Oflewyn was expecting a baby she could not keep. She wanted to know if they would take him. A few months after that, they brought Emyr home.

Emyr has traveled to Oflewyn with his parents more than once. He's met his birth mother, one of Kadri's cousins. Though I've always been curious about her, there doesn't seem to be much of a story there.

"Please, everyone, take a seat." Leonidas is still smiling, and he claps me—hard—on the shoulder, too startlingly fast for me to react.

As we sit, staff begin pouring out of the kitchen, pushing carts laden with food and drink. They arrange our food in golden bowls, pour wine into matching glasses, and set down the goldenware with quiet clinks before slipping away again. Best not to be in sight unless they're needed, I guess.

"I hope you're still a fan of kavera, Wyatt." Leonidas is watching me, still smiling that big smile. "It was your favorite when you were little."

Kavera. My stomach gurgles at the thought, tongue rolling up against the roof of my mouth as I look down at the bowl in front of me.

Kavera is a dragon meat stew, made with a dark red, almost black, bone broth, melt-in-your-mouth slices of meat, potatoes, carrots, and onions. The best part, though, is the topping. The stew is topped with thin pieces of dragonskin, deep fried and sprinkled on top as a heavy-handed garnish.

I don't even bother answering the king, spooning a giant pile of it into my mouth and practically moaning at the sharp, earthy, *so ridiculously good I could actually cry* taste.

Okay. So, the human world might have McDonald's, but you can't get kavera anywhere else but a fae kingdom. I guess I can see *one* upside to sticking around.

Leonidas doesn't seem bothered by my bad manners, as he chuckles and digs into his own food. I grab a piece of toasted bread from the center of the table, ladle some stew onto it, and tear into it with my teeth in one big bite.

For a while, we eat in silence, apart from the sound of utensils clinking and my occasional groans of pleasure. The queen is the one who speaks next.

"I apologize we were unable to see you before tonight, Wyatt." Kadri's voice is smooth and slow, as if she is choosing her words very carefully. "Given the circumstances of your arrival, we thought it best to wait until the trial had come to a close. There are already so many whispers of your preferential treatment, after all."

She's watching me, dark eyes sharp. I'm being tested. I know this. I can see it on her face. But I don't know what the test is.

"It's fine." I shrug. "It's over now."

Kadri tilts her head toward me. "Indeed."

Suddenly, finally, Tessa breaks her silence. "You truly still intend to go forward with this marriage?"

The queen slides her discerning gaze to my sister's face, while Leonidas continues smiling in a way that doesn't quite crinkle around his eyes. It's he who answers her. "Of course. There is no union more sacred than that of fated mates."

"You don't believe choice matters as much as fate?" Tessa demands. Her tone is sharp, a blade fresh off a whetstone, but her posture remains loose. Her hands remain folded over her belly, her thumbs circling each other slowly.

I'm not sure where she's going with this. Briar and I exchange a look.

"Well, certainly the choices we make are important." Leonidas speaks slowly, choosing each word carefully.

It almost seems as if he and Tessa are playing a game. A game I don't have a rulebook for. A game for which the winner's prize is beyond me. They stare one another down from opposite ends of the table, green shards of broken glass against purpling bruised knuckles.

"But Wyatt and Emyr have chosen to be here today," he continues.

"Not exactly." I offer the room a smile when all eyes flick toward me. "Under threat of a blood contract and all."

I can *feel* Emyr's glower burning the side of my face before I look at him. He's slumped forward with his chalice in the palm of his hand, grip so tight I think his black claws might rip right through the metal.

I smile. He bares his fangs at me, and the hair on the nape of my neck rises. I flash one black slicked middle finger in his direction and his wings twitch over his shoulders.

"Well…" Leonidas coughs, dragging the attention back to him. "Yes, there is that. But you are still making the choice to be happy in this arrangement. And that's something."

Oh, am I? That's what I want to ask. But Tessa doesn't allow me the chance.

"It was also his choice to murder our parents. To burn them alive, to *cook* them like meat until they couldn't be saved by any Healer in Asalin."

The only part of her statement that takes me off guard is when she genders me correctly.

Briar decides to take up the torch on my behalf, though. Because of course she does. "Your parents attacked *him* that night. And not for the first time. What happened was an accident, but it never would have happened if he'd been given an ounce of compassion. If he'd been allowed around other witches so he could learn how to use his power to begin with."

Tessa stares, unblinking. "My parents loved her—"

Ah, there it is, the inevitable slip of the tongue. Tension cords it way up my shoulder blades, screws tightening in the bones in my back.

"Him."

I expect the correction to come from Briar. And it does. But only at the same time it comes from Emyr.

He took me by surprise when he asked for my pronouns in Laredo, and he's managed to do it again. It sets off something inside me I don't want to name, some warmth that wiggles down from my chest, my gut, into my thighs, my freaking toes. *Fondness*, maybe. Ugh.

I shoot him a look, some petulant part of me wanting to tell him I do not *need* him to defend me, I do not find anything *heroic* or *charming* about the simple act of not being a transphobic asshole. The bar is not set that low! I refuse to be tricked into having gay thoughts about him just because he isn't *as* terrible as he could be!

But he isn't looking at me. He's looking at Tessa.

She takes a deep breath. To my continued surprise, she simply says, "Yes. My parents loved *him* the best they knew how. They were not perfect. But they did not deserve to die."

"And Wyatt did not intend to kill them," Emyr says flatly. I wonder if he believes that, or if he just needs it to be true.

"When someone is pushed into a corner, bad things happen." Briar swallows, shaking her head. "You could have stepped in long before that night. You could have given him an ally."

"So, this is my fault?" The knife of my sister's voice edges closer to Briar's throat.

"I can't answer that for you," is all the comfort Briar offers her. "Besides, you are not the only one who saw abuse happening and did nothing."

Her words hang heavy in the air around us. Too heavy. I go back to focusing on my bread.

Leonidas gives another uncomfortable cough. "Yes, well, all things being equal, the Guard has made their ruling. Wyatt is not guilty. Hopefully, moving forward with this wedding will allow us all a chance to heal. To focus on the future, instead of continuing to dwell on the unfortunate circumstances of the past."

"Sounds like a fairy tale," I say, and I don't know if Leonidas can't hear the acid in my mouth or if he's choosing to ignore it, because he smiles and nods.

"There is, of course, the issue of Derek Pierce."

My spine goes tight at Kadri's words.

Leonidas sighs. "Yes. As you may or may not be aware, Wyatt, Derek has gotten it into his head that *he* should be king of Asalin."

"Derek has always believed he would be king of Asalin." Tessa sounds almost bored. She's slumped back in her seat again, body relaxed, holding her wine with loose fingers and a blank expression on her uncanny face. "After all, that's what you told him."

"A very, *very* long time ago," Leonidas chuffs. "Before we knew we would be gifted with a son of our own."

Had Kadri and Leonidas not adopted Emyr, Derek would have been the next in line. He would've been nearly a teenager by the time they brought Emyr here, with an entire childhood spent believing he would one day rule. No wonder he's such a dick.

"Derek does not see eye to eye with Emyr's decision-making," Kadri says, swirling her wine, watching the red liquid spin. "He believes Emyr has rejected the ways of Faery."

"Of course Emyr respects the old ways." Leonidas shakes his head. "It's only that...we must adapt. In some ways, we all must adapt to the world we live in. Derek will come to realize that eventually. Surely, in time, he and Emyr will find a middle ground between remaining rooted in the past and throwing away all we hold near and dear."

Throwing away all we hold near and dear? Leonidas doesn't sound nearly as progressive as his wife and son.

"Perhaps," Kadri answers, in a way that indicates she in no way believes Derek will come to realize anything eventually. "But his fear of being discovered is what holds him back from wanting to evolve. It is not a fear without basis."

"Being discovered?" Tessa's voice contains not even the barest hint at emotion. She raises one eyebrow, the only crack in her heavy armor. "You can't mean by the humans."

Leonidas sighs, waving one hand dismissively. "It is always a possibility, and one we must be prepared for. Ultimately, I believe it is unlikely. But should the time come, we will do what must be done. Perhaps a peace could be found. And if not, Emyr will lead us into war. I have all the faith in the world in him."

"There are other ways," Emyr adds quietly.

When I turn my head to look at him, he isn't looking up anymore. His gaze has fallen to his hands, studying the curve of his own claws.

"Other ways than what?" Leonidas asks the question slowly.

Briar and I exchange another *what is happening this time* glance.

"Beyond going to war." Finally, Emyr looks up. His expression is hesitant, as if he'd rather not say whatever it is he intends to.

Here, now, in this moment, staring at his mother and father, he looks very much like an eighteen-year-old boy. Not the imposing prince he's been since our reunion. This Emyr is so much more familiar. So much more similar to *my* Emyr.

I cut that thought off before it gets carried away.

"And what does that mean?" Leonidas demands.

Emyr exchanges a look with his mother. I think I see Kadri give the slightest inclination of her head.

"I know Faery was a brutal place when you returned. I understand people died. But you lived. Others lived. And you've said yourself, if you'd gone better prepared—"

Leonidas does not let him finish. "No. Out of the question."

"But with the proper Healing magic—"

"Faery was destroyed a long time ago. There will be no attempts to return. I will not let you take the same risk I did." Leonidas gnashes his teeth. "End any fantasy of this now, because it will not happen. Not under your rule. Not ever. Do you understand me?"

Emyr falls quiet, his shoulders slumping, his body seeming to sink in on itself. "Yes, Father."

The sound of breathing and cutlery tapping expensive golden bowls is too loud.

After a long moment of silence, Kadri clears her throat. "Yes, well. Be that as it may, it does not help matters that this wedding is the source of much ire from Derek's followers." The words are said calmly and factually, but they still manage to sting.

"Why?" Briar demands. "Because of the fire?"

"Because they don't want one of his kind on the Throne," Tessa responds. She isn't looking at us. She's staring at the tabletop, though the glazed look in her eyes leads me to believe she's somewhere else entirely. "You would be hard-pressed to find a fae in the kingdom who supports this wedding."

"For now," Leonidas amends, sounding more certain than he has any right to be. "I have all the faith in the world that Wyatt will be able to win them over."

Whoops. I hope you aren't a gambling man, Leo.

When Emyr taps his talons on the table and clips out, "Right, with his charming personality," what I think he means is, *We'll be lucky if this little shit doesn't burn the village down again.*

I'm pleased to see the softness he'd displayed only moments earlier seems to have evaporated. Good. I prefer playing with this version.

When I lean forward and smile, stage whispering, "Oh, darling. You know I reserve my best charms for you," what I mean is, *You wanted me, now you got me, fucko.*

He sneers. The sight of his long fangs pressed against his plush lower lip is enough to have me curling my nails into the palms of my hands. "Lucky. Me."

"Splendid!" Leonidas is beaming as if his son and I aren't throwing invisible daggers across the dining room table.

Kadri sighs, pressing her thumb to the bridge of her nose and closing her eyes. "This is why I tried to have the contract annulled."

"What?" Immediately, the vibe in the room shifts, like we've gone and doused ourselves in cold water. I glance from the queen to Leonidas, who's looking uncomfortable, to Emyr, who won't meet my eyes. "What are you talking about?"

"Emyr didn't tell you?" Kadri lowers her hand. "The animosity from Derek's faction has become so vile I thought this union would only serve to fuel them. I called upon the Court to dissolve your blood oath. We couldn't come to a unanimous vote, and so it remains."

"No. Emyr didn't tell me." But I think she already knew that.

Why wouldn't the Court throw out our contract? What possible benefit could it have for them, the royals I've never met, from fae kingdoms I'll likely never step foot in? And why did Emyr not tell me this, when I pleaded with him to go before the Court himself?

When I finally manage to drag my gaze away from the queen's face, I catch Tessa staring at me. *Hard.*

The same way I wondered what Emyr saw that night in Texas, the first time he'd laid eyes on me in years, I wonder what Tessa sees when she looks at me. Does she feel the same uncomfortable communion between us, this strange and unshakable sameness? Does she look at me and see who she might've been had she been put together the wrong way?

Does she really wish I was dead, or did she just say that to hurt me?

I'm going to leave this dinner with way more questions than answers.

Briar's hand finds my thigh beneath the table. Through my jeans, I can feel the warmth and softness of her palm.

All around me, I watch the way her yellow sunlight drapes across my skin. Before I met Briar, I never really understood the term *sun-kissed*.

It's the only thing that keeps me from going aflame when Leonidas says, "So, let's set a date, shall we?"

CHAPTER NINE

I AM AN ANT

The date we set is the last day of October. A Halloween wedding, though that means nothing to the fae. Five months away, the furthest out I could get Emyr—and Leonidas, who was somehow even more annoying—to agree to.

I am not spending my Halloween getting married. I'm dressing up and going trick-or-treating, one of my most beloved human traditions in the world, before I start looking too adult to get away with it. There is no way I'm letting a wedding interfere with that.

Which is how I've ended up *here*.

"You know, normally I would try to discourage this kind of self-destructive behavior." Briar tosses her braid over her shoulder and flashes me a dimpled grin. The afternoon sun beats down hard as we trudge up the hill, making her dark eyes glint. "But this sounds like fun for me, so."

Today, I've decided to steal a dragon.

Specifically, I've decided to steal the *king's* dragon. I remember the beast well enough from all the time Emyr and I spent riding him with Leonidas once upon a time. I think there is a favorable chance he isn't going to take one look at me, open up his jaws, and swallow me whole. And if I'm very wrong, well, at least I'll die for a worthy cause.

Anyway, if anything might turn the people here totally against me, I think *yeehawing* with the fifty-thousand-pound, hundred-year-old flying monster who's belonged to the royal family since he was a hatchling...will probably do the trick. Proximity to the dragons has always served as something of a status symbol for the fae. Not just anyone can show up and hop on one of these bad boys—at least, not just anyone is *supposed* to. Especially the one reserved for the king. It'd be like hijacking *Air Force One* to go joyriding.

But Briar did say she wanted to meet the dragons, after all. Who have I ever been to deny Briar anything when I have the ability to give it to her?

"I am not being self-destructive," I huff, struggling to suck in enough air, struggling to keep my legs pushing my body upward instead of collapsing into a heap in the grass. Were I less weighed down with emotional baggage, I might've considered leaving my hoodie behind on this abysmally hot day. Every inch of me under the heavy black fabric is covered in sweat, and we've barely even gotten started. "I am...pursuing the greater good."

Briar, when I finally gave in and explained Derek's scheming to her, was less than impressed. Between the two of them, I'm fairly certain she prefers the idea of King Emyr over King Derek, though that's probably because Emyr isn't the one who tried to have me executed when I first arrived. But, like, bygones and all that.

Still, despite her general disapproval, she hasn't tried talking me out of it. Not really, though I can see the cogs turning in her head when she scrunches up her nose and makes a *face* at my words. As if our ideas of the greater good are at odds, for the first time.

Whatever she might be considering saying to me, though, it doesn't matter. Because when we finally crest the hill, both of us panting and leaning forward to press our hands to our knees, the dragons come fully into view. Up close and personal this time. And all thought of anything else goes directly out the window.

From the balcony of our bedroom, it's hard to tell how big these creatures are. Here, standing in the grass not fifty feet away from where they're clustered together and bathing in the sun, it's clear they're the size of *houses*. They come in varying colors, no shade quite the same, much like the energies we carry around. Their scales catch the rays of the sun and reflect it into the air, creating soft little prisms of light all around them, making it hard to see without squinting. A few raise their heads, twisting their long necks to glance in our direction when they sense they're no longer alone, but none seem all that interested. They're used to dealing with people. We are probably as exciting to them as ants are to us.

"Wyatt," Briar breathes quietly at my side. Yellow buzzes

around her shoulders, twists down her arms to knot around her fingers.

"I know." I reach out to give her wrist a gentle squeeze. "Wait here until I say otherwise. If shit looks like it's going to hit the fan, you turn around and *roll* down the hill if you have to."

"I'm not going to leave you."

"You sure as fuck are." I squeeze again, brushing my thumb against the back of her hand. "What would you do to save me, anyway?"

She bites her lip, and I can see the acceptance finally settling on her face, even as she huffs out, "I'm very charming. I might be able to talk him out of eating you."

"Mmm-hmm." I let go of her wrist and start walking deeper into the clearing.

It isn't hard to find the beast I'm looking for.

Summanus is not colorful like many of the others. His scales are black as pitch, every inch of him so dark it's like staring into a void. He's stretched out near the center of the field, probably a hundred feet long from the tip of his snout to the end of his tail, which is spiked and rounded at the tip like a morning star.

I swallow any lingering fear and throw back my shoulders, and then trek right through the cluster of dragons sunbathing around him. One of them, obviously young because she's hardly bigger than a hatchling, with baby-pink scales and bright red eyes, rolls from her back to her belly to consider me. I worry she's going to rise to her feet and come romping over to investigate, but she seems content with watching.

The rest of them don't even bat an eye. I am an ant. I am fine with that.

Finally, I come face to nose with Summanus. He lets out a snore that sends a wave of hot air blowing against my legs, and I am reminded in the most gentle way possible that he could, with very little effort, turn me into a toasted marshmallow. And what would I do if he did?

Not shit, that's what.

Even though it's been a few years and I'm probably definitely rusty, I remember enough of this little ritual to know what I'm supposed to do. I take a deep breath and rub my sweaty palms against my thighs before crouching down. My knees settle into the grass in front of him. My hands slip into the front pocket of my hoodie, fingers twisting together uncomfortably.

A beat passes and he doesn't move.

I clear my throat.

One eye pops open and stares right at me so quickly and with such sharp intent that I stop breathing. Summanus's eyes are as black as the rest of him, two starless skies in the center of his long, keenly angled face. He stares at me. I stare back. Neither of us moves for what might be a very long time or might be only seconds.

And then, as if it takes an enormous amount of effort for him to lift the great weight of his own skull, he begins raising his neck. He bobs slowly closer until he can press the warm, wet weight of his nose to my neck.

I swallow. He takes a deep inhale that threatens to drag me like a speck of dirt right into his lungs. And then he pulls back again.

Summanus's mouth splits open, revealing row after row after row of metallic teeth, as long and sharp as swords. His forked tongue flicks out and whispers across my cheek, smoke billowing around us as he does. My heart threatens to give up its post.

And then he lowers his head again, the moment gone. Only this time, those endless black eyes remain open, fixed on my face. Waiting. And I have my answer.

I deflate like a water balloon exploding on impact. Maybe I'm not going to die today.

Well, Summanus isn't going to eat me today. But the day is still young. I've plenty of time to annoy someone else into doing it for him.

Raising my hand toward the hillside, I crook two fingers, motioning for Briar to come over to us. She gives a too-bright grin and books it across the field, scurrying her way past the other sleeping bodies, only nearly tripping three times in her combined haste and awe. When she finally stumbles up against my side, gasping for breath and beaming at the massive creature in front of us, I grip the spot just below her elbow to steady her.

God forbid she trip and land on this dude's head.

Summanus doesn't seem phased by Briar, though. He blinks at her in an assessing sort of way, then goes back to looking at me.

Oh, I see. *I* needed to pass the sniff test, but one look at her and she's in the clear.

Well, actually, that's not all that surprising, I guess.

A blush settles on Briar's cheeks and she flashes me a gap-toothed smile. *We're good to go?*

I give her a nod. *As good as we'll ever be.*

Still holding her arm, I move her to the base of Summanus's neck. "You wanna sit down in the space right between these spikes. Like a built-in saddle."

"Reminds me more of the bars on the roller coaster bucket seats," she amends with a thoughtful hum, but does as I say, stepping up and over him to straddle his neck.

He lets out a loud sigh, more smoke leaving him.

As soon as Briar is settled, I crawl into the space behind her. There's a rather large dragon spike between my stomach and her back, but that doesn't stop me from leaning as far forward as is physically possible so I can curl my arms around her middle, twining my fingers together just beneath her chest.

"Squeeze with your thighs. And wrap your arms around his neck in front of you."

"What if we fall?"

"We won't. He's trained not to let that happen."

"But what if we do?" She turns her head over her shoulder just enough to catch my eye. Our noses nearly brush.

I take a deep, slow breath. "We don't have to do this. We can go back to the castle."

"No. No, I want to. Just." She swallows. "Don't let go of me, okay?"

Never.

I nudge Summanus's throat with my knee and cough down at him again. I don't actually know how to get this part started, so I just shoot with a "Hey, bro, we're ready."

It should not work. But seconds later, the creature is pushing his body up on all fours. We jostle as he moves, the spikes on either side of me digging into my body. My arms tighten reflexively around Briar.

Summanus spreads his wings underneath our feet, unfurling them hard enough to create a breeze that blows all the grass and tree branches nearby. I swallow at the casual display of power.

And then his wings are flapping hard, harder, making the whole world around us billow out. He's running, racing from one side of the field to the other, and my ass can't even stay seated on his back, my whole body lifting up and into the air every time he takes another step. My stomach flips around so hard I think I might spit it right out.

And then he's taking off, his whole body lifting into the air, and we're right there with him.

"Ohmygodohmygodohmygod," Briar squeals, but it sounds more like a whisper over the wind rushing all around us.

Finally, when we reach the highest we're going to go, when Summanus's body can coast a little instead of flapping harder and harder, and some of the turbulence finally settles, I look down at the world underneath us. All of Asalin spread out, thousands of feet below. Mountains and forest and fields and streams and gardens and homes and businesses and the palace, right there in the center of it all.

It reminds me of the night in the tower with Emyr, looking out over Asalin together. I think I prefer the way it looks at night.

I tuck my face between Briar's shoulder blades and close my eyes, enjoying the weightless feeling of flying and the smell of her hair. For a moment, I can forget why we're here. I can forget my goals of causing chaos for the sake of chaos, for the sake of being hated. I can forget *being hated.* For a moment, it's just Briar and me and the feeling of being weightless and free and okay.

The moment does not last.

When Briar tugs aggressively at the sleeve of my hoodie, I finally pull my gaze up to her face. She's staring straight ahead, brown skin a shade grayer, lips parted. I follow her line of sight to...

"Is that Jin?" I demand, but I don't know if Briar can hear me over the sound of the wind.

I'm pretty sure it is Jin, though. I can just barely make out their electric purple energy crackling behind the dragon they're mounted on. This one is smaller than Summanus, with blood-slicked-red plates of armor for scales and eyes so bright they might be white. And the two of them are barreling straight toward us.

"WHAWEOO?!" Briar shouts, and it's only through our near-telepathic connection that I understand what she's asking.

I don't know what we do, though. I didn't really expect to get this far, much less get caught by Jin.

I wrap one of my arms tighter around Briar's middle so I can release my other one, grabbing one of Summanus's spikes and yanking to the left. The dragon seems to get the idea and suddenly swirls his massive body, turning the other direction.

Not that it matters. Jin and their dragon are at our side within seconds. It's definitely Jin, too. This close, I can see their face.

They do not look particularly happy to see me.

"LAND!" I can see them mouth the words, even if I can't

hear them. They enunciate it with a sharp jab at the ground with their thumb.

NO! I nudge Summanus's side with my heel, trying to spur him to move faster. He gives a disgusted grunt, but obliges me, picking up a little speed. Briar's hair whips hard against my face, obscuring my vision.

And then I feel it. Summanus shifts underneath us as something *knocks up against his side*. I have to grab Briar's hair and yank it out of my way just to look over and see that Jin is *banging up against our dragon with theirs*. In mid-fucking-air! Are they trying to kill us?

See, I knew it was too early in the day to say I wasn't going to die.

"LAND!" they shout again, and this time Summanus turns his head to blink over his shoulder at me.

He's waiting for me to tell him what to do.

I came here to steal the king's dragon.

Briar twists her body around to press her face against my neck, wrapping her arms around me as Summanus picks up speed for the second time. And this time, I yank at his spikes to direct him *upward*. Higher into the air. Higher above Asalin. Let Leonidas and Kadri see us. Let *Emyr*. Let them—

Summanus lets out a too-human scream, fire erupting from his throat and exploding into the air in front of us. When I jerk my head around, I see that Jin's dragon has clamped her mouth down on his tail. He twists his massive body in the air, yanking backward and rolling around, thrashing the lower half of his body to try and throw the smaller dragon off him.

My stomach is somewhere near my tonsils. I can feel my

thighs losing their grip on his scales. I can feel Briar shaking with fear, pressed against me.

What have I done?

That's the last coherent thought I manage before we slip from the dragon's back and plummet toward the ground.

You know, I've always heard your life is supposed to flash before your eyes when you're dying. That's not true. At least not for me. It isn't my life I see. It's everyone else's.

Will Tessa mourn me, or is this what she wanted all along? Will she cry at my funeral, finally realizing that I was the last blood kin she had left in this world, that I was her last living connection to being a Croft, or will she refuse to attend at all?

The wind rushes in my ears, a high-pitched whistle that would set my teeth on edge if I weren't about to die, anyway.

Will Sunny and Nadua ever forgive me for being the reason their daughter dies here in my arms? Will the fae manage to get her body back to them? Will they even bother to do it? Or will the people who've fed and clothed and housed and loved me, accepted me, treated me like a son for the last two years, have no idea what happened to either of us? Will they go the rest of their lives waiting for our ghosts to come home?

In my arms, Briar gives one long, heartbroken scream. My stomach flops like a fish tossed on the beach.

What about Emyr?

Overhead, Jin's dragon finally releases Summanus, and he yanks his body in the other direction, flying back toward the field I grabbed him from. The smaller red creature wheels around and beelines for us. I can make out those brilliant white eyes as she speeds closer. Her mouth opens, revealing her own rows of fangs.

The ground looms beneath us.

The dragon snakes out her claws and yanks us into her grip, talons curling around us until she can, as gently as her kind is capable of, toss us onto the grass.

"Good girl, Auriga," Jin says with a click of their tongue, tall and muscled body leaping from the back of their steed's neck to drop to the ground in front of us. They place their hands on their hips, raising their eyebrows high. "You wanna tell me what's going on here?"

I open my mouth to answer and bile comes out.

While I empty my stomach into a cluster of wildflowers, Briar is having a meltdown. In hysterics next to me, she warbles, "It was a stupid plan! We just wanted to have a little fun! Why would you try to kill us?"

"Kill you?" Jin groans. "I was trying to save you. Do you have any idea who you decided to take for a joy ride?"

"The king's dragon," I finally mumble, wiping spit and vomit from my mouth with the back of my hand, then wiping the back of my hand on my jeans.

"Right. The *king's*. And are you the king?"

"Not yet." *Not ever.*

"Yeah, and you're lucky he didn't just swallow your twink ass," Jin scoffs, reaching up to rub their palm against Auriga's neck. "His loyalty isn't to you. You had no idea what you were getting yourself into."

"I—I am *not* a twink!"

Jin just rolls their eyes.

"We're sorry," Briar says softly, finally stumbling to her feet, swiping tears from beneath her eyes. "It won't happen again."

"Damn straight it won't. Now come on. Let's get you back

to the castle. Hopefully, I'm the only one who saw your little grand-theft-dragon act over here." They click their tongue and flick three fingers at Auriga. The smaller dragon lets out a loud huff, turns, and takes off into the sky, following Summanus.

When Jin turns their back to us and starts heading away, Briar quickly shuffles along after them. With a heavy sigh, I follow their lead.

Ahead of me, I can hear Jin start in on their lecture. "You *never* just go and climb on someone else's dragon. Well, not unless you're like me."

"Like you?" Briar tucks a stray strand of hair behind one ear, turning her head up to look at Jin's face.

"*I'm* a professional." Some of the annoyance has bled away from Jin's tone, replaced by an obvious bit of pride. Maybe even a little smugness. "Not to mention the only witch to ever hold my position. It's how Emyr and I became friends actually. He noticed I was interested in them. Kept sneaking out to watch them up close. 'Course, I was never so reckless as to try and steal one..."

Disinterested in being chewed out yet again, I pretend I can't hear them and instead drink in my surroundings.

We've landed on one of the mountains, dumped on high ground, the back end of the castle in view. Asalin doesn't seem so big, or imposing, or powerful. Up here, I don't feel like an ant. I feel like I could do anything. Even appreciate the beauty of this place, without getting sucked in to all the ugliness that lies underneath.

When I rejoin the conversation, they've veered into wildly different territory. Jin is in the middle of saying, "Gender is weird, you know? I mean, I always knew I was *something*. I've been out as nonbinary forever. But it wasn't until I started dating Clarke that I realized how deeply being a *lesbian* was tied up in my gender, too. How I felt a connection to womanhood because of that."

Briar hums, nodding along in understanding. "You credit Clarke for that?"

"Well…no, not credit. Clarke's just the first girlfriend I've ever had, is all." They laugh, rubbing the back of their neck. "I don't know how I got so lucky on my first shot."

"I'd say you both got lucky," Briar points out. "You're a catch."

Jin flushes. "Thanks, but she's… Well, you've seen her. Seriously, I didn't even think she knew I existed. I never would've tried anything with her. But then one day, she just waltzed her little ass right up to my place and banged on the door. Said she'd bonded on me *months* ago, the first time she saw me with Auriga, and had been dropping hints that she wanted me to ask her out ever since. Got fed up with my being obtuse."

"You're a mated couple?" I hasten forward a little, raising my eyebrows to consider Jin. "Fated mates?"

"Yep." Jin shrugs. "We're not exactly traditional, but we fit."

Not exactly traditional is putting it lightly. I've heard of fae being bound to witches before Emyr and me, sure. But I've never actually met another couple like us.

Oh. Wait, no. No, no, nope. Emyr and I are not a couple. *Not.* No.

"Anyway, enough about me and Clarke. What about you, Wyatt?"

"I don't think Emyr and I fit all that well." And we are not a couple!

"Okay, well, agree to disagree, but that's not what I was talking about." Jin snickers. "What was it like for you? Figuring out you were trans. Was it easier, in the human world? I sort of thought it would be. I didn't even really know being an enby was a *thing*, outside of myself, for a long time."

"Oh. Uh." I rub a hand over the back of my neck. I don't really want to talk about it. Not in detail. Not because it's a bad story or whatever, just because discussing the intimate details of my life with someone I barely know sounds like some kind of torture designed for me specifically. "I guess I was just angry all the time."

Jin raises their eyebrows.

Begrudgingly, I add, "I felt defensive over anything gendered, for what I thought was no good reason. And any time I was around a guy I thought was hot, I was, like…mad at him."

"You were mad at him," Jin repeats, sharing a concerned look with Briar. "I don't get it."

I scrub the tips of my fingers against my face, struggling to explain without sounding like a freak. "Right. For looking the way he looked. Because I wanted to make out, but also, like…steal his face. *Especially* trans guys. I was obsessed with trans guys. Obsessed. But also hated them, because they…got to be trans? And then one day I was, like…hey, dumbass, uh, you can be trans, too."

Jin laughs out loud, seemingly startled into it by my answer, and even Briar chuckles a little.

Whatever. Gender *is* weird, the rules are all made up, and people should just do whatever they want.

"How did you pick the name Wyatt?"

"Oh, I dunno. I liked the meaning, I guess." *Brave in war.* Maybe I'd like to think I could be brave someday.

Briar releases a too-loud *"HA!"* and rolls her eyes. "Do not let him lie to you. I made him watch *Charmed* and he wanted to bang Dark Future Wyatt Halliwell."

"Okay, I desperately wanna get that reference, but...?" Jin's eyes glint, looking between the two of us.

"Early 2000s TV show. All about what humans think witches are. It's on Netflix. Maybe we could double-date sometime and watch it."

"I would love that!"

Briar grins and Jin grins back and it's like we're all hunky-dory and best friends and I hate it here.

The three of us fall into easy silence, trekking down the side of the mountain. It's gotten cooler since Briar and I first climbed the hill to see the dragons, and walking down is a whole hell of a lot easier than going up. I can actually enjoy the light breeze blowing at the back of my neck, the clear sky overhead.

After a while, Jin breaks the silence by addressing Briar again. "Now, you're cis, right?"

Briar makes a face. "I don't...*like* the word *cis*. Not to describe myself, anyway."

Something akin to abject horror appears on Jin's face. "Tell me you aren't one of those people who thinks *cis* is a slur."

"Oh, no. No. That's not it. It's just..." Briar lets go of both of us so she can gesticulate awkwardly with her hands. "My

father is Seminole, and my mother Diné. Before settlers, there
was no *cis* or *trans* for any of my people. We recognized from
the beginning of time that there are more than two genders,
and someone's genitals are only one part of the bigger picture. I've never felt a connection to cis womanhood the way
other people talk about it, but I do feel a connection to ma-
triarchy, especially within my community. Calling myself cis
feels like playing by someone else's rules. But so would calling myself nonbinary."

"Huh."

"But I mean, yeah, I was assigned female at birth." Briar
shrugs. "What about your people? You've always had traditional gender roles? Male and female? Even back in Faery?"

Jin frowns. "I… I guess I don't really know what things
were like back in Faery. I mean, I guess so? Probably so."

"Don't think the fae would stand for anything abnormal
mucking up their traditions," I offer as politely as I can.

"The fae aren't that bad," Jin mumbles, looking sheepish.
"Not most of them. Like, my parents weren't exactly happy
to have a nonbinary witch for a kid, but they could've been
a lot worse. *Most* of the fae could be a lot worse. It's just…the
worst ones are usually the loudest. Same as anywhere else in
the world."

"Sure, yeah." Briar nods. "And when you're backed by in-
stitutional power, it's easy to be as loud as you want."

Jin watches Briar, and I watch Jin for a long moment. Finally, Jin turns their eyes toward me, something hesitant in
their dark gaze. They open their mouth to speak, seem to
think better of it, then close their mouth again.

"What?" I ask, raising my eyebrows. If they have something to say, they should get it over with.

Jin casts another look at Briar before sighing, softly, and reaching up to run their fingers through their short hair. "There is...a group that I'm part of. That you two might have some interest in meeting."

"A group?" Briar asks, leaning her head to the side. "What kind of group?"

"A witches' group." Jin reaches up to curl their fingers around the base of their throat, awkwardly brushing their thumb against their skin. I get the impression they aren't used to talking about this with outsiders. "We meet every other week to discuss the goings-on in Asalin. Things have gotten...tense lately. More so than before."

Derek said as much, that my impending marriage was doing more harm than good for fae-witch relations.

"There's actually a meeting tonight." Jin worries at their lower lip. "They asked me to invite you, but I wasn't sure you would be...interested."

Interested is definitely not the word they intended to use, but I'm not sure what was. I look at them, considering, eyes narrowed.

Briar answers before I can. "Of course we're interested."

I snap my head to look at her, eyebrows shooting up toward my hairline. "Oh?"

"Yes," she pushes. "These are your people. You're going to be their king. Don't you want to hear what they have to say?"

Briar knows I have no intention of actually becoming their king. I don't know what she's playing at.

"If you decide to come," Jin continues, not waiting for me

to answer Briar's question, "we meet at nightfall, in the cottage across from the bakery, with the blue door. Come around to the back and someone will let you in."

"We'll be there," Briar promises, flashing a reassuring smile.

I grit my teeth and will myself to say nothing. Silently, the three of us continue to make our way toward the castle, looming ever more ominously as the distance closes.

CHAPTER TEN

A CLUELESS SEVENTEEN-YEAR-OLD WHO DIDN'T ASK FOR ANY OF THIS

A statue of Vorgaine sits in the center of the village, just down the street from the bakery and the little cottage where we're meant to be meeting the witches after dark. The god stands ten feet tall, her body carved from marble and silver. Her curls are wild, as if blowing in a breeze, her head tipped back, mouth open in a silent scream, showing off the long, murderous lines of her fangs. Her wings stretch over her head in an unmoving flurry, and all of her many eyes stare unseeing at the dusky night sky above us.

It's sort of a horrifying image, really. Looking at her for too long makes me uncomfortable, but Briar wanted to stop and examine her more closely. So here we are. I can feel eyes on me as villagers mill about the square, most of them probably coming home at the end of the day. Just like in the tribunal room, I fight not to meet anyone's stare. I don't want to see anything they might be feeling reflected back at me.

People leave offerings at the foot of Vorgaine's statue. Random things that don't make sense out of context, but meant something to the people who left them. Pages ripped from books. Drawings and letters folded up to conceal their contents. Money. Jewelry. I spot a sheet of paper scrawled with sigils, a carved wooden dragon, and an old glass thermometer.

"Have you ever left anything?" Briar asks, cutting a look at me. "When you were a kid here, when things started to get bad. Did you ever think about asking her for help?"

I make a face.

Some in Asalin still *genuinely* believe that Vorgaine is watching over them, that she'll grant their wishes and take care of them if they leave her some worthless little trinket. But I think, for most people, this is superstition. Like throwing salt over your shoulder or not walking under ladders in the human world. Most people don't really believe it, but it's better safe than sorry.

My parents believed Vorgaine died when Faery did. She was the god of that world, but not of this one. And if this world has a god, we haven't met them.

And still, my answer is, "Once."

"What did you ask her for?"

It should be too intimate a question for her to ask, but the boundaries between appropriate and not have always been a bit fucky when it comes to Briar and me. There isn't much we don't tell each other.

The one and only time I left an offering was in the weeks leading up to the fire. I was too big for my body. My skin no longer fit. I flinched at every whisper or sidelong look from the fae, in the village and at the palace. Emyr kept trying to fix it, kept asking me what was *wrong* so he could just *fix it*, but he didn't get it, and I didn't get it, and everything hurt, all the time, both in ways I *had* words for but was too afraid to say aloud, and ways I didn't yet.

"I just wanted to be happy again." I shrug. "But it didn't matter. Even if she were answering prayers, I don't think she can hear mine."

At least that's what the fae say. Vorgaine is *their* god. The witches are her children's unwanted abominations. She would not lower herself to heed the call of one like me.

I can feel Briar staring at me, but don't meet her gaze.

Instead, inclining my head toward the bakery, I say, "C'mon. You wanted to see the snacks here, right?"

She hesitates before reaching for my hand, and I lead her away from the creepy tribute.

The moment we step inside the bakery, my stomach gives a loud rumble. The entire little storefront smells of carbs and sugar, two of my most favorite things, and I swallow back a mouthful of saliva as it blooms between my teeth.

Glass cases are set up displaying the different pastries and snack foods, an assortment of vivid colors and sticky, gooey goodness. Rovuri, round balls of puffy, light pastry filled with sour berries, honey, and cream. Voleia, a loaf of bread that's hard as rock on the outside and as soft as feathers within, dusted with powdered sugar and filled with nuts and sometimes chocolate. Kytur, a savory pie filled with white cheeses, leafy greens, and shredded or ground meat—peryton, traditionally, but chicken or beef are common substitutes.

I am truly, one hundred percent a food bitch. Maybe, if my plan works, if I get myself out of here and into the real world, in an apartment with Briar somewhere far away and filled with queers, I'll go to culinary school. Maybe I'll open up my own little café, with a weird menu and even weirder customers.

It's a dream I've never let myself consider, not really. I've lived the last three years constantly wondering when I would start to feel fae breath at the back of my neck, when everything I'd started to build would finally be ripped out from under me. Things were as happy as they could've been in Texas, with Nadua and Sunny and the rest of Briar's family, but some part of me knew it wasn't forever.

If I can find a way to pull off Derek's plan, I'm staring down a forever of my own making.

Briar makes a delighted sound and sets about bending over to examine each and every item behind the glass. But my eyes shift to the baker himself.

The fae man stands with his arms crossed behind the counter, a white apron drooping off his thin frame. Brown wings are pulled tight against his back, the claws on one hand tapping against his countertop with impatience. Murky yellow energy bubbles like angry pus around his shoulders. He narrows his eyes as he watches us, suspicious, hateful.

I know that look. I grew up with it following me everywhere I went. I anticipated it tenfold, coming back to Asalin after the fire. If it were up to me, I wouldn't mingle with these people at all. The situations I'm willing to put myself in for Briar...

"We should probably hurry up," I say to her back without looking away from his face. He sneers at me, upper lip pulling up over his teeth. His canines are smaller than most of his kind. They remind me of a dog's.

"I want this one, I think." Briar grins, looking at me over her shoulder and pointing to the halyic in the case. A wonderful—and unsurprising—choice, the dessert is basically a bunch of wafer-thin cookies stacked on top of each other, stuck together with syrup, then drizzled with a thick, tart, multicolored icing. It's served on a stick, because it's a mess to carry. Kids love it.

I approach the fae behind the counter and he tenses, tilting his chin back to look down at me. I smile just enough to flash my own fangs.

I promise you, I'm a hungrier stray than you are.

"We'll take two halyics." I produce a single, crumpled-up ten-dollar bill from my back pocket, and slide it across the counter.

The baker looks at the money, then back at my face. "Sorry. Fae currency only."

I'm... What?

I look to the glass cases. Clear as day, the prices for each pastry are written on little notecards next to their display, each one written in USD. As it has been for my *entire life*, everywhere in Asalin.

Fae currency still exists, sure, but it came from Faery. It's the same few thousand coins that've been floating around for the last five hundred years. Most people won't spend them anymore, if they have them, just hoarding them in keepsake boxes and passing them down to their children. For a while in the very early days after their arrival here, fae relied on bartering as a means of currency, but long before I was born, they'd started integrating money from the human world into their system. It was one of the earliest ways they adapted, one of the smallest, simplest steps they took.

There is no such thing as a store that accepts only fae currency.

"That's bullshit," I answer him finally, though I do snatch the money back.

He smiles as if amused by my answer. "That's business. I don't have to serve anyone who doesn't follow my rules." I want to hit him until his smile turns red. "Not even the prince's little friend."

"Now, wait just a minute." Briar slaps her hand against the countertop, her own yellow energy, brighter and bolder than the baker's, flaring to life. "That's discrimination!"

He looks into her face and laughs. *Laughs.* "And?"

Blackness blooms along my fingers, stretching up to my palms, along my wrists. Though I can't see it through my sleeves, I know it's crawling its way to the insides of my elbows. I grit my teeth, hands balling into fists in front of me even as fire licks beneath the surface of my skin.

Years, I went without my magic flaring. Years, I managed to keep the fire at bay.

These people bring it out of me. This ugly thing I have no hope of controlling. They turned me into this monster. And as long as I'm around them, it's all I'll ever be.

The baker's laugh disappears. "Get out of my store, you little freak." He motions to Briar with one clawed hand. "And take your empty sack of flesh with you."

The wood of his countertop beneath my fists begins to smoke and singe. His eyes widen, and he takes a step back, disgusting yellow energy spilling into the air around him.

"GET OUT! NOW!"

"Wyatt—"

"Is there a problem here, Norman?" a familiar voice lilts from the front of the store.

"Clarke." Briar lets out a shaky breath, one hand shooting up to grab my shoulder, the other motioning to the baker. "He won't serve us."

"As is his right." Clarke's heels click against the ground softly as she approaches, coming to a stop at my other side. Her soft-pink energy thrums up against my black. "Just as it is your right to choose not to patronize such an establishment. My many, many connections at the palace and I have that same right."

"Miss Pierce," the baker begins, shaking his head frantically, shoulders drooping. "You cannot—"

"I would give serious consideration to telling me what I can and cannot do, Norman." Clarke turns her head to look at me. At length, I manage to pull my gaze from the baker's face and meet her stare. "C'mon, Wyatt. It's after dark."

The witches are waiting, she doesn't say.

I manage to nod, pulling away from the counter and turning to follow her out of the bakery. My fists leave two black, burned holes in their wake.

★ ★ ★

There are maybe twenty or thirty witches piled in the back room of the little cottage across the street. I've never been surrounded by so many witches before. I was never *allowed* to be around so many witches before. While the rest of my kind mingled in the streets and made their own little community within Asalin, my parents kept me in a viselike grip, watching my every move, making sure I didn't associate with those they considered beneath them. They wanted so desperately to believe I wasn't like the others—and eventually, that desperation lead to their own downfall. If I'd been allowed the resources I needed, if I'd been supported in learning to control my magic, how differently my life might've shaped up...

But I wasn't, and I wasn't, and it didn't, and now here I am, surrounded by strangers, every single one of them staring at me.

"Found them," Clarke says in a sort of singsong as she closes the door behind us and slides a dead bolt into place. "They were at Norman's."

"Oh, you do *not* want to go there," announces a girl who appears a few years older than us. She's striking to look at, a few inches taller than me, built thick and muscular, with cool-toned black skin and sharp features. Her hair is left long and braided on one side, dyed a deep shade of purple, while the other half is shaved. The leather jacket and combat boots make her look like she's ready to fight, if needed. "The stale food is not worth his even staler attitude."

"Yeah, we gathered as much," Briar mumbles in response. I'm still bristling from the encounter, my heart bouncing against my breastbone so hard it might break, like an alarm clock ringing itself right off the shelf.

The room is dark and cramped, everyone squished together on old, antique-looking furniture. This place isn't decorated the way I'd imagine a top-secret meeting room for a rebellious witch alliance should be. There are little cat trinkets on the shelves, a tray of snacks and tea on the coffee table, and doilies. Like, so many doilies. Everywhere.

Though, as Clarke ushers us to one of the couches, where Jin is sitting, I can make out the sigils painted on the walls. Well, sigil. The same one, repeated over and over again. The one I saw that first day back in Asalin, on the front of the abandoned building.

"What's it mean?" I ask Jin when I drop down next to them.

They glance at the walls, tilting their head down to whisper at my ear, "It's a barrier. Keeps the fae out."

"*Most* of the fae," Clarke amends, tugging up one sleeve to flash me a sigil painted in black ink on the inside of her forearm. It looks almost the same as the one on the walls, except this one has a single, thin slash running through it.

Sigils are witch magic. She couldn't have given that mark to herself, not if she wanted it to actually work. Must've been Jin's work.

"So the fae are barred from entering this place, unless invited by a witch? What's with all the secrecy, then?"

"Just because they can't get in here doesn't mean they wouldn't wait for us to come out," snaps a guy about the same age as the purple-haired witch, from where he's leaning against the table nearest her. He's got the most skeletal face I've ever seen, eyes sunken into his head, gaunt cheek-bones, made up for only by full lips and an array of piercings that help fill things out. He's pale enough to look half-dead, too, and his limp brown hair hangs unkempt to his shoulders. "Drag us into the dungeons, interrogate us about our *plotting*."

"Roman, that only happened once. And it was fine." Jin makes a face, like they don't really believe their own words.

"It was not fine," Clarke argues, taking her girlfriend's hand and giving it a squeeze. "They treated you like a terrorist."

"The Guard will jump at any excuse to get rid of us," Roman snaps the words, hard, like a bite. And he's watching *me*. "What are you going to do about that, *witch king*?"

"Excuse me?"

"Roman—" Jin tries to interrupt, but this guy clearly has a bone to pick.

"They think you're some kind of savior. That you're going to lead us to salvation. But you don't look like a messiah to me. And forgive me, but I don't see how continuing to play by their rules is going to get us anywhere we haven't already been." He raises his eyebrows, like he's waiting for me to argue back.

I blink. I got nothing. He's *right*.

"We *just* got started," comes a tired, tired voice from the dining table at the far wall. The woman sitting there appears to be in her eighties or older, gray hair pulled up at the top of her head, a notebook open in front of her and a pencil in one hand. She's wearing a pink floral muumuu. "Can we at least get through the recap before we start throwing curses?"

"Of course, Lav." Jin gets up and moves to stand behind the

woman, placing one large hand gently on her back. "Wyatt, Briar, this is Lavender. This is her home. She started this group back in the seventies."

Lavender. The name brings back a stark memory, one that I didn't even know existed until this moment.

I'm young, maybe six or seven, and I'm following at my mother's back through the village. We've just come from the palace, where she spent the day at work and I spent the day hiding in Emyr's chamber. These are my favorite days, but this is my least favorite part. I wish I could go back. I wish I could be with Emyr all the time.

"Isobel, you cannot avoid me forever," comes a harsh voice from behind us.

When I turn to try and get a look at the woman, my mother grabs my upper arm and yanks me around so that I'm behind her legs again.

"This is becoming harassment, Lavender."

"I'm sorry you feel that way." I can only barely make out hints of the woman, a pantsuit and sensible beige shoes, nothing particularly descript. Certainly not to a child. "But you're leaving me very little choice. This is important. Your daughter—"

"My daughter is no concern of yours. Your little cult is not going to get their hands on her."

Lavender sighs. I think she tries to lean around my mom to look at me, but my mother takes a step back, continuing to block her view. "Someday, she's going to sit on the Throne. She'll rule over all of us. What you do now, the choices you make, will shape the person she is when that time comes. Don't you want her to know everything about herself? To be in control of the magic in her body?"

"She'll be fine. But if you continue trying to induct my child, you won't be."

With that, my mother drags me away, grip on my arm tight enough to bruise.

When I blink myself back into the present, Lavender's eyes are trained on my face. "I started *something* back in the seventies." She sniffs. "Things are very different now."

Jin slides their hand up to squeeze her shoulder before moving to one corner of the room to grab a little tea trolley with a laptop set up on top of it. Like Emyr's cell phone, at first glance it looks inconspicuous enough. But when Jin pushes the lid of the laptop open, I realize the logo etched into the metal isn't actually a logo at all, but another sigil.

"What is that?" I lean in closer to Clarke.

"One of their many projects," she answers with a small shake of her head.

The laptop's screen is black for a moment, then kicks on to reflect...the room itself. It's as if a tiny camera that we can't see is buzzing around the room, flitting from person to person, zooming in on everyone's face before finally landing on the notebook in Lavender's hand. When it does, a light on the other side of the computer turns on, and the image on the screen is projected onto the far wall, big enough that we can all see.

Clarke explains, "They've been building their own version of the internet. They've already mastered sending spells through the phone. The laptop's a bigger version of that." She grins, pride etched on her pretty face as she talks about

Jin's accomplishments. "They've even uploaded your contract onto the net."

"Huh?"

"The blood oath that ties you to Emyr. He gave them access to it and they designed magic that would make it digital. They've been doing it with other old documents, too."

That's...interesting. The important part of the contract isn't necessarily the paper it was written on. The magic that happened when Emyr and I mingled our blood, when the Court came together and sealed out fates—it's inside us now. Part of us. That's what blood magic is. That's why, if I broke the contract, it would kill me, no matter where I was.

Clarke isn't done with her bragging just yet. "The laptop also has something they're calling Fae TV."

"Fae TV?" Sounds terrible.

"Mmm. Lets us send a broadcast to anyone with one of these magicked laptops. Was meant to make it easier to connect with people in the other kingdoms, to send messages that we wouldn't want intercepted by the humans. We record these meetings in case we ever need to publish them on there, to prove we haven't been doing anything unscrupulous."

"Huh. Who all has one of these laptops?"

"Jin and Emyr. And they sent one to all the royal families, too."

"Okay. First things first." Jin claps their hands. "Is everyone here tonight?"

"I don't see Alice and John," someone offers up.

"Anyone know where they are?" Jin asks.

"Probably in bed. I hate newlyweds." Lavender clicks

her tongue disdainfully, scribbling the two names into her notebook.

Jin makes a face. "I'll talk to John tomorrow. I seriously doubt either of them has been compromised."

I look at Clarke and raise my eyebrows in question.

She lowers her voice to say, "Like, uh, they've turned on the group. Passing information to the Guard or something. Technically, what we're doing here isn't illegal. But there are things we talk about that...well, we wouldn't want them getting back to my brother, so long as it's avoidable."

"All right." Jin clicks their tongue. "Let's recap. What have we noticed the last two weeks?"

"Five more Faery flags went up." The words come from a tall, thin boy with skin the color of dried tobacco and coily hair pulled into a ponytail. His cat-eye glasses sit poised at the tip of his nose, and his oversize pink sweater threatens to swallow him whole. The purple-haired girl is seated next to him, one hand on his thigh.

"Five? In two weeks?" Jin rubs a hand over the back of their neck.

"Yeah, well, two of those went up days after Mrs. Carwin and Mrs. McCough caught Roman lecturing their six-year-olds about their fae privilege." He pushes his glasses up.

Roman scowls. "Teach them young, and maybe they won't grow up to be such shits."

"They are not your children to teach."

"And thank fuck for that, because if I had some fae brat as my kid, I would—"

"Stop!" The purple-haired girl casts an angry glare between the both of them until they settle back down in their seats. She looks at Clarke and sighs. "I'm sorry. I try to control them, you know."

"It's all right, Lorena." Clarke shrugs one dainty shoulder, reaching up to flick her blond curls behind her back as she stands in a flourish of pink energy and gauzy fabrics. She curls her arms around Jin's waist from behind, settling her cheek against the center of their back. Even with her massive heels, she doesn't even reach their shoulders. "If the worst I get called is a brat, I'd say that's still privilege."

Jin smiles, rubbing their palm against the back of Clarke's hand, tilting their head back to kiss her gently.

Roman makes a face at the two of them before looking back to the sweatered guy. "Solomon, she talks about us like we're her dogs instead of her boyfriends."

"You are a dog," Lorena and Solomon answer in response.

Roman throws his hands up.

"I'm going to have to insist that Jin bars you two from these meetings if you keep monopolizing every single conversation." Lavender taps the tip of her pen against her notebook. "Five new flags. Anyone know what brought about the other three?"

"Not exactly." Lorena clears her throat, glances at me and then quickly away. "Though they did all appear after Wyatt's return."

All eyes on me again. I would like to disappear forever. I would like to stop embodying a physical form altogether. Thanks.

"Right..." Lavender slides her tongue against her front teeth. "Anything else?"

"Delilah has decided to leave Asalin," a soft-spoken witch,

probably in her thirties or forties, pipes up. The man beside her takes her hand. "She says there's nothing for her here. She wants to go to a human school in New York City. She's been working on fabricating transcripts to apply."

Delilah must be their kid. Statistically speaking, fae/witch couples are only a *little* more likely to produce witch offspring than fae/fae couples, but witch/witch couples have the highest rates by far. For that reason, witches are usually dissuaded from procreating at all.

At least, witches who aren't bound to the fae prince.

"Oh, Miranda." Jin turns away from Clarke to look at the woman, shaking their head. "I know you wanted her to stay. But maybe she'll be happier."

She'll definitely be happier, I want to say. I don't know much about what the witch children in Asalin get up to, because I was never allowed to know. There's a little school I always wanted to be part of, though I have no idea what the lessons are like. Once they graduate, most of them end up working for pennies at the palace. Or leaving. Witches like Jin, with high-ranking, important careers and connections to the royal line, are practically unheard of.

"And what could I even say to convince her not to go?" Miranda asks, eyes wet as she squeezes her companion's hand. "She isn't wrong, is she? Every day, it feels more and more like she's right. There's nothing here for her. Or any of us."

"That's not true." Jin moves across the crowded room to crouch in front of Miranda, arms balanced on their legs. "We won't see the kind of changes we'd like overnight, but we're doing what needs to be done. We're sticking together.

We're supporting one another. And soon, with Wyatt on the Throne—"

"Give me a break, Jin." Roman doesn't let them finish. "The poor woman is terrified about sending her only kid off to a world she knows nothing about. Don't condescend to us about how *Wyatt the Awaited One* is going to swoop in and save witchkind. It was hardly believable before he got here, and it's not any more so now. For crying out loud, *look at him*."

I was really enjoying everyone definitely not looking at me, too focused on the arguing and the back-and-forth. But now, all the eyes in the room snap right back toward where they started, scrutinizing me like some kind of bug. I want to burst into flame.

Of course, Briar refuses to take the criticism lightly. "Wyatt *could* do a lot of good for Asalin. He's a good person. He will make a great king."

She says it with so much conviction, as if she doesn't know I have zero intention of sticking around and doing any good here. Besides, I will *not* make a great king. I know it. And I suspect most of the people in this room know it.

"King of what? King of the witches? We're hardly people, as far as the fae are concerned. King of the fae? They'll never recognize his authority. He's going to be king of sitting next to Emyr North and looking pretty for the next eighty years." Roman might as well have plucked the thoughts from my head. "I say Delilah is right. Screw Asalin. This place isn't doing anything for us. We should *all* leave. Now. Take root in the human world." His eyes glint with something fierce and familiar.

"I don't think it will be what you're imagining. Even in

the human world, we will be expected to play by fae rules."
Miranda shakes her head.

"They can expect whatever they want! What are they
gonna do to us if we just *bounce*?" Roman laughs. "They
won't risk exposing themselves to humans, even if it means
not keeping us in line."

Oh, okay, I think I might be falling in love with Roman.
I bob my head as I say, "That's what Derek is afraid of. That
integrating more and more risks exposure."

Roman points one gnarled finger at my chest. "Do not say
that cretin's name in my presence."

Lorena frowns and offers Clarke another apologetic look.
"Sorry."

Clarke only shrugs.

"Witches leaving Asalin behind will do nothing but give
the fae precisely what they want—our exile. And then what
will we do? Force ourselves to play by the rules of humans, to
avoid risking *exposure* ourselves?" Solomon's tone is scathing.
"We have been robbed of feeling at home anywhere we go.
Of having anything that *belongs to us* anywhere. But we have
just as much right to Earth and to Faery as anyone else." His
voice rises an octave higher.

"Oh, shut up about Faery!" Roman throws back at him.
"Faery is dead! The only people with any *right* to that realm
are a bunch of corpses!"

"That isn't what Emyr thinks."

Briar's voice is even and soft, but it manages to quiet the
whole room. Everyone turns to look at her, including me. She
flushes under the scrutiny but juts out her chin all the same.

"What does that mean?" Lorena demands.

"Well..." Briar glances at me. "Isn't that what he said the other night at dinner? That Emyr thinks Faery might be inhabitable? That it could be healed with the right magic?"

Slowly, I explain, "He mentioned that. But he doesn't have any proof."

"How would we get proof?" Solomon is leaning forward, eyes sharp and intense. Too intense. It's unsettling, really.

"I don't know."

"Emyr wants to go through the door," Briar pushes. "That's what you said, right? He's trying to convince his father to open it and send another team through, Healers instead of warriors this time."

"I remember when Leonidas's group went through the door the first time," Lavender says, tone grave. "Many died. I cannot imagine he will let his son try it. No, that door stays locked for a reason."

"But if the prince is right..." Solomon presses, standing up and pacing back and forth across the floor, nearly jostling other witches with his elbows as he does. "If we could open the door to Faery and *survive* on the other side—"

"The fae could return there," Briar finishes for him, her dark eyes alight. "And the witches could have Asalin for themselves."

"And every other fae village across the globe," Solomon snaps, standing up straighter. "Our persecution is not limited to our own borders. Our siblings across the seas face similar circumstances."

Briar leans in closer, the two of them clearly sharing some kind of moment. "You could all finally be free. You could even begin to integrate—"

"Into the human world! And when witches are born into Faery—"

"They could pass them back through the door to you, here."

A beat goes by before Clarke says, "Well, if no one else is going to say it, I will. You are off your rocker, Sol."

The room erupts in shouting. People keep throwing fingers in each other's faces, spewing obscenities and accusations. Jin towers above them all, trying to quiet the chaos by asking, over and over again, that everyone please sit down so they can have an earnest conversation.

Solomon says something to Roman that makes him so angry he storms out the back door. I wait a moment more, and when the fighting doesn't stop, I stand and try to ease out after him.

Lavender catches me just before I manage to bolt. "Wyatt!"

Her eyes are so icy blue they could be white, and they're boring into me when I turn to look at her. She pushes herself up from the table, shuffling past a few people still scream-ing at each other, to join me in front of the door. "Perhaps, when things are less...*loud*, you could come back and see me. Just the two of us."

I want to make a joke about her not being my type, be-cause I think it would be very funny. But something about this woman is unsettlingly authoritative, and instead I just say, "Um, sure."

"You are very behind in your development." Oh, okay. I mean, she's not wrong, but ow. "It'll take a lot to get you back on track, but I'll do my best."

As she toddles away, toward a little trolley with a teakettle,

I lock eyes with Clarke across the room. She snickers, like she finds it funny I'm *underdeveloped*.

I huff, and finish my escape outside.

Roman is leaning against a tree in Lavender's backyard, his maroon red energy sizzling and crackling around him like a firework about to go off. His head jerks up when he hears me approaching, and he scowls.

"Leave me alone, Croft. I don't want to hear about your grand plans for witch revolution."

"I don't have any grand plans." I lean against the other side of the tree, shoving my hands into the front pocket of my hoodie. "I'm a clueless seventeen-year-old who didn't ask for any of this."

Roman snorts out, "Weird flex, but okay," and I sense he agrees with me. At least about my being clueless. After a moment more, he asks, "Does your boyfriend seriously think he could get back into Faery?"

I bristle at Emyr being referred to as my boyfriend, but there's really no use arguing about that. Not right now, anyway. "He thinks there's a *chance*. But he also thinks he and I are going to live happily ever after, so, you know."

"So, he's even more clueless than you are?"

"That's what I'm thinking, yeah."

He snorts again, then sighs, casting a look toward the back of the house. "They all just want something to believe in. No matter how ridiculous, they want to feel like they have choices that aren't just…"

"Burning it all down?"

Our eyes meet, and he inclines his head. "Burning it all down."

"But you know better?"

He considers me for a moment, as if debating how much he wants to say. Finally, he turns his head back to the sky, offering me the bony slope of his jaw. "My parents are both in the Guard. They've got six kids. I'm the only witch." He smiles a smile that isn't really a smile, that's just a show of teeth. "They were on their way to leave me in the woods when Lavender stopped them. Begged them to let her take me. Promised she'd never tell me who they were, never tell anyone. That their *shame* could stay buried."

I frown, raising my eyebrows. "How'd you find out, then?"

"Uh, because I have two brain cells? Because people in Asalin don't know how to mind their own business, ever? There was a pregnant woman, and then she wasn't pregnant anymore, but there was no baby, and then *Lavender* mysteriously shows up with a kid? It was an open secret." Roman slides his teeth against his lower lip. "One day, Lorena, Sol, and I are about thirteen. We're playing in the creek in the woods. Using mud to draw runes on stones and casting them, trying to see our futures. And my *father* shows up. Starts accusing us of casting hexes. I don't know why. Don't know where it came from. Guess he saw some magic he didn't understand and got scared. Or maybe he'd just been waiting for thirteen years to finally get rid of me."

That sounds ominous. I frown, shuffling a few steps closer to Roman. "What happened?"

"He tried to arrest us. I may have gotten a bit angry. I told him I knew he was my dad. And he…" A haunted film settles across Roman's dark eyes. He's here, but he isn't. "Anyway, Lorena's mom is in the Guard, too. Solomon's dad is one of

Queen Kadri's personal attendants. If they hadn't both spoken out on my behalf, well. I think Daddy would've gotten what he wanted."

To finally get rid of him.

Roman coughs into his fist, finally dragging his attention back to me. "Suffice to say, I know the issues between the fae and witches aren't going to be solved with fairy tales or hugs or a wedding between two clueless kids."

I slide my tongue against my teeth but say nothing. He isn't wrong. The witches are looking for liberation. Maybe, as king, I would have the power to give it to them. Or at least to influence things to move in the right direction.

What does it say about me that I intend to run instead?

CHAPTER ELEVEN

SOME THINGS NEVER CHANGE

Since stealing one of their dragons did nothing for my cause, today I'm going to steal the fae's drugs.

Well, technically it isn't a drug. *Technically* the morghira is a flower.

Potato, pot*ah*to, whatever, I'm going to steal it and I'm going to smoke it.

Briar trails after me the next evening, and I can feel the bleakness in her expression even though I refuse to turn around and look at her. She was overjoyed that no one besides Jin seemed to have caught on to our little adventure with Summanus, that the only consequence we faced from the ordeal was spending a night with the witches—a night she seemed to enjoy, at that.

"You know, they say curiosity killed the cat, Wyatt."

"And they say that satisfaction brought it back, Briar." I look over my shoulder to grin at her. "Besides, I'm not *curious*. I know exactly what I'm doing."

"Mmm-hmm. And what was today's card?"

I roll my eyes at the question. "Six of Cups. Nothing in the reading that said I was going to put myself in mortal peril by having a little fun."

And maybe, if I'm being honest, breaking into the fae's greenhouse and stealing the morghira has way more to do with having fun than it does actually getting into trouble. It's obnoxious, and reckless, and against the rules, all of which technically is in line with Derek's plans, but that's not really the motivation here.

It's been a long, *weird* time lately. I miss Laredo. I miss Nadua and Sunny, because texting and the occasional FaceTime call isn't the same as being home with my family. I miss the dogs and the dry, overbearing Texas heat. I miss walking a mile down the road to get cheap soda from the gas station, and meeting up with Briar's friends, and feeling seventeen and normal. The last couple of years are the only time in my life I've ever felt normal.

So, okay. Maybe I haven't thought this one through. But what's more normal than a teenager doing something remarkably asinine in order to get inebriated?

Briar huffs, jogging a little to catch up to me as we head toward the woods. "You said yourself you've only seen other people use this stuff. You have no idea how it might affect you. What if you hate it?"

I shrug, casting a glance around us. We've left the palace

yard behind, and there aren't many fae lingering about to hear. Though why I'm trying to be sneaky when being caught and punished is the entire point, I'm not sure. "It's less about the smoking and more about the stealing. I'm just trying to cause a disturbance. Or have you forgotten the end game already?"

"No, I remember." She pins me with a pinched expression. I can read her thoughts clearly, but I choose not to and instead look away.

"Once we get beyond the tree line, stay close to me. The last thing we need is a goblin trying to abscond with you and make you their wife." Goblins are known to do that, trapping people in unhappy marriages by tricking them into ancient, confusing rituals.

Perhaps Emyr has taken a page from their handbook.

"Mmm-hmm."

Truthfully, it is perhaps at least a little about the smoking. I need something to take the edge off. The meeting from last night has left me feeling frayed, confused, wide open.

"You know, if we're going to be out here getting into things we shouldn't anyway, maybe you could take me to see the door to Faery," she suggests, because of course she does. Because of course that's where her head is, after last night.

I slide one sharpened tooth over my lower lip and shrug. "It's not really much to look at."

"Oh."

I glance back at her and stop in my tracks. Her bright energy has dulled, albeit only a little. "We don't have to do this if you really don't want to."

Because I am weak and helpless to do anything that might make Briar unhappy. Because she has me curled around her finger, even if she's not cunning enough to do anything with that power.

She meets my eye and shrugs. "Promise you'll take me to the door later?"

It's a ridiculous request, but I nod, anyway. "Promise."

She grins, flashing a hint of dimple, and reaches out to take my hand. "Okay. Let's go steal the magic flower."

Asalin's woods are thick and dark and filled with things that would likely enjoy seeing both of us dead, but I don't feel unsafe here. I never have. All my memories of these woods are good ones: Emyr and me disappearing together into the brambles, sneaking off to have our own adventures. Back then, I felt more like myself out here than I ever did in the castle or at home with my parents and sister.

Besides, I'm probably a bigger monster than anything that lives in this forest.

"The greenhouse is just up ahead. But a little farther beyond, there's a clearing where the peryton flock like to gather. We can go check them out, yeah? They're a little shy, but as long as we keep our distance they shouldn't fly away."

Briar grins again, and this time her dimples make craters in her cheeks, her energy as bright as day. She squeezes my hand tighter. "Okay."

She's practically vibrating she's so excited. Good. All it takes are a few magical creatures to sway Briar to the side of chaos. And I guess I understand that. When you've never seen this shit before, Asalin must be pretty enthralling.

I remember the time after I ran away, when I disappeared into the human world. I was alone and afraid. Hungry. Traumatized. Angry. I didn't have time to stop and take in the things around me. I barely had time to *breathe*. I slept in shelters, or abandoned cars, or bathroom stalls. I ate what I could steal, or beg for, or I didn't eat at all. There was a moment, completely by myself in the world with nothing left to hang on to, when I realized how much easier it would be if I just let go. If I just stopped trying to survive.

Nadua found me shortly after that. She took me in, and Briar stitched me back together again. And eventually, I could relax enough to realize how unbelievably cool humans are.

Hell, the idea of twenty-four-hour fast-food places still gets me pretty worked up. You can just go! Get chicken nuggets! At any time of day or night! How is that not magic in and of itself?

Asalin's greenhouse is tucked behind an army of honey locust trees, a cluster of them grown in a circle around the glass dome. Their limbs stretch up and over it, parting just enough around the top to let the waning sunlight in. I'm not sure if that's a work of magic, or a work of nature, or some combination of the two. The greenhouse itself is a perfect half circle, a little bubble made of glass so thin it might be invisible if not for the multitude of colorful plants climbing it, reaching toward the sky.

Birds gather here, singing to themselves and hopping at the top. A particularly suspicious-looking wood thrush flutters down to a low-hanging branch to eye Briar and me with what I imagine is contempt.

Perhaps even the damn bird knows I'm not supposed to be here.

"Wyatt." Briar drops my hand and takes a few steps to the

side, leaning forward to try and peer around the edge of the greenhouse. "How do we get in?"

That isn't a terrible question. A little more investigating proves that, yep, no, there doesn't appear to be any door. At all.

If I were to wager a guess, it would be that the fae who tend to these plants use some bippity-boppity-boo shit to get inside. But I don't have any idea what I'm doing, and I do not have the time or inclination to learn. Instead, I find the biggest rock in the vicinity and scoop it up into my palms.

"Oh, for crying out loud," I hear Briar mumble, seconds before I pull my arm back and send the rock hurtling through the glass.

It shatters. And I mean…the whole thing. Fucking shatters. I guess that glass really was *wafer thin*, because taking one hole out of it brought the whole thing crumbling down, shards of glass erupting through the trees as the dome caves in on itself. The birds screech and take off, all except the wood thrush, who's still glaring at me.

Whatever. Damn judgmental bird. I swat at the thing until it takes off after the others.

"Did you mean to do that?" Briar has crossed her arms and is glaring at me from the other side of what used to be a greenhouse the size of a small home and is now a pile of glass and sad-looking plants.

"Ah. No. But! This will definitely piss people off, right?" If someone was alerted by the sound and comes running to investigate, at least I'll have the satisfaction of being caught red-handed. That's, like, the whole point, anyway, right?

Briar pinches the bridge of her nose.

The soles of my boots make extremely satisfying crunches as I step past the line of trees to wiggle my way into the remnants of the greenhouse. I toe a few things, flipping them over and investigating each one.

All right, maybe I *shouldn't* have done this. The greenhouse protects the most rare plants in Asalin, the ones gathered by Leonidas and his crew during their brief time in Faery. It was never my intention to *destroy* anything. And no matter what I might feel about the fae, the witches use these plants in all kinds of concoctions. My heart pangs sharply.

Still. There's nothing I can do about it now.

The morghira flower is swirled with shades of deep green and blue, with flecks of red along the edges of each petal. They grow to be about the size of my fist, but this isn't the height of their season, and for now they're rather small. I can fit three in my palm. I shove as many as I can gather into the pocket of my hoodie, shaking glass off each one, and then crunch my way back to Briar.

"All right, you ready to go see—"

The bushes shift in the most unnatural way. Without thinking, I reach for Briar's hand and yank her behind me, eyes narrowing. There are too many things out here in the forest. There's no telling what I might've attracted with the sound of breaking glass.

"Wyatt?"

"Shh." My eyes narrow. "Who's there?"

A growl vibrates from the shrubbery, low and guttural. The hair on my body stands on end, a chill creeping along every inch of my skin. Not fae, nor witch. Something even more animal than either.

"Wyatt?" Briar whispers at my back.

I give the barest shake of my head. I won't let anything happen to her.

The bush shifts again, and this time the creature emerges. It looks like a wolf, only bigger. Easily four feet tall and eight feet long, it's covered in shaggy black fur that stands up straight down its back. The hellhound stalks toward us, its shoulders rolling, a predator hunting its prey. Its red eyes flash, slobbery tongue flicking out to lick its massive jaws.

Briar sucks in a breath. I can hear the way her sandals move against the forest floor underneath us, her feet sliding beneath her on instinct, her body no doubt telling her she needs to run.

"Don't move," I whisper, even as the creature inches closer. You never run from a hellhound. They'll always be faster.

It's only a few feet away from me now. It lowers its upper body toward the ground, black tail swishing back and forth as it stares into my face. The creature's lips pull back from its teeth as it inhales the scent of me. We meet eyes.

The hellhound lunges. Behind me, Briar screams.

Pinned to the ground underneath the animal, I can hear my heart thundering in my ears as he bends down, opens his mouth above my throat, and begins licking his way across my neck and face. I reach up to scratch my nails into the fur at his neck, scrubbing against him, grinning wildly.

"Who's a good boy? Is it you? Are you a good boy?"

Boom, the pup Emyr and I rescued once, a long, long time ago, jumps off me to spin in circles in front of us. His massive body bangs against a few trees, knocking loose a couple branches, but he doesn't seem to notice. He snaps his teeth at the air in front of himself, excitement making him throw back his head and howl.

I laugh, hoisting myself to my feet and throwing my arms around him, pressing our foreheads together and kissing his snout. "That's right, you're a good boy."

He licks my face even more aggressively and then bounds away, running between the trees, back and forth, barking at Briar and me all the while.

She blinks at me. "You two know each other?"

"His name's Boom." I can't stop smiling, watching the big, goofy dog run circles around us. "He's mine."

"Yours?"

"Yeah."

"You haven't been here in a long time."

"Yeah, well." I shrug. "Some things never change."

Some connections are too important to be broken, no matter the time or distance between people.

Briar raises an eyebrow at me. I think she's going to say something I don't want to hear, but she doesn't get the chance. Boom comes to a screeching halt in front of me, kicking up dirt and rocks underfoot as he throws his head back to howl again. I can't help but laugh.

When he runs off in the direction of the peryton clearing, I motion for Briar to follow me and head after him. He disappears into the trees ahead and I quicken my pace, desperate not to lose sight of him for long.

After a minute of power-walking through the thicket of trees, we break into the meadow at the heart of the forest. When Briar bumps up beside me, I turn and press my finger to my lips, making sure she stays quiet. Then I point in front of us.

Peryton are basically white-tailed deer with huge, hawk-like wings. There are about fifty flock members in Asalin, bucks and does and fawns all spread across the field before us. Some stand and nibble at the grass under their hooves. Others lie in the last rays of the fading sun, warming their feathers and fur. Still others buck their horns together, play fighting.

Briar brings her hands to her mouth, covering her lips to keep from screaming. I grin and turn back to scan the area for Boom. He seems to have really disappeared this time. I want to call his name and see if he'll come to me. Though if I do that, all the peryton will fly away and Briar will be upset. So, I don't.

The meadow looks the same. Ever since I crossed the threshold back into Asalin, unwanted memories from my childhood have begun to resurface, a youth I've tried to bury regenerating sharply in my mind's eye. I have so many memories of trekking to this meadow with Emyr, hiding behind the line of trees to watch the flock from a far distance so as to not spook them. We would climb into the branches and lounge next to one another, hold hands, talk about the future. If I didn't know better, I would think no time had passed at all.

But plenty of time has passed, and things are different now—really different, including *one* thing about the meadow itself. After I scan for a few seconds, I notice something new, something that definitely wasn't here back when Emyr and I used to spend our time hiding in the woods. There's a little cabin tucked away on the other side of the clearing, a tiny log house decorated on the outside with climbing ivy entwined with rows and rows of flowers.

Huh. Who lives out here? Maybe that's where Boom is.

I take Briar's hand, pulling her along the edge of the tree line to make our way toward the cabin without cutting through the clearing and disturbing the flock. She stumbles along behind me, refusing to look away from the creatures gathered in the sun.

As we make our way up the stone pathway to the cabin, I see the freaking wood thrush sitting on the window ledge. It looks smug. Smug!

I don't have time to choke the damn bird before the front door of the cabin swings open. Boom comes bounding out barking, running circles around us again. A few of the peryton take note and ruffle their feathers, but they don't seem all that disturbed by his obnoxiousness. And he isn't alone— clearly, he didn't open the door himself. Seconds after Boom bounds away to try and goad a few bucks into playing with him, Emyr steps out of the cabin.

Oh.

Oh, no.

Oh, shit.

I'm so *gay*.

He's shirtless and barefoot, dressed in only a pair of sheer black pants that appear to be made of tightly woven mesh. They're low slung on the waist and oversize on his legs, then fitted to his ankles. They show off the dip of his V, and underneath there appears to be an opaque swath of black fabric around his waist like a skirt. He scratches his long black claws across his happy trail, dragging them up and down his muscled stomach. His eyes are tired, his wings drooping as if they haven't quite woken up yet. His golden energy drags along on the ground behind him.

Sleepy and half-naked Emyr is apparently my homosexual kryptonite, because I feel like I could combust.

"Evening," he grumbles, sleepiness making his words rasp out. He yawns big and wide, flashing those huge viper's fangs. I think I can feel my knees wiggle underneath me. "Were you looking for me?"

"We had *no* idea you were out here," I quickly retort. I so do not want Emyr thinking I wanted to see him. Especially not right now, when I'm barely suppressing my inexplicable desire to, like, lick him or something.

"Hmm." He curls his hands behind his head and arches his body forward, stretching out the curve of his spine. I force myself to glance at the sky. "S'my cabin. Came out here to do some reading. Must've dozed off. What are you doing?"

"Just looking for a place to hook up with my concubine," I say, because I know Emyr has convinced himself I'm banging Briar and because I want to irritate him.

What I don't expect is for Briar to give me a wholly disgusted look. What? There was a time she wouldn't have been *that* opposed to sleeping with me.

Emyr either doesn't notice the unamused expression on Briar's face or doesn't know her well enough to read it properly, because he glowers at me like he's thinking about snapping me in half. *Go ahead and try it, pretty boy.*

As Boom continues his tussling with two young peryton bucks, Briar's attention drifts after him. Her dark gaze follows the animals this way and that, delight etching itself into her round face as she clearly forgets to be annoyed at me.

Emyr tells her, "You can get closer, if you want. They're pretty friendly, at least with my friends."

She doesn't wait for a response from me, nor does she give him any answer of her own. Instead, she hightails it toward the field, getting as close to a fawn and its mother as she can before crouching down to stare at them in wonder.

I watch her for a long moment before turning back to Emyr. "You two are not friends."

"You want to come inside?" he asks, ignoring my statement. "I have ileiva."

A beat passes before I nod, and the two of us move into the house. Because, okay, he's not my friend or Briar's friend, and I definitely didn't come here looking for him. But I do want ileiva.

The inside of the cabin is decorated much the same as the outside. Live plants cover most of the walls. It's laid out like a studio apartment, with a small kitchen and an attached bedroom. A circular hammock bed hangs from the ceiling and a plush-looking, ridiculously oversize dog bed is on the floor next to it. One door probably leads to a bathroom.

As Emyr begins heating up a coffee percolator over a wood stove, sleep still trying to creep along the edges of his eyes, he pushes a plate of ileiva toward me. I haven't had one in years. They're completely self-indulgent without any real nutritional benefit, just spun sugar figurines dusted with some kind of crushed nuts. The ones Emyr offers me are shaped like succulents and covered in green pistachio powder. I eat three before I speak again.

"So, this is, like, your secret hideout?"

"Something like that." Emyr shrugs. "It's nice to get away from the castle sometimes."

"I bet." I shove a fourth ileiva in my mouth—who even needs asshole bakers when Emyr is around to provide this—and accept the cup of black coffee when he hands it over to me. Typically, I prefer it with heaping amounts of sugar and cream, but this'll work.

Boom comes trotting through the door and pushes his nose against my side until I reach over to scratch him behind the ears.

"He missed you," Emyr says, watching us.

"Of course he did, I'm great." I grin at the hellhound, moving my nails to scratch under his chin. "I'm surprised you're still taking care of him. I thought maybe he would have rejoined the pack or something."

"Of course I'm taking care of him. He's ours."

Briar enters just in time to hear Emyr's words. She raises her eyebrows at me, silently asking, *Oh, you two have a child together?*

I roll my eyes. *Shut up.*

To avoid the heavy scrutiny of her gaze, I stand up to explore the rest of the cabin. There are a few things that give hints to the sort of person Emyr might be underneath it all—glimmers of the boy I used to be friends with shining through his new princely demeanor. A stack of books—mostly nonfiction, mostly medicinal, but a few graphic novels tossed in, too—in one corner, topped by a moleskin journal and a very fancy-looking pen. A pile of knit blankets are stacked in the corner by the window, next to a pair of wooden knitting needles and a basket full of yarn. His laptop, nearly identical to the one Jin used at the witches' meeting, is tossed on his hammock.

"What were the two of you *truly* getting up to out here?" Emyr asks, and I spin around to catch him looking between Briar and me with skepticism.

She stomps right over to me and shoves her hand in my pocket.

"Hey!"

That doesn't deter her. She pulls out a handful of the morghira flowers and moves to Emyr's kitchen island, slumps against it, and holds them out until he offers her his palm. When he does, she drops them in his hand. "You know what to do with these?"

Suddenly seeming far more awake than he did a second earlier, Emyr blinks down at the flower. Then up at me. "Where did you get this?"

I smirk, sidling over to rest at Briar's side, my elbow brushing hers. I don't want her being annoyed with me anymore. "Wouldn't you like to know?"

And he will, soon enough. Can't exactly hide the damage done to the greenhouse. There is a good chance Emyr is going to wring my neck for what happened back there.

Ah. Hmm. I am *not* thinking about Emyr touching my neck in any way.

Emyr huffs at my nonanswer, curling his fingers to press one of the flowers into his palm. His tongue flicks out against his lower lip, and finally, with a long-suffering sigh, he asks, "Do either of you have a lighter?"

I'm so confused by the question I almost miss the very pointed look he gives me. Almost.

"I can't just do it on command." I shove my hands into the front of my hoodie. "What do you need a lighter for?"

"I thought you wanted to smoke this."

"Are you serious?"

He raises his eyebrows and leans forward, considering me. He is *far* too close. He smells like sugar and books and freshly tilled earth. My tongue presses against the back of my teeth. I want to scream. "Do I seem facetious to you?"

My nails dig into my palms, fists twisting in my pocket. "You seem like an uptight dick."

"Maybe you don't know me as well as you think you do."

"I have a lighter." Briar shoves her peach Zippo knockoff into the space between our mouths.

When did Emyr get so much closer to me? When did *I* move closer to *him*? I growl and step back.

He plucks it from her fingers with two of his claws, sharp talons clicking against aluminum. "Well, come on, then."

When we step outside again, the sun is lower on the skyline, painting everything in warm tones. Emyr hands Briar all the flowers back but one, which he nestles into the palm of his hand. He looks up, considering us through his eyelashes as if double-checking we aren't going to back out. When he seems satisfied with whatever it is staring back at him, he brings the lighter to the tip of one petal and flicks the flame to life.

Instantly, the morghira seems to simply *evaporate* in his palm. One moment it's there, a perfectly composed flower, and the next there is nothing in his hand but a cloud of deep gray smoke.

Emyr tilts his head forward and inhales.

Not one to be shown up, I lean forward and do the same.

The scent is what hits me first. It's deeply floral, which isn't unexpected, but it isn't exactly sweet. There's something *spicy* about it, cinnamon and black pepper that burns my nose hairs. And there's an undertow of earthiness to it, a heavy, rich, damp smell, like mud puddles in the heart of the forest after it rains.

The ground rises up to meet me. That or I fall to my ass. Either is possible.

I can *feel* the smoke inside me, the way it winds its way from my face down my throat, into my chest, spreading into my arms, my stomach, down into my legs. The way it makes me feel heavy, too heavy to stand, but also light, like I might float away at any moment. The way it makes my face flush with heat, warmth chasing the smoke like embers from a fire, but it isn't anything at all like the fire I feel beneath my skin. There is nothing uncontrollable about this feeling, nothing to be afraid of. No. Right now I could be a goddamn fat cat curled up in front of a fireplace.

My vision shifts next. It's hard to explain. It looks as if someone grabs the edges of the world like a bedsheet and *shakes* it, sending ripples dancing in front of my eyes. Colors blend into one another—greens and browns and blacks and the rainbow of flowers decorating the walls of Emyr's cabin—all swirling together like they aren't sure where to settle. I roll onto my stomach and press my face into the ground, laughter bubbling up and out of me without warning. Grass tickles my cheeks.

"What—" Briar, seated somewhere behind me, takes a deep breath and tries again. "What is this supposed to do, anyway?"

I know Emyr is a few feet away, but his voice is so close he might as well be on top of me. I can imagine it, his body draped over me, mouth pressed to the shell of my ear, those viper's fangs brushing against my lobe…

What is Emyr saying? Right. Something about what the morghira does. I miss the first part of his sentence because I'm too focused on the sound of his voice—it reminds me of warm honey drizzled over fresh, crusty bread.

"—long as you don't try to fight it, nothing bad will happen. Just relax. It'll wear off in a few minutes."

Relax. Hmm. I cannot, in that moment, imagine doing anything *but* relaxing.

I laugh again, quiet enough that it might be silent, and turn my cheek so I can look up at Emyr. The sun setting behind him sparks a halo of light between his horns, making them glow along with the tips of his wings and that gold hoop in his nose. He's already staring at me when I find his face. His tongue wets the corner of his mouth.

"Didn't think you had it in you, Your Highness."

"You should really stop underestimating what I might have in me, firestarter."

"Hmm." Another soft laugh and I have to turn my eyes away to look down at the ground again. "Pity about this whole marriage and monarchy thing. We might be able to have a bit of fun if we could fuck off to the human world together."

Briar makes a *delighted* sound, and I turn my head to look back at where she's sitting up with Boom's massive body stretched over her knees, her hands working their way up and down his back. "Fun!"

"Were it that simple," Emyr drawls, "I might consider it."

When I look back at him, he's closed his eyes and tilted his head back. The long line of his neck is exposed, the apple of his throat, the tendons and veins that stretch down to the sharp planes of his shoulders. The sunset bathes his black skin, illuminating him in iridescent light. Or maybe that's the morghira.

"Why isn't it?" I can hear the pout in Briar's voice.

"I have responsibilities."

You'd think he'd just informed us all he was going to have his eyeballs removed, for as excited as he sounds about the prospect of becoming king.

Or perhaps it's more about the prospect of marrying me.

"Still don't understand why you can't put it off for a while longer." I sigh, tongue trailing my own dry mouth. I can already feel the morghira beginning to wear off, as if the smoke in my body has found an air vent and has begun leaking out. "You're eighteen. Why do your parents want you taking over already?"

Emyr doesn't answer, but I've never been particularly good at letting things go.

"You're being very shady about this whole thing, you know." I draw lines in the dirt with the tip of my finger, connecting swirls and slashes. They look like sigils. Maybe they are sigils, buried somewhere deep in my subconscious, untouchable magic that I've been trained not to go anywhere near. "Why is it so *pressing* that you step up and take on the Throne? They're old, but they're not decrepit."

"My mother is dying."

He says the words so softly, so earnestly, that it forces the world to stop spinning. My hand freezes, my head snapping up as I stare across the grass at Emyr's profile. He's pointedly not looking at me, gazing down at Briar's lighter, still in his hand. His wings curl in toward his body, as if he's trying to lock himself away. The golden glow of his energy is so dim it could be the sun, almost gone over the horizon.

"Oh, Emyr." Briar has her arms wrapped around Boom's shoulders, her face pressed into the fur of his throat, and her dark eyes have gone huge and wet. "What's wrong with her?"

He flicks the lighter open, one tiny little flame budding to life in his hand. Then flicks it closed again. "She nearly died once before, you know. A long time ago. It took all the best Healers in Asalin to save her."

I know he's talking about the night Kadri fell from the tower.

Or the night she jumped.

Or was pushed.

Whatever happened that night, I also know she didn't merely almost die. She did die. They managed to bring her back, the kingdom's most powerful Healers pouring their strength into her to breathe life back into her body. But she did die.

Still, I don't correct him.

"But it's been years since then. The magic that's kept her alive all this time is starting to waver." He sniffs. His claw flicks at the lighter again. On. Off. On. Off. "We've met with other Healers. Influencers. Feelers. They've done what they

can, but the truth has become clear. She's been living on bor-
rowed time for a while now. She won't make it much longer."

Well...fuck.

I want to try and offer him some companionship, to find
some camaraderie in the dead-or-dying-parents club. But
I can't imagine he would want it from me. After all, Emyr
isn't the one responsible for his mother's death. And the two
of them actually seem to care for each other. All of his innovations in Asalin, his technological advances and the agenda
he's trying to push forward, his mother has cosigned right
alongside him.

Boom gives a soft whine and untangles himself from
Briar's body, then lopes over to Emyr and flops down against
his thighs. He nuzzles at his belly, whimpering quietly until
Emyr lowers one hand to tangle in the fur at the top of his
head, thumb grazing the hellhound's soft ear.

Briar scoots closer to me, and I roll onto my back and push
myself into a sitting position. She takes my hand—I think
maybe because she can't take Emyr's.

"If they saved her once before, can't they do it again?" Her
yellow energy crawls across the ground toward him, like it's
testing the water. Emyr's gives a hesitant slither in her direction before giving in, and the two of them push up against
each other.

For the first time, I'm forced to acknowledge how *similar*
the shades of yellow and gold are. They're still discernible
from one another, Briar's brighter and more inviting, Emyr's
glittering and toasted. But they're close.

If our energies are meant to be a reflection of who we are
as people, it stands to reason that anyone with similar energies

would be kindred spirits. What might it mean that I disappeared into the human world, only to attach myself to someone whose energy was a near-mirror of my fiancé's?

I decide I'm having this thought only because I'm high, and yet it's right out the mental window.

"They've tried. *I've* tried." Emyr looks small, somehow, like this, lying on the grass and staring up as the sky turns purple and pink overhead and the sun disappears. He is suddenly *my* Emyr again, not the prince, not my future husband, but my best friend, the one who writes shitty poetry and chases me through the halls of the palace with our laughter trailing after us. I hate it. It makes me want to pick my own skin off. "But she uses up the healing faster and faster each time. Soon, it won't be able to sustain her at all. She may simply slip away, unable to ever be revived again."

He curls a palm over his face and trails his claws down the bridge of his nose, over his mouth. "When that happens, my father will not be able to rule Asalin without her. I have to be ready to ascend when the time comes."

"Why? Why would Leonidas need to step down?" I pick at blades of grass next to my thighs, absentmindedly tearing them from the ground and tossing them into a pile at my side. "He was king before he met her."

Emyr does not answer. Instead, he takes another flower from the pile he gave back to Briar, then holds it in his palm and uses her lighter to set it ablaze. He dips his head forward, inhaling the smoke as it rises.

Briar and I lean forward in unison, breathing in that floral, heady scent. The effect is immediate, another wave of calm washing over me. Once again, the colors at the edges of my vision tug and swirl together, brighter, closer. I drop onto the ground again, on my side, elbow keeping me raised a little.

When Emyr finally speaks, he's still staring at his palm. "It is very difficult for a fae to survive the death of their fated one. Imagine that a piece of your own soul has been carved away. He will not be fit to be king."

Though I don't know what that means, the finality in Emyr's tone tells me he probably knows what he's talking about. I swallow.

"Did you think Wyatt had died?" Briar asks suddenly. I can feel her at my back, but her voice sounds far away. She's floating somewhere, an ocean on another planet. "Tessa did. When he disappeared. Did you?"

Finally, he turns his head to look at me again. "No. I knew he was alive."

"How?" Who asked that question, me or Briar? I guess it doesn't matter.

"Because I felt it. Every day. Every hour. Every minute. It was the first thing I felt when I woke up in the morning. It was the last thing I felt before I fell asleep at night. I knew you were out there. I knew I had to find you. And so I did."

I can't look away. He doesn't, either. How have I never noticed before that Emyr's eyes are the same shade of brown as the wet soil Asalin is built on? As if this kingdom built this boy from the roots up. The fae might not've come from here, but these forests are in Emyr's bones.

What's that human saying? Bloom where you're planted. That's Emyr.

Briar hums, suddenly draping forward and pressing her body atop mine, nuzzling her face into my shoulder. I can hear her thoughts playing like Briar Radio in my head, a singsong collection of incoherent babbling that makes me feel close to her and disconnected all at once. She's happy, I think. She's full of love.

The world tugs at the edges again, a swirl of incomprehensible color until it all narrows down to a single pinpoint. Until all I can see is Emyr, and the lighter in his hand, and Boom curled up in his lap.

"What does the bond feel like?" This is probably the hundredth time I've asked over the course of our lives. I don't know why I can't let it go. "You can't avoid the question forever."

He studies me through the veil of smoke just beginning to disappear between us, gaze heavy enough to press me deeper into the grass. Or maybe that's just Briar's body weight on top of mine. When he finally looks away, I can just make out the way his throat bobs as he swallows. "Do you remember the first day we met?"

"No," I answer, like a liar.

"You tried to steal my shoes." Emyr laughs. "Your mother had made me a custom piece for a dinner my parents were hosting. I was trying it on, and you waltzed right up, all forty pounds of chaos, and grabbed my shoes. They were these…slip-on things with gold chains that jingled. I think you liked the jingling. Anyway, your mother's yelling, I'm yelling, you're running down the hall, I'm chasing you, half-naked, utterly indignant at having my shoes stolen by some *tiny fiend*. And finally I caught up to you."

I didn't steal the shoes because I liked the way they jingled. I was angry. I was sad and lonely and tired of being shoved in the corner by my mother, the child no one was supposed to see, or hear, or know. I wanted someone to look at me. I wanted someone to *see* me.

Still, I don't correct Emyr.

"My first thought when I grabbed you was, *Who does this little asshole think he is?* But then... I looked into your face. And I really *saw you* for the first time. And I was drowning."

I press my fingers deeper into the dirt.

"I barely had time to process what was happening before your mother caught up to us. She was livid. I thought she was going to hurt you. And all I can remember thinking is...if this woman raises a hand to him, I'll kill her."

It doesn't slip my notice that he's not misgendering me, even when relaying a story from the past. Most cis people have to be *taught* that. I guess I probably have Jin to thank for Emyr's education. Or else he just gets it.

Either way, some part of me makes a note and tucks it away, unsure what to do with it right now.

He continues on, unaware of my internal scribbling. "I was barely bigger than you were. I didn't have any idea how to fight. She could have picked me up and thrown me across the hall if she'd wanted. But I knew I'd do whatever I had to do to protect you. It was the only thing that mattered. And so there I was, all four feet of me, telling this grown woman to stand down."

She had stood down, of course, because Emyr might've been a child but he was still the prince of the fae. And what he wanted mattered. It certainly mattered more than I did.

But that was only one moment in time. Emyr wasn't always there. He couldn't always protect me. Especially when he didn't know what I needed protecting from.

"It didn't matter that I didn't know your name. It didn't matter that we hadn't spoken a single word to each other yet. I saw you, and everything in me shifted. I saw you, and it was like someone had pulled me to the cliff's edge of my heart—and pushed me over."

Briar grazes her fingers down my thigh, curling her hand around the back of my knee. "Like love at first sight?"

"No." Emyr shakes his head, adamant. "No, I didn't love him. I didn't even like him. Because I didn't *know* him. What I did know was that this insufferable, weird-ass child was suddenly the air I was breathing. I needed him. There was no going back."

"We should head back to the palace." I push myself to my feet and scrub my palms on my jeans.

The morghira has worn off. I don't want to talk about this anymore.

"Oh." Briar frowns but stands up next to me. "Yeah, okay."

Emyr clears his throat and joins us in the land of the vertical. "I'm staying out here tonight, but I'll walk you back."

"You don't need to do that."

He has the audacity to roll his eyes at me. "It's late, and there are things a lot scarier than Boom in that forest. You're a human and a witch who doesn't practice magic. I'm walking you back."

I don't bother trying to argue. My head is filled with rocks. Maybe this is an aftereffect of the drugs. This is why people shouldn't smoke.

Boom trots ahead of us as the last bits of sun finally disappear and we make our way back into the trees. It's quiet, the only sounds our breathing and the woods rustling as they make way for our bodies.

The destroyed greenhouse comes into view, shards of glass reflecting the moonlight overhead.

Emyr freezes at my side. "What the fuck?"

"What the fuck indeed," a too-familiar voice bites out.

From the other side of the debris, Tessa is standing with her hands on her hips, Wade at her side. She glares at me until I can't feel the rocks in my head for her knife in my chest. "What the hell did you do?"

CHAPTER TWELVE

CURSE YOU THROUGH THE PHONE

"What makes you think this had anything to do with me?"

It isn't the right question, and I know it isn't the right question as soon as my sister's eyebrows slowly rise toward her hairline, her expression somehow managing to be both utterly blank and radiating with hatred at once. That's the face you see right before you get murdered, I think.

In this moment, she doesn't look *exactly* like me anymore. Actually, she kind of looks like our mother.

"*What. Did. You. Do.*"

I open my mouth to tell her I'm pretty sure it's obvious what I did, because if she wants to fight, we might as well knuckle up, but Emyr cuts me off.

"This was an accident."

Like hell it was! And I don't need *him* defending me, either! I am not the little shithead stealing the prince's shoes anymore, and—

I flick my eyes toward Emyr's face and, if Tessa looks like she's thinking about murdering me, Emyr looks like he's already mapping out where he's going to bury my body.

Okay. So. Maybe I don't argue with Emyr right now. Maybe I let him get me out of trouble with Tessa and then argue with Emyr later.

Tessa, meanwhile, has gone from glaring at me to staring at Emyr with her mouth hanging open. Next to her, Wade rolls his eyes and throws his hands up in exasperation, turning his back to us. It's possible he's having a conversation with the nearest tree. I really can't say.

"How far are you willing to go to make excuses for him?" Tessa demands.

A nerve in Emyr's jaw ticks. I think I know what he's thinking. I think he's thinking he doesn't know yet, either. He doesn't answer.

Briar pipes up. "It really was an accident. It was my fault. We were exploring. I got a little too curious. As soon as it happened, we went looking for Emyr to try and fix it."

"You did this?" Tessa blinks at her, then gives one small, irate shake of her head. "You shouldn't even be here. You need to go back where you came from before something worse happens."

"Is that a threat, *Tee*?" I snap, baring my teeth.

My sister's face shutters closed.

"Besides, Briar's lying. She's trying to protect me. I did it. You know how *uncontrollable* my magic is."

Tessa's face does not change, but I think, maybe, her wings pull in tighter to her spine.

"Enough!" Wade spins around on his heel, dangly earrings clinking together as he does. "Crofts, you can both stop swinging your silicone dicks around now. Tessa, Emyr, the two of you should be able to take care of this together. Yes?"

There is a single bulging vein that keeps jumping in Tessa's temple. I watch it move like a dancing blue worm beneath the surface of her skin.

"Technically," she finally bites out. The faintest lisp creeps into her voice as her tongue presses against the back of her fangs.

I'm not sure what they're talking about for a single, suspended moment. And then lavender begins streaking its way from my sister's fingertips up her hands, crawling up to her elbows. Her eyes illuminate like two pastel purple orbs, her wings stretching over her head and catching the rays of moonlight filtering through the tree branches.

When she lifts one palm, the soft glow of her energy stretches from the center of it, a single tendril of soft purple that floats out of her body and toward the remains of the greenhouse. When it reaches the pile of glass and plant carnage, it becomes a thin, translucent dome, taking up the space where the greenhouse stood hours before.

And then shards of glass begin floating up from the ground, shaking themselves free of the dirt and greenery, and piecing themselves together.

Briar gasps, very softly, at my side, reaching over and taking my hand. I squeeze.

I've seen Influencer magic before obviously. I'm more familiar with fae magic than I am with witch. But it never stops being kind of cool.

Not that I would tell Tessa that.

Bit by bit, the greenhouse comes together again, my sister's purple energy sealing the individual pieces of glass together until they're finally all fitted back into one. She lowers her arm and the lavender recedes, slipping back down and disappearing beneath her claws once more.

"Your move, Your Highness."

You know how some people manage to say something really respectful but it totally sounds like *eat shit and die?* Tessa has mastered that art. So much so that Wade groans, as if she's just spit in Emyr's face.

Either Emyr does not notice her tone, or he simply does not intend to lower himself enough to care. He steps away from Briar and me, moving until he's about a foot away from the glass half-bubble. Silently, he lowers himself to the ground, one knee connecting with the dirt, his wings billowing behind his body when he does.

Gold spills out of his talons and creeps up his arms. I can't see his eyes from here, but I know they're glowing golden, too. And then he reaches forward and sinks his fingers into the dirt, burying his hand in the soil.

Seconds later, a golden glow emanates from beneath the ground. It snakes away from Emyr's hand and moves in a million tiny threads, like roots spreading beneath the greenhouse walls, inside of the barrier. The entire greenhouse lights up with a golden shimmer, as if a tiny, personal sun has just risen inside.

And then the plants—plants that were destroyed either

when they were knocked out of place by their home being shattered or when they were crushed underneath my stomping feet —begin to…rise. Stems tremble up from the ground. Blossoms shake themselves awake. Vines slither out of hiding. With his Healing magic, Emyr breathes new life back into everything I ruined.

But it does not slip my notice that, even as the plants inside the greenhouse begin to heal, the forest around us seems to shrink away. The leaves on one tree branch shrivel up and fall, dead, to the ground.

Magic gives, and magic takes away.

Still, by the time Emyr pulls his hand from the dirt and turns back to us, the greenhouse looks as if it was never harmed at all. I can't stop staring at Emyr's body, long after the gold disappears and he's only himself again.

Healers are more rare than Influencers, more rare than Feelers. Seeing one in action is not an everyday occurrence.

Seeing Emyr in action is not something I think I'll ever get used to.

My teeth rattle when I realize my lips are parted, and I snap them shut.

He's staring back at me with something inscrutable in his dark gaze. The anger seems to have been leached right out of him. Finally, in a tone of finality, our eyes still locked, he says, "No harm, no foul."

Tessa does not try to hide her disdain when she answers for me. *"This time."*

It's very late at night when my phone dings on the bedside table. Briar is already asleep, soft snores blowing through her lips as she lies curled up against my side, her head on my shoulder. I've spent the last hour or so staring at the ceiling, trying to shut my thoughts off. Any excuse to grab my phone and provide my rabid brain with the immediate satisfaction of techy interaction is welcome.

My wallpaper's a selfie of Briar and me back home, our faces smushed together, both of us smiling so big it looks like our cheeks might crack. It makes me smile every time I look at it.

I have three new messages. As soon as I open the thread, my heart sputters indignantly.

The first is a picture of Boom, lying in front of the closed door to Emyr's cabin, as if waiting to be let outside.

UNKNOWN NUMBER
I think he's waiting for you to come back.

This is Emyr.

I consider asking him how he got my number, but that feels like a pointless question. He's the prince. Of course he could get my number if he wanted it.

Should I pretend to be asleep? It's late enough to be believable.

But I'm bored. This is as good an excuse as any to avoid sleep for a little longer.

I save him as a new contact before messaging back.

poor guy. i'm very missable, after all.

he could come stay with me. plenty of room at the castle.

ROYAL PAIN
You are moderately missable.

He doesn't like leaving the forest. I think the number of people at the palace make him uncomfortable.

                                                                    mood.

What does *moderately missable* mean?

ROYAL PAIN
You're up late. Are you and Briar having another adventure?

Another subtle accusation. I huff.

briar's asleep. i'm having adventures with my other concubine.

ROYAL PAIN
There is another?

                                                        ...joking, dude.

ROYAL PAIN
Oh.

Haha.

That was the most dry, unamused reaction I've ever read in my life. So much so that I can't help but snort to myself in response. I roll onto my side, tucking my phone under the blanket so the light from the screen won't wake Briar.

so, i go away for a little while and you give my dog anxiety.

ROYAL PAIN
I did not give him anxiety. Perhaps being abandoned by his other father gave him anxiety.

i would have taken him with me if i could.

ROYAL PAIN
What about me?

> i guess you would have had to get a new dog.

ROYAL PAIN
No. I mean, would you have taken me with you if you could?

The question throws me off guard so hard my head spins. My stomach roils at the mere *idea* of doing even the barest amount of introspection required to answer that question honestly.

Would I have taken him with me? At the time, feeling the way I felt about him back then? We were fighting all the time; I wasn't sure what to do with all the big emotions trapped in my body. It wasn't really Emyr I was angry with, though. It was our circumstances. It was the kingdom. If I could've had Emyr, my best friend, away from the responsibilities and pressures of the Throne, would I have?

I refuse to think about it too long. I don't want to get anywhere *near* those feelings.

> you wouldn't have come. responsibilities to the throne and all.

ROYAL PAIN
Back then, I might've been able to be persuaded.

> what are you doing awake?

I don't want to have this conversation. I refuse to keep it going.

ROYAL PAIN
Can't sleep.

If you're not having adventures with another concubine, what are you doing?

can't sleep.

There is a horrifying moment when the little bubble appears to inform me he's typing a new message that I think to myself, oh, shit, he's going to ask me to meet up with him. What will he want to do? Dragon riding? Goblin watching? We could pick mushrooms from the pixie clusters, or take Boom for a walk near the creek a mile north of the castle. All things we used to do as kids.

Will I say yes? I mean, I don't want to, not really, but it isn't like I have anything better to do. I guess it wouldn't hurt to climb out of bed and go see him again, just the two of us, getting—

His message comes through.

ROYAL PAIN
It appears you have trouble sleeping often. You always have dark circles under your eyes.

Oh, *okay.*

we can't all afford a royal skin-care routine.

ROYAL PAIN
Are you implying I have nice skin?

Seconds later, another picture message comes through. Emyr's face lights up my screen. He's lying in the hammock in his cabin, one arm behind his head. He's smiling, a coy sort of smile that doesn't show off his dimples.

I swallow.

                              how do i curse you through the phone?

ROYAL PAIN
You can't, unless you have Jin's phone.

                              jin better watch out for a pickpocket.

ROYAL PAIN
Be careful, you don't want to end up in the dungeon again.

                  eh. i always suspected prison might be where i wound up.

ROYAL PAIN
Keep pulling stunts like you did today, and you might just make good
on that.

You did not actually intend to destroy it, did you?

                                                      does it matter?

ROYAL PAIN
Why wouldn't it?

                              intention only exists in our heads.

ROYAL PAIN
It's still important.

                                                    not to everyone.

ROYAL PAIN
You mean to Tessa.

Are we talking about the greenhouse, or are we talking about your
parents?

                                        we're not talking about either.

ROYAL PAIN
Okay.

I take a deep breath, press my forehead against the screen, and close my eyes.

There are a lot of things I don't want to talk about. I'd rather not think about them, either.

ROYAL PAIN
I'm not very fond of your sister.

lmao. mood.

ROYAL PAIN
I know there is pain there, between the two of you. But I can't imagine not at least wanting to try to repair things. Especially when you are the only family the other has.

But you will have your own family. And she need not be part of it, if that's what she wants.

please do not use this as a segue to talk to me about the royal baby again. because i will seriously set your dick on fire next time i see you if you do.

ROYAL PAIN
Oh, is that what you're into?

EXCUSE ME?

There is absolutely zero possibility I am reading that message correctly.

ROYAL PAIN
I wasn't going to mention any royal babies. But you will have a family of your own someday. One of your own design, who treats you the way a family should.

My gaze shifts to Briar. I already have a family of my own. It might be small, and it might be untraditional, but that doesn't make it less important.

I know what Emyr's getting at. He wants me to think I could be happy here. That I could belong here. Put down roots. Find love and connections.

But he doesn't get it. There is no eating an apple from a poisoned tree without getting sick. The tree here is a kingdom that hates witches and *really* hates me, a contract I'm bound to by threat of death, and a fiancé who's made it perfectly clear he'll use me for his own gain no matter what I want.

Any attempt at winning me over with promises of love and happiness is pure manipulation. He doesn't care if I'm happy. Not really. I have *got* to remember that.

i should try to sleep. and you should, too. otherwise, that face might start looking as bad as mine.

ROYAL PAIN
I'm not going to call you beautiful again because you scare me a little.

Good night, firestarter.

good night, your highness.

CHAPTER THIRTEEN

THAT'S ENOUGH CIS MEN FOR TODAY

The main dining hall, entirely separate from the private dining room of the royal family, is the largest room in Asalin's palace. It's sort of narrow but *long*, stretching out to take up more than half the length of the lower floor. The high ceilings are hand painted, with little depictions of pixies and peryton and other Faery creatures slashed across their surface in shades of gold and silver. The three long tables have benches covered in bright white satin and stuffed to be made utterly plush.

I hate it here. I hate the lack of windows. I hate the fact that there's only one door in or out, and that everyone in the castle crams inside for meals three times a day. The whole thing makes me feel claustrophobic. And that's nothing compared to how much I hate every memory I have of this room.

The staring. The whispers. Being forced to parade around in front of the fae, Emyr's pretty little wife-to-be, the future queen no one wanted.

Whatever. I know I'm being a baby about it, so I didn't bother to tell Briar no when she asked that we go down and eat breakfast with everyone else. Since we arrived, food has been delivered to our room three times a day every day by kitchen staff. I'm not sure who told them to make sure we're being fed, though I suppose I could wager a guess.

Anyway, that's how I end up sitting on one of these god-awful benches, Briar next to me, Jin and Clarke across from us, a mountain of fae breakfast food stretched out in the middle.

"It was *incredible*, right up until the minute I was pretty sure I was going to die." Briar is grinning, relaying to Clarke her experience with flying dragonback. "We should all go together sometime. I think I've recovered enough to find it fun again."

"Oh, Clarke doesn't do dragon." Jin chuckles, wrapping an arm around their girlfriend's shoulders, behind the downy feathers of her white wings. "Darling thing is petrified."

Clarke's cheeks turn a soft peach, and she scrunches up her nose at us. "I am not *petrified* exactly..."

"The dragons can sense fear, and it lights up their predator drive. The first time Auriga met Clarke, I had to convince her not to eat her."

"Okay! Well!" Clarke throws up her hands, then presses them over her face. "Can we not talk about this?"

Jin grins, tilting their face down to kiss the tip of one of Clarke's antlers. Then they turn back to look at us. "If you wanted, though, I'd be happy to take the two of you."

"No thanks," I mumble.

"I would love that," Briar says at almost the exact same time, grinning wide enough to split her face.

Purple and yellow energy buzz around each other over our heads.

"Well, okay." Jin nods. "It's a date, then."

I pretend not to notice the way Briar's cheeks warm, or the fact that she won't meet my eye.

"Wyatt?"

That deep, rolling voice is so lyrical it sounds like music when it hits me from behind. I still flinch, jerking around to look up at Derek, looming over me.

He's dressed in all black today, a black suit with a black button-down underneath, black knitted leather dress shoes. It contrasts sharply with his blond hair, slicked back over his skull, and those bright blue eyes that cut to my center.

"What?" Perhaps not the most polite I've ever been. Or maybe it is actually, since I've never been polite at all.

"Might we have a word in private?"

Clarke huffs. "Derek, what are you doing? What could you possibly need to talk to Wyatt about?"

Derek narrows his eyes at his sister. "A *private* matter."

"I'm not sure you should be having private matters with seventeen-year-old boys," Clarke says in singsong, and I nearly choke on my own tongue.

"I am coming to Wyatt as the head of the Guard. And what I need to discuss with him is a private *legal* matter." Derek raises one perfectly groomed eyebrow. "Have I sated your curiosity enough, dear sister?"

"It's fine." I stand, black energy sliding against Derek's blue

when I do. The azure fog envelops me. "I'm happy to talk."
Anything to get me out of this damned dining room.

When Briar goes to stand with me, Derek puts one hand
on my shoulder and drags my back toward him. My ass nearly
connects with his thighs. "Must I explain the definition of
private?"

I jerk myself out of his grip, scowling, and reach down to
tuck a curl behind her ear. "It'll be fine. I'll be back soon."

Briar doesn't look convinced, her gapped front teeth chewing at her lower lip, dark eyes focused and hateful on Derek's
face.

Jin reaches over and presses their hand to her elbow. "Don't
worry. We'll keep you company."

I can feel Briar staring woefully after us as Derek and I
exit, side by side.

He leads me through the winding hallways of the palace,
nodding at other fae as we pass, occasionally stopping to exchange a few words with another member of the Guard. It
isn't until several minutes have passed and we've gone up a
flight of stairs to the second floor that I realize I should maybe
be more concerned about where this grown man who hates
witches is leading me. I was so eager to get out of the claustrophobic dining hall I didn't ask enough questions.

"Are you going to take me to the tower and push me off?"
I ask, and a passing fae in a cleaner's uniform shoots us a concerned look.

Derek looks down at me and scowls. "Not today."

That's encouraging, I suppose.

Finally, we appear to reach our destination. Derek pauses
in front of a door, glancing down either side of the hallway.

Upon confirming we are alone, he opens the door, grabs me by the back of the neck, and tosses me into the room like a dish towel.

"Hey!"

Losing my footing, I reach out and grab the first thing I can to steady myself. In this case, it happens to be the footboard of a large, four-poster bed. Another few seconds, and I realize we must be in the bedroom Derek shares with his wife. The bed sits in the center of the room, with an oil painting of the two of them hanging above the headboard. A massive wood desk is on one side, a striking gold vanity on the other. The thick red curtains leading to their private balcony have been thrown open, the table sitting out there covered in a stack of books.

Derek steps in behind me and wraps his arm around my front to grip my chin between his thumb and index finger. He turns my head until I'm looking up at him, our eyes locking. His fangs press against his lower lip when he parts his mouth, his gaze sharp and unyielding. I can *smell* him again, that scent that manages to be both masculine and elegant.

He shoves my back suddenly against the foot of his bed, his claws pressing against the underside of my jaw, a promise of pain as of yet unfulfilled. Even as my black energy drapes over me like a shield, his blue finds the cracks like a noxious gas, seeping in to press against my skin. It sends a chill over me, goose bumps rising down my neck, spreading over my arms.

"I thought we had an agreement, Wyatt."

It takes me a moment to start processing the English language as I blink up at him. When I finally do, all I can manage to say is, "Huh?"

He scowls, dipping his head. Those fangs are entirely too close to my face. Are there any major arteries in the face? Fuck, I don't know.

"The last time we spoke, you were meant to be getting yourself chased out of Asalin. So far, all you seem to be doing is getting cozy with the prince. And my sister."

Finally, my head seems to catch up with the rest of my body. I huff, jerking my chin out of his grip. "I've been *trying*. And last time we spoke, I'm pretty sure I told you to back off and stop putting your damn hands on me."

I go to push around him, to put some space between his body and mine, and his wings shoot out on either side of me, trapping me against the footboard. My own energy tightens around me like some kind of body bag.

"Are you trying, Wyatt? Or are you getting too comfortable here? Perhaps you're beginning to have regrets about our agreement." He cocks his head, and something wild burns behind those dazzling eyes. How are his eyes *so blue*? "Perhaps you've been swayed by the prince's charms."

"I have not been *swayed* by anyone." I bare my teeth at Derek, willing myself to jut out my chin and glare up at him as if I am not very aware that he could do anything to me in this room, anything at all, and I wouldn't be able to stop him. "I don't want Emyr. I don't want the Throne. And I'm working on it."

"Well, work *harder*."

Derek sighs, as if suddenly distraught. Again, he raises a hand to me. Only this time, his touch is almost tender when he presses his palm against my cheek. Almost tender, because he still manages to grab me by the jaw and yank my face closer. His thumb rests at the corner of my mouth, his fingertips curling around the curve of my jaw and pressing into the space where I can feel my pulse pounding. "I only want what's best for you, Wyatt. I hope you know that."

I want to disappear. Acid gurgles in my belly and crawls up my throat, threatening to choke me. I can't answer.

And so he continues, bending down to me until our noses nearly touch. "I don't want to hurt you. But consider what I might have to do, should I no longer be able to trust you. Should you become a liability."

The world threatens to short-circuit. Everything goes dark at the edges until it's just Derek and me and I can't breathe, or think, or feel anything but cold fear and fire threading its way through my veins like a promise.

I don't trust myself to speak, but I don't have much choice. "I get it," is all I manage. I need to get out of here.

Derek considers me for a moment before nodding and stepping back. Freed from the intimate closeness of his body, my knees practically give out underneath me. I have to grip the bedpost to stop myself from hitting the ground.

"Good," he says. "Now, should your little friends inquire as to the purpose behind this conversation, you'll tell them we were discussing the matter of your fine. Which, were you curious, dear Emyr has paid in full."

Right. He said his family would take care of that. I sort of forgot all about it until this moment.

"Otherwise, do get to work. I would hate to see things around here go from bad to worse."

I don't bother asking what he means by that, because I don't want to stick around long enough for him to answer.

Instead, as soon as my legs are steady enough to walk on, I bolt for the door. And I keep bolting until I've put as much distance between Derek Pierce's bedroom and my thundering heart as I possibly can.

After a while of wandering and trying to ease the frantic twitching in my nervous system, I come to a halt and focus on my surroundings. I know exactly where I've ended up. It's been a long time since I've been in this part of the palace, but I wouldn't be able to forget it. Besides the woods, this is right down the hall from the very room where the best memories of my childhood were formed, where I spent some of the happiest nights of my naive little life.

An idea begins to form. A terrible idea probably. An idea that could certainly cause a lot of trouble.

But isn't that the point?

Mind made up, I head to my once-familiar destination.

After having seen the cabin in the woods, Emyr's suite seems...un-Emyr. The giant, imposing bed at the center, covered by a red-and-black silk duvet. The matching desk and dresser. The balcony overlooking the courtyard in front of the castle. It reminds me not at all of the little cottage surrounded by flowers, filled with plants and books and his hammock.

Whatever. I don't stop to investigate all the nooks and crannies, don't pause to rifle through his belongings in search of something that actually seems like Emyr, because I'm here on a mission. And what I'm looking for is sitting on the bedside table, as if waiting for me. The magicked laptop.

I pick it up and flip the lid open. If this doesn't get me thrown out of Asalin, I really don't know what will.

★ ★ ★

Twenty minutes later, I've just snapped the laptop closed and shoved it back where I found it when the door opens and Emyr walks in.

He freezes. I freeze. The two of us stare at each other.

I am still gay, for anyone wondering. This is emphasized by my reaction to the fact that Emyr is carrying a *sword* slung over one shoulder, all casual and shit like that's an everyday sort of occurrence. He's wearing what looks like a leather breastplate and pauldrons that make him look even more broad than he is, and matching leather pants slung low on his hips.

He's *sweaty*. And *flushed*. And I'm going to *die*.

"What are you doing?" I demand, because, seriously, what is he doing?

He throws the sword off his shoulder and places the tip on the ground, leaning forward with his palm curled around the hilt. "Excuse me?"

"What are you doing with a sword?"

"Firestarter, you're the one in my bedroom. What are *you* doing?"

Oh. Right. "Uh, I was looking for you."

He raises his eyebrows as if he knows this isn't true but has no proof. I smile back, because I know he knows this isn't true but has no proof. And we stare at one another like that for a long moment.

Finally, he huffs and tosses the sword onto his bed, all casual and careless and shit. "I was working out."

"*This* is how you work out?"

"Did you think it was easy to maintain my body type?"

"I—" That's enough cis men for today. I would like to can-

cel all cis men and go take a nap. "I don't ever think about
your body."

"Okay." He does not sound convinced.

What if I threw myself out the window?

"Why *swords*?" I ask, turning away from him to wrap my
hand around the handle. I try to pick it up and swing it around
all laid-back and sexy, but I can't even lift it more than a few
inches off the bed. The thing has to weigh a metric fuckton.

"Why not swords?" He moves to his wardrobe in one corner and pops it open, then reaches down and unstraps himself from his top.

I am pointedly looking at anything else. "Maybe because
it's not the 1500s anymore? They sell weightlifting sets at
Walmart, you know."

He laughs. Laughs! All melodic and happy, totally at ease.
I'm gonna kill him.

"Yes, well, my family's been collecting their weapons *since*
the 1500s. My father's passed down blades to me since I was
big enough to carry them. Healing won't do me any good in
a fight, after all. I've got to train for combat."

A memory threatens to drag me down. It's Emyr and me,
and we're standing in the armory, where he keeps the weapons his dad has given him. I'm trailing my fingers against a
spike on the end of a very old club, and Emyr is explaining
its history to me. I'm not really listening, I just like the sound
of his voice.

I grit my teeth and force myself back to the present.

"Right, in case you should ever need to run into battle
against the United States military." I roll my eyes. And then,
thinking aloud, add, "I want a sword."

"You're *still* not big enough to carry most of them."

Oh, I'm definitely gonna kill him. I turn around to glower in his direction and discover that he's stripping out of his pants now. I look back down at the blade. "I don't remember you doing all this *training* when we were kids." Of course, I try not to remember anything at all.

"I was more interested in other things back then."

Another part of Emyr's new persona I don't recognize. Though I guess I don't hate this part as much as I hate some of his other princely attributes.

Something *thunks* onto the bed, and I look over to see Emyr has produced a dagger from somewhere in his wardrobe and tossed it to me.

There is a part of me that is deeply offended by the fact that I've been offered the children's version of a sword, but another part of me just wants to play with it. I pick it up by the handle, feeling the surprisingly heavy weight of it in my hand, and twirl it around experimentally.

Emyr chuckles. When he steps back into my line of sight, he's changed into a pair of white *lace shorts* and a tan shirt that looks like something a pirate would wear, all billowy and hanging off his shoulders.

I'm not even going to address this look.

"This does not seem nearly as threatening as that one." I hold up the dagger in his face and jerk my chin toward the sword on the bed.

Emyr shrugs, stepping in closer until he's nearly pressing himself against the tip of my knife. "The size of the blade isn't nearly as important as knowing what you're doing with it."

I—

Okay.

Instead of responding to that statement, I decide to try and stab him. I swipe the knife at his chest, and he manages to curl his body backward and avoid being sliced open.

Instead of fear, when Emyr looks down at me wielding a knife on him, he looks...excited? Light burns in his dark eyes, a dangerous kind of smile playing at the corner of his mouth.

I thrust the blade out again, and this time, when he maneuvers away, he yanks the sword up from his bed and uses it to block my assault. Steel clashes against steel, the sound ringing throughout his bedroom.

He continues like that, never trying to hurt me but blocking my every strike with ridiculous ease. I step this way, he steps that. I throw my body forward, he slides his back. It's a strange sort of dance I didn't know I could enjoy until this moment.

"Don't get cocky," I mumble, licking my lower lip, watching him for a weak spot. "You've got years of practice on me. Give me time and I could totally beat your ass."

"I don't doubt it," he says smoothly, in the sort of way that makes me want to beat my *own* ass. He seems to think this is my admission of defeat, that I've given up, and he kneels down to open the trunk at the foot of his bed, presumably to store his sword.

That's when I press the dagger against his carotid.

Emyr freezes. The only parts of him that still seem to be working are his eyes, which flick up to meet mine, and his pulse, which I can *see* fluttering against the tip of the blade.

I've got him on his knees in front of me, I've got a knife on his throat, and he's looking at me with a mixture of fear and that familiar, inscrutable expression I've come to expect when his gaze lands on me. And I'm...

Incapable of coherent thought.

"Like I said," he finally whispers, so quiet I nearly don't hear him. "It's about knowing what you're doing with it."

The door to his bedroom opens again and I almost fall on my ass I scramble back so quickly, the dagger falling to the floor between us.

Kadri is standing in the doorway, expression tight, gray energy as fierce as a tornado around her shoulders. "I apologize for the intrusion."

Emyr scrambles to his feet, dropping the sword into his chest like a toy. "Ah, no, it's fine, Mother. Did you need something?"

"There are protestors gathering outside on the steps."

"Protestors?"

"Derek's men." Does she shoot me a foul look, or do I imagine that? "I would feel more comfortable were you to come and wait with your father and me until they disperse."

I wonder if it's as exhausting having people protest your legitimacy as it is comforting having a mother who cares about your safety.

"Oh. Of course." He nods, rubbing a hand against his throat, talons pressing into the spot where the knife was only moments ago. The gesture appears to be a subconscious one.

"Wyatt, you should return to your room, as well," Kadri says plainly.

"Mother, if there are safety concerns at play, perhaps Wyatt and Briar should join us." Emyr's gaze flicks quickly between my face and Kadri's.

"I'd rather not." The words come tumbling out before I can stop them. But, seriously, I think it would do me and my hormones some good to not be so close to Emyr for a while.

Kadri appears skeptical. "We'll install a Guard outside your door to make sure you and your companion are left undisturbed."

"Oh, yeah, okay." I nod and head toward the door. I need to find Briar. Hopefully, Jin's made good on their promise to keep her close, even though I've been gone longer than I imagined I would be.

"Hey," Emyr calls at my back, and I look at him over my shoulder. "You were looking for me. What did you want?"

"Oh." Shit. Um. "I just, uh. Wanted to say hi."

Emyr raises his eyebrows. I scramble out the door and away from this side of the palace as quickly as I can.

CHAPTER FOURTEEN

MY BODY IS NOT MY BODY AND I AM NOT MYSELF

By nightfall, the protests have escalated. The number of fae traditionists—their own word for themselves—on the steps has risen steadily all day and now there are dozens of them out there, shouting obscenities. Their energies converge into a buzzing, multicolored hive of little creatures, all screaming in unison and swarming in the air around us.

Their chants climb the walls of the castle until they reach the balcony outside my and Briar's room, where I'm watching the crowd.

FAE FIRST, FAE FOREVER!
FAE FIRST, FAE FOREVER!
FAE FIRST, FAE FOREVER!

A trickle of fear tiptoes across my shoulders like a crawling spider.

Jin and the other witches have gathered on the other side of the lawn. I can see Roman, Solomon, and Lorena there, front and center. They have chants of their own.

FASCIST FAE? NOT TODAY! HAVE OUR BACKS OR GET OUT OF THE WAY!

FASCIST FAE? NOT TODAY! HAVE OUR BACKS OR GET OUT OF THE WAY!

The Guard stands between the two sides, armed fae in full battle uniform. I've never seen the battle uniforms in person before, only in illustrated copies of our history books. They differ from the typical uniforms in that these black shirts are made of something thick and leathery, like shields wrapped around their bodies. They're also sporting red cloaks, clasped across their throats and trailing down their backs, hoods pulled high. A glimmering magic can be made out inside the hood, no doubt some sort of Influencer magic intended to shield their faces.

A shimmer of pink and green catches my eye, and I turn my head to look away from the protestors to the edge of the woods. I have to squint, but I manage to make out Clarke and Wade standing by the tree line. Wade throws his arms out, yelling something at his sister. Clarke reaches for him to grab his hand, and he pushes her away. She says something else, holding her hands out to him, as if she's pleading. He shakes his head and crosses his arms.

Wonder what that's about. Maybe Clarke is trying to sway Wade to the witches' side? I don't know much about this guy and his politics, but he is Derek's brother. And if his relation-

ship with Tessa—whatever they are to each other—is any indication, he probably hates my guts.

A knock on the door tugs me from my observation and I
slip back into the room as Briar opens it.

Emyr steps inside, looking far more haggard than he did
this afternoon. He's changed clothes again, too, now wearing
a simple pair of brown trousers and a black cloak. It doesn't
look like *him* at all. "There was supposed to be a Guard at
your door."

"There was." I shrug. "He decided about an hour ago that
he'd rather be outside with all the excitement."

"Of course he did," Emyr snarls, flashing fang, and that
definitely is not exciting to any part of my body at all. "I was
concerned you might've decided the same."

"Worried I might have the audacity to stand next to the
other witches and demand equality?" I ask, sliding my hands
into the front pocket of my hoodie and leaning against the
bedpost.

Emyr scoffs, dark eyes rolling. He opens his mouth to
speak, but Briar interjects before he can.

"What set this off tonight?" She tugs nervously at a curl
hanging down her chest, gaze flitting from Emyr to the window and back again.

I'm curious about that, too. There's no way it has anything
to do with what I did in Emyr's room earlier, on his laptop.
I'm not sure if anyone's seen *that* yet, and even if they have,
it wouldn't have reached these particular protestors. So, why
the outburst tonight?

Emyr runs his claws over the back of his neck. "This has
been building for some time. Now that you're here and my

parents are beginning to make arrangements for the wedding, things have gotten worse. This was inevitable. We should have been better prepared for it."

"I don't understand the hatred for the witches." She shakes her head, wrapping her hand around the bedpost by my hip, resting her chin against the side of my head. "It's not as if they're a different *species*. They're your children, your siblings, your cousins. They're your neighbors and, for some of you, your friends. Why this divide?"

Emyr looks to me as if he expects me to answer. I just wave him on. I have my own ideas about why the fae hate us, but I'm curious to hear what his reasoning is.

He sighs, hard, reaching up to tug at his curls. "It is an old prejudice. There are people who will hate anything that's different from them. The witches are something different. That's all."

"Humans are different, too. Do you hate them as much?"

"*I* don't hate anyone." Emyr presses each word out slowly through his teeth. "But yes. There are some among us who hate humans."

"The fae came here from Faery. Sought safe haven here when your own world was collapsing. And now you hide away in these kingdoms, plotting for some confrontation the humans don't even know might be coming, and throwing your unwanted children into our world to die." Briar is clearly upset, her hands clenching and unclenching at her sides, yellow energy shaking all around her.

Again, Emyr looks at me. But I see him only in my periphery, because I'm too busy watching Briar, concern tugging my eyebrows together.

We've talked before about the fae penchant for abandoning their witch children outside of the kingdom. How my parents thought I ought to feel lucky for not being left for dead. I didn't realize that story had affected her enough to stay with her, but clearly it did.

It almost doesn't matter, though. Because Emyr doesn't get a chance to respond.

An explosion *BOOMS* across the night, rattling the stone floor beneath our feet, the mirror on the dresser falling and shattering into thousands of tiny shards.

I reach for Briar's hand, yanking her toward me. "What the *fuck?*"

Terrified screams filter up, mingled with bloody war cries and a stream of curses. Another *BOOM* nearly knocks Briar and me off our feet, and Emyr's hands reach out to curl around each of our sides, steadying us. My legs shake so badly I'm not sure I would be able to stay upright if not for his warm grip on my waist. Bile rises in the back of my throat, threatening to gag me as fear begins threading its way through my body.

The windowed doors that lead to the balcony burst open with a ball of fire, more shards of glass erupting into the bedroom with the force of the blast. Emyr's wings snap out to create a blockade between the glass and our bodies, but I still feel a dozen tiny fragments slice my skin.

Flames lick their way into the room, blackening the walls and turning the curtains to ash. It won't be long before they reach the bed and grow out of control.

"Come on!" Emyr motions for us to follow him out of the room. As he does, our magic begins to twine together again, black and gold weaving into one another to create a bubble around our little trio. Briar's energy trembles quietly at the center.

As we make our way down the hallway, inhabitants of the palace—off-duty Guards, Committee members, and their families—pour out of their rooms, shouting, wailing. A window down the hall bursts open as another gust of flame eats its way into the castle. A servant girl, a little witch, frantically whispers an incantation, and frost builds along her hands and arms. She tosses bundles of snow toward the flame, but it doesn't do anything to subdue the quickly growing inferno. She keeps trying, even as the flames slither closer to her body, until an older woman grabs her and drags her away.

I watch them flee, feeling helpless in the face of the fire. *Fire* is the only magic I know, the only thing that ever came naturally to me when I was forbidden from learning anything else. What good would fire do me now?

Emyr isn't good for much in this moment, either, though I take some comfort in knowing he'll be able to heal Briar if she gets hurt. That's more than I'll be able to do.

"Derek's men are trying to bring the palace down," Emyr growls, flashing his huge fangs, gold dripping into his eyes and sliding against his arms. "We have to get outside. I'll take you to the cabin—you'll both be safe there."

"We'll *all* be safe there," Briar corrects. "If they burn the castle down with you inside, Derek gets the Throne."

My heart beats a little faster in my chest, adrenaline and fear making my palms slick with sweat. I glance at Emyr's face and see nothing but a hard, emotionless mask.

"Either way, we have to get out of here," is all he says.

We wind our way down a flight of stairs to the floor below.

It's even more frenzied here, people screaming and frantic bodies pushing and pulling at each other, trying to escape. The fire is worse on this level somehow.

I wrap my arms around Briar's shoulders, and Emyr stands tight to my back. The three of us move in tandem along with the rest of the crowd, making our way toward the next set of stairs.

What we find there is chaos.

Both groups from outside have infiltrated the palace. Fae Influencers, the only fae with the ability to manipulate the elements, throw balls of fire like tiny blazing meteors into the walls, making mountain rock crack and glass shatter under the impact. Some have rendered themselves invisible, balls of fire, more elegant and controlled than anything I've ever managed to wield, appearing from thin air. Others practice protective measures, sending debris flying another direction when it threatens to come down on them. It looks, for all intents and purposes, like they're trying to bring the place down from the inside.

Still, Jin's group of witches fight back against them. They toss vials of potion at the flames, some concoction that stamps out the magical fire—but not without consequences. Everywhere the fire is extinguished, black smoke bubbles up, thick and noxious, making my eyes sting and my throat tighten. They use their magic against the fae, too. Some of the witches have cloaked their bodies the way the Influencers have. Some draw sigils on the walls with their own blood, pressing their palms against them to radiate magic that robs the fae of their breath or steals their senses. Others wield knives coated in

black liquid, no doubt some kind of toxin, swiping out to
slash the skin of the fae.

Fae Feelers sense the intentions of the witches before they
can strike, using their inhuman speed to counter their attacks
before they can even move. Their Healers erase their wounds
before they succumb to them.

Lorena, in the heart of the chaos, reaches into a satchel at
her side and produces a handful of black powder. She tosses it
into the air and, when it connects with the fae, it burns their
skin, leaving them stumbling away and screaming in pain.
Iron filings? It won't be enough to stop the assault, but it's
certainly enough to slow it down.

I've wondered before what would happen if the witches
rose up, who would come out on top if the playing field were
truly even. If an equal number of us could form a united front
against them. Maybe tonight we'll find out.

As the Guard rush into the fray and civilians around us
scream, Briar turns in my arms and pushes at my chest. "Go!
We have to find another way out!"

Emyr wraps one long arm around us both, steering us away.
"Come on. I know another route."

We slip away from the screaming battle, down a small ad-
jacent hallway. The echoes of the clash die out behind us and
it gets quiet, almost painfully so, the only sound our footsteps
and labored breathing.

"How much farther?" I ask as we make our way down a
small staircase and into a narrow hallway. I have no idea which
part of the castle we're in now, and I can only hope Emyr still
knows where we're going.

"Not much."

We round a corner and find the hallway filled with even more smoke, so thick that everything more than a few feet in front of us is obscured. Briar's hand tightens in mine.

"We have to turn around," she manages to cough out. I shrug out of my hoodie and hold it to her mouth until she takes it from me. I am not going to let her die here.

Emyr stays close behind us, one hand on my shoulder, the other on Briar's back. "We can't. We have to keep moving or we'll end up trapped in the castle."

He stoops forward and puts an arm around the back of Briar's knees, then hoists her up as easily as lifting a feather. He turns his back to me, wings spanning the hallway. When he glances at me over his shoulder, I can only stare openmouthed.

"You must be joking."

"I can get us out faster if I carry you. She can't breathe this smoke much longer."

There's nothing I wouldn't do for Briar… I groan and reach for the back of his neck, then pull myself up his body. I curl my arms around his chest, reaching down with one hand to hold my hoodie tighter to Briar's mouth. My knees tighten around Emyr's slim hips. "Do not drop me."

"I would never," Emyr huffs. And then he takes off at a run.

There is nothing even remotely pleasant about clinging to Emyr's back while he races through the smoky halls. Within seconds, I'm nauseated enough that I have to press my face into the back of his neck and squeeze my eyes shut, willing myself not to vomit across his wings.

One of his curls tickles my nose. I nuzzle my face tighter against him. I think—and I'm probably totally imagining this—I hear him purr.

When Emyr comes to a stop, I assume we've reached our destination. But when I open my eyes, I find we've stopped for another reason altogether.

"Is that...?" Emyr asks, squinting at the body on the floor.

"Tessa?" I leap down and take a few steps closer.

My sister lifts her head and meets my eyes. She's tucked in on herself, knees against her chest, arms around her legs, wings creating a bubble around her body as much as they can. When she looks at me, I see that her mascara has made tracks down her face and her pale cheeks are tinted red from crying.

When she sees me, she gives a warbly kind of scream and shrinks back, holding up the palms of her hands like she thinks I'm going to attack her. "Please—please don't. I'm sorry. I'm so sorry, I'm so sorry, I'm—"

"What?" What is going on? I shuffle a little closer but draw up short when she shrinks even further into herself. "Are you... Are you afraid of me?"

"Please just—just put the fire out." She coughs around a mouthful of smoke, and another violent sob wrenches through her body. "Fire— I can't— Just— Please. Please."

"Tessa, I'm not doing this. This fire isn't mine."

She doesn't seem to hear me; she just starts crying louder. She presses her forehead against her knees again, rocking back and forth, sobs shaking her.

I turn back to Emyr and Briar, holding my hands out. I don't know what the fuck to do.

"Leave her." Emyr shakes his head. "She'll be fine here."

And she probably will be. If the roles were reversed, and it was me lying in a hallway having some kind of crisis, she would leave me. It isn't a poor suggestion. Emyr and I are the ones with targets on our heads. Briar is the one with fragile human lungs. We should go.

And still, I find myself hesitating.

"Goddammit," I grumble, turning back and stomping over to her. She winces when I reach down and grip her elbows, then yank her to her feet. "I'm not going to hurt you."

"I'm sorry," she says again, and she stares into my face like she's seeing me for the first time tonight. Really seeing me, and not a ghost.

"Whatever."

I drag Tessa along with us, following Emyr as we make our way into another hallway, this one even more smoke-filled than the last. And we run into another problem.

A figure blocks our path, a fae shrouded in darkness and smog.

I leave Tessa at Emyr's side and move to stand in front of them, squinting to get a better look.

"Well, well, well," the fae drawls, feathered wings fluttering around him. "When they asked me to block this route, I didn't think I'd run into you—"

And then he says it. My deadname.

My skin crawls. I could vomit from the wrongness of it, the dissociation that comes from hearing someone address me as anything other than me. It's always like this. The feeling that my body is not my body and I am not myself.

Behind me, Emyr snaps, "By order of the Throne, you are commanded to vacate our path."

The stranger laughs. "The Throne? I don't answer to *your* Throne. Soon, none of Asalin will."

Briar makes a noise like she's trying to speak before erupting into a fit of coughs.

"Who the hell are you?" I snarl.

He laughs. "What? You don't recognize me?"

The fae turns his head to the side and I see it, the telltale sign. One single horn, poised in the center of his head.

He raises his hand and a bright, white light erupts from his palm, lighting the entire hallway. I can make him out clearly now. Same freckles and bright orange hair. Same smug, taunting smile.

Moisture beads in my mouth, saliva collecting behind my teeth and against my gums. Nausea makes my insides curdle.

Unicorn Boy's gaze flicks behind me to Emyr and Briar and he laughs, this hateful little sound, before he comes back to me. "How does it feel, bitch? Knowing you're the one who's going to burn now?"

"BY ORDER OF THE THRONE," Emyr bellows. "YOU ARE ORDERED TO SHUT THE FUCK UP AND GET OUT OF THE WAY."

Unicorn Boy is on a roll, though. He continues on as if he didn't hear Emyr speak. "We picked the fire just for you, you know. A little present, after what you did. You psychotic little—"

As black magic slicks across my body and drips into my eyes, a blue lasso of flame shoots from my hand and curls around his throat. It tightens, constricting his breathing and burning through his fair skin all at once. He tries to scream but he can't. He tries to claw at the rope, but all he does is burn his hands. His own magic flares, his energy swirling as it paints across his body, desperately trying to defend himself.

But he can't defend himself. Not against me. Not against this fire. It comes as naturally as breathing, when I finally let it. I'm not aware of how much effort I expend pressing my magic down until I stop trying to control it. Until I let it take the reins.

I still feel like I'm going to be sick. I sway on my feet, held up by sheer spite and rage as I watch my fire eat away at his flesh.

"Enough! We have to go," Emyr warns. I look over my shoulder to see he's holding Briar one-handed now, his other hand around her throat. Soft golden light emanates from his fingertips into her skin. He's healing her, helping to keep her breathing through the smoke. "He'll get what's coming to him soon."

Next to him, Tessa's eyes have glazed over. She's staring at me, but again she doesn't seem to really see me. I recognize the dissociation. She needs to get out of here as badly as Briar does, for entirely different reasons.

I look back down at the fae's body, now crumpled on the ground. His throat is red, bloodied and burned under my flame. He can barely raise his hands anymore.

Finally, I tug the lasso back. It recedes into my palms, disappearing back into my body.

"Someone should teach you some manners," I whisper on a rasp, voice roughened from breathing in soot for too long. "Let's go."

We move around him and after a few steps I can make out light at the end of the hallway. We're almost outside. The smoke begins to dissipate and Emyr lowers Briar to her feet.

But I can hear shuffling behind me. When I turn, I find

Unicorn Boy has somehow stood, blood dripping from the burned, bubbling skin of his throat. He stumbles toward us, his white magic dripping from his body to leave a trail behind him.

"You will die," he whispers, and I can barely make out the words, garbled and twisted as they are. A bubble on his neck bursts, spewing blood from the open wound. "And your human will die, and your bodies will nourish the earth for the fae."

"That's a cool story," I offer coldly, masking the way my gut churns at his ominous warning.

"Cocky, two-faced little girl." He spits out a gob of blood mingled with black soot. "Playing at a game you can't understand. You should have stayed dead."

His hand shoots out, the white light in his palm returning. It blazes brighter and brighter until it feels like the sun has been trapped in this hallway with us.

Briar screams, and Emyr slaps his hand over her eyes. "Close your eyes! He's trying to blind you!"

Unicorn Boy's mouth warps into a smile, teeth coated in ash. Black ribbons of burned flesh flutter against his neck as he drags his twisted body closer. The light dancing in his fingers grows brighter until it illuminates every inch of him like a broken, unholy angel.

"The truth is always pulled into the light eventually," he whispers. Bile, blood, and white magic drip from the corners of his mouth across his chin.

We are going to die here.

My eyes burn, but I can't look away. Emyr grabs my arm, trying to drag me back against him. Briar gives a terrified cry.

I can feel the way the light in Unicorn Boy's palm begins to burn away at my skin, can feel blood rushing from my face, my eyes aching as if they're going to turn to ash in my head.

Unfamiliar fingers wrap around my other arm, Tessa's soft hand trying to pull me to her. "Wyatt," she whispers in that voice that could almost be my own.

She raises her other hand, purple energy radiating out and yanking stones from the very walls of the castle. They plummet in Unicorn Boy's direction, assailing him, but he sidesteps each one.

She's trying, but she's not really here. And he's stronger than she is.

I'm going to die here. And Emyr is going to die here, and Briar is going to die here, and Tessa is going to die here.

And then... Then I'm not entirely sure what happens. One moment everything is shrouded in too-bright light, and the next we're blanketed in darkness. The world is pitch-black around me, and my heart plummets into my stomach.

Did it work? For the briefest moment, panic seizes my chest. Did the fae blind me?

But no. No, I don't think so. Because in the darkness, I hear him give one gurgling scream...and then nothing. Total silence settles among the blackness, interrupted only by the sounds of our breathing.

Slowly, the black begins to fade—and I realize it came from me. It draws itself up against my body and glides against my skin, disappearing under the surface just like my fire does.

With the moonlight glinting in from outside, I can make out Unicorn Boy again. Or at least, I can make out what's left of him. I struggle to breathe. His body looks like it's gone through a blender, scraps of skin torn asunder and decorating the walls of the castle. Blood, muscle tissue, and bone shrapnel lie in puddles across the floor. His single stupid horn glints at my feet.

Briar loses the contents of her stomach.

Emyr and I are silent, taking in the carnage. Finally, he raises his hand to heal the burn marks on Briar's body, a flash of gold before her deep brown skin is left unmarred once more. He reaches for me next but I push him away, even as my face aches from the attack. I don't know if it's a good idea for anyone to be touching me right now.

Finally, as Emyr heals himself instead, Briar asks, "Wyatt, what did you do?"

I meet Tessa's eyes. She looks as afraid as she should be.

We both know what I did. I just killed my third victim.

But how?

CHAPTER FIFTEEN

POLITICS AS USUAL

Outside in the fresh air, Tessa hits the ground again, this time leaning forward to press her face to the earth, fingers digging into the grass. She is clearly going through it, but I don't think she wants comfort from me. Not that I have much to offer.

This is not the first time I've been up close and personal with gruesome, ugly death. Not the first time I've watched my magic mangle someone's body right in front of my eyes. The only thing I can do to survive it is to feel nothing at all, to detach myself completely.

Besides, Emyr, Briar, and I have a date with a cabin.

Before we can make our escape into the woods, Jin's voice calls out, "Emyr!"

Emyr turns in the direction of their voice. The crowd

outside isn't so bad anymore. It looks like most people have either invaded the palace or fled to the village. On this side of the palace, it appears to only be us, and Jin, a few yards away.

"Please help me." Jin's voice is choked, like they're trying to talk through a mouthful of cotton. Or on the brink of having a serious breakdown. "It's Clarke."

Emyr moves toward them. I have every intention of staying the course and heading to the cabin, finding Boom, and bunking down for the night. But Briar hastens after him, leaving me no choice but to follow.

Clarke doesn't look much better off than Unicorn Boy back there. She's unconscious and spread across her girlfriend's lap. Organ meat and bone are visible beneath flaps of torn skin, her stomach ripped open. Bubblegum-pink magic drips pathetically from the corners of her eyes, her cracked lips, beneath the sharp edges of her white claws, as her body struggles to fight against death.

I know I should feel something about this. The sight of her, this gruesome display of gore, should have me retching the same way Briar did back there. But I can't seem to summon any feeling at all. It's like I'm here, but I'm not. This is real, but it isn't. It's like I'm watching my life happen through a screen.

Emyr hits his knees next to her and presses his palms against her chest. Immediately, gold slicks across his skin and his hands begin to glow.

Nothing happens.

Briar sinks down behind a sobbing Jin, wrapping her arms around them. She kisses the side of their face, their hair, holding them tight.

Emyr whispers, "Come on. Come *on*."

Only the most powerful Healing magic in the world can bring someone back from the dead. Clarke isn't dead yet, but she's getting there. And it looks like Emyr isn't strong enough.

"Should I try and find help?" I ask, hanging back from the others. I don't know how to be helpful in this moment. I barely know how to be, period.

Jin's cries grow harder, more frantic. A bead of sweat trickles down Emyr's forehead. He's so focused on what he's doing I don't think he heard me.

Briar meets my eyes over Clarke's body. She nods. *I don't think she's going to make it. But hurry, find someone just in case.*

I nod back, turning to do just that. I don't get more than ten feet away before I hear Emyr say, too quiet, "No. You don't need to do that."

Shit.

She's too far gone. I knew she was. Everyone else knows it, too. Nothing's going to bring her back. Clarke is going to die here tonight. I move back to them, expecting to see the last spark of light fading from Clarke's body.

Instead, I get there just in time to see the skin of her abdomen stitching itself back together.

"Oh, shit." The words come tumbling out before I can stop them. "You're doing it."

Emyr doesn't give much of a reaction to my words. But I think I see a hint of a smile.

A few minutes later, the four of us sit around Clarke as she slowly starts coming back to herself, now without a single organ on the wrong side of her skin. She blinks her blue eyes open and stares up into Jin's face, a little pout settling across her rosebud mouth.

"What happened?"

"I think you finally got tired of all my bad jokes and decided you'd had enough," Jin mumbles, swiping at their eyes and making a face down at Clarke. "Well, guess what, sucker? It didn't work and you're stuck with me forever."

"Hmm," Clarke sighs, nuzzling her cheek into Jin's knee. "That's okay."

"What *did* happen, Jin?" Emyr asks.

Jin sighs. "I don't know. I was helping a group of servant kids escape out one of the back entrances. Clarke and I got separated. I found her like this. She—" Their eyes widen, head snapping back over her shoulder. "She wasn't alone. There was a body. Another body."

Briar pushes herself to her feet and moves in the direction of Jin's stare, disappearing behind one of the castle walls. A moment later, she returns, round face gray, mouth open.

"Did you find someone?"

"It's, um. It was." She swallows. "Lavender. It's Lavender."

The old witch whose home the meeting was held in.

Jin gives a startled scream and folds themself in half over Clarke's body, pressing their face into her bloodied blond hair. Clarke simply stares, unseeing, at the night sky overhead.

Near-silence settles over us, the only sound Jin's quiet sobs and the ongoing clash in the distance. No one seems sure of what to say, so no one says anything at all.

After a while, I notice Emyr staring at me.

"The wounds on your face will scar if you don't let me heal them."

I shrug, reaching up to brush the tips of my fingers against the charred burns along my nose and cheeks. "I'll probably look pretty badass."

Emyr's gaze doesn't waver, though he does turn his attention downward. It takes me a second before I realize what he's looking at. Scars. Ugly, mottled, twisted scars where my flesh was burned away from my bone, covering both of my arms from wrist to elbow. In all the chaos of the evening, I forgot I'm not wearing my hoodie anymore, that I'm laid bare for everyone to see.

There is a reason I don't walk around in public like this.

As if reading my mind, Briar drops the hoodie back into my lap. I yank it on, disappearing under the black fabric, oversized enough it's practically a tent on me.

Emyr is still staring. I meet his gaze and hold it.

Finally, having regained some control of their weeping, Jin looks back up at us. "Are you three okay? The first blast was practically a direct hit to your room, Wyatt. It looked like Derek's groupies were trying to blow you right off the map."

"They did their best." I shrug. "But I'm better."

Briar leans her head on my shoulder. I twist my neck to brush a kiss into the tangles of her hair, closing my eyes to take a deep breath. To breathe in the smell of her. Cocoa butter and fresh air. The only good thing in the world.

It centers me just enough to finally ask myself: *What the hell happened tonight?*

Not the protests, the rioting, the attack on the castle. The death. I get that part. That seems like politics as usual. Humans and fae don't differ much in that area.

But what did I *do?* And more importantly, *how* did I do it? I've only ever seen anything like it once before. The way the blackness took over, suffusing everything around it, engulfing us all in darkness and claiming its victim.

The same thing happened the night I killed my parents. In my memories of that night, I've always focused so much on the fire that the moment everything went dark has never stood out to me as much. Until tonight.

Tonight, I'd felt helpless, dependent on Emyr in a way I didn't know how to deal with. And then seeing that *kid*. Bigger and older, a man now instead of a child, but the same hateful, evil little brat he'd been the night he'd pushed me into the dirt and shoved his hand up my skirt. I could have killed him with the fire. I could have lost control, could have let my rage and bitterness eat me up inside until it took his life. The same way it took my parents' lives.

But I didn't. I knew I had to get Briar away from the smoke. Taking care of my best friend took precedence over getting revenge. I'd found control and managed to walk away in order to save the people I cared about.

It didn't matter, in the end. Because I killed him, anyway.

But *how*?

Briar nudges me and nods at something behind us, pulling me from my thoughts. A small cluster of Guards trail onto the front lawn and start approaching stragglers. The sounds of chaos from inside have died off.

"Still think we should spend the night at the cabin?" I ask, swiveling my head toward Emyr.

He doesn't answer me. He looks so tired.

When one Guard wanders over to us, Emyr stands to speak to her. "What damage was sustained inside? Have the aggressors been taken to the dungeons?"

"The fire is out, Your Highness. The Committee and the servants are clearing the smoke and debris now, and most repairs will be completed before sunrise. Almost all aggressors have been accounted for, except this one." She motions to Jin. "Jin Ueno. You are under arrest for inciting a riot. Will you come peacefully?"

Her words set off five shouts in near-unison.

"Seriously?"

"What the hell?"

"What is the meaning of this?"

"Jin didn't do anything wrong!"

"Are you out of your goddamn mind?"

The Guard takes a surprised step back, but then her face turns stony. She addresses Jin to say, "You are the leader of the anti-fae hate group. You were at the center of tonight's events. Of course you are under arrest."

"Our group isn't anti-fae." Jin shakes their head. "We're pro-witch. Meanwhile, one of our kind was *murdered* tonight. You'll find the body of Lavender Nott around that corner. And the fae protestors tried to do the same to Wyatt, and my girlfriend."

"I would like to speak to the commanding officer who gave this order." Emyr is using his princely voice, the one that makes him sound like an authoritative asshole whose eyes I want to claw out. But in this case, it's useful.

The Guard narrows her eyes, glancing between our ragtag little ensemble. Finally, she grits her teeth and mumbles, "Fine." Turning her head over her shoulder she calls out, "Derek! We've got some trouble over here!"

Derek? Seriously?

Briar and I exchange a look.

He would have his own sister's girlfriend arrested? She frowns.

I shake my head. *I don't know what he's capable of.*

But that's a lie, I realize as soon as I think it. I have a feeling I know exactly what Derek is capable of. I just don't want to admit it, even to myself.

Derek's mouth is set in a thin line when he makes his way to us, followed by one very, very round woman. This must be his wife, Martha. I've heard mention of her around the castle. Except for her belly, which looks like an overinflated beach ball, she's tiny. (Though still a few inches taller than I am.) The second largest thing about her is her red hair, a mess of tangled curls sticking up at odd angles all around her face. Her wings are delicate and velvety like a butterfly's, her horns too small to make out under all that hair. She's dressed in a nightgown and a pair of slippers, as if the attacks roused her from bed. A soft teal energy floats around her stomach, protecting the center of her body and nothing else.

"What?" Derek snaps, coming to a halt at the other Guard's side. He seems to realize Clarke is with us, his eyes widening slightly at the image of his sister sprawled in Jin's lap, the edge of her shirt torn. "What's going on? What happened to you?"

"Well, right now..." Clarke groans, pushing herself into a sitting position. I think she must still be in pain, despite Emyr's impressive healing. "You're trying to have my girlfriend arrested."

Derek narrows his eyes, gaze flicking to Jin and back to Clarke. "Jin was responsible for inciting this riot. Of course they are under arrest. I would not be surprised if they were to face execution for this."

"EXECUTION?"

"What the fuck?"

"There has to be some mistake!"

Emyr moves to stand between Derek and Jin, planting his hands firmly on his hips as he eyes his head Guardsman. "Derek, I don't know what scheme you're trying to pull here, but Jin did nothing wrong. There are dozens of witnesses who will attest to that. If you wish to remain in charge of the Guard, I would think very carefully about your next move."

Hatred bubbles in Derek's blue eyes. His energy cracks like a whip around him, restless, eager for a fight. By comparison, Emyr's energy is calm and steady, a golden glow that spreads out on all sides as if he thinks to shield Jin with his magic if necessary.

"Are you threatening me?" Derek demands.

"No." Emyr shakes his head. "I am *warning* you."

"I am aware you have a soft spot for the witches," Derek seethes. His gaze darts to me, there and gone just as quickly. "But there was violence on both sides tonight. We cannot absolve them of all guilt because of your disdain for your own kind."

"If there was so much violence on both sides, why are you not arresting the fae?" Briar demands. "Maybe because too many of them were Guards out of uniform?"

Derek stares at her, and my black energy drapes itself over her shoulders to keep him away. I can feel her warmth pulsing under it as easily as if I've touched her with my hands.

"What's going on here?"

Wade comes into view, Tessa tucked into the crook of his elbow. He seems to be carrying her, more or less. She doesn't look at me even when they stop only a few feet from where we're standing.

"Derek?" Wade asks again. "What's going on?"

For a moment, Derek doesn't answer. And when he does, he isn't looking at Briar, or Wade, or Jin, or even Emyr. Now he's looking right at me, in a way that sets my teeth on edge. In a way that makes me feel like I'm alone in his bedroom again, no matter how many other people are around.

Like he could do anything, *anything*, and nothing would be able to stop him.

"It is time for the witches to face retribution."

CHAPTER SIXTEEN

YOU DON'T WANT TO LOOK

Hours later, in the dead of night, Lavender's house has filled with people, but only five of us are still awake.

"FOOLISH boy!" Roman is in the middle of shouting, the way he's been doing on and off for the last hour now, since we arrived. "I told Solomon—I said when the Guard shows up and starts disappearing people, you *get out of there*. And what did he do? What did the little twerp do?"

"He tried to reason with them," Briar answers softly. She doesn't look up from her reading, one of Lavender's many spellbooks that are scattered around the house. She's heard this story a hundred times already, because we've all heard this story a hundred times already.

"Reason! As if the Guard know anything about reason!"

Roman sits back down, skinny body dropping onto the arm of the couch where Lorena is sitting, staring blank-eyed at the wall in front of her.

Solomon was arrested, along with Jin and a handful of others from their group. Lavender appears to have been the only casualty of the riot, besides Unicorn Boy, but we won't know for sure until later.

And she won't stay the only casualty. Not if the Guard makes good on their threat to execute the provocateurs. They'll burn the witches at the stake for no goddamn reason. Legal murder.

Derek's words from earlier that day play on loop in my head. *Get to work. Before things around here go from bad to worse.*

In retrospect, the words feel every bit a direct threat. And though I haven't told the witches what he said to me—as that would require outing our shameful alliance—their version of events does match up with the idea that Derek knew what was going to happen tonight.

According to them, the fae protestors started gathering after word spread about the Committee moving forward with arrangements for the wedding. Jin's group arrived on the scene to counter their protests, a show of strength and unity among the witches. Whispers started on the other side about how none of the fae would recognize my rule, were I to become king. The fire hit my room soon after, a clear attempt to make sure I never took the Throne.

When the fae stormed the castle, the witches believed they were doing so in order to find me. They followed to protect me. To make sure the fae were cut off before they could actually get their hands on me.

If all of that's true, Jin and Solomon were arrested because of me.

Lavender lost her life because of me.

She's not the first.

"What are we going to do?" Clarke whispers from where she's folded into herself in the corner of the sofa. Her wings are drawn tight against her back, her eyes wide and vacant, her claws digging into her calves as she wraps her arms around herself. "I didn't—I never thought they would actually *kill* them. Not Jin. This wasn't supposed to happen."

"And why didn't you protect them?" Lorena asks, as if suddenly coming to life for the first time tonight. "You were right there. You couldn't put yourself between Jin and the Guard? You really think you couldn't have forced your own brother to back down?"

Clarke blinks.

Lorena is clearly not finished. She speaks in a furious stage whisper, trying not to wake the rest of the witches scattered around the house sleeping. "*Months* I've spent defending you to this group. *Clarke isn't like the rest of the fae. Clarke is on our side.* But when it came down to it, you just sat back and did nothing. *Nothing.*"

"I nearly died for the witches," Clarke bites back. "I was still half-dead when they dragged *my mate* away! And what about you? Your mother's in the Guard, isn't she? Which side was she on tonight?"

"This isn't going to help anyone."

It's only when everyone looks at me that I realize I was the one who spoke. With the room's attention on me—including Briar, finally tearing her gaze away from the sigils she's been quietly studying—I want to shrink, want to disappear. But I don't. I can't.

I owe it to everyone here to fix this. However I can. "Whatever we did or didn't do before doesn't matter. We can't change that. All we can change is what we do next."

"And what do you suggest?" When Roman asks the question, it lacks his usual venom. And I realize he's serious. He's looking to me for an answer.

They all are.

"We can't let them go to trial," I find myself saying. "We have to get them out of there."

A beat passes. Briar shuts her book. "Wyatt, are you suggesting we break them out?"

Am I? "Yeah."

"How are we supposed to do that without ending up behind bars ourselves?" Lorena demands.

I slide my tongue over my fangs. "*You* aren't."

If I'm understanding things correctly, Roman has done a good job at making himself a target in the months leading up to today, pressing fae buttons by lecturing their children and just never shutting up. Lorena was at the front of the battlefield, making more moves than anyone except Jin themself. And Clarke… Clarke doesn't exactly look like she'd be much good to anyone right now.

When I head for the door, Briar jumps to her feet and scurries after me.

"What do you want us to do?" Roman asks at my back.

"Stay here and stay out of trouble." Since when did I start giving people orders?

"What's your plan?"

I glance at him over my shoulder and shrug when I meet his eye. "I'll burn it all down if I have to."

Outside, the world feels too still. A glance at my phone tells me it's past two in the morning. Everyone's retreated to their homes for the night. The air smells like darkness and smoke still coming off the palace.

Briar touches her knuckles to the back of my hand. "I guess if anything was going to get you thrown out of Asalin, helping a terrorist group escape from jail is probably it."

I don't say anything back. I'm not sure what to say, since it's the first time that occurred to me tonight.

Wanting to get Jin and the others free has nothing to do with my own plans to cause chaos at every turn. I'm not going to examine what that might mean. Least of all right now.

It's a ghost town in the village. Not even the animals in the forest around us make a peep. It's eerie. As if all of Asalin has fallen still. Eventually, the cobblestone streets turn to dirt, and the turrets of the castle come into view. The smell of smoke is stronger the closer we get, though I'm pretty sure the fire's out by now. People aren't running around screaming, so that seems like a safe enough assumption.

Good. I have *no* idea how I'm going to get the witches out of the dungeon; I don't need the added stress of fighting a fire while I'm at it.

"Hey!"

Briar and I freeze at the sound of a stranger's voice, and when we turn, we see a man in a Guard uniform crossing the path to get to us. He glowers, hand already poised on the iron cuffs at his hip.

"What are you two doing out here?"

"Just heading back to the palace, sir." Did I just call this man *sir*? Has someone taken control of my body? Is this what dissociating feels like? "Is there some kind of problem?"

"You're damn right there's a problem. Your kind tried to burn the palace down." His eyes narrow. "Where've you been all night, kid?"

"With me."

That warm, familiar voice hits me hard enough it almost takes my knees out from under me. When I look up, I see Emyr walking toward us from the direction of the castle.

And he isn't alone. Tessa and Wade flank him.

After Jin's arrest, Emyr went to meet with his parents in their chamber while Briar and I left for Lavender's house with a beside-herself Clarke. We haven't seen one another in a few hours.

He looks exhausted. The kind of exhausted that doesn't come from staying up until two in the morning, but from watching everything around you burn to the ground.

The Guard looks skeptical. "Your Highness, what are you—"

"I am here to accompany my mate to the palace. He has spent the last few hours grieving the senseless death of an elder in his community, and now I intend to make sure he gets back to his room safely. What are *you* doing?"

Exhausted Emyr does not have time for this man's shit.

And, unlike Derek, this Guard does not seem to have it in him to argue. He stumbles over his own words—*something something apology something*—and darts off down the street toward the village. Probably to try and find some other witch

to terrorize. I hope Roman and Lorena heed my command
to stay out of trouble.

We wait. We watch him disappear. We say nothing, not
until his shadow has long gone and the world is too silent
once more, and even then we say nothing. As if sharing a single brain cell, the five of us turn and head into the woods in
search of a moment of privacy, putting as much distance between us and the rest of the world as we can. The farther we
retreat, the darker it gets. The quieter. The creepier.

Briar is the one who speaks first. "What is *that?*"

It isn't until she says it that I realize where we are.

Wade is the one who answers her. "That's the door to
Faery."

Although "door" is pretty far from what this thing looks
like. I remember venturing here once as a child, Emyr and I
sneaking out to catch a stolen glimpse at the dark and twisty-
looking portal from which our ancestors came. It looks just
the way I remember it.

Two elm trees, dead and blackened, have grown together to
form one ugly, unnatural archway. Their branches, dark and
sharp like talons, twist around each other and jut out at odd
intervals, creating bleak silhouettes against the sunrise. Between the tree trunks, beneath this abysmal arch, is…nothing.

I don't know how else to describe it. My eyes can't focus
on it. When I try, it makes my jaw hurt, the sound of static
like crinkling aluminum blaring in my head.

Witches can't see through the door, but fae can. It's sort
of the way humans can't find Asalin on their own because of
the cloaking magic, but they can get here if they're brought.
The first time Emyr and I wandered over to sneak a peek at

the door, I was *so* angry that I couldn't see it. I stomped my feet and curled my fists and gnashed my teeth, confused and hurt because I wanted to know! I didn't understand why I couldn't look!

But Emyr, crouching down next to me, little body trembling, whispered, "You don't want to look."

I still don't know what he saw that day. But the doorway gives me the creeps. I look away from it.

"Are the two of you all right?" Emyr reaches for me, and I don't shove him away. He takes my hand and tugs me closer, as if to examine me, but instead presses his nose to the top of my head and takes a deep breath. I lean my head against his chest, warm and solid, my eyes sliding halfway closed.

"As all right as anyone is tonight," Briar answers from behind me. I hear something tucked into her tone that I don't want to recognize, so I ignore it. "How did your meeting with your parents go? Are they going to do something about the arrests?"

Emyr says nothing. His hand settles on the back of my neck. Have I been this tired all night? I feel like I could fall asleep on my feet, that I could lean into him and close my eyes and drift right off.

But I can't. And after a moment too long of quiet, I pull away, shaking myself free of him, blinking up into his face. "Your parents?"

"It—"

"They aren't going to do shit," Tessa offers succinctly. "They are choosing to defer to Derek Pierce and his infinite wisdom."

"Are you serious?" My eyebrows draw together as I stare

at Emyr. He can't seem to meet my eye. "They're going to let them die."

Emyr swallows. "Derek is the head of the Guard. He holds a considerable amount of power, and—"

"YOUR PARENTS ARE THE KING AND QUEEN!" Briar throws her hands up. "What exactly is the point of the Throne if the Guard can do whatever the *fuck* they want?"

Emyr—well over six feet tall, with his horns and wings and fangs, with all his magic and his money and his power— takes a step back when Briar yells at him. He stares at her, lips parted, for a long moment, before saying, finally, "The Throne makes the rules. The Guard enforces them. My parents can stay an execution, but…"

"But?" My hands clench.

"But I don't know if they will. Not when…" He stops again.

Briar growls, "Just spit it out!"

Emyr doesn't. But Wade does speak up. "Not when the Throne is already seen as too sympathetic to witches."

So, this is my fault.

One way or another, I am responsible for everything that happened tonight.

I don't have time for this. Don't have time to wallow in my guilt and feel bad for myself. That can come later. After the witches are out of the dungeon and far away from here. I turn to Wade and Tessa. "What are you two doing here?"

"Officially, I'm on duty tonight." Wade shrugs and tucks one strand of blond hair behind his ear. "Unofficially, we were looking for you."

The Throne makes the rules. The Guard enforces the rules. The Committee makes sure everything runs smoothly.

I think I know a way to get the witches out. It's blooming in the back of my mind. I just need a minute to let it get there.

Tessa is staring at me. I meet her eye. Neither of us blink.

"And what are you doing out here, Wyatt?" She asks the question like she already knows the answer.

We have always been more similar than Tessa would like the world to believe.

"We're going to break the witches out of jail."

Wade, Briar, and Emyr burst into a cacophony of arguing, but I'm not paying them any mind. I know what I'm doing. At least, I have some idea. And Tessa's staring back at me.

I think of her dragging those stones out of the wall to toss at Unicorn Boy's body. Neck-deep in her own panic, nearly drowning in whatever flashback she was having, and still trying to fight back. I don't know what that means.

"We've tried doing things the right way." I speak, and the others stop arguing long enough to listen. "And if we don't try doing them the wrong way, Jin is going to die. Derek is going to kill them." My gaze flicks to Emyr. "*Jin*. Do you really trust that your parents will come through with a stay of execution at the last minute? Enough to risk Jin's life?"

Emyr stares down at me. A moment ticks by. Another. Finally, he folds his arms over his chest. "How are we going to do it?"

"*We* aren't going to do anything. You're going to stay as far away from this as possible. Derek's goonies are already looking for anything they can use against you."

"But—"

"No. Go back to the cabin. Tell people I was with you all night."

Briar is staring at me. I don't stare back, but I can feel her question boring into me, anyway.

If my goal here is to help Derek get his Throne just so I can waltz out of Asalin a free man, wouldn't it serve my purpose to drag Emyr into this with me?

And the answer to that is yes.

But I can be introspective about all of this later.

"How are you going to do it?" Tessa asks.

I look at her and swallow. She looks back at me. Finally, she nods.

"Okay. Right." She turns to Wade. "We're going to need your keys."

"Excuse me?" He looks at me, then toward her with an eyebrow raised. "Really?"

"Would you rather innocent people be put to death?"

"Well, no, but—"

"The keys, please, darling." She holds out her hand, crooking her fingers toward the center of her palm.

Wade hesitates only a moment longer before pulling the keys free from his belt. As he drops them into Tessa's hand, he mutters, "Absolutely ridiculous. This timeline is completely fucked. I hate it here."

"I know." She slides the keys into her back pocket.

Briar glares with all the rage of a wild dog, staring at Tessa like this is some kind of trap. "Why would you help us?"

"I'm not helping you. I'm helping my best friend's sister's girlfriend."

That sounds like bullshit, and I don't care. There's a lot

going on tonight that will need to be unpacked in the day-
light. But I can't worry about any of it right now.

Emyr clears his throat. "You'll need to make it look real."

"I know." Tessa has already picked up a rock. She tosses
it up and down, and it makes a quiet thud each time it connects with her palm.

"Make what look real?" Briar asks, and I put an arm around
her waist.

Wade glowers. "Not the face. I am far too pretty."

"Turn around, then."

"*I hate it here.*" But he does as Tessa says, turning around
and hitting his knees.

Tessa raises the rock.

Briar gasps at my side. "Oh, shit."

It takes three swings for Wade to collapse to his front, his
blond ponytail bloodied, the rock falling to the ground beside him. Tessa rubs her red-slicked hands against her jeans.

"Emyr, could you—"

"Yes." He moves to Wade's side, kneeling down and gently touching the side of his neck. "He'll be fine. You three
go, now."

We don't need to be told twice. But as we start to walk
away, Emyr calls out, "Wait!"

He's risen from his post at Wade's side, moved closer to us.
He lowers his voice. "No one knows what happened to the fae
who attacked us. No one but the four of us. Keep it that way."

In all the events of the night, I'd nearly forgotten about
Unicorn Boy. "Or else I'll be the one in the dungeon?"

Emyr need not say anything in response. I know. I got away
with it once. I won't a second time.

"Whatever." I turn away, start to walk off again. "He's lucky he lived another three years after the first time he attacked me."

"Wait, hey—" Emyr snatches my arm, forcing me around to face him. "What are you talking about? What attack?"

"What are *you* talking about?" I demand, reaching down to shove his hand away from me. "The group of fae who assaulted me. The attack that started the whole goddamn fire."

A second ticks by and my body begins to grow cold.

Emyr has no idea what I'm talking about.

I guess I'd always thought there would be some investigation into what I'd done. And that, eventually, someone would have said something. That one of the boys would come forward, or one of Asalin's citizens who *had* to have seen what really happened that night. I guess in some part of me I always imagined they wouldn't just think I'd committed arson, and murder, for no reason. That they would at least dig until they found a freaking *reason*, even if they thought I did it on purpose.

But no. Apparently not.

"The night I left Asalin, that one-horned piece of shit and a group of his friends surrounded me on my way home. They pinned me down—" I swallow. I can't say any more than that. "That's when the fire started."

Reading Emyr might not be as easy for me now as it once was, but I can see the wheels rolling in his head. He steps back, wings snapping shut. "I didn't know. No one knew."

I look from him to Tessa. Her face has gone perfectly impassive again.

But I think her bloodstained fingers are shaking.

"What, you thought I started the fire for fun?" I look back at Emyr. "You thought I left your bedroom and went home to kill my parents for no reason?"

Silence.

A broken laugh escapes my mouth. "And you accused *me* of not knowing *you*?"

I can feel his stare on my back as I turn, and Briar, Tessa, and I race to the palace.

The castle is more awake than the village is, but somehow that works in our favor. As witches and fae alike sweep this way and that, trying to put the palace back together again, no one has time to stop and question what we're doing. No one looks up from their tasks long enough to realize we're there.

The dungeon is quiet and damp and dark, the same as it was the day Briar and I spent locked down here.

"Wyatt?"

There are six witches in the holding cell. Jin, Solomon, the older couple I remember from that first night, a girl with a shaved pink head, and a kid who can't be older than six.

"Holy shit." Briar curls her fingers around the bars, looking in on them. "Are y'all okay?"

"We're...fine." Jin rubs a hand over the back of their neck. "We're fine. What are you doing here?"

Tessa is already undoing the lock on the cell door, shoving it open. She goes to the little kid first, kneeling down so she can get the cuffs off their tiny wrists. She has to shrug out of her jacket and wrap it around her hands so she can touch them without being burned. "You lot any good with Influencing magic? You're gonna need one helluva glamour to get past the barriers undetected. Guard are prowling all over the village right now."

"Why is there a baby in here?" I demand, throwing my arm out at the kid who's sitting there, little body quivering. Like, hello, am I the only one seeing this shit? "Why was there a baby at the riot?"

"She was in the palace when shit got bad, ended up caught in the crosshairs," Jin explains when Tessa pops their cuffs off. They tug the kid against their legs. "We have to take her to her parents."

"No, you don't." Tessa shakes her head. "Because you do that, and you risk getting caught, and shit getting worse. You need to leave Asalin. Immediately."

"Fuck." Jin reaches up to press their fingers into their temples. "I—I don't have anything to make sigils with. Crap, I don't even have my phone—it's back at my place."

"Here." Briar reaches into the front pocket of her overalls and produces a Sharpie and a pocketknife. She grabs Jin's arm and pops the cap off the marker with her teeth, scribbling out a phone number. "This is my mom's cell. Get out of Asalin. Get somewhere where you can borrow a phone, and give her a call. She's got a whole network of people, all over the country. They'll help you get somewhere safe."

"Humans?" The older woman—I think I remember her name being Miranda—demands, shaking her head. "What are we supposed to say?"

"Tell her I sent you. Tell her you're family. That's all she needs to know. And take this, just in case." Briar presses the knife and the marker into Jin's hand, and they immediately start drawing sigils onto their other arm, moving on to the kid when they've finished with themself.

Like nearly all of witch magic, these sigils are alien to me. I don't know what they're meant to do, but I hope like hell it's something that'll get them all out of here.

"Have you seen Roman and Lorena?" Solomon asks, rubbing his wrist, expression soft. "Are they safe?"

"We just left them." I nod. "They're scared shitless for you, but they're fine."

"God, Roman's gonna kick my ass when we get back together. He told me to run."

"Yeah, I know. He won't stop bitching about it."

If nothing else, that makes Solomon laugh a little.

"Okay, are you finished? We need to hurry this show along. Now." Tessa tosses the keys to the cell onto the floor, glancing up the steps in the direction we came. "Wade's shift is supposed to be over at sunrise. Won't be long after that before someone comes down here to check on you."

Jin grabs me, hands pressing into my shoulders. "We have to fix this, Wyatt. This shit is getting so much worse, and I don't—I don't know how to fix this from out there. You have to do something."

My chest hurts. I open and close my mouth. I don't know what to say.

"Briar." Jin wheels on her now instead. "Clarke."

"I know. I've got her. Don't worry."

"Okay."

"You have got to *move*," Tessa snarls.

Jin scoops up the little girl. Her cheeks are fat and tearstained, eyes red-rimmed and near-vacant, like she's disappeared to someplace inside of herself. That's probably for the best.

"This is on you now, Wyatt." Jin shakes their head. "I'm sorry."

"Me, too." Because I don't think I'm the hero any of these people need.

Jin presses their fingers to a sigil on their arm. One minute, they're standing in front of me, and the next, they're not. One by one, each of the witches does the same thing, disappearing in front of my eyes.

Eventually, it's just me, Briar, and Tessa, alone in the dungeon. I guess now I know what those sigils are for.

CHAPTER SEVENTEEN

LIKE DAY AND NIGHT

For two days, I don't get out of bed.

On the first day, someone comes in the morning and stitches together the damage done to the room the night before, waves their magic around and watches as evidence of the fire disappears.

I pull a card. Eight of Swords.

Briar gets up and heads into the village alone to check on Clarke, returns with more of Lavender's spellbooks, and sets up shop on the balcony, reading silently except for asking if I'm still breathing every half hour.

No one comes to arrest me. That seems like a good sign.

Briar tells me that her mother heard from Jin, another good sign, because it means their group got out and into the human world. I don't know exactly what story Briar spun for Nadua, but it doesn't matter. The witches were sent to an activist commune somewhere near Geneva. They're safe, for now.

Jin's words keep playing over and over in my head. *You have to do something.*

All I can seem to do is stay in bed.

I pull the Eight of Swords again the second day.

Trapped.

In the middle of the afternoon, I get a message from Emyr.

ROYAL PAIN
Do you know the names of the other fae?

It takes a minute for me to realize what he's talking about, and when I do, I desperately regret ever learning how to read.

He wants to know about Unicorn Boy's accomplices. The ones who helped him get away with what he did.

> i don't. and i probably couldn't pick them out of a lineup, either, if that was going to be your next question.

> and also i'd really rather not talk about this.

His reply comes almost immediately.

ROYAL PAIN
I'm sorry. We don't have to discuss anything that makes you uncomfortable.

Well. Good, then. I lock the phone screen and roll onto my back, content to leave it be. For, like, eight seconds. And then I pick my phone back up and type a new message.

    you seriously thought i just went, like, full-blown anarchy
and tried to burn down a bunch of houses for no reason?

ROYAL PAIN
Of course not. I've told you, I never thought you did anything on purpose. I thought you'd just...lost control. You'd been so angry for so long at that point. I guess I thought you finally snapped. And no one had any answers for me. You were gone. I woke up one morning and you were just gone. I had to make up the story in my head.

I think of Emyr, *that* Emyr, *my* Emyr, the one I left behind. The one who existed before this version, this prince caught up in his diplomacy and his political strategies. I think of the boy who wrote poetry and nursed our puppy back to health and giggled at my silly jokes. I think of him waking up one morning to realize I was gone. That after I'd been so shitty to him, so angry and volatile for months leading up to it, I was just...gone. No explanation. No goodbye.

My throat tightens.

i'm sorry.

Because I am, and because it's true, and because, really, I don't know what else to say.

ROYAL PAIN
Please don't apologize.

Briar is back on the balcony today, flipping through a spellbook. She looks up when she hears my phone go off for the fourth time.

"Everything okay?"

"Mmm."

She nods and goes back to her reading.

i'm just saying. no wonder you turned into such an asshole.
i traumatized you.

It's supposed to be a joke, but it doesn't land like one.
Three little dots appear. Then disappear. Then appear again.

ROYAL PAIN
I don't try to be an asshole.

And it sucks in particular because I know he doesn't. I'm
starting to piece that together.

There are two Emyrs. There is Prince Emyr, His Royal
Highness, who barks orders at the Guard and develops technology for the kingdom. Who trains with his swords and
studies the history of Faery. The one who dragged me here
on threat of a blood oath to *procure heirs.*

But then there's my Emyr. The one who reads graphic novels
and knits blankets. Who makes ileiva and smokes stolen morghira
and tends to the peryton. Who sleeps in a hammock surrounded
by plants and dresses like no one else I've ever known.

Three years ago, maybe he was just a boy. But then his mate
disappeared and he found out his mother was dying and he
split in two, because he had to, because he couldn't be just
Emyr anymore.

Now, I want to strangle one version of him and hold hands
with the other.

I might want to make out with them both.

I hate this.

everything okay? i haven't heard anything.

ROYAL PAIN
Nothing to hear. No one knows what happened.

derek must be beside himself.

ROYAL PAIN
Oh, certainly. I'm expecting poison in my wine anytime now.

I think that's supposed to be a joke, too. It just makes my stomach hurt.

"Hey." At some point, Briar must have moved from the balcony to the bed because now she's there, at my side, her fingers wrapping around my elbow. "You okay?"

All I can do is laugh. "I swear, humans have magic of their own."

She raises her eyebrows. *The hell are you talking about?*

I shrug. "You *feel* things like no one else I've ever known."

"Hmm." Her fingers brush up and down my arm. "Well, I've always suspected I was magical." Her gapped teeth nibble at her full lower lip before she shoots me a smile. "Bright yellow magic. Like sunshine. That's me."

"That is you." I laugh, softly. "We're like day and night, you and me. Good and evil."

"Hey." Her face has suddenly gone hard. Apparently she didn't find my joke funny. "Black magic isn't evil. Why would you say that?"

Well, it seems pretty obvious, but I don't say that to her. Instead, I offer, "Uh, you know. Black…magic. Don't people usually associate that with being evil? Plus, um. Well, I have magically murdered three people without even trying."

"They were going to kill *you*. The fae the other night was probably going to kill all of us. What you did was save us. You, me, Emyr, Tessa. That's not evil." Briar's words are urgent, intense, as if she desperately needs me to hear and understand what she's saying. The hand on my arm squeezes a little tighter. "And anyway, I don't believe black magic is evil. Maybe we're taught to believe *darkness* is inherently tied to *badness* because racism is everywhere. But, I mean." She takes a deep breath. "Haven't you ever heard the phrase *under the cover of darkness?*"

I can only nod, because I have no idea where she's going with this.

"Well, people say that because it means the darkness is keeping them safe. It means they can move freely without being seen."

"Yeah, seen doing shady shit."

"Maybe. Or maybe not. Just because something happens in secret doesn't mean it's evil." Briar groans, running her hands through her hair. She places her palms on either side of my face, looking me directly in the eye. "Darkness means safety. It means *protection.* Just like you protected yourself, and everyone else, from the fae that night."

I suddenly feel very uncomfortable. I don't know what to say to that.

"You are not a bad person, Wyatt. You are not evil. Your magic is not evil. You know that, don't you?" She's pleading with me now. I can hear the desperation sliding into her voice. "I know the kind of person you are. And you're *good.*"

Briar and Jin. Both of them looking at me like that. Like I can save the world.

I can't save shit. I am not the good guy other people want me to be.

"C'mon, it isn't that serious." Or maybe it is. I don't know. I don't want to talk about it anymore.

Briar hesitates. Clearly, she wants to keep at this. But she finally sighs, pulling back and climbing out of the bed.

"You should get up. Get some fresh air. I'm going to go check on Clarke. And Roman and Lorena, too. Why don't you come with me?"

The way Briar loves, the way she cares about people, and causes, it's one of my favorite things about her. The passionate, full-hearted way she throws herself into things is something I've always admired.

I'm never going to care the way she does.

"Nah." I roll onto my stomach, nuzzle my face into the pillow under my head. "Think I'm gonna stay here. Jerk off and take a nap."

She scoffs but doesn't argue. "Yeah, okay."

A moment later, she dusts by me and brushes her fingers over the top of my head.

"Tell Emyr I said hello," she trills. "That is who you're texting, isn't it?"

I huff.

"Mmm-hmm. If I didn't know any better, I'd think you have a crush on him."

"I do not have a crush on him." I might have a little bit of a crush on him. "Why would I?"

"Maybe because he's gorgeous and you're gay and horny."

That much is true. "He isn't my type."

"Yeah, okay." Briar scoffs. "Why? Because he doesn't look like a twink who watches too many YouTube documentaries about aliens?"

"There are some *very* interesting YouTube documentaries

about aliens," I counter. "And there's nothing wrong with a good twink."

"I can't stand you," she says, but I know she doesn't mean it. She leans down and kisses my temple, and then she's gone.

My phone dings again.

This time, it's a picture of the most beautiful plate of cookies I've ever seen, next to what appears to be black coffee topped with thick whipped cream. I can just barely make out Boom's nose in the corner of the photo, like he was thinking of stealing a cookie for himself.

ROYAL PAIN
New recipe.

i'm a little turned on rn i'm ngl.

ROYAL PAIN
...Oh?

asdfghjkl

I pitch my phone across the room and make good on that nap.

CHAPTER EIGHTEEN

IT'S FUCK FAE HOURS

Three days after the riot, I wake up to pounding on my bedroom door.

"We have a problem," Wade announces when I fling it open to find him standing on the other side with Emyr, Tessa, and Clarke.

"Is your problem that no one here knows how to let me rest?" I ask, rubbing sleep from my eyes and moving back to the bed to shake Briar awake—only to find she's propped up with her book in her lap and her hair in braids. "Because I agree. That is a problem."

"Why are you still asleep, anyway?" Wade snaps. "It's noon."

Ah. Well, whatever.

I wave him off with a yawn. "What's the big emergency?"

"I have been trying to handle this myself. I didn't want to drag everyone into it, in the wake of the other night. But as it turns out, even my charming ass can't fix what you screwed up."

"What the hell did I do?" I demand as Briar sets her book down and shifts her legs to the side of the bed.

Emyr sets his laptop down on my bedside table. Until then, I hadn't realized he was holding it. He opens the lid and pulls up a video.

On screen, I'm standing in his room.

The afternoon before the riot.

Oh, shit. With everything else going on, I'd *completely* forgotten about this.

On-screen Wyatt waves at the camera, a shit-eating smirk tucked into the corner of his mouth. On-screen Wyatt has yet to live through the next twenty-four hours of his life and has no idea that everything is about to start feeling very, very fucky, and that maybe his priorities are not the best. On-screen Wyatt is a douchebag.

"What's up, Fae TV, it's ya boy, Wyatt Croft." The only way I am going to survive having to watch this thing is if I pretend it isn't me. Did he just say *ya boy*? What if, perhaps, I simply died? "And I am coming at you today with a very important announcement."

In real time, I make eye contact with Emyr.

I do not think I've ever seen someone look *less* impressed with me.

On-screen Wyatt continues, unphased. "Fae ain't shit."

Next to me on the bed, Briar groans. "Oh my god, what the hell is this?"

"Please, keep watching," Tessa says simply, arms crossed, standing at the foot of the bed.

I put my head in my hands. I *cannot* keep watching.

Doesn't stop me from having to listen to it. The recording of my voice—and seriously, my voice cannot actually sound like this to other people—blares from Emyr's speakers.

"Fae really and truly are not shit. I don't know why anyone would appoint you as kings and queens of anything. You don't deserve your own Facebook page, much less entire kingdoms to run. But that's okay. That's okay, you know why? 'Cause I'm about to take over. And when I do, I plan on making some big changes. Number one—it's fuck fae hours 24/7."

"Okay, that's enough." I scramble forward and slam my hand on the spacebar to pause the video.

"You're right. That alone probably *was* enough to piss off every other kingdom around the globe. To say nothing of the fact that you proceeded to go on and list all the ways you in-tended to…overhaul the system." Wade actually might look less impressed with me than Emyr does.

"Wyatt." Briar puts her face in her hands.

"Well." I cough, rubbing my hands on my thighs. "I was having a bad day."

"Your bad day has cost the entire Committee three days of trying to placate the very high emotions of a bunch of powerful fae monarchs," Wade snaps. "And it could not have come at a worse time."

"Well…had I known what would happen later that night, I wouldn't have done it."

"Why would you do it in the first place?" Emyr demands, leaning forward with his claws digging craters into the tabletop.

"I was PMSing," I offer, in the hope it'll make him uncomfortable enough to drop it.

Emyr just stares at me.

Wade pushes on. "Because I am brilliant, I've managed to quell the rage of three of the other four families. But Paloma and Maritza are threatening to start a war."

I manage to drag my attention away from Emyr to look back at Wade. "Paloma and Maritza?"

"The queens of Eirgard." Clarke crawls into my bed and drapes herself onto the pillows next to Briar.

There's an alternate reality version of me who might be very excited about two girls in my bed.

Wait, *queens*?

"The Eirgard monarchy is *gay*?" I ask, because I feel like someone should have told me about gay fae queens, like, the second I stepped foot back in Asalin. No one ever tells me anything I want to hear.

Eirgard is the fae kingdom in South America. The five kingdoms don't have much to do with one another, except for occasions when the Court needs to come together. I have vague memories of Paloma, now that the name has been stitched together with the kingdom. She took over the Throne from her parents a couple of years before the fire, and in that time she never came to Asalin. She definitely did not have a wife at that point. I would've remembered.

"Quite sapphic," Clarke confirms with a bob of her head.

"What, did you think you and Emyr would be the *only* queer royals? Please. The kings of Monalai just had twins."

Monalai is the farthest kingdom from Asalin, an island tucked away somewhere off the coast of New Zealand.

And I *do* remember those kings. I would just like to be kept more up to date on *all* the gay happenings, is all.

"Right. Anyway." I rub the back of my neck. "So, uh. How do we avoid a war?"

Without warning, Emyr reaches down and places a hand on my shoulder, too warm and too familiar. He's getting used to this...this *touching* me whenever he feels like it, this casual intimacy, like we're some real, actual couple. And apparently I'm getting good at pretending it doesn't bother me, because my black energy doesn't even spike, doesn't seem to notice or care. Instead, it stretches out underneath his palm, flexing into his touch. "Well, firestarter, why don't you tell me? You're the one who got us into this."

He isn't *wrong*. Looking back on it now, the video was... ill-advised. I can't believe that's the person I was only a few days ago. It churns my stomach with embarrassment.

"I'm not sure they'll want to see me," I begin, shaking my shoulder so his hand falls away. I really don't like the mental picture of my energy as a housecat that's purring for the prince.

"I'm sure there are many people who don't want to see you," Wade agrees.

"But," I snap, narrowing my eyes at Wade. "I guess...if they'll agree to it...it would make sense for me to go and beg for forgiveness in person."

I hate this idea. I don't want anything to do with it.

But eventually, I'm going to have to start accepting the consequences for my actions. On the long, long list of my sins, this is nowhere near the worst thing I've ever done. It's a start, though.

Wade rubs a hand over his stubbled jaw, considering me before looking to Emyr. "It isn't a terrible idea. Maritza is probably the one who threw out the idea of war. And Paloma would drink up a little ass-kissing."

"It isn't terrible," Emyr agrees. He's still staring at me. I can feel his gaze on my throat and I pointedly don't tilt my head in his direction. "But can we leave the kingdom right now? Think of the optics, with the riot and the prisoners' escape. How will this be interpreted?"

"The optics of a war will be worse," Tessa offers. When I look up at her, though, she isn't looking at me at all. She's watching Clarke and Briar, snuggled together in the bed behind me.

I bring my hands to my face, rubbing my palms against my cheeks with a groan. "She's right." At the time, pissing off the whole fae world seemed like a very good idea. Now, I can't remember what purpose it was supposed to serve. I suppose Derek will be ecstatic.

Emyr clears his throat. "All right. I'll make the arrangements for you to go and grovel, then."

"Wait." Without thinking about it, I reach out and grab his wrist. When I realize what I've done, my fingers wrapped around his warm skin, I let my hand fall away. "I can't leave Briar. Even if Derek doesn't know I was behind the witches' escape, someone probably suspects. She'll be walking around here with a target on her back."

Especially when he realizes I'm on my way to Eirgard, to try and undo the one thing I've done *right*, in his eyes.

"I'll take care of Briar," Clarke offers, pink energy swirling like cotton candy surrounding Briar's yellow.

"We'll all keep an eye on Briar," Tessa amends.

"I don't have a passport, either."

"The Committee will take care of that," Wade says.

I look at Emyr again and he raises his eyebrows.

All right. I guess my apology tour is going international.

That evening finds Emyr and me thirty thousand feet in the air, back in first class. Most of the afternoon leading up to this moment is a blur. A loud, annoying blur.

Clarke and Wade dragged me off to find clothes to wear in front of the queens. Apparently, they were horrified at the idea I might show up in Eirgard looking as put together as I do every other day of my life. And apparently, if I don't let them wash the hoodie while I'm gone, they're going to incinerate it.

I've managed to glimpse a few looks at myself only in passing, but every time I do, I want to rip my own eyes out.

I understand the need to look presentable, especially when I'm groveling for forgiveness. But why in the hell was Wade's idea of a compromise sticking me in *pastels*?

Seriously. I look like an Easter egg. The light green pants are cuffed at my ankles. The white button-down is embellished with a rose on the front pocket. And of course the outfit wouldn't be complete without some ugly canvas slides. Hey, my socks have the same rose on them as my shirt does. Wow, I hate every single thing about this.

I look like a middle-aged heterosexual whose wife dressed him for church photos with the kids. I'm positive Wade and Clarke did this with the sole purpose of humiliating me. And it's working wonders. At least Clarke was generous enough to offer me a glamour to hide the scars.

"I'm starving," I announce, breaking my self-imposed silence to finally twist away from the window and glare at Emyr.

He doesn't look up from the book he's reading, one of the graphic novels I'd previously spotted on the floor of his cottage. They stuck him in the same pastels that were forced on me, but somehow he looks perfectly acceptable in his floral button-down and purple chinos. Although he looks just as ridiculous without his wings and other fae appendages this time as he did the first, hidden beneath a glamour of his own to appear perfectly human. Or *supposedly* perfectly human. I still think he sticks out. There's something too…much about him. Maybe it's the gold energy thrumming everywhere, practically suffusing everyone else in the cabin.

"Mmm. If you call a flight attendant, they will provide you with a menu."

"I still don't understand why we couldn't stop at the drive-through on the way here!"

"We were running late."

"We were not! And the drive-through takes, like, three minutes. We could have wasted three minutes getting my chicken nuggets."

"You wanted *one hundred* chicken nuggets. I sincerely doubt that would have only taken three minutes."

"Oh, please!" I throw my hands up. "Everyone knows

they're already cooked and just sitting under a heat lamp for hours. All they had to do was throw them in a bag."

He finally raises his eyes to look at me, disgust flitting across his face. "Why would anyone choose to eat at such a place?"

"Uh, because it's delightful. Do you not understand how many chicken nuggets a hundred chicken nuggets is?"

Emyr groans at me, reaching above my head to press his finger against the call button.

I huff and drop back against my seat. When I do, my elbow brushes against Emyr's invisible wings once again, bare skin to velvet softness. I refuse to pull back and cower, so it stays right where it is. I don't look at him when he glances down at me.

"Everything okay over here?" A human woman appears too quickly at our side, smiling mechanically. Her cucumber-green energy seems to be settled all the way down at her feet, hovering against her shoes. I get the impression she hates her job.

"My fiancé would like to see a food menu," Emyr drawls, going back to his book.

"Of course!" She whips the laminated paper from the front pocket of her apron so quickly I think it could have sliced someone's head off if they were close enough. "Because this is an international flight, you'll have access to our full menu today. Just let me know what you want and the chef will prepare it right away."

I take the menu from her with furrowed brows. "Seriously?"

She blinks robotically. "Is there a problem?"

"Uh. No." This is weird. I mean, I'm not used to flying,

but the idea of having a chef make a full-blown meal for me while I am in the sky just seems bizarre. I look down at the menu, scanning the items listed. Jeez. Salmon? Steak? Roasted asparagus and mushrooms with fingerling potatoes?

From a foodie standpoint, this is amazing. But I still find the whole thing sort of unsettling.

"I'll take the cheeseburger. And a Coke."

Her smile never wavers as she takes the menu from me and shuffles to the kitchen to put my order in.

Emyr is studying me like he's trying to see past a two-way mirror. Finally, he says, "I know you worried about leaving Briar, but I thought you would be in a better mood than this."

"Oh, yeah, because going to beg for forgiveness from two dramatic lesbians is exactly how I wanted my day to go." I pinch the bridge of my nose. I know this was my idea, but *why* was this my idea again?

He scoffs. "Perhaps you should've thought of that before you posted that video. I still cannot comprehend what the point of that was. And you have the audacity to call anyone else dramatic?"

He…might have a point.

"Whatever. Still don't know why you thought I'd be happy to make this trip."

"You're back in the human world. At least for the duration of this flight. And you certainly seem to prefer this one to your own."

"Okay, first of all, Asalin is not my world. It's yours. I don't get a world. Second of all, this? Not the human world." I laugh. "I mean, okay, it is. But this isn't, like, the universal human experience or anything. Trust me when I say one hundred chicken nuggets for seventeen bucks is way more relatable than a private chef cooking me a first-class meal on an international flight."

"Hmm." Emyr settles back against his headrest, eyes flicking up toward the TV set in front of him. He raises his hand and drags his fingers against his chin. I can see the way his claws, even invisible, scratch little scuffs against his dark skin. "I'm sorry we didn't stop for the nuggets, then."

The apology catches me so off guard I don't know what to do other than stare at him. After a moment, I turn away, rolling the words around in my head.

"So," I say finally, running my tongue against one sharp canine tooth. "This is all you know about the real world? First class?"

Emyr shrugs. "Other than traveling between the kingdoms, I've never needed to enter the *real world*." I can hear his annoyance at my choice of words. "Except for when I was searching Laredo for you."

"You have to have some familiarity with humans, though. I mean…" I reach over and tap one nail against the book in his lap. "I don't think this is fae-made."

"No…but this is not about humans. It is about aliens."

"Aliens, huh?" A graphic novel is not the same thing as a YouTube documentary. "Very much part of the collective human experience." I narrow my eyes at him. "You know, when you think about it, the fae *did* come here from another planet. That *kinda* makes you an alien."

He glares at me. "And what would that make you?"

"I dunno. Very cool?"

"Hmm." Emyr rolls his eyes and turns his attention back to the book in his hands. "I do enjoy online shopping for books."

"Online shopping, also super human."

"Maybe I would like your world if I got to see more of it," he muses.

"Sure. Maybe Taco Bell could cater the wedding."

"Or perhaps we could take a...honeymoon. It isn't traditional, but neither are we." He smiles and flashes those dimples. "We could spend a few weeks eating as many drive-through chicken nuggets as you wanted. You could show me your world."

There is so much sincerity packed into his tone I don't know what to do with it.

My nails dig into the armrests and I finally pull my arm away from his wing.

"Yeah, maybe," I mumble, but the mood is gone.

The flight attendant brings me my burger.

Emyr and I don't speak for the rest of the flight.

CHAPTER NINETEEN

LITTLE SHADOW

"Where the hell are they?" I snarl, leaning against the wall, arms crossed. My heinous bad mood from earlier has returned in force. We've been standing in the Eirgard palace throne room for twenty minutes.

The layout of their kingdom—queendom? no one has ever accused me of having a strong grasp on the intricacies of the English language—reminds me of Asalin's. The village is down the hill, a collection of hundreds of houses and a dozen or so businesses. The castle sits way at the top overlooking the surrounding populace. But that's where the similarities begin and end.

Eirgard's village was alive with bustling people and energized music as Emyr and I rode through. The homes and businesses are beautiful here, brightly painted and built close together. I noted an eclectic mix of classic and newer cars parked all along the stone-paved streets between vendors peddling foods that made my mouth water. I also spotted more than one little old lady—fae and witch alike—with a string of rosary beads around her neck. Apparently, the people of Eirgard have less interest in Vorgaine than those of Asalin.

Even the palace itself reminds me a little of a church, like those old-timey cathedrals made of stained glass and domed rooftops. Only there's very little about the interior that screams *old-timey*. Everything has been renovated to reflect the most modern standards, from the fingerprinted keypad at each door requiring a waiting servant to let us inside, to the marble floors, to the *rec room* we passed where a cluster of witches and fae were gathered in front of a big-screen TV.

Seriously, what kind of castle comes with a rec room? This place might be some kind of royal paradise if it weren't for the fact that I've been standing around twiddling my thumbs for twenty godforsaken minutes.

Seriously, has someone *died*? Was there a *coup* just before we got here?

Emyr shrugs. He appears utterly unconcerned, which sort of makes me want to strangle him. "They're probably hoping to make an entrance. Just be patient."

"I am being plenty patient," I snap back at him.

Another minute ticks by. I tap my toes against the gold floor.

"Do you think this is their payback? Forcing me to wilt away here?"

"I suppose it is entirely possible that they are surrounding us to take our heads as we speak." Emyr could not possibly sound more bored if he tried.

Another minute. I pace from one side of the room to the other.

"You're going to drive yourself over the ledge if you don't learn to relax." Emyr sighs.

"You're going to drive yourself over the ledge if you don't learn to relax," I repeat back at him in a high-pitched, mocking rendition. I hoist myself onto one of the bases for a marble pillar at the bottom of the stairs that lead to their matching plush, ornate thrones. My knuckles tap a frantic tune.

Another minute. "You have got to be fucking kidding me!"

The door to the throne room bursts open in a gust of *green flames*. I let out a panicked scream, falling off the base and hitting the floor with a thud. Black magic erupts from my body, a protective wall forming between me and the fire. Emyr's wings spread out behind him and he turns toward the doors, gold magic defensively spreading across his arms.

This is the second time this week someone has thrown fire at me. I'm unamused. What exactly is the universe trying to tell—oh, holy shit, what the hell?

Seconds after the flame comes a flash of vibrant cyan scales. They shimmer in the low light of the throne room as a massive jaw and rounded head covered in row after row of spikes slowly appears. A huge jaw filled with hundreds upon hundreds of razor-sharp teeth parts just enough to let a red tongue flick out. Yellow eyes with slits for pupils, the size of dining room tables, slowly blink at us.

"That is a dragon!" I shout at the back of Emyr's head. "An indoor dragon!"

"Yes." He turns his head over his shoulder, sighing. He holds out his hand for me, palm up. "I told you the queens would make an entrance."

What?

The dragon bows its head, extending its long neck toward the ground. A woman slides down the length of it, her heels clicking against the floor when she lands.

She looks soft, too soft to show up on dragonback. A swath of yellow covers her body, a shapeless, gauzy sort of dress that makes her look as if she's covered in spun sugar. Her skin, as dark and flawless as fresh ink, shimmers with a fine layer of dusted gold body glitter that covers her curly hair, as well. Thin black horns, more like antennae than anything else, droop down from either side of her face to touch the long, sharp points of her ears. Pink and yellow wings, covered in a thin layer of fluff, rest against her back. Her baby-blue energy sparkles like the afternoon sky around her shoulders.

"Paloma." Emyr inclines his head.

She giggles—not exactly the reaction I was expecting. "Emyr, you've gotten so *tall*."

Another woman comes sliding down next, leaping from the dragon's body halfway down its neck and landing with a clang next to her wife. Where Paloma is soft, this woman is hard. Her red leather dress clings to her olive skin, showing off the lines of her body. A black holster holding a long blade is strapped to each of her plush thighs. Her horns remind me of a Texas longhorn's, her wings made of tawny and white feathers and pulled tight against her back. She smiles in a way that tells me she could kill me if she wanted. Her burnt-umber energy blows back and forth around her like a dust storm.

"Maritza." Emyr still hasn't lowered the hand he's holding out to me. "Thank you for having us."

"Of course," Maritza answers coolly, eyeing me in a way that makes me distinctly uncomfortable. "Though I can't imagine why little Wyatt would want anything to do with this meeting. Considering how he feels about the fae."

Emyr gets called tall. I get called little. That does not slip my notice.

Still, I manage to swallow back any kind of retort and say, "I have no good excuse for that video. But believe me, it is not an accurate representation of my feelings today."

"Mmm-hmm." Paloma clicks her tongue, stepping away from the dragon just vibing in the doorway. She reaches out to brush her hand against her wife's bicep. "I told you this would work out. Now, boys, shall we adjourn to the dining room? I'm sure you two are hungry after your travels."

Emyr looks at me. I take a deep breath, reaching out and finally putting my hand in his. He threads his fingers with mine, touch warm and gentle as he guides me after the queens.

I guess we're doing this.

Whatever *this* is.

After sitting down to eat and begging the queens to please not murder any of us just because I am a gay little worm who makes terrible life decisions, I've determined two things.

The first, everything is easier to handle on a stomach full of good food. I already knew this, but it's nice to be reminded regularly. The plane food was okay at best, but whoever staffs the queens' kitchen clearly knows how to cook. They serve a dinner of empanadas stuffed with dragon meat, phoenix ajiaco, and patacón that somehow leaves me about to burst *and* wanting more. Seriously, I love a Big Mac and some greasy French fries as much as the next guy, but this is incredible. Nothing, not even my ridiculous outfit, seems as bad once I've eaten.

The second, Paloma and Maritza were clearly not as mad as they'd led everyone to believe. It didn't take much ass-kissing on our parts to get them to forgive and forget. Which would make me angrier—and a whole lot more confused—if I didn't think they were sort of...fun.

They're younger than I expected, probably in their thirties. Talking to them doesn't feel like talking to authority figures, even though they're the queens of their own queendom. A few times, I actually find myself accidentally laughing at Paloma's jokes. It seems almost easy here, with them. Not what I expected at all.

But maybe that's the guaro they let me have with dinner.

Things are starting to wind down, the sun having set some time ago through the open windows in their dining hall. It's been a long day and I'm even more tired than I was before thanks to a full stomach and a little bit of alcohol, but I'm holding it together for now. Besides, I'm kind of enjoying their company.

"So tell us," Paloma says, leaning against the table, balancing her chin in her hand. "Do you two plan on bringing us beautiful little witchling babies soon?"

Okay. Good mood immediately ruined.

I open my mouth, knowing something bleak is about to jump off my tongue, but Emyr beats me to speaking.

"Now, now, Paloma. You and Maritza haven't had any children yet." He chuckles, waving between the two of them. "Where are *your* beautiful babies?"

"Oh, please." Paloma rolls her eyes. "We are *not* having children. My poor mother. All her life she waited for me to find my bonded mate, and here we are—someone who can't give me babies and wouldn't even if she had the equipment."

"The two of you are fated mates?" I raise my eyebrows in Emyr's direction, then flick my gaze back to Paloma. "How's that work?"

Because if the lessons I've always had shoved down my throat are meant to be believed, fated mates is all about genetics. Who's best suited to *procreate* with each other. How would that work between two cis women?

But Paloma just shrugs. "Same way it works for anyone else, I suppose. And, really, can you imagine? Us? Mothers?" She shudders, as if that's the most tragic thing she's ever heard.

"It's true," Maritza agrees, leaning back in her chair, arms resting gently at her sides.

"How will you choose an heir?" Emyr frowns.

Paloma shrugs, appearing unconcerned. "I suppose it will fall to my brother. Or perhaps there will be a war. Either way, we won't be around to deal with it."

"That's certainly one way of thinking," Emyr agrees.

"I would probably make a terrible parent, too," I offer with a shrug. Am I trying to save Emyr from this conversation? No. That is not my responsibility. But he does look awfully uncomfortable with Paloma's flippancy.

"I don't think that's true, little shadow." Paloma sighs dreamily. "I think you're going to make a great father someday. And a wonderful king."

"This coming from the woman who doesn't care if our kingdom falls to ruin once we're gone," Maritza reminds us, probably trying to make sure I don't go and get a big head from Paloma's compliments.

Paloma chuckles, leaning over to gently tap her wife on the nose with the tip of one finger. "When we're dead, we won't have the time to care about what happens. We'll be far too busy doing ghostly things, yes? But I think we've got another sixty or seventy years left in this life. Plenty of time for Wyatt to screw things up for fae everywhere and ruin our lives."

Something sparkles in Paloma's eye and she shoots me a smirk. Maritza sighs, reaching out to run her fingers against the inside of her wife's wrist.

"But to be clear," Paloma continues. "You are going to make a great king, Wyatt. Regardless of the petitions Derek's followers have sent us and the plans they may have. Regardless of Kadri's attempts at annulling your contract. Regardless of your own plans."

Something unsettling sweeps across the four of us. My hackles rise as the energy in the room shifts, Paloma's magic sweeping like a fog overhead, Maritza's rumbling like an earthquake at our feet. Emyr and I exchange a look.

What the hell is happening here?

"You were the ones who voted *no* on the annulment." It isn't a question. A rough touch has slid into his voice. When they say nothing back, he asks, "Why? What do you know?"

"We know nothing for certain." Paloma shrugs. "But I'm a Feeler. I've seen things. I wanted to get you here in person to see with my eyes this time."

"What sorts of things do you mean?" I ask, sitting up straighter.

Maritza nails me with a dark look. "I'm not sure you want her to say."

"That sounds almost threatening, Maritza," Emyr growls.

"Only almost?"

"The future will come as it is meant to," Paloma says. "All we can say for certain is this union is fated. The contract was not meant to be dissolved. What happens afterward is only speculation."

I think she's lying.

"I'm tired," I say, instead of calling the queen of another kingdom a liar and starting another war. "Can we go to our room now?"

Maritza chuckles in a way that sounds like an incantation, leaning back in her chair again and staring at me.

Paloma smiles. "Of course. Mateo!"

The door to the dining room opens and a young witch with a big smile stares at Paloma. "Yes, my Queen?"

"Please, show our guests to their suite, my love."

Mateo flushes and turns his head to look at Emyr and me. "Come along, then."

I stand, pushing my chair back from the table. Emyr joins me.

"Thank you for the lovely dinner." He inclines his head at them. "We will see you in the morning."

Paloma's smile is unwavering. "Sleep well."

The three of us travel in silence to an elevator, where Mateo presses the fifth-floor button. God, they've even got elevators here? We've got to get on this back in Asalin.

We? As if I intend to stay there for much longer. Do I?

No. I need to remember what my endgame here is. I need to remember I'm the bad guy, that I'm working on my *own* agenda, and all I want is to be free. Selfishly, blissfully free.

I catch Emyr watching me and offer him a raised eyebrow.

His lips part, and then he sighs, pressing them together again. He shakes his head.

When we reach the fifth floor, Mateo motions down the hall. "Yours is the first room at the right. The red door. No keypad required for the guest rooms. If you need anything, there is an intercom system in the room connected to the servants' quarters. Is that all I can help you with today?"

"Um. Yep."

"Have a good evening." He dips back into the elevator and the doors close behind him.

Emyr and I stare at each other for a long, long moment in the hallway. Something lingers in the air between us, but I'm not sure what it is. Black and gold crackle against each other like hissing alley cats.

Before Emyr can say whatever it is he's going to say— because I know he's going to say something, and I don't think I want to hear it—I clear my throat and jerk my head down the hall. "I really am tired. And I'd like to get out of these ridiculous clothes."

He considers me for a moment longer, and then breathes deep. Maybe he's resigning himself to shutting up and letting me sleep. Maybe this means we won't have to discuss dinner with the queens.

Good. Because I don't want to talk about it.

Together, we approach the room with the red door. Emyr reaches down and twists the handle, pushing it open.

In the center of the room sits one bed.

CHAPTER TWENTY

WORRIED YOU MIGHT ENJOY YOURSELF?

As if totally unfazed by our predicament, Emyr lopes into the bathroom. By the time he emerges, minutes later, suit jacket shed, belt and shoes gone, I'm still standing there with my mouth open. When he starts pulling his T-shirt from the waist of his pants, I make a strangled sound that pulls his attention back to me.

"What?"

"We are *not* sharing a bed."

He looks down at the mattress as if just realizing there's only one, then looks back up at me. His eyebrows knit together and he shrugs. "Why not?"

"I don't share beds."

"You share a bed with Briar every single night."

"Yeah, well. You're not Briar."

"No. I am your future husband."

My mouth sets into a firm line. I don't have a decent comeback for that. But that's mostly because he's gone back to taking off his shirt and the sharp planes of his abdomen are coming into view.

God, he's hot. I have accepted the fact that there's probably no one as unfairly attractive as Emyr North.

Once, I'd looked at Derek Pierce and thought he was the most beautiful man I'd ever seen. And in some ways, maybe that's still true. Derek looks like someone who just stepped out of a cologne commercial. He looks like the kind of guy whose pictures get circulated online with the caption "daddy" and water spray emojis. You don't expect to see a guy like him just walking around in real life, un-Photoshopped.

But there are plenty of guys that look a lot like Derek. Most of them are named Chris, and they all live in Hollywood. There isn't anything special about him, not once you get past the charm and the magic.

And he's kind of a *huge* dick.

Emyr doesn't look anything like a Hollywood Chris. If Derek belongs in a cologne commercial, Emyr belongs on an avante-garde runway, showing off weird-ass clothes that no one would ever actually wear in real life but still look incredible on him. His features can be deadly and soft at once, like a killer's fangs framed by a plush mouth. His body is somehow slender and muscular in a way that doesn't entirely add up. Something about the way he moves is both wild and regal, the boy who tends to hellhounds and peryton existing in perfect harmony alongside the man who sits on the Throne. It's unsettling.

I've never questioned that he's attractive. Emyr has never *not* been beautiful. But the longer I'm around him, the more time we spend together, I realize Emyr is like a work of art. Like expensive paintings hung up in museums I'll probably never go to. Like a bunch of abstract shapes twisted together that make something phenomenal, but you have to pay attention to see what it is. The longer you stare, the more you see.

Well, I've been paying attention. I think I'm finally beginning to see him in his entirety. And Emyr is incomparably, undeniably, really irritatingly beautiful.

And hot, which is a completely different monster altogether. He is so, so hot.

We are definitely not sleeping in this bed together.

As if oblivious to the meltdown happening inside my head, Emyr continues taking his clothes off. He strips until he's wearing nothing but his boxers, miles and miles of skin exposed before me, and puts his hands on his narrow hips. Like this is a challenge!

I cross my arms. "How am I supposed to fit in this bed with you?"

"I was thinking I would sleep on the left side, and you could have the right."

I do not find his joke funny. At all. I narrow my eyes. "I *mean*, I don't know if I'm going to fit next to your giant wings, asshole."

"Surely it can be done. Many fae are coupled. Presumably, a majority of those couples sleep in the same bed." He stretches his arms over his head and his wings stretch with them, spanning out behind his body and flexing. "We'll need to get some practice in, anyway."

"Practice."

"What's the matter, firestarter?" He tosses the edge of the blanket back and knees his way onto the side of the bed. "Worried you might enjoy yourself?"

Is he—I'm sorry, is he *flirting* with me?

I will rip your throat out with my teeth.

"Hardly."

"Not at all concerned you might get turned on again?" He smirks.

I regret every life decision I've made that's brought me to this point. "Not even slightly."

"Then what's the problem?"

"Maybe I'm worried *you'll* enjoy yourself. Too much."

He raises an eyebrow and then seems to concede. At least enough to say, "Sleep on the floor, then."

"That's not a denial."

Emyr fluffs his pillow. "I'm not going to lay a hand on you unless you want me to." He stills, tilting his head up and meeting my eye again. "If that's really what this is about, I can go to the queens and ask for separate rooms. I'm sure there's somewhere else in the palace for me to sleep."

Ugh.

Bitterly, I stomp into the bathroom.

An assortment of toiletries have been set up for us on the counter. I don't even know what half of this shit is for. Why would two overnight guests possibly need this many skin-care supplies?

When I glance up and catch my reflection in the mirror, I

nearly jump. I haven't paused to look at myself since the night of the riot, and while I knew Unicorn Boy's blinding light had sliced my skin open and left me with some new scars, this is the first time I've surveyed the damage. Little white streaks run from my jawline down the sides of my neck.

They aren't so bad, I guess. They're not as noticeable as the ones on my arms, except for the fact that they're *on my damn face*. Oh, well.

I tug my phone out next, shooting off a message for Briar, then get to work brushing my teeth. And trying to figure out what the hell I'm going to do about these sleeping arrangements.

It's been a long day and I'm exhausted. There's no way I'm actually going to sleep on the floor, not when I have to fly back to New York tomorrow.

Emyr offered to go and talk to Paloma and Maritza. I should have him do that. I should go back in there and tell him I don't want him anywhere near me and I'll be taking this room on my own.

Definitely, I should do that.

It's definitely what I want.

I have absolutely no reason not to want that.

So, I have no idea why I don't.

I spit into the sink and rub my moist hands on my pants before stalking back into the main room. I kick off my shoes with too much heat, sending one flying into the wall with a thud. Emyr's chuckle curls up and dies in his throat when I shoot him a glare. I hesitate after pulling off the hideous green pants, unsure what to do next.

With Briar, I usually just sleep in my boxers. But there's

nothing to be nervous about when it's just Briar and me. There's no question of will-we-won't-we when I'm in bed with Briar. With her, it's like I'm sleeping alone, only warmer.

The same can't be said of Emyr.

"Something still wrong?" Emyr asks, stretched out on his stomach with his wings folded against his back. He rests his cheek on the pillow, gaze following my movements.

I waffle some more. Shirt on? Binder on? Just boxers? Secret fourth option? Oh my god, this should not be as hard as it is.

And it isn't really about my body in the sense of me being dysphoric. I don't have a huge issue with my body. Actually, if we're being totally honest, I kind of like the way my body looks. Being trans comes with plenty of downsides, but being forced to hate every second I spend trapped in my own skin isn't one of them.

It's more about the way other people think about my body. And I don't know if I want to open myself up to Emyr treating me differently because he sees me without my extra layers on.

There's also the small, insignificant issue of not totally trusting myself to be half-naked in bed with him.

He's just…so…hot.

"Hey, I'm being serious here, are you okay?"

"Yeah, yeah, I'm fine." I've been standing here too long. I don't want to sleep in this button-down, so I opt for gathering up Emyr's discarded cotton undershirt and turning around to get undressed. Offering him my naked back, I strip out of the button down and my binder and tug his shirt on. After plugging my phone in on the side table, I climb into bed, tossing the blanket back as I do. I keep as close to the edge as I can, maintaining as much distance between us as possible, the mattress stretched out between our chests.

Emyr and I stare at each other for a while.

Finally, in an attempt to break the quiet, I ask, "Did you know before tonight that Paloma and Maritza were the ones who refused to break the contract?"

He shakes his head. "I had no idea. I didn't even know it was a unified couple. I sort of thought one of the *no* votes might've been my dad."

Well, that's interesting. Leo not as happy to see me as he seemed to be the night we sat down for dinner? Hmm. I file that away for later. "You wanna explain to me why you made it seem like you were refusing to go to the Court to ask for the contract to be dissolved when you knew you couldn't actually do it in the first place?"

Emyr winces, rubbing a hand over his face. "My answer would've been the same, either way."

"Yeah, well, I would've been a lot less annoyed at you if I'd realized from the jump that it was out of your control."

"Well..." He pauses, then sheepishly says, "I didn't want you to think my mother disapproves of our marriage. She had extenuating reasons for going to the Court."

I blink. "You didn't want me to think your mom disapproved of me?"

Emyr huffs.

There are so many things I want to say to that, starting by calling him a mama's boy. But Kadri is, like, actively dying. So I don't say any of them.

My tongue flicks out against my lower lip. "What do you

think Paloma was talking about? When she said she's seen things?"

"I don't know. But it didn't sound good, did it?"

"Not even a little. You sure you still wanna marry me?"

It's meant to be a joke, but somehow it isn't.

His dark gaze feels as heavy as a touch as his gaze slides over the place where his shirt rests against my throat. He swallows, lips parting as he drags in a deep breath, not looking away for even a moment.

"That looks nice on you," he finally manages to say.

I frown. "It's a white T-shirt."

He shrugs one shoulder.

"Well, I'm glad you approve," I finally mumble back at him. "I wasn't keen on sleeping naked."

This is some, like…some *guy* thing, right? Seeing me in his clothes? Some weird hyper-masculine territorial thing? That's why he's into it?

Or else he can totally see my nipples through the fabric. Shit. I glance down at my chest to make sure that isn't the case. Nope. Totally opaque. I'm in the clear.

It actually isn't all that difficult, sharing a bed. Maybe psychologically, but not logistically. His wings are tucked behind his back, the tips stretching over his shoulders into the air above my head, still leaving plenty of room for us both to get comfortable. I can make out the blue veins threaded through them, see a hint of shine as moonlight from outside catches one clawed tip.

Briefly, I have the ridiculous thought that I want to reach out and touch one. I want to graze my fingers against the wing and feel the softness under my palm.

I don't, though. I'm not actually masochistic enough to do that.

My black aura settles down, sinking lower and lower into the mattress with every deep breath I take. The golden glow of Emyr's energy washes over us both like a warm blanket. That shouldn't feel as nice as it does.

After a while, Emyr says, quietly, "It didn't occur to me that you might be uncomfortable sleeping together because you would be more...exposed."

I scoff. He's not saying it, but he's saying it, in his own delicate, roundabout, Emyr kind of way. I think about not responding at all. He didn't ask a question. But, after a moment, I shrug. "I know you know I have tits. It's not like this is some big secret. Everyone knows."

"It isn't your fault you were born in the wrong body," Emyr begins, and I really don't care where he's going with that, and I definitely don't let him finish.

"Oh, god, no, shut up. Stop." I wave my hand at his face. "Somewhere, at some point in time, some random cis person who's probably dead now decided all trans people were stuck in the wrong body, and that became law. But I'm not a boy trapped in a girl's body. My body is a boy's body because I'm a boy and it's mine. My body isn't wrong. Okay?"

My sharp teeth and soft edges and blood and sweat and zits and, yes, boobs. They're all mine, and they're fine. I spend enough time being angry at other people. Why the hell do I have to waste time being angry at my own body?

Emyr frowns, but he hears me. He nods. "Okay. I'm sorry. So...what is it?"

"I just, uh. I don't know. I didn't want you getting weird

around me or anything. That would be incredibly annoying." I crinkle my nose and roll my eyes for good measure. "And frankly, you're annoying enough already."

His frown deepens. "I know you think very little of me."

No, I don't. The thought surprises me, and even more surprising is the realization that it's true. Emyr definitely isn't my favorite person, considering the context of our relationship. But he's not a *bad* person, either. He's a boy capable of acts of both awesome power and immense gentleness. He's clever, and beautiful, and there's something wild in him that the wildness in me recognizes.

I think, in another world, under another set of circumstances, I really could have fallen in love with him.

Instead of answering him, I just shrug. "I think very little of most people."

"Except Briar."

I am so sick of him bringing her up every time we have a conversation, a hint of accusation always hidden behind the corner of what he's saying out loud. "You have *got* to get off the Briar thing."

He considers me for a moment before admitting, "I don't understand your relationship."

"She's my best friend. It's not complicated. Haven't you ever had a best friend before?"

"Yes. You."

Don't say shit like that to me. I don't answer, just stare at him. I have no idea what to say to that, anyway.

We were more than best friends, once. We were…we were something I don't have a word for. At least, not a word I can let myself think. Once. But then I got older and angrier, and Emyr got older and princelier, and everything fell apart because we live in a terrible, horrible, unfair world where everything sucks.

Or maybe because I am a terrible, horrible, unfair boy. Looking back now, I can still see myself for who I was then. Angry at the fae for treating me like a second-class citizen. Angry at my parents for treating me like my only value was in my engagement to Emyr. Angry at Emyr because he'd come to represent everything that felt wrong about my life, when for so long he'd been the best thing about it.

I let my bitterness at the rest of the world turn me against him. And it poisoned everything.

Finally, Emyr adds, "I just worry if you're in love with her that you'll be—"

"Dude, I'm gay. Okay?"

He raises his eyebrows.

I shake my head. "Very, very gay. I love Briar. I would die for her. I would definitely kill you if she needed me to. And, like, sure, a long time ago I might've grabbed her ass a little, but—no. Okay? She's not my type. Not anymore."

"Oh."

Silence settles over us again.

I close my eyes and press my head into the pillows. I need to get some sleep. The drain of the last day is really, really starting to get to me. My head is pounding. Although, again, I could blame that on the guaro.

But before I can turn my brain off, Emyr speaks again.

"So, what is your type?"

I groan, rucking up the neck of his shirt to put the cotton over my eyes. I do not want to look at him. "Wingless human boys who are a good few inches shorter than me."

"I imagine it would be very hard to find that many boys shorter than you."

"Hey now, wait just a damn minute—" I tug the shirt from my eyes to scold him, but find Emyr isn't looking at my face. He's staring at my stomach, at the line of skin exposed between the hem of his shirt and the elastic waistband of my boxers.

I know that look on his face. I recognize the way his throat bobs. When his horns darken and twist, the tips of his ears twitching, I yank the blanket higher up my torso.

Not because *he* needs to stop looking at me, but because *I* need him to stop looking at me.

Has it always been this warm in the bed? Have I always been able to feel the heat coming off his body and pushing up against mine? Were we always this *close*?

I am not—repeat, NOT—going to have sex with Emyr Leonidas Mirac North. EVER.

Well, maybe.

He drags his gaze back to my face, seeming to shake himself out of it. "Um. Is that really your type?"

Why does his voice sound all raspy now? No. I am not doing this!

"I don't have a type." I shrug. "Do you?"

"Do you want me to answer that honestly?" he asks, and I don't.

I don't want to ask, because I've spent a lot of time telling myself I definitely don't care, but the timing's never been more perfect than it is right now. And I figure, I'm already making some pretty questionable choices. What's one more?

"So…was Jin right about you? You a little gay?"

Emyr frowns, rubbing a hand over his mouth. "Honestly, I'd never really thought about it until I realized you were a guy."

"You've only ever been with girls before?"

"Ah…" Emyr shrugs.

The moment stretches on a bit before I ask. "I mean, you've been with other people, right?"

"No, I haven't."

"You cannot be serious. You're telling me you walk around looking like—" I bite the inside of my cheek and start over. "You're telling me you're a *prince* and you're a *virgin*?"

Emyr seems utterly unbothered. "Is that really so surprising?"

"Uh, yeah. How've you not had your bones jumped?" I am going to yeet myself out of the airplane on the way back to New York, but still. I have to know.

"It isn't like people haven't tried." His tongue flicks out to taste his lips. "But I was never interested."

"Never? Not even a little?"

Another infuriating shrug. "You talk like wanting to sleep with everyone I meet is normal."

"Well, not *everyone*," I mumble. "Maybe like a quarter of people."

"That is…absurd."

"Whatever, I'm horny, leave me alone." I look away, study the arch of the ceiling.

Emyr is quiet for a moment, before he asks, "So, have you? Been with other people?"

Oh, here we go.

"Couple people. Guys I met after I came out, friends of friends of Briar's."

"Hmm." Emyr props his chin up on his fist, considering me. "Did you love either of them?"

I don't mean to laugh, but I can't seem to help it. "No. God, no. I just, uh... I don't know. They were there. And I knew them well enough to know I could probably trust them, but not so well that I'd be heartbroken if we never talked again 'cause shit got awkward."

"They were there," he repeats, and I flush.

"Don't slut shame me."

"I'm not. Or I don't mean to be." Emyr sighs softly, arches his back a little, hips rolling against the bed underneath him. "I want to ask you something, but I don't want you to get offended."

Oh, here we *really* go.

"Starting any question off like that is a red flag, but sure. Let's hear it."

Emyr's front teeth scrape against his lower lip. "What exactly did you do with them? I mean... Did they— Did you—"

"Please stop before you hurt yourself." I sigh, reaching up to rub a hand over my chest, pressing my thumb against the dip of my sternum. "I did...just about everything...to them." It feels weird, wrong, to be talking about this at all, but especially with Emyr. It makes my mouth wet and my stomach flip and I can't meet his eye. "I don't like taking my clothes

off. But it's less of a dysphoria thing and more of a not wanting to explain the scars thing."

I glance down at my arms. Clarke's glamour is damn long-
lasting, still in place now, making them appear smooth. I'm
not sure how long it'll keep.

"Hmm. So, they didn't do anything to you."

"I mean, not *much*. They did enough."

"Hmm."

I groan, rubbing my palm against my shaved head. "Stop
that. What does *hmm* mean? Are you pissed that I went and
fooled around with other guys while we were engaged?"

"No." And when Emyr says it, it doesn't sound like a lie.
Which would be something to think about if every brain cell
in my head didn't fly out the window when he followed it
up with, "I was just thinking, *I've* already seen your scars. I
know exactly where they come from. You wouldn't have to
explain anything to me."

I am going to straight up mcfucking lose it.

"You— I thought you didn't experience sexual attraction,
or whatever."

"That isn't what I said. I said I never wanted to sleep with
anyone *else*."

"I—" I roll onto my side so that my back is turned to him,
because I can *feel* my face heating, and we are *so* not doing
this. "Is that a mated fae thing?"

"Not at all. Plenty of mated fae have other partners who
they aren't bound to. Not every bond is even sexual in nature at all, beyond the need to reproduce. This... It's a me
and you thing."

"Well, that sucks for you. What a shitty deal you got." I motion to myself with a flick of my wrist.

Emyr says, point-blank, "I don't think so."

Oh, for crying out loud.

I roll back over, if only to make a face at him. "I really don't get it. You said yourself the bond wasn't like falling in love. And if the bond doesn't make you like me, or love me, or want me, then why would you?"

"Are you fishing for compliments, firestarter?" Emyr smirks.

"Yeah. Indulge me."

"You don't let me get away with anything," Emyr starts, reaching up to run his fingers through his curls, "which is completely infuriating. But no one calls me out like you do. Everyone else has a game to play, some agenda they're hoping to twist me toward. You wear everything on your sleeve."

He doesn't have any idea how wrong he is about that.

"You have a sharp tongue that keeps me on my toes. You aren't afraid of offending people or challenging the status quo. You do what you believe is right, no matter the consequences. You're *good*, but you aren't afraid to get your hands dirty, either."

I don't think that's true. I don't think I'm good at all. And it makes me very, very uncomfortable to hear Emyr say he thinks otherwise.

"It helps that you're nice to look at," he adds, taking me off guard.

I scoff, fumbling over my own tongue as I struggle for a retort. "That hardly seems like enough foundation for a *marriage.* And what about this whole babies thing? You were looking for someone who was gonna lie back and be your little incubator, and, my dude, I am so not it."

Emyr watches the ceiling. "I've always imagined biological children. I... I thought it would help."

"Help?" I prop my head up on my fist. "Help what?"

"I love my parents. And I'm very close with my mother. But..." Emyr swallows. "There's always been a distance between my father and me. I feel like there's something between us, like he doesn't trust me the way he should."

It's a quiet, vulnerable admission that makes a little wrinkle settle between Emyr's eyes. I have the absolutely out-of-my-mind thought that I want to reach over and press my thumb there, and smooth that worry away.

I don't, of course.

At least we're no longer being horny.

"Is this about you wanting to go back to Faery?" I ask, thinking about the awkwardness of dinner with the king and queen, the king's sharp retorts to Emyr's ideas.

Emyr shrugs. "That's part of it."

"Why would you want to do that? It seems dangerous to even try."

He opens and closes his mouth, then exhales. "I don't know if you would understand."

I roll my eyes. "Try me."

"This world is all I've ever known. But it's...it's not a world that was meant for us. It's not where we *belong*." He reaches up to rub a hand against his mouth. "I don't know how I can miss a place I've never been, but it's as if my *bones* know they don't come from here. They belong in Faery. They want to go home."

After a quiet moment, Emyr shakes his head. "It sounds ridiculous, doesn't it?"

I stare at him for a long moment before swallowing. "No. It doesn't."

Because that feeling he's describing is exactly the way I feel now that I've been away from the human world for a while. And though I'm hard-pressed to admit it, it's also the way I felt for years, being away from Asalin.

Quietly, I ask a question that's bothered me for years. "When you look through the door to Faery, what do you see?"

Emyr frowns. "Nothing much. It's a wasteland, just like my dad says. But…there was one time…once, back when we were kids, I thought I saw something else."

"What?"

"You probably wouldn't believe me if I told you." He laughs softly, shaking his head. "No one would."

"Try me."

Heaving a deep breath, Emyr rubs a hand against his bare chest and finally says, "I thought I saw a *person*. And they were terrifying."

I blink at him. He's right, I don't believe him. "How would that be possible?"

"I don't know. I've thought about it a lot. Maybe my dad is still sending people over in secret for short missions. Maybe they're collecting intel, and he won't tell me because he thinks it's too dangerous. Maybe that's what his secret is. Maybe it was something else, someone from Asalin who managed to get through. Or…maybe it was the overactive imagination of a child. After all, I haven't seen anything like it since."

I watch his face. His expression is screwed up in concentration, like even now his mind is trying to sort through what he knows. The furrowed line between his eyebrows appears again.

"It doesn't matter, though," Emyr continues. "The issue of biological children, that is. I've thought about what you said, and you're right. We're young. We don't need to rush into figuring out our heirs. We can decide the details later. Whenever you're comfortable."

I swallow and flop onto my back to blink up at the ceiling. This is so *frustrating*. Emyr is changing. He sees me, and he's adjusting.

But I've already made my deal with the devil. Could Emyr ever forgive me if he knew?

And even if he could…could I really ever be happy as a king of the fae?

Briar, Jin, Emyr. All of them look at me and see what they want to see, instead of who I actually am. They don't know that I am the monster. I don't know how they could've missed it, though.

Emyr looks straight at me. "Look, I want to be with *you*. Maybe it's ridiculous to you, but I know this is the way things are meant to be me. You and I are supposed to make each other happy. And that means, for me, you're it. Whoever or whatever you are. However my life may change because of it. You're it."

I have no idea what to say to that. I stare at him for a long

moment before dragging the blanket over my head and closing my eyes.

It comes to me after Emyr falls asleep, when the soft sound
of his snoring fills the bedroom. This twisted, warped rev-
enant crawls out of the deepest, most buried part of me and
latches itself into my mind. I've been trying *so* hard not to
think about it. But it's too late.

*The sun is beginning to set over the mountains that surround
Asalin. I know I should go home soon, but I don't want to. There's
nowhere I would rather be than right where I am.*

*Emyr's fingers rest in mine, the pad of his thumb stroking my own.
We're lying on the balcony of his bedroom in a tangle of blankets,
our makeshift fort, watching the sky erupt into pinks and oranges.*

*The rest of the world can be bad sometimes, but I always feel safe
with Emyr. When the fae whisper awful things about me behind my
back, when my parents yell at me for not wanting to act the way they
tell me to, when my sister is cruel…there's always Emyr.*

I know I should go home soon, but home, for me, is wherever he is.

*"My parents found the deck of tarot cards you gave me," I say qui-
etly. "They got so mad. They burned them all right in front of me."*

*Witch magic is forbidden in my house. They don't want me prac-
ticing it. Don't want me rubbing my abnormality in their faces.*

*Emyr brushes his nose against mine. "I don't understand why
they're so mean all the time."*

*"They want me to be more like Tessa, I guess." I sniffle and reach
up to rub my eyes. I don't want to leave. I don't want to go back to
my family's house. I want to stay here.*

*Emyr takes my hand, pulling it away from my face and squeez-
ing my fingers. "I like you just the way you are."*

"You wouldn't change anything about me?"

"Of course not." He frowns. "Then you wouldn't be you. Besides, when we're married you can have as many spellbooks as you want. They won't be able to do anything about it."

Tears blur my vision as I stare into his face. Hesitantly, unsure of myself, I lean forward and brush my lips against his. It's only a whisper of a kiss, and my tears are still warm between us.

Still, when I pull away, Emyr smiles, dimples breaking out on either side of his mouth.

I sigh and lean into his side, and the two of us snuggle up in that blanket fort until servants come to send me home.

Pain rips through my gut so ferociously it threatens to tear me in half. This is not a new pain, but a familiar one. A gaping, raw loneliness I've felt every day since I ran from Asalin. I've gotten good at acting like it doesn't exist, at ignoring it and shoving it down. But it's never gone away. It's always been there, just beneath the surface.

I missed him so much.

That is the ugly secret I've tried not to look at since the day I left for the human world. The secret I knew I would have to burn alive if I wanted to change my fate. It isn't possible I could maybe, someday, in another universe, love Emyr. I already love him. I have always loved him. Maybe I'm not *in love* with him, maybe not in the way you love someone you marry, I don't know. But definitely in the way you love someone who's got his claws in part of your soul. Emyr's had his claws in me since we were kids, and anything I did to hurt him would end up hurting me, too.

It was just so much easier to do that when I could pretend it wasn't there at all.

I roll onto my stomach and press my face into the pillows. As quietly as I can, hoping I won't wake him, I cry myself to sleep.

CHAPTER TWENTY-ONE

ME OR THE THRONE

Everything is warm.

Not *hot*, not like being on fire, but warm like sitting *next* to the fire. Like lying under the sun. My body feels loose, muscles relaxed, bones eased up like someone's shot me up with morphine while I wasn't looking.

I arch back, seeking more of that warmth behind me, and the warmth rolls forward to meet me. It slides against the backs of my thighs, crawls up my hip to curl around my waist and press into my belly, nuzzles against my throat. I reach down to tangle my fingers with the warmth's, to drag its hand from my stomach to my chest to my face, to press my mouth into its palm.

It occurs to me, in some distant part of my brain, that the

warmth is Emyr. But that part of me is so quiet. And the part of me that craves touch is so, so much louder. So, I ignore it.

His fangs dance pinpricks against my neck, hints of sting at my pulse. His claws trail from my jaw to my collar to my ribs, a ghost of touch so as not to hurt.

I reach back and curl my fingers around one thigh, my own nails sinking in hard enough to pull a rumble from his chest, a rough growl pressed into my ear.

Fuck. I wanna do whatever I have to do to make him do that again.

I jostle my hips enough to roll over, opening my eyes to look up at the underside of his jaw. It's dawn now, I think, the room lit in soft shades of orange and pink leaking through the window. When I press my mouth to his clavicle, his wings curl in tighter around us like a cocoon, and he swallows.

My hand presses to the elastic of his boxers, blunt nails crawling up the sharp planes of his stomach, up over his broad chest, finally resting at his throat. My thumb strokes up in a long sweep, cresting over his Adam's apple and resting in the notch under his jaw where I can feel his heart beating.

I think I feel him trembling.

That's around the same time I notice Clarke's glamour has worn off, and the scars are back.

It shouldn't be a big deal. I'm used to seeing them. Every morning in the shower, every night when I get into bed. It's an errant thought, really.

Oh, the scars are back.

And it's about the scars, but it isn't about the scars.

I see the scars and I can feel fire and shadow mingling to-gether in my blood to make poison. I feel the poison and remember who I've used it on. I remember my ghosts and re-member the contract that promises my own death. I remem-ber that oath and remember a fresh one, a bargain made with Derek Pierce for my freedom.

If Emyr had any idea who I really was, he wouldn't want his hands on me.

He's noticed my stillness and matched it with his own. His touch does not stray, body poised in the last position it held. I'm not even sure he breathes for a moment, waiting, wait-ing for me to reanimate.

When I do, it's only to roll my way out of his arms, throw my feet over the side of the bed, and jump up.

"G'mornin," he drawls at my back. "You sleep okay?"

"Morning. I slept fine."

I snatch my phone from the bedside table and frown. Still nothing from Briar.

This wouldn't be concerning most of the time. She can leave her phone lying on the charger for days without care, completely lacking my rabid need for constant entertainment to fill some void. She'd rather be outside getting her hands dirty.

But she knows I'm in another country, on another conti-nent, with some queens who maybe wanted to kill me. She knows I'm worried about her being left there without me to look out for her. Why wouldn't she text me back?

My concern must be bleeding out all over my face, because Emyr asks, "Everything okay?"

"Yeah. No. I don't know. I haven't heard from Briar since we landed in Bogotá."

He's up and grabbing his own phone from the dresser immediately. "I'll get in touch with Clarke. I'm sure they're probably together."

"Yeah. Probably." I stare at the screen a moment longer before shooting off another text, just a series of question marks, double checking that the ringer's on the highest volume, and setting it down. "When are we getting out of here?"

"Should start getting ready and head down to say our good-byes. We'll need to be at the airport in a few hours." Emyr sets his own phone down and turns back to me. Tentatively, as if worried I might bespell him, he reaches out one hand for my arm. I think he might be going to stroke his knuckle down the ragged scars trailing from my wrist to my elbow.

I step back before he can.

His hand falls limply to his side. "Did I...have I done something wrong?"

Shit. I don't want to do this. "No. Not any worse than usual."

"I'm being serious."

"So am I."

He stares at me for a long moment and then nods, reaching up and twisting his fingers through his curls. "I just want to understand what the rules are."

"What are you talking about?"

"Sometimes you like me, and sometimes you don't. Sometimes I can touch you, and sometimes I can't. I just want to understand where the boundaries are, so I don't cross them." He holds his palms open at his sides, a surrender. "I'm not trying to be an asshole."

He isn't being an asshole. He's being a perfect gentleman, and I want to stab myself in the neck.

"I don't know what to tell you." I move over to my suitcase and pop it open.

"Yes, you do." Emyr moves up behind me and presses his hand down on the suitcase to close it. I note that he's careful to keep his body from brushing mine, no matter how close we are. "You know exactly what I'm talking about. Just say whatever it is that's on your mind. Just let me know. *Help me.*"

"Help you?" I wheel around, eyebrows rising, throat catching. "You forced me to be here. You dragged me away from the life I was *trying* to build, to come here and be your *perfect biological match*, and now you're asking me to *help you*?"

He looks at me like I've attacked him. He steps back, wings drooping down toward the floor, eyes soft and molten. "I thought... I didn't realize you were still angry about that."

I'm not, really. I'm not angry.

I want to be. I really, really want to be angry at him, because being angry at him would be so much easier than what I actually am right now.

"Yeah, well, I have plenty of anger to go around. For you, and the Guard, and all the other fae who treat witches like shit." And for myself. I've got plenty of anger saved up for myself.

"You know I'm on your side!" Emyr throws his hands up. "What else can I do? How else can I prove to you that I want to protect the witches? Would you like me to break fae law—*again*?"

I don't know what else he could do. He's trapped in the contract as much as I am. Maybe more so, because of his goddamn bond. What more could he do to show me he wants what's best for my people? That he isn't like his cousin? The cousin I've made a *deal* with. The cousin who's made it perfectly clear he has no problem doing something terrible if he doesn't get what he wants.

My chest hurts.

"Please," Emyr says when I've been quiet for too long. "Tell me what you want from me."

What do I want? Not just from Emyr, but in general. What do I want?

I flounder, tongue twisting behind my teeth, before finally blurting out, "Do you even want to be king?"

Emyr can only stare back at me. Clearly, that wasn't what he was expecting.

I wasn't expecting it from me, either. But here I am. And now that I've started, I can't seem to stop. "You know I don't want to sit on the Throne."

Actually, he can't know that, because I don't even know that anymore. I could do some good for the people of Asalin, I think. I might not be a great person, I might even be a terrible king, but I could help. I could be better than *Derek*.

But Derek's threats linger like smoke in the back of my mind. He's never said it outright, but I think he'd kill to be king.

What do I want? I want to protect people. I want to protect Emyr. From Derek. From myself. From the deal I stupidly, selfishly made.

I babble on. "And you didn't choose this life any more than I did. Is it really what you *want*? To spend the rest of your life bound in politics, fighting with the Guard—is that really who you want to be? Because I'm looking at you, and I... I don't think it is."

He looks down at his claws.

"I think the you who lives in the cabin in the woods, the you who helped me break the witches out of jail, and reads graphic novels about aliens? I think *that's* the guy you want to be."

"You're still not giving me—"

"So, let me ask you something." I cut him off. "You forced me back here to help you secure the Throne. Because you thought you needed me to be king. But what if you don't... what if you just don't need to be king? What if I was willing to give myself to you completely, and the only thing I asked in return was that you walked away from the Throne?"

At that, Emyr raises his eyes.

"What if we could disappear together? Start over? Fuck Asalin. Fuck the Throne. Let Derek have it. Let someone else fight for it. I don't care. I want you. I want *you*. But I don't want this."

My knees threaten to give out underneath me. Emyr stares, openmouthed, like I've just struck him.

"Given the choice, what would you choose? Me or the Throne?"

It isn't fair, and I know it isn't. The truth of my deal with Derek, the fear that something really, terribly awful is going to happen if Derek doesn't get the Throne, sits at the back of my throat, threatening to spill out. I should tell Emyr. I should tell him everything.

That I think I love him. That I think I've always loved him. But that I fucked up. I keep fucking up, and now I don't know how to fix it except to run away again.

I'm always running away. Because I'm weak. See? I really would make a terrible king.

Emyr's silence could smother me.

One moment ticks by. Then another. Silent moments bleeding into one another until they're one long stretch of quiet that holds my unspoken answer.

By the time Emyr finally manages to mumble, "It isn't that simple," it doesn't matter, because I already know.

"Yeah." I nod, looking away. "You're right. It isn't."

Because I'm a coward, I still don't tell him. But I know I have to. Sooner rather than later, I'm going to have to face up to everything I've done. For the first time in my life, it's time for me to fight to make things right, instead of disappearing.

Emyr deserves that much from me. All of Asalin does.

CHAPTER TWENTY-TWO

TO BE SEEN AS I AM

By the time we make it back to Asalin, I still haven't heard from Briar. Emyr got a single text back from Clarke saying she would go check on her, and then nothing more from her, either.

I have every intention of having a hard conversation with Emyr. Every intention of opening myself up and bleeding all over the metaphorical place. But only *after* I've made sure my best friend isn't sprawled out dead in a ditch somewhere, that the women in my life aren't being picked off by a magical serial killer.

Emyr calls after me when I practically tuck and roll out of the car as it crawls to a stop at the palace steps. I turn my head and raise my eyebrows.

"You want me to come with you?"

Because I'm gay and pathetic, I almost tell him yes. What I actually do is give a quick shake of my head and take off. Being around him hurts. And I need to focus.

Briar isn't in our bedroom, though I expected as much. Her *phone* is, though. I pluck it from its resting spot on the bedside table. She's got seven unread texts from me, one from her mother, one from a number I don't recognize and that she doesn't have saved.

POCKET GOBLIN
we just landed, thank fuck.

i don't think i like first class as, like, a concept.

eat the rich, basically.

maybe some of the rich can be saved. these queens are probably loaded but they're not terrible.

gonna head to bed soon. text me when you see this, please. love you.

??????

okay, hey, you're really starting to freak me out, bri.

I try not to be *too* indignant about my contact name. I've bemoaned it plenty of times. She maintains it's cute.

MAMA
Promise me you're being careful. You don't know what they're capable of, even the ones you call friends.

Well, that's…cryptic. I try and scroll up to read the rest of the conversation, but there's not much. Only texts every few days, one or two at a time, Nadua checking in and Briar confirming everything's okay. More often than not, they talk on the phone. I wonder what they talked about during their last call.

I haven't had time to sit and think much about Nadua since everything blew up and I found myself headed back to Asa-lin. I haven't had time to sit and ruminate on her reaction to Emyr, the steadiness of her hand on the shotgun, the complete and utter lack of surprise as she sized him up.

But reading the message now, I have to ask again. What does she know? What more might Briar have told her?

My damn head hurts.

UNKNOWN NUMBER
Why are you ignoring me? :(

There's one other message from the same number, from the night before, the last message it looks like Briar actually read.

UNKNOWN NUMBER
Hey, dollface. (: It's Jin. Clarke finally managed to smuggle my phone out to me. Can we talk?

Huh. That's interesting.

There's nothing in any of the messages that tells me where Briar might've disappeared to. I don't know if that should make me feel worse, but it sure as shit doesn't make me feel any better.

My beloved black hoodie is clean and folded on top of the dresser, so I snatch it up and tug it on before shoving Briar's phone in the front pocket. I don't know why. Like maybe at some point, someone will send a message that gives me an idea of where she might be. I pull a pen from her stash of art supplies tucked under the bed and rip off a piece of sketch paper to leave a note on her pillow.

Where are you?
Meet me at the cabin tonight.
Please.

The rest of the castle feels too normal. Service workers—maids, tailors, butlers, almost all witches—bustle to and fro. I pass Guardspeople and Committee members as I head for the castle's exit again, each of them glancing in my direction with expressions ranging from a hint of concern to blatant hatred.

Right. I expected that. I'd worried about Derek piecing together I'd been behind the witches breaking out, and that he and his people would have it out for me now. But in the midst of everything else, somehow I'd managed to forget.

And speaking of Derek.

"Wyatt Croft!"

That lyrical voice sounds a whole lot less so when he barks my name down the hallway. I stop only long enough to turn my head over my shoulder and catch sight of him, shoulders pulled back, mouth set in a furious line, blue energy in convulsions around his body.

Nope. Do not have time for this. Gotta find Briar. I wheel around and pick up the pace, desperate to make my way into the woods. Maybe she went to see the peryton again. Maybe she and Boom are curled up together in Emyr's cabin right now. Maybe, maybe, maybe...

Fingers dig into my arm so hard I can't help but to *yelp*. It feels as if my bicep nearly disconnects from my shoulder as I'm yanked back. Derek slams my body into the nearest wall and inverted stars, little bursts of black spots, erupt in my vision as my skull cracks against stone.

"Don't you *dare* walk away from me, witch," Derek snarls, horns shooting ramrod straight atop his head. He's managed to trap me in the one deserted hallway. His wings flare out to either side of him. "Who do you think you are?"

I think, *No one*. But fire burns underneath my skin and black magic slides its way between our bodies like a shield and I say, "If you don't get your hands off me, I'm gonna be the guy who turns you into pâté."

Unicorn Boy learned that lesson the hard way.

Derek's lip comes up over his fangs in a sneer. "And now you threaten me to my face? I should have gotten rid of you when I had the chance."

"Yeah, well, you didn't. You dropped the charges, I'm a free man, sucks to suck. Now, if you don't mind, I've got shit to do, and—"

"No, I should've disposed of you *long* before the trial." Derek breathes the words right into my face, the overwhelming scent of his cologne nearly choking me. "I *knew* you would grow up to be a thorn in my side. I never should've let you."

The weight of his words slams into me so hard I can't breathe for a moment. I'm standing there, pinpoints of my body already throbbing from his manhandling, and he's telling me he should have murdered me when I was a kid.

Was there really a time when I *wanted* Derek Pierce?

What is wrong with me?

"We had an agreement, Wyatt. I did what I said I would

do. And what have you done with that good faith, hmm? Are you even *trying* to uphold your end of our deal?"

The answer leaves me before I can tame my tongue and force it back down my throat. "Not really."

When Derek's hand squeezes tighter, I feel my bones shift. Pain radiates through my entire arm, and I give a shout of pain, trying to wrest my body away from him, but I can't.

"Look at me, Wyatt," Derek growls, leaning his head closer to mine. *"Look at me."*

I meet those bewitching blue eyes again. His energy snakes along my body, wrapping around my skin, tugging at me as if to pull me closer. I can smell him, that crisp, moneyed, masculine scent.

Maybe he's right. We did have an agreement. Briar can wait…

Wait, Briar can wait? I frown. Something tugs at my subconscious. This isn't right.

His energy is all over me.

Influencing me.

My stomach drops. Rage builds like an inferno in my belly. "How long have you been fucking with my head, Derek?"

Fire burns in my palms. Blackness shoots up my fingers, slides into my eyes, and flame bursts to life in my hands. I shove at his chest with as much strength as I can summon in my free hand, and my fingers leave five singed holes in his no-doubt-stupid-expensive button-down.

Derek doesn't hesitate, just reaches down to grab my other arm and shove it back, hard, until my elbow smacks against the stone wall. The cry it wrenches from me reverberates off the walls, filling the hallway with the sound of my pain.

"Ahem." A quiet voice clears their throat from down the way, and an older woman in a servant's uniform blinks at the two of us. "Is everything all right?"

No, everything is not all right, everything is extremely not all right, but her question gives Derek enough of a pause that I can finally rip myself away from him. I take off for the doors at a sprint, moving as quickly as my legs will carry me, doing my best to ignore the throbbing in my arm.

Derek's voice follows me, brushes at my back: "You could have avoided what happens next. Remember that."

I don't have time to think about the threat in his words. I have to find Briar.

The world outside is warm and still. It's too nice a day, I think, for what's going on in my head. Where are the storm clouds, the thunder and lightning, the sun eclipsed in the sky? How can the world go on spinning, pretty and peaceful and utterly unbothered by the fact that every single thing in my life feels like it's falling apart around me?

The woods, at least, are dark. The trees press in tight, branches trying to snag my hoodie and jeans as I stomp in the direction of the clearing.

It's only when I've walked halfway there that it occurs to me: What if Derek has Briar?

I freeze.

Is *that* what's coming next? Would he do something to her to try and get back at me? To force my hand in some way? What about Clarke? Emyr hasn't heard back from her, either. Would Derek be willing to hurt his own sister in order to further his agenda?

The question doesn't linger for long, because I already

know the answer. Derek Pierce would do anything to anyone to get what he wants.

I have to go back to the castle. I have to find Derek again, demand he tell me what he knows.

The rest of the world seems to warp in my vision. I turn, but I'm not sure where I've turned. My body feels hollowed out, like someone's reached into me and made a chasm of my chest, a gaping hole where my heart and lungs used to be. I can't breathe.

Trees move in my vision, or maybe my vision moves against the trees, the world tipping in a way it isn't supposed to. I have to find Briar, but I can't find my own feet. Where am I?

Why can't I breathe?

Something bites my hand.

It barely registers the first time, but the second bite is harder, more determined. My brain has detached from my body, but I manage to turn my head on a robotic impulse, looking down. At first, I can see only roving shadows. I blink away unshed tears I didn't know had pooled.

Boom stares up at me. When our eyes meet, he whines, licking a slobbery, warm trail up the back of the hand he was just gnawing on.

Seeing him here, this far away from the safety of his clearing, is enough of a surprise to jar me back from the edge. Just a little. Enough that I no longer feel I'm about to topple over.

I press my palm against the top of his head and scratch behind his ears. He whines again, turning his head against my fingers to lick my wrist.

My lungs inflate. But the tears *really* come as soon as I'm breathing again.

Ass, meet dirt. I drag my knees up near my shoulders, and Boom presses in between my legs, shoving his massive body against me as tight as it'll go.

My nose finds his neck and I bury my face in his thick, black fur, letting the wave crash over me. My body heaves, torso rolling like it's trying to force the emotion up and out of my mouth, like I could simply expel it from my system. My hands shake, wrapping around the back of Boom's front legs, cleaving to him while he nuzzles and licks my head.

Why am I crying? I have shit to do, important shit to do, and I'm sitting on the forest floor crying like some kind of ridiculous baby.

I need to get up. I need to get up, but I can't seem to make my legs work, can't seem to do anything but cry, and the longer I cry, the angrier I get at myself for the crying, and the angrier I get, the harder I cry. I'm going to throw up. I'm going to lose my lungs again.

What is wrong with me?

"Oh, shit. Tee, it's Wyatt."

"Wyatt?" A rustling to the side of me, and then a voice at my back, words floating delicately around my skull to tickle at my earlobes. "Oh, Wyatt. Hey. Hey. Wade, give us a minute."

A hand presses against my spine, and a soft touch sweeps its way up and down, from the back of my neck to the waistband of my jeans. Even through the thick material of my hoodie, I can feel the cooling whisper of Tessa's hand, lavender energy sliding over me, blanketing me.

For some reason, it only makes me cry harder.

"Big-ass dog, move," Tessa mumbles, pushing at Boom's

shoulders until he gives a little growl and pulls away from me, only enough to lie down in the dirt at my side.

One of my hands stays tangled in his fur. The other rises to my face, desperately trying to rub away the tears and snot and puffy redness that's taken over.

"Wyatt, what happened?"

"I fuck everything up!" And I didn't know I was going to say it before I say it, but then I say it and it's like the last piece of the dam has burst, like the last determined stitch trying to keep my body glued together has finally snapped and all my insides are suddenly spilling everywhere, all over the forest floor. "Everyone I love gets hurt. Or dies! Because of me. Mom and Dad and Briar and Emyr and—and why? Why am I still here? What is the point of *me* if everyone around me just—"

I can't finish the thought, at least not out loud. I reach up to dig my nails into the top of my shaved head, curling in on myself. I want to disappear. Maybe Derek was right. Maybe he should've gotten rid of me when he had the chance.

"Oh, Wyatt." Tessa's hands settle on my shoulders and she pulls me against her chest, gathering me up and wrapping herself around me. Her cheek rests against my temple and she presses one single, tender kiss. And in that moment, she doesn't remind me of me, or our dead mom, but just her, just Tessa, my angry, sad, determined sister. "Wyatt, Wyatt, Wyatt, Wyatt. It's okay. You're okay."

"NOTHING IS OKAY!" I press my face to her jaw, tears making a waterfall of her throat. "How can you say that? How can you tell me it's okay? You *hate* me."

"I don't hate you."

"Bullshit. You told me you wished I was dead."

Tessa doesn't say anything for a long moment and I think, Well, there it is. She does hate me. Of course she hates me. And why shouldn't she? I killed our parents.

I *killed* our parents.

I. Killed. Our. Parents.

She has no reason not to hate me. No one has any reason not to hate me.

When she pulls back from our embrace, it doesn't take me by surprise. But the tears I find shining in our identical eyes do.

Tessa's voice warbles when she says, "That was a very unfair thing of me to say. I was hurting. And so confused. But I didn't mean it. Or maybe I did mean it, in that moment, but I shouldn't have said it. And I don't feel that way now."

I press the back of one hand to my eyes and wipe the salt water away. When I lower it to the ground, Boom licks the tears away and rests his muzzle against my wrist. "You don't?"

"No, Wyatt, I don't."

Silence settles between us again. My fit seems to have ended, my body finally rejecting all of its untapped emotion. Though the look on Tessa's face seems to indicate a fit of her own may be right around the corner.

She doesn't cry, though. Instead, she reaches up and tugs her fingers through her hair, tucking it behind her pointed ears and taking a deep breath. "Our parents were horrible, abusive people who treated you like shit every day of your life and brainwashed me into thinking what they did was okay. I don't know exactly what happened that night, but—"

"They were trying to kill me." I blink. Swallow. "I was

attacked, and I was terrified, and I didn't know anything about controlling my magic. It got out of hand, and they... were going to kill me to make it stop."

Another moment of silence passes. Tessa stares at me and I stare at her and I don't think either of us breathes.

Finally, she nods. Looks down at her claws. "Then they deserved to die. Your magic was protecting you. I—if I had spent one day protecting you myself, if I had realized what was happening earlier, maybe it wouldn't have happened. But I didn't, and it did, and we can't go back now."

I wrap my arms around my knees, rest my chin against my thighs. "You were just a kid."

"Yeah, well, so were you." She lets out a quiet laugh. Less like wind chimes, more like birdsong. Her fingers brush against that scar on her belly, the mark that stretches across her pelvis. "I got this the first year after you disappeared. It's the date of the fire, written in the Old Language. The last time I saw you, or them."

"Why would you want *that* on your body forever?"

"A reminder of the worst parts of ourselves." Her fingertips brush over the white lines. "A reminder to never go back there."

I think about the scars on my arms. Tessa and I and our many, many similarities.

She continues. "I don't want either of us to spend the rest of our lives feeling like this, Wyatt."

And I don't have to ask what she means, because I know. Guilt and anger and heartache, my familiar companions, are Tessa's, too.

"How do we fix it?" Maybe she'll have some magic for

me. Maybe she can wave her fae hand and all of this pain will simply go away.

But it isn't that simple. She shakes her head and meets my eye again. "Time. Hard work. We could probably both use several hundred hours of therapy."

It's a joke but it isn't a joke and neither of us laugh.

Tessa reaches forward and rests her hands on either side of my face, pressing her thumb underneath my chin and raising my head up to meet her eyes.

"You are not a bad person. Sometimes people get hurt, and you can't save everyone from everything, but that is not your fault. Your value as a person is not based on how much you can do for other people. You are valuable, Wyatt. *You.* All on your own. For exactly who you are."

More than a pawn. More than a means to an end. That's all I've ever wanted, to be seen as a whole person, to be seen as I am. I just didn't expect that acknowledgment to come from my sister.

Somewhere in my chest, something begins to stitch itself back together.

I don't have the chance to respond, though, because Briar's phone pings in my pocket and snaps me back to reality. Shit. Briar. I push myself to my feet and pull it out.

UNKNOWN NUMBER
Where are you?

Fuck if I know, Jin!

"Not to dramatically change the tone here, but have you seen Briar?" I shove the phone back in my pocket and raise my eyebrows.

Tessa frowns, gracefully hopping to her feet. "Ah…a few hours ago actually. She was in the village. Think she was leaving Lavender's place. Why, what's up?"

"I haven't been able to get in touch with her for days. Can't find her anywhere. And then Emyr talked to Clarke and she said she'd look for her, but then Clarke stopped responding. And I found Briar's phone in our room, with missed messages from me, and her mom, and Jin."

"Jin?" Tessa's eyebrows shoot up toward the sky.

"Yeah. I guess Clarke smuggled their phone out to them?"

"Huh…" Tessa frowns, reaching up and rubbing a hand over the back of her neck. "That's…interesting. You can't find either of them?"

"I mean, I haven't really looked for Clarke. I'm just worried about Briar."

"Right, yeah. I tell you what, Wade and I'll go into the village, hunt around, see if I can find her, and bring her to you. You have any other ideas where she might've gone? Any place in particular that she was interested in?"

After a moment, I nod. I don't know why it comes to me, but it does, suddenly slotting into place in the back of my mind. "Yeah, one."

"Okay, you check there." Tessa reaches over and squeezes my arm, and only then does my body register it's still in pain from Derek's assault. "We'll find her. Wade!"

He appears with a rustle of branches, and I don't know how much of that exchange he heard, but I don't have the mental capacity to be embarrassed about it right now. Together, the two of them head off in the direction of town.

I watch them go for a long moment before finally heading to the one place I think Briar might be. Boom follows, a shadow at my back.

CHAPTER TWENTY-THREE

HOW IS THIS WORTH DYING FOR?

The closer I get to the door of Faery, the worse I feel.

I can't explain it. My stomach is in knots. The hair at the back of my neck stands on end. Saliva blooms under my tongue, between my teeth.

Humans have excellent instincts. Somehow, they're genetically predisposed to sense danger. They feel it before it happens, the coming threat, red flags shooting to mast.

Fae don't have that. Witches don't have that. We throw ourselves headfirst into whatever bullshit we come up with and hope for the best. So, this? This feeling? This gut feeling telling me, *Stop, turn around, god have mercy on all who enter here*? I don't know what it is, or where it's coming from. And I make a point to ignore it.

The trees around the door seem quieter than the rest of the woods. Here, the birds don't chirp, the leaves don't crunch underfoot. Even the sunlight streaming in through the tops of the trees seems dimmer, this part of the forest awash in shades of gray.

Has it always been like this? Not that I can remember. The door's always felt creepy, but never *ominous*.

Doesn't matter, though. There's no time to worry about it. I just keep putting one foot in front of the other, Doom at my back, until we get where we're going.

Curiosity killed the cat.

But satisfaction brought it back.

I repeat those words to myself, a silent mantra.

The small comfort they have to offer disappears when I finally reach the elm trees whose tangled, black branches form the archway that leads to Faery.

"Briar?"

I've found her. There should be relief. The anxiety I've been carrying around with me all day should dissipate, at least some. Derek doesn't have her. She isn't hurt.

But...is she?

She's standing in front of the door, her back to me, black and blue curls cascading down her back in a frenzied mess. She turns at the waist at the sound of my face, deep brown eyes widening slightly.

"Briar, what are you doing here? I've been trying to reach you all day."

In one hand, she's holding a book, spine cracked open against her forearm. That same book she's been carrying

around since the night of the riots, the one she's been studying in our room.

The fingers of her other hand drip with blood. Her own
blood, running from a cut down the center of her palm.

There is no relief to be found here. There is only the silence of the forest, the heavy weight of an unseen threat
pressing around us from all sides, and the cold dread creeping into my chest.

"Bri, you're bleeding."

I say the words even as I know she knows them. Her black-
shot eyes flick from my face to her bloodied hand. From her
hand back to my face. From my face to the twisted archway
of the door.

My gaze follows hers there. I realize, that sickening feeling growing worse and worse, that the elm arch is covered in
her blood, too. Sticky and wet with a trail of red sigils Briar
has drawn.

I don't know anything about witchcraft. I don't know what
any of these are used for, not separately and certainly not when
all combined together.

But that dread begins to flood into the rest of me. Everything goes cold.

Behind me, Boom gives one long, pained growl, and every
strand of hair on my body stands at attention.

"I'm sorry, Wyatt."

She presses her wet palm against the tree. The elm arches
twist and sizzle, her bloody sigils seeping into the wood and
disappearing, the strange magic of them being absorbed right
into the door itself. Her yellow energy flares out from her

body like the blast of a bomb, rattling the air so hard that it
knocks me off my feet and my head cracks against the ground.

Through the archway, I see the usually staticky view begin
to dissipate. Maybe it's because my head's fucked up from the
fall, but I swear, for the first time I actually manage to *see* beyond the veil, into the world of Faery itself.

And before I lose consciousness, Faery stares back.

When I wake, everything hurts, but the woods feel normal
again. Briar's jacket is rolled up like a pillow under my head,
and Boom is sleeping next to me, my face against his back. I
blink up at the sky, catching hints of the sunset through the
tree limbs.

"Was worried I lost you there for a minute," comes Briar's
voice from somewhere to the side.

I turn my head and my neck aches. She's sitting on the
ground a few feet away, perched in front of the door. She looks
at me, and I look back, and we say nothing for a long moment.

Before now, before this exact moment, we've always been
able to say whatever we needed to say without any words at
all. But I can't even begin to guess what Briar's thinking.
Not now.

She's the one who breaks the silence, her gaze going back
to the archway. "I didn't really think it was going to work."

"Are you sure that it did?"

She frowns, sitting up straighter and twisting her fingers
in front of her belly. "No. But I think so."

Yeah. I think so, too.

I am pretty sure that Briar just yanked down the whole

doorway to Faery, leaving nothing but an open hole in its wake. A hole anyone could walk through, anytime.

"You owe me a giant explanation," I snap. I'm not used to snapping at her. It doesn't feel right. It doesn't feel okay.

But Briar also doesn't feel like *Briar* in this moment. She definitely didn't feel like herself when she was standing there painting sigils with her own blood.

"I know," she says quietly, shoulders sagging. "I know. I meant it when I said I was sorry."

I stare at her more before shaking my head. "Start at the beginning."

She nibbles at her mouth, watching me again. She might know she owes me an explanation, but she clearly doesn't want to give me one.

Still, at length, she asks, "Did you really never think about the witches who were abandoned in the human world?"

That is...not where I expected this story to begin.

When I say nothing, my brain floundering inside my head, she finally sighs. "The fae toss their unwanted babies past the borders and you never thought to wonder...if any of them might've survived? You just assumed they were, what, eaten by wild animals? That none of them were ever found? Rescued? Raised by humans?"

I...

No, I guess I never did consider that before.

Pieces start moving in my mind, things clicking together bit by bit, but my head hurts and everything else hurts and it's been a long day and I can't get to where I'm going without a little more help. I ask, "Briar, what do you know about the abandoned witches?"

"Only what my mother's told me." She swallows, shifting from one thigh to the other. "The stories I grew up on."

I stare at her again, waiting for her to continue. To explain. When she doesn't, I ask, "Like... Native American legends?"

Her nervousness seems to dissipate some with that question. She glares at me like I've given her a small stroke. "No, Wyatt. Not like *Native American legends*. Like a family history. Passed down from one generation to the next."

I press my palms to my face and scrub at my temples to try and ease the pounding behind my eyes. "What does your family history have to do with the witches, Briar?"

I know. I already know. The pieces are all there, but my brain won't shove them together. Everything hurts too much.

When her voice comes again, it's so quiet I almost don't hear it at all. "A long time ago, my great-great-grandmother found a child in the woods."

"Fuck."

"My family spent years uncovering the fae's secrets after that. And still, I never really believed my mom's stories. How could I? It was ridiculous. It sounded like a fairy tale." I look up to see her shaking her head. Her tongue slides over her lower lip. "But then she brought you home."

But then she brought me home.

It makes sense now. The ease with which Briar accepted my story, those years ago, when I told her the truth about who I was. Her mother's reaction to Emyr, cold and calculating more than afraid. Even Briar's interest in the other witches, which I'd never thought to question much because it was so very her to want to fight for the underdog, makes more sense in the context of her believing her family is con nected to my people. That any one of us could be her distant cousins or some shit.

I look at my hands. "You're a witch."

"We call ourselves changelings."

My nails curl into my palms. "I told you everything about me. And you hid this. I told you everything about me, and you looked me in my face and lied."

Who *is* she? I'm going to be sick. I have to stand up to suck in a deep breath, tilting my head back to catch the smell of the trees and fresh air breezing around us. Everything hurts, but nothing hurts as badly as what's going on inside my chest.

For so long, Briar was the only good thing in my world. If I can't trust her, the other half of my soul, a piece of my heart walking free from my body, what does that say about the world?

"*No one* knows about us. Not even my father. My great-grandfather, my grandmother, my mother, they all taught the same lesson. Fear the fae. Do not open your mouth and reveal yourself, because if the fae knew we existed—I mean, look at how the witches here are treated!" She takes a deep breath, joining me on her feet. "I wanted to tell you. But I didn't know how."

"By opening your mouth and saying it!" I've never yelled at her before. It feels ugly and warped and heavy in a way I can't tolerate. "I'm—I'm *me*! We're *us*! We don't keep secrets! We're—we're—"

I don't even know how to say it. My lungs feel tight again.

At my side, Boom lets out a pitiful cry.

Briar stares at me for a long moment. When she finally speaks, I expect another apology. I deserve another apology, right? Instead, she says, "Do you have any idea how hard it is being everything you need me to be all the time?"

My hands shake. My stomach hurts so badly I think I'm going to be sick. "What does that mean?"

She scrubs her hands against her own eyes, and some of the still-wet blood there rubs off on her face. "Never mind. It's not what's important right now."

Then why did you say it? I think the question but I don't say it, and I don't think she hears it, because whatever door has hung open between us for so long is closed now.

Finally, I say, "You convinced your parents to let you come to Asalin. Even though your mom knew where you were going, how dangerous it would be. How?"

She meets my eyes again. She looks like she's going to cry. "My family has as much reason to hate the fae as yours does. I wanted to learn everything I could about them. My mom... she told me to be careful. But to find out everything I could."

"So you started spending time with the witches."

"So I started spending time with the witches."

"And you got it in your head you could send the fae back where they came from."

"And I got it in my head I could send the fae back where they came from."

"You wanted to be a hero."

"I *want* to be a hero." Her voice warbles. "I want to *save* people. I want *justice!* Is that so bad? The fae have been allowed to do as they please for so long, without repercussion, without anyone keeping them in check. That kind of power, it only breeds more and more corruption. It destroys every thing around it. I wanted to do right by my family *and* the witches."

"And you still didn't tell me."

"I was neck-deep in secrets at that point!" She paces back and forth, leaves crunching beneath her feet. "I thought maybe if Solomon and I could get the door open, if we could see what was on the other side, I could tell you then. But then Solomon had to escape, and it was just me, and I thought, well, there was probably no way I could do it by myself, anyway. But then you started waxing poetic about me having my own kind of magic. And I thought…well, you aren't wrong about that, are you? There's magic in me, somewhere. I thought… maybe I *could* do it."

She holds out the book she's been carrying around. After a brief hesitation, I snatch it from her and flick it open. It's nothing but sigils, each one painted by Lavender, an explanation of their uses scrawled in her handwriting next to them.

"So, I waited until I was alone. I've been out here, working, trying, for two days. Trying to open this damn door. And it wasn't cooperating. Nothing was happening. Until I saw you. Until I looked into your face." She chokes back a sob, tears streaking her round cheeks. "You need the fae out of your life. And I need to help you. I am always trying to *help* you, because I *love* you. And it was like…as soon as I felt that…as soon as I looked at you, I knew I could do it."

She's handed me all the pieces, but my brain doesn't want to connect them. I want to go back to yesterday, before any of this happened. I want a do-over.

Why can't I have a do-over?

"What would you have done? If you'd been standing there

alone, and the door had opened. Were you planning on just waltzing through?"

She frowns and wipes her face. The blood on her hand has dried by now, but it mingles with her tears to smudge her cheeks some more. "I guess. Just to see what was over there. If Emyr was right, if it was inhabitable."

"And what if he was wrong?" I narrow my eyes at her. "Leonidas said his people, the *fae*, the people who *came* from that world, couldn't even survive it. What if you died, Briar? What if you just fucking died over there and no one ever knew what happened?"

"You—sometimes you have to be willing to die for the things you believe in!"

"How is this worth dying for?!" I toss the book to the forest floor and raise my hands in defeat. "You would be gone. No goodbye. No explanation. Just me, left here wondering where you disappeared to and spending the rest of my life blaming myself for ever bringing you along. And all for what? The chance to send the fae back to Faery? Who says the fae even want to go back to Faery? Who says opening the door would make anyone's life any easier? For crying out loud, did you think about this *at all*?"

Briar's impulsivity, the way she jumps headfirst into things because of how passionate and loving she is, has never bothered me before. The fire in her belly that keeps her fighting, constantly, for other people has always been admirable to me.

Until now.

She doesn't answer my questions, staring at me with her lips parted, her body trembling.

"You're not going through that door. Neither of us is." My

nails make pinpricks on the top of my head when I drag my fingers over my skull. "We have to tell Emyr. The door is locked for a reason. We have to make sure it gets closed again."

"You can't tell Emyr." Briar shakes her head frantically, curls bouncing. "The fae can't know about my family. Emyr— I like him a lot, I want to trust him, but—"

"Seriously? You're still protecting this secret?"

Briar sniffs. One shoulder rises and falls. "I'm sorry, Wyatt. I'm so sorry."

I can only stare at her for a long, long moment, feeling as if I'm seeing a stranger. Finally, I say, "Then I hope that book can tell you how to fix this."

I reach into my hoodie pocket, pull out her phone, and toss it over to her. She barely manages to catch it in her blood-ied hands.

"And clean yourself off before you go inside," is all I say before I turn and storm away, unsure where I'm going, leaving Briar crying, quietly, at my back.

CHAPTER TWENTY-FOUR

THIS MOMENT IS ALL THERE IS

There have been days in my life that moved like humming-birds, buzzing from one perch to the next, flying so quickly their movements aren't discernible as individual motions. Others have rushed by like river water, rarely slowing down but still allowing me to climb in or out at the shore. Sometimes, the grass grows between each ticking of the clock.

Today is the second day since being back in Asalin that's felt like an entire lifetime all in itself. How is it possible I woke up in Eirgard this morning, Emyr's hands on me, mouth at my ear, warm blankets around us to block out the rest of the world? That couldn't possibly have been today. I was another person then. That was a different universe.

But it was, and I wasn't, and it wasn't.

I don't really realize I'm going to the cabin until I'm already there. Maybe I never intended to head this way. Maybe I was just following Boom, the big hellhound's paws making a path a few feet in front of me, the two of us weaving like matching shades between the trees. Doesn't matter, though, because I'm here, just standing here outside of Emyr's cabin, staring straight ahead, unable to keep moving. There's a little yellow light visible through the window. My heart *wants* so badly it hurts. Or maybe it just hurts.

Boom circles me and nudges the small of my back with his muzzle. I stumble forward, hands shooting out to steady my fall against the front door, but then it's opening and instead of grabbing the door I'm grabbing onto Emyr's arms as he reaches for me.

He asks, "Wyatt?" against the top of my head, and I want to cry again, want to lose my shit again, but I can't. I don't think I have enough energy to fall apart, and why did I never realize it took energy to fall apart, and—

Emyr's hands settle on my hips, and my hands reach up to curl in the front of his shirt, and I say, "I don't want to talk about it. Take me inside."

And he does.

"Wyatt," he whispers my name again, one hand slipping around my chest and the other settling on my lower back.

I like my name. I picked it. But I like it even better when it's coming from his tongue, like the way his mouth forms each letter, like the way the sound slides over me like hot water. I want to make him say it again. I don't want him to ever stop saying it.

That familiar golden glow spreads out from his palms,

wraps around my rib cage, and circles my body like a serpent.
I'm flooded with warmth, Emyr's warmth, seeping right into
the core of me. I didn't realize how much pain I was in until
I'm not anymore, the blows to my head, my arms, all of it
fading away until there's nothing but this cabin, and Emyr,
and Emyr's hands, and me trying to sink into it to forget
everything else.

I think, *If today was a lifetime all on its own, does that mean
tonight could be a rebirth?*

"I don't want to talk about it," I repeat, lifting my head to
meet his dark eyes.

That wrinkle settles between his eyebrows. His worried
fangs press against his bottom lips, the corners of his mouth
tugged down into a frown. One perfect black curl reaches
forward to touch the bridge of his nose. "Okay," he says in
that voice like honey.

He smells like mud and smoke and *sugar* and I want to
taste him.

"Can I kiss you?"

I don't know what will happen next. I don't know if there
will even be a *next* to happen. Briar and the door to Faery.
Derek and his bid for the Throne. Either one of them could
wipe us all off the planet tomorrow. Nothing is guaranteed,
nothing is permanent, and all I know is that I have to kiss
him now, here, while I still have the chance.

"What?" He pulls back, only slightly, only enough to really look into my face.

I want to go back to this morning. His hands. My body.
The bedsheets. Before everything got turned upside down.

Why didn't I kiss him this morning? Why am I such a coward?

"I really, *really* want to kiss you," I repeat, and I close the gap between us again, hands sliding up his chest to touch the hollows of his collarbones.

"I thought you were angry at me."

I am. I was. I don't know what I am anymore. "I'm tired of being angry. Emyr, *can I kiss you?*"

There is nothing human about Emyr, there never has been. But the sound he makes, the growl that crawls up out of his chest, vibrating the tips of my fingers before it slides from his throat, is the furthest from human he's ever been. My whole body clenches in response, even before he adds, *"Please."*

My fingers tighten in the front of his shirt again, dragging him down to meet me. His lips are soft and yielding under mine, his mouth opening to let my tongue explore him. I give an experimental flick against one fang and he growls again, something in me blooming in response. I pull him tighter, wanting more, *needing* more. His hands find my waist and curl around me like he's tethering himself here, to me, to this moment.

This moment is all there is. This night, this cabin. Emyr's mouth.

I love him, and I want him, and I don't care anymore. I need something to feel *real*, to feel *good*. Even if I know it can't last.

When I tug our mouths apart, he gives the softest groan, gazing down at me with his eyes half-closed. But when I reach down to grip the end of my hoodie and tug it off my

torso, tossing it away to reveal the white shirt and scars underneath, those eyes blow wide.

"Are you sure?"

"Yes." I curl my hand around the back of his neck and
press our lips together again, because I *am*, I really, really am.

When my free hand slides beneath the silk of his shirt,
exploring the finely honed ridges of his torso, a shock trails
up my spine. When his hands dip under the fabric covering
me, his talons making pinpricks on my hips as his grip urges
me closer, that same shock echoes through every other inch
of my body.

"Okay, okay," I mumble, pulling back a second time. One
of his fangs catches on my lower lip, tugging at it and leaving
a flash of iron in my mouth. I shiver, turning away from him,
albeit begrudgingly. "Boom, you gotta go outside, buddy."

The hellhound gives me a head tilt, wide, wet eyes blinking up at me all pleadingly.

"No, absolutely not. Outside." I open the front door for
him, waving my arm demonstratively until he finally huffs,
stomping out into the night like a petulant child.

Whatever. I slam the door closed behind his tail.

Where was I?

Right. Shock waves.

"C'mere." I reach for Emyr again, my hands finding the
slim muscles of his waist, dragging his body against mine.
This time he bends down to meet me, our foreheads knocking together just before our lips touch, the base of his horns
brushing the short bristles of my hair.

Emyr's hands cover the entire expanse of my lower back
when he pushes up my shirt to press them there. I can feel his

palms, roughened from his years of swordplay and romping in the woods, the clawed tips of his fingers, the warm magic that burns right out of him. He strokes them higher, higher, until his hands are resting on the outside of my binder, my shirt rucked up underneath my arms, and only then does he break the kiss.

"Can I—"

"Yes." I raise my arms, help him tug the shirt off me and toss it away.

For the beat that follows, Emyr and I simply stand facing one another. I watch his face as he takes me in, takes in this body that could not be more different from his own. My soft stomach, wide hips, hourglass waist. The black binder I've definitely been wearing too many hours by now judging by the way it's starting to dig into my sides, flattening my chest as much as is reasonable. The twisted white and red scars running the lengths of my arms, trailing from my wrists up above my elbows, wrapping down and around my rib cage on either side, nearly connecting in the space just above my naval.

He looks at me. I look at him looking at me. And then he steps in again.

Emyr's ears twitch as he leans forward to brush his mouth against the crook of one elbow. When he nuzzles his mouth deeper and his fangs graze the vein there, goose bumps flutter their way across my shoulders.

But when he slides to his knees in front of me, my mouth goes dry. My breath hitches in my nostrils, and my legs suddenly feel as sturdy as a spider's web, trembling like they might give out underneath me.

Emyr seems to recognize that, and he reaches up to curl

his palms around the backs of my thighs, stilling my shaking, holding me steady. His mouth presses featherlight kisses down that same arm, trailing lower and lower, my wrist, my knuckles, the tips of each finger, the center of my palm. With every press of his mouth against me, my body gets looser and heavier all at once, and it seems impossible I should still be on my feet right now.

When he switches sides and starts kissing his way up my other arm, I groan, unable to take another second of it. Both of my hands shoot out and curl around the base of his horns.

My only goal was to get him to pause what he was doing long enough that I could catch my breath. I don't anticipate the way the horns darken and curl in my hands. I don't anticipate Emyr's wrecked gasp, the way all the air in his body shoots free of his lungs at once. He thrusts his head back into my hands, staring up at me from his knees with the beautiful, elegant slope of his neck bared for me.

My sharpened fangs throb behind my lips. Every part of me *throbs*. My hands tighten, fingers giving an experimental stroke along the cool ridges of Emyr's horns. A shudder ripples through his entire body, wings shooting out on either side of him. Even they appear to quiver.

"*Wyatt.*" This time when he says my name it is not only my name, it is a growl, and a plea, and a hollow ache at the center of him that a matching ache in me desperately wants to fill.

I have always been more feral than not, but in that moment I lose any semblance of civility. Hands tightening around Emyr's horns, I use them to push him back, off his knees and onto his ass on the floor, dropping on top of him with my thighs on either side of his hips. He still towers over me like this, but it doesn't matter. I feel *powerful*.

There is a power in being seen and wanted as you are, a power I hadn't grasped until tonight, here, with Emyr's eyes, and hands, and mouth. It's a better high than the morghira was.

Our mouths crash together again and my fangs sink into his lower lip, gently enough not to do any real harm but not so gently to be considered anything other than a bite. I open my mouth to swallow the cry he lets loose. I like the way it tastes.

At some point, Emyr must shrug out of his shirt, because the next thing I know my belly is pressing into bare skin. Only then do I release my grip on his horns, my hands trailing down the sides of his face, his throat, sweeping over his broad shoulders to wrap around his back. My curious fingertips find the spot where his wings meet his back, that delicate muscle and bone where skin turns into velvet. Emyr shivers and rolls his hips up underneath me. He earns a growl and another bite to his lip in reply.

When his hands dust up along the edges of my binder, an unspoken question hanging in the air between us, I pull back enough to shake my head before sliding my mouth to the notch of his jaw. Immediately, his hands skirt away, pressing into my hips instead, pulling me down as he rolls up again. This time it's his neck that my teeth find themselves buried in.

My fingers slide back to his front, running over his chest, slipping lower until they reach the hem of his pants, and then—

"Wait." Emyr sucks in a breath, pulling back enough to

put some cool air between his chest and mine, to pause the moment.

I freeze, hands exactly where they are, eyes meeting his. "Hmm?"

"I, um. Well, I don't have any protective tonic." A witch concoction, old fae birth control. "Or a condom."

"I do." Tucked in my phone case, a little emergency *what if*. Don't come unless you're prepared, or however that saying goes.

"Oh." Emyr's eyes shift from my face to my mouth to the floor.

A beat passes. "But we also don't have to. We can be done." I shift in his lap, pulling back slightly so I'm resting closer to his knees than his hips. "Do you wanna be done?"

"No! No, I just... Not *that*. Not yet. That okay?"

It occurs to me that I'm the first and only person Emyr has ever kissed, and this night has already probably been a lot for him, going from zero to a hundred in a few strokes, so: "Of course that's okay."

I reach up to press my hand to his neck, thumb brushing at his jaw, nail scratching gently up behind his earlobe. "What do you want to do?"

Emyr's tongue trails against his lower lip. I watch it slide between his fangs. He looks like he's about to say something, lips parting wider, then sliding closed. Finally, he lets out a heavy breath. "I want to do something *neither* of us has ever done before."

Oh.

Oh.

Emyr must take my blip of hesitation as something it isn't,

because he quickly starts to add, "We don't have to. I know you said—your scars—it's just—"

"You've already seen my scars," I remind him, and I roll off his lap.

One of his knit blankets finds its way beneath my head. His mouth finds its way to the scars on my rib cage, my belly button, lower, lower. My hands find themselves on his horns again.

I can't see his face when Emyr whispers, *"Fuck,"* but I can feel his hot breath against my skin.

And this moment *is* all there is.

This night.

This cabin.

Emyr's mouth.

After, his claws scrape little white rivers up and down my belly while I stare at the ceiling and try to remember what breathing normally feels like.

"I've been thinking about what you said this morning," he says quietly, thumb claw circling my naval, scratching the edges without hurting. "About giving up the Throne for you."

"Not right now, okay?" I mumble, reaching down and pressing my mouth to his palm.

Somewhere across the room, Emyr's phone dings. He ignores it, watching me kissing his hand, eyebrows tugged together.

"We're going to talk about it. I just want to pretend everything's okay for another minute."

He looks like he's thinking about saying whatever it is, anyway. His phone dings again. Then again. He growls, glancing in its direction.

"Go talk to whoever that is instead, Your Highness," I mumble, swatting lightly at his hip.

Emyr rolls his eyes, pushing himself to his feet and loping to the counter.

I find my discarded boxers, tug them back into place, then go in search of my own phone, shoved away with my hoodie. There are three missed texts from Briar.

Just seeing her name is enough to bring me crashing back down to reality. The door to Faery is out there standing wide open. Anyone could accidentally crawl through it at any time, could end up in that same desolate wasteland that killed Leonidas's soldiers. There are plenty of awful people in Asalin, but there are just as many, maybe more, who are just trying to live their lives and do their best. We have to close the door. And if Briar can't figure out how to fix it, I'm going to have to tell Emyr, even if she hates me for it.

Although, with all his interest in Faery, he may not be so keen on closing it right away, either. In which case, I have no idea what I'm going to do.

The content of her messages, though, is possibly even more concerning.

MY GIRL
Wyatt, I know you're angry at me, and you have every right to be, but I need to talk to you. It's important. Meet me in our room and bring Emyr.

I AM NOT KIDDING. WHERE ARE YOU?

We're coming to the cabin. You better be there. If Emyr is with you, DO NOT LET HIM OUT OF YOUR SIGHT.

Something inside my body *jolts* forward. It's like I've had the air snatched out of me, like someone's just reached into my body and yanked something free from my skin. I yelp, jumping and shaking my limbs out to try and rid myself of the overwhelming feeling of weirdness that's suddenly all over me. It isn't really *painful* so much as surprising and...odd.

"Hey, what—"

A crash interrupts me, and my head shoots up.

Emyr is back on the ground, only this time he's barely holding himself up on one palm. His wings have shot straight back, their protective spikes ejected, each one convulsing. Blood mingled with black sludge begins to trickle from his mouth. He turns his eyes to me—gold magic has spilled into them, but it's now spilled out of them, too, leaking down across his cheeks.

The world narrows down to nothing but his body on the floor. I race to him. I think I'm screaming but I don't know what I'm saying. I don't know if I'm making any sound at all or if the words have been snatched from my chest. My knees hit the floor at his side.

Maybe I'm screaming his name.

His golden eyes widen as he looks up at me. One hand reaches for my wrist, curls around my fragile bones, and squeezes. His claws dig into my skin until I'm bleeding over the both of us. I reach out with my other hand, curling my fingers around his neck.

Maybe I'm still screaming his name.

I think he tries to speak, but only more sludge bubbles out.

The cabin door flies open. We aren't alone anymore. Bod
ies are suddenly filling the space, crowding in all around us.

But it doesn't matter. Beneath my touch, Emyr's pulse slows
and slows until the rhythm ends altogether. His heart stops
beating.

He's dead.

CHAPTER TWENTY-FIVE

THE UNDERBELLY OF PREY BEFORE
A PREDATOR STRIKES

From the moment I first set eyes on Emyr after all our years apart, that split second in Texas with garden shears stabbed through him, when my heart tried to claw its way out of my throat and throw itself into his arms, I'd known I didn't *actually* want to hurt him.

Love, this kind of love, the kind that grows up and out of your bone marrow like roots curling in tight, isn't that easy to get rid of. It doesn't always mean it's healthy. Love can cleave to your insides, envelop and consume you, overwhelm you, and still be bad for you. Sometimes you gotta take a knife to love, you gotta cut it out, cauterize your wounds, and move on.

That's what I thought I was planning to do. I was going to cut Emyr out of me, and cut out whatever part of me had to go in order to do it.

It took remembering who Emyr was, seeing that the boy I knew still existed, for me to realize I was wrong. Cutting him out of me wouldn't be like removing bone rot with a scalpel; it'd be like amputating a perfectly healthy limb with nothing but a pocketknife.

Because he was *good*. He was good and he was gentle and he was kind in ways I have no idea how to be, and he made me feel things no one else ever made me feel, and even if it meant giving up on everything I'd ever wanted for myself, there was a part of me that wanted to say yes.

But it doesn't matter. In the end, none of it meant anything. Not his goodness. Not my bleeding, naive, feral heart.

Because now Emyr is dead on the floor in front of me. He's just dead. He's never going to make coffee again or tend to his flock or take a long nap in his hammock. He's never going to travel the world with me like he wanted, seeing human sights and reading human books. He's never going to smile again so wide that dimples etch themselves into the corners of his mouth. His energy is never again going to glow so brightly it outshines the sun.

I know there are others in the room, people trying to pull me away, people trying to check on Emyr, but I can't comprehend what's going on. I don't see them, I don't hear them. There's only Emyr's lifeless body, still warm and soft but covered in blood and bile and black muck.

Am I still screaming?

"Wyatt." A choked whisper cuts through the static in my

ears. A familiar warmth drapes across my back, Briar pressing herself into me from behind, holding me as tightly as she can. I can feel her energy overtaking me, pressing past the boundary of my body to sink into my very skin. Like the strength of her love might be enough to keep me together, to keep my bones from coming undone. "Oh, Wyatt."

How is Emyr dead? How is he the one lying on this floor, lifeless, when he's the good one? He's soft and radiant and kind and he would have made a *good* king. He was a beautiful boy with a beautiful heart and a warm soul and he didn't deserve to die. And I'm nothing. I'm just an asshole with a violent streak who's never cared about anyone except myself. And I'm here, breathing air I don't deserve.

I would do anything to trade places with him.

And then the world goes black.

At first, I think I did it. Somehow, I did trade places with Emyr, and now I'm dead and he's going to come back to life. But I can still hear Briar whispering my name. And there are other voices, too. The king and queen crying out for their son. Tessa, Wade, Clarke. Derek? All of them are here with me, in this cabin, in the dark.

I'm not dead. The blackness surrounding us now is the same darkness that settled over us the night of the riot, the darkness that ripped Unicorn Boy to shreds. A magic I don't understand, that feels even more impossible to control.

Is it going to kill *me* this time?

Maybe it should. Without Emyr, what good is Asalin? Without his light and strength, without his sharp mind and tender heart, what is there in this kingdom that's worth saving?

Maybe this magic should take me out before I make good on my threat to burn it all to the ground.

Beneath my skin, Briar's energy shifts and tugs, pulling at the ventricles of my heart. I can feel her breath against the back of my neck. In my arms, Emyr's body is still warm.

No.

No, I'm not going to do that.

I don't want to destroy anything else.

Slowly, the darkness all around me is joined by something new. Flecks of light begin to appear, tiny specks of gold weaving themselves into the fabric of my black magic. One or two at first, then a dozen, then a hundred, then hundreds of tiny stars lighting up the darkness like constellations. Hundreds of little suns warming up my personal midnight sky.

Just as it did the first time, it recedes into my skin, black and gold disappearing *together* into my body.

And Emyr lies in my arms, his pulse even against the palm of my hand, his big brown eyes blinking up at me.

"Wyatt?"

Behind me, Briar pulls back and whispers, "Holy shit."

My universe tilts.

"Emyr." I lean down to press my face into his throat, dragging in the smell of him, the warmth of him, the *alive-ness* of him.

Kadri hits her knees beside us, brushing her fingers through Emyr's hair, kissing his face. "Sweet boy. Beautiful boy." She whispers the words through tears. "How did you do this? How did you bring him back?"

I don't know. I don't know anything about my own magic. I never have.

I do know that Healing magic is the rarest and most complicated of all the fae skills. Even Emyr struggled to heal Clarke when she was close to death's doorstep, and she was still alive.

Kadri was brought back once, and it took a congregation of the most powerful Healers in Asalin.

Seriously...what the hell did I do?

"I died?" Emyr asks, still staring at me.

I brush my fingertips against the base of one horn. "You died. And it was a real dick move, I gotta tell you. Talk about hit it and quit it."

The joke might've been funnier if I'd managed to stop myself from breaking into a sob halfway through.

Emyr swallows. "Sorry. Won't happen again."

I curl myself around him, holding on to him as tightly as I can while not shoving his mother away. Every breath he takes feels like a gift. I can't lose him.

How did I ever think I could cut this boy out of my chest?

"That Wyatt brought him back is irrelevant," Derek says, shaking his head. He waves a hand at a small fleet of Guards at his back, fae I hadn't even realized were here until now. "When we know he's the one who killed him. Take the boy into custody."

Wait, what?

"It wasn't him!" Briar jumps to her feet and flings her whole body in front of the Guard who takes a step toward me, yellow energy exploding out in every direction.

I can't seem to make myself let go of Emyr, but my black flies forward to twist itself together with her yellow, our energies weaving into each other.

"He was the only one here, was he not? And we know his motives. We've all seen the video."

"What video?" I ask, glancing around the room, hands tightening on Emyr's bare skin.

Tessa makes a face at me. "Derek has shown us all a clip of you…in the maze garden. Telling him you would do whatever it took to get out of this engagement."

"You were recording me?" Only the part of the conversation that made me look guilty, it would seem.

"I was." A hint of a smile, cruel as a blade, teases at Derek's mouth. "It would appear Emyr's modernizations are useful, after all. I never would've had the phone to make the recording without his *upgrades*."

I can only blink at him for a long moment.

You could have avoided what happens next. Remember that.

Derek did this. Somehow, he's the one who killed Emyr. And now I'm being framed for it.

"Take the boy into custody," Kadri growls, reaching up to slam her hands against my shoulders, trying to shove me off her son. "Now!"

"Wait." Emyr groans, struggling to sit up, to push his body between his mother and me. "It wasn't him. I know who it was. It just…doesn't make any sense."

The Guards look to Derek. Derek is glaring at the floor, pale face mottled with furious red splotches, nostrils flaring. "Who?"

Emyr shakes his head. "Jin."

"Jin Ueno?" Kadri demands, eyebrows shooting up. "How is that possible?"

"They sent me…a document… I downloaded it, and…"

He frowns, voice trailing off, eyes sliding across the floor to that magicked iPhone-knockoff.

The dings right before he...*temporarily* died.

Me, refusing to talk to him about our future, telling him to go talk to his phone instead.

"Jin Ueno is long gone from Asalin by now." Leonidas claps his hands together with authority. "We will gather a search party to find them. They cannot outrun this."

"With all due respect, Your Majesty," Tessa says in a way which conveys she believes absolutely no respect is due, "we have been *trying* to explain to you that Jin Ueno is no longer in possession of their phone."

The messages in Briar's phone.

Hey, dollface. (: It's Jin. Clarke finally managed to smuggle my phone out to me. Can we talk?

Why are you ignoring me? :(

Where are you?

Derek growls. "You can prove nothing."

"We can, though," Briar snaps. "Jin and I have been in contact since they left."

"A crime for which you will be sentenced to death in ways far more unpleasant than you would in a human court," Derek responds, shaking his head.

"Eat me, knockoff-Nazi." Briar rolls her shoulders back. "Jin was wrongly imprisoned to begin with. And it wasn't *them* who was trying to hunt me down today."

And then, in her usual fashion of overdramatics, Clarke *sighs*. "Oh, give it up, Derek. They have all the pieces put together. It's over."

Every eye in the room turns to her. Her shoulders straighten, her chin tilting up. And her energy...

I can't explain it. It's not different, not changing, but it's like for the first time I'm seeing it in a new way. The soft pink cradling her body isn't cotton candy or bubblegum, it's not sugary sweet the way I always thought it was.

No. This pink is the underbelly of prey before a predator strikes. It's the sky before the sun vanishes and night descends. It's the glistening snakeskin shed by a copperhead. It's blood and water running in diluted rivulets down the drain, hiding evidence of her crimes. It's organ and muscle tissue when flesh has been ripped open.

Clarke did this.

"I am so sick," she finally says, "of men screwing everything up."

"So, you admit to this?" Leonidas asks, voice roughened with shock. "You used the witch's phone? You tried to kill my *son*?"

"Of course I did." She shrugs one delicate shoulder.

One of the Guards grabs her arms and yanks them behind her back, snapping those iron cuffs around her wrists.

She doesn't seem fazed. In fact, she *giggles*. "You know, Wyatt, I really thought you would have figured it out a long time ago. After your magic tried to off me."

"What are you talking about?" I can barely form words my head is spinning too fast.

"You're the one who killed the witch," Tessa says behind me. "Jin found your bodies together. You did that, didn't you?"

Lavender? Clarke...

Clarke killed Lavender.

But what does that have to do with my magic?

Clarke just shrugs. "Mmm. Really, Wyatt, your little black hole trick seriously did not like me. It tried to stop me from ripping the witch's throat out. Too late, though."

I was the one who almost killed Clarke the night of the riot? If what she's saying is true, when the darkness jumped out of my body and consumed Unicorn Boy, when it tore him to shreds, it tried to do the same thing to her, hidden just outside. Only we didn't realize it at the time.

Seriously, *Clarke* is the one who killed *Lavender*?

Briar shakes her head. "What about Jin? How could you do this to them? You're *bound* to each other. You love each other."

"I am not allowed to love them." Clarke's pretty blue eyes have taken on a wild quality, too big for her face, too glassy to see clearly. "The bond was unexpected, but it presented an opportunity. Do you know how easy it is to convince a room full of people you're on their side once you learn the language? All I had to do was be self-deprecating and talk about all my *fae privilege*, and every fool there was lapping it up."

She laughs like glass breaking.

This is going to kill Jin, I think. I'm just glad they aren't here to see this.

Clarke sighs. "I kept my eye on Wyatt here, and it didn't take me long to realize there was no way he was going to go through with Derek's plan—oh, you don't know about that, hmm? Right. Derek thought he could convince Wyatt to ruin Emyr's shot at the throne all by himself. *I* was only ever the backup plan. But as it turned out, the little witchling couldn't even get *fucking up* right. Why do we ever send men to do women's jobs? I only needed to get my hands on Jin's phone. The arrests certainly made that more convenient, didn't they?"

Leonidas appears to be getting with the program. "The riot was started on purpose. As a means to this horrific end."

"How did you ever think you were going to get away with this?" Fury seeps into every inflection in Briar's voice.

"Well, I never planned on Emyr rising from the dead and opening his big mouth." Clarke tilts her head at Wade. "And I certainly never planned on my own brother selling me out to his girlfriend. Tessa's been on my ass since the protests."

"You knew about this?" Emyr demands, gaze shooting to Wade.

Wade, horrified, shakes his head. "No! Well." He frowns, hands curling and uncurling. "I knew, that night, whose side Clarke was really on. That she was only pretending. But I never thought she would do this—I thought I could convince her to change her alliance. If I'd had any idea…"

His voice trails off, and he and Emyr stare at each other.

The night of the riots, when I saw Wade and Clarke arguing in the woods. I'd thought it was Clarke trying to convince her brother to stand with her, to stand with the witches. But she wasn't. It was the other way around.

Planned. This whole thing's been planned, maybe since the moment I got here. I was always going to be their scapegoat.

"You'll be executed for this." Leonidas shakes his head, staring at his niece as if seeing a stranger. "Have you no remorse?"

"Remorse? I did what needed to be done. I am a *heroine*."

"For attempting to kill your own cousin?" Briar demands.

"For trying to assassinate the prince, just so your brother can have the Throne? In what world does that make you a good person?"

"Do you think this is only about Derek?" Clarke scoffs, shaking her head. "You people really are so shortsighted. I am *saving everyone*."

"From what?" The question snaps from my tongue like the crack of a whip.

It's Derek who speaks up. "From the destruction of life as we know it. Every move Emyr makes puts us in danger. Coalescing with the humans? Thoughts of opening the door to Faery once more?"

It takes every ounce of willpower I have not to look at Briar.

Oops?

"Reopening that door would kill us all, wouldn't it, Uncle?" he continues, raising his eyebrows at Leonidas.

Slowly, my gaze drifts across the room to land on the king. Stiff, staring slack-jawed at his nephew, he can only shake his head. "I don't know what you're talking about."

"Really?" Clarke giggles that maniacal giggle again. "Because Derek told me all about what *really* happened in Faery, and—"

"Enough!"

The force of Leonidas's roar is enough to rustle the wings of every other fae in the cabin. I press myself tight to Emyr's body, black barbs threading into the air around us. I do not like listening to cis men yell. It makes me want to rip out their larynxes. And after the night I've had, Leonidas North does *not* want to push me.

"Leonidas?" Kadri's voice is cold as she rises to her feet and turns toward her husband. "Is there something you would like to tell us?"

The king's face pales.

Clarke sighs, shaking her head so that her bundle of blond curls bounces around her face. "I suppose I'll have to be the one to do it. So, here it is. Are you ready? Faery is inhabitable. And Uncle Leo knows this."

Wait...what? Briar and I find one another's eyes again, but I quickly look away. We still haven't heard any accusations about the open door. I don't want to draw attention.

The group gathered casts their glances around, confusion bubbling along the energy in the room. Even the Guards standing attention at Derek's side don't seem to know what's really going on.

"Leonidas," Kadri says firmly. "You will stop gaping as if your brain is oozing from your eardrums and tell me what these children are speaking of."

Leonidas winces, and his voice is soft when he begins to speak. "When our group entered Faery, it was a wasteland. But things...were not as bad as they could have been. Over time, it appears the climate there has shifted back. Life is possible in that realm. We encountered some of it."

"Life? Like nature?"

"Yes...among other things." He swallows, eyes unfocused as if he isn't in this room at all. As if he's reliving the story itself. "There were animals. And—and fae. But you have to understand, these fae were like animals themselves. Primitive, wild. They've adapted to their new world by turning to carnage. They attacked us as soon as we were spotted."

"Why?" Wade demands. "Why would they attack their own kind?"

"Because five hundred years ago, we left their ancestors to rot," Derek offers. "We fled to Earth to escape Faery's destruction and we left them to deal with it alone. Everyone believed they would all die, that no one could survive what was happening to that planet. And perhaps death would have been kinder than what they actually became. Now, they aren't only beasts. They're beasts whose history paints us as the greatest villains of all time."

My blood runs cold.

No. That can't be right. What they're saying definitely cannot be true, because—

"Why keep this a secret?" Tessa asks, shaking her head. "Why lie about what you saw?"

"Because if he did that, he'd have to come clean about the people he killed while he was there," Derek answers smoothly. "Anyone in his own group who wanted to reason with the inhabitants of Faery, who wanted to try and bring them back through the door to Earth. My father and a small handful of others were the only members of his campaign to make it back alive."

"It was a risk we could not take!" Leonidas argues. "You didn't see these creatures! You don't know what they are capable of!"

And Briar's impulsive blood magic has left the door wide open for them to walk right through whenever they want.

"You killed Lavender because you wanted the witches disbanded," Briar says quietly, eyes on Clarke. "Because they were beginning to talk about opening the door."

"I was protecting the whole world," Clarke says, and I think she believes it. "Sometimes people have to die for the greater good. You don't understand that yet. But you will, soon. Soon, you will *all* understand."

"For the love of shit, what is she talking about now?" Wade groans, snatching a fistful of his hair.

Clarke turns her big, glassy eyes on him. "Can't you feel it? *This world* is dying now, too. Just like Faery was, all those years ago. But we have the chance to save it. If all the humans were gone, we might have a chance of saving it. This is why integration is not possible. This is why Emyr's plans to modernize and adapt *hurt* us more than help. We cannot acclimate any longer. We have to overcome."

The ease with which she speaks of genocide silences the room in one hush.

It's Briar who finds her voice first. "You really are like every other colonizer who's come before you, aren't you?"

Clarke's gaze flicks to Briar's face. *Don't like that, don't like that one bit.* My black magic swirls up and around her body, a cloak. "You think that now, but you don't understand. We are the victims here. We are forced to live in hiding, to protect ourselves from what the humans might do, from what *Faery* might do. We are only trying to survive."

"You are not hiding," Briar snarls. "You sit comfortably in your kingdoms, using prophecy and influence to grow richer instead of doing anything to help heal the planet you've usurped. You say you fear what humans might do if they find out about you. But those humans, the *rightful* inhabitants of the ground you walk on, have no idea there are real-life mon sters lying in wait for them. You are not victims. You are a plague, biding your time."

A beat passes. Clarke juts out her lower lip. "That was not very nice."

"Take them to the dungeons," Kadri demands, and all eyes turn to look at Derek.

Clarke might've been the backup plan, but Derek was still the one moving pieces on the chessboard.

The Guards at either side of him hesitate. They don't grab for him, don't reach for their cuffs. Not right away. They give him a moment's head start to throw open the front door.

Boom leaps up, snarling, saliva dripping from his massive teeth. His paws fall heavy against Derek's shoulders and nearly take the fae off his feet.

Instead of falling, Derek wheels around toward us again, like he's looking for another way out. His wings shoot out, his eyes going wild. Magic begins to build in his hands and spread up his arms, something dangerous and electric sparking along his skin. That blue energy, like a fog, begins to fill the cabin, and as his magic swells, the very plants lining Emyr's walls begin to wither and die right before our eyes.

"You will never—"

Wade's fist slams hard enough against Derek's jaw that something *cracks*. Derek lets out a yowl, and the magic sloughs right off him as he hits his knees. The Guards finally seem to remember their jobs, scrambling to get him in the cuffs.

"Anyone else tired of listening to straight men speak?" Wade asks, shaking out his fist and looking down at his knuckles. Tessa *tsks*, taking his hand in hers.

As the Guards drag the siblings from the cabin, everyone

moves to the sides to clear a path for them. Only Emyr and I stay where we are, him still lying across my lap, my arms still curled around him.

Clarke meets Briar's eye as she passes and gives a small, nearly imperceptible shake of her head. "It's a pity. You really are so cute. I was even thinking of letting you live."

Tessa curls her free hand around Briar's shoulder. It might be the only thing that prevents another Pierce with a broken jaw.

CHAPTER TWENTY-SIX

LONG LIVE THE KING

The next day, Tessa comes to my room and tells me Leonidas and Kadri are stepping down from the Throne. I suspect, and she does, too, it's because of what happened in Faery, the truth Leonidas has been hiding from everyone, even his wife. The rest of the Court is headed to Asalin for an emergency conclave to crown Emyr. He'll be king before the week's end.

I text him from my bed.

can we talk?

i heard about your parents. are you okay?

please say something.

Briar comes in and out. We don't talk much. At least not

with our mouths. She touches the back of my hand. I squeeze her wrist.

The door between us reopens.

We'll be okay. We'll figure it out. Just not right now.

I forget to draw a card.

The day after, Wade, Tessa, Briar, and I sit on the balcony and watch as members of the Court start to appear.

"Amin and Pari Darwish, King and Queen of Oflewyn, the fae kingdom of Eurasia," Wade whispers.

Amin Darwish's energy is *bright* red. It sort of reminds me of a candy apple from the fair. It bounces around the court-yard as soon as his car door opens, the first thing any of us can see. He's smiling when he steps out, dark brown hair fall-ing in the sort of devil-may-care way that *looks* effortless but probably takes a lot of time to perfect.

His wings are ridiculous. They look like peacock feathers, massive blue and green swirls sticking straight up from his back. Two simple, nondescript black horns sit on either side of his forehead.

Amin takes Pari's hand and the two of them make their way up the steps to the spot where Kadri and Leonidas are waiting, looking somber. Pari's energy couldn't be more dif-ferent from her husband's. Hers is a dark navy blue that wraps around her like a cocoon, a protective shield between her and the world. Her baby-pink headscarf and bright white dress clinging to her rounded belly are a stark contrast to her golden skin, nearly every visible inch of which seems to be decorated with tattoos, intricate designs in dark brown ink.

Her wings are strange, thin strips of what looks like scales sliding down behind her back. But it's her horns that are the most unusual thing about Pari. They start at her temples and wind *down* instead of up, like most horns do. They slope down to meet in front of her nose, the tips of each horn almost touching each other just above her upper lip.

She's one of the most unique-looking people I've ever seen.

As soon as they reach the top of the stairs, Pari and Kadri embrace like long-lost friends, the queens wrapping their arms around one another. Pari says something against Kadri's ear and Kadri smiles, reaching down to press her hand against the other woman's baby bump.

"Robin and Gordon Bell," Wade tells us sometime later when the next car arrives. "King and King of Monalai, the fae kingdom of Oceania."

Robin Bell is a mountain of a man, taller even than Jin and almost as wide as he is tall. His oversize brown wings and massive antlers, the furs he wears around his huge body, and the giant, bushy beard hanging down to his gut only make him look bigger. As if to avoid taking up any more space than he already does, his energy, a diluted yellow-green color, just sort of flops around him.

On the contrary, Gordon Bell is built more like me than his husband. He's a tiny, slender little guy with fluffy gray wings and sharp silver horns like blades. His energy is so dark gray it could be black in dim lighting, and it spreads across the courtyard like smoke.

Their driver, a witch, unloads a wheelchair from the back of the SUV, and Gordon slides into it. Another witch holds her hand above the palace steps until they transform before our very eyes into a ramp.

From inside the car, Robin produces two very fat, happy-looking babies, and hands one to his now-seated husband.

"So many babies," Briar coos, leaning forward to watch the tiny fae children bouncing in their fathers' arms. Their itty-bitty wings jut out from their onesies, the twins' teeny little horns almost concealed behind tousled curls.

"Must be mating season," I mumble in response, watching as the family of four walks right past Kadri and Leonidas and into the palace.

Wade drags one claw against the balcony railing. I don't know how much time has passed between one kingdom's arrival and the next. "Loureen and Calvince Muia, Queen and King of Kitaraq, the fae kingdom of Africa."

I assume—and seriously hope—these people aren't lugging around a baby with them, because they look to be about seven billion years old. Or at least a hundred.

Loureen's horns—long, slender, and brown—are curled in a circle around the top of her head. They're tangled in with the white coils of her hair, the whole thing looking sort of like a (very elegant) bird's nest. Her wings are huge, gray downy feathers, hanging down gracefully from the tops of her shoulders. She moves slowly but fluidly, like she's gliding through water, and her movements don't betray her age the way her many wrinkles do.

Calvince's horns—either brown or black, it's hard to tell from here—curl out from either side of his head, his delicate, translucent wings wrapped around his shoulders. He looks tired and more than slightly irritable. Loureen reaches out and takes his hand, and he relaxes, albeit only slightly.

But it's their energy that fascinates me the most. *Energy*, singular, because I have no idea where hers ends and his begins. One color surrounds them, a sparkling, pearlescent white, speckled with hints of green and pink and purple, like the surface of an opal.

It's beautiful. You know, for old people.

By the time the last car arrives, it's past nightfall.

"Paloma and Maritza Pereira—"

"I'm well aware of who these two are," I cut Wade off, shaking my head.

Paloma slides out of the back seat, dragging Maritza along with her, a wicked grin stretching wide enough to take up her whole mouth.

Leonidas shouts something, pointing an accusatory finger in their direction. Angry for the late hour?

Maritza takes a step forward, but Paloma wraps an arm around her wife's middle and kisses her neck, that smile never fading. She says something in response to Leonidas's yelling, and whatever it is must shut him up. Because the queens simply drift right past him, up the stairs.

Just before going inside, Paloma turns her head up and finds my eye. Despite the distance between us, I know she's looking right at me. And she *winks*.

I text Emyr.

> i would really like to be there. i know you're upset with me, and i understand why. but i'm still your fiancé, right? i should still be with you when you take the crown. i want to be there for you. please.

No answer ever comes. Hours later, on the edge of sleep,
I try again.

has it already happened?

Still nothing. I dream of dragons setting Asalin's forest
ablaze.

"How could you be sure I hadn't done it?" I asked Briar
the next afternoon as we walk through the woods to reach
the cabin. "When all of you burst in and saw him lying
there. You'd seen Derek's video. You knew I was trying to
get out of the contract by any means necessary. How could
you know, beyond a shadow of a doubt, I hadn't done something to him?"

"I just knew."

"*How?*"

Briar sighs. There's something haunted in her expression.
"You didn't see yourself, Wyatt. You were...you were torn
open by what'd happened. I took one look at you and I just
knew. There was no way you could've done it." She shrugs.
"Besides, we were pretty convinced by that point that Clarke
had done something somehow. Just didn't know exactly what.
God, this is going to *kill* Jin."

I shake my head. "No, trusting Clarke might've killed Jin.
This is going to save them."

Briar catches my eye, hesitates, then nods.

After another beat of silence, I ask, "Has anyone mentioned
the door? Have you heard anything?"

Briar sighs, shaking her head. "No. Nothing. You?"

"Nothing." I take a deep breath. "Briar, you know— "

"I know. It was one thing when we thought there was no one on the other side. But if what Leonidas said is true, if there are...worse fae over there, we can't keep this between us. I'm still working with Lavender's sigils, trying to piece together the spell to close the door. But if I can't...we have to tell Emyr, either way."

I'm glad she was the one to say it. Even though we both know it's true, I understand now how important her family's secret is to her. I didn't want to be the one to force her to reveal herself to Emyr. The healing happening between Briar and me is tenuous, her words still hovering at the periphery of my thoughts.

Do you have any idea how hard it is being everything you need me to be all the time?

It's possible I haven't been the kind of friend Briar needed. While I was figuring myself out, while I was trying to survive being in my own head, she was always there keeping me upright. Hell, even when I broke up with her, hurt her, she didn't let it show, not once, that things weren't going to be totally okay. I should work on being a better friend.

"All anyone can seem to talk about is Derek and Clarke," I finally say.

Briar makes a face, shaking her head. "What happened with them, anyway?"

"The Court has sentenced them to death for their conspiracies." I heard the ruling come down this morning. "Derek's wife, Martha, managed to convince the Court she didn't know anything about her husband's plans, but I think they probably just felt weird about burning a woman alive when she's nine months pregnant."

"Huh." Briar clicks her tongue at me.

Huh indeed.

I also haven't spoken to Emyr since that night, since Kadri finally pulled him from my arms and took him back to the palace. I have no idea what'll be waiting for me when I walk into the cabin. I know he's there only because Wade told me—after swearing me to secrecy, like the two of us were committing treason—he'd seen him slipping out earlier in the morning.

Boom lets out a loud bark when we come into view of the flower-speckled cabin and its field of peryton, racing up to meet us. He noses Briar's hand until she reaches under his chin to give him a little scratch.

After a moment, she awkwardly clears her throat. "I'm gonna go check on the flock. Holler if you need me."

"Okay."

She squeezes my hand. *I hope this goes the way you want it to, Wyatt.*

I squeeze hers back. My chest hurts. *Yeah, me, too.*

Boom trots behind me as I head to the front door, and I reach down to rub him behind his ears. "Your other dad inside?"

He woofs at me, moving back into the house. I follow after, tucking my hands into the front pocket of my hoodie.

Emyr lies in the hammock in the center of the room, staring blank-eyed up at the ceiling overhead. His energy is small and dull, a foggy hint of gold clinging to his skin. He doesn't turn his head my way, not even when I silently climb into the hammock at his feet.

"Hey."

"Hey."

Upon his head, intricately shaped to accommodate his horns, sits a circlet made of finely woven gold and multicolored gems.

Long live the king.

"How are you feeling?" It's such a weak question and I know that, but I don't know what else to ask.

"Okay, I guess."

Silence settles over us. Boom makes a disgruntled noise before curling into a ball on his dog bed.

Finally, Emyr asks, "So, when are you leaving?"

"What?"

He looks at me for the first time, raising his eyebrows. "You're going back to Laredo with Briar, aren't you? Now that all of this is over?"

"I..." I shake my head. "Sorry, what? Why would I do that?"

"Because you aren't trapped in the contract anymore."

I can only blink at him. I don't understand. I mean, I know the meaning of the words he's saying individually, but it's like, together, strung in a sentence, my brain has no idea what to do with them.

"What?"

"No one told you? I assumed it would be all over the palace by now. You know how quickly gossip moves."

I shake my head. I can feel acid rising in my stomach and worming its way into my chest.

He considers me for a moment. I don't dare to interrupt the silence. Finally, he asks, "Do you remember the terms of our contract?"

"Of course I do." We were so young when it was written. But it was the center of my life for so long. I went over it, with my parents, with Emyr, alone in my own head, over and over again, until I knew it backward and forward.

"The termination clauses?"

"Obviously." I can't seem to make myself move, body made of lead. "If either of us broke the contract, the other could trigger the blood magic. It would...our blood would destroy us from the inside...that's what happened to you?"

Emyr turns his head away and nods. "Only, instead of calling it in on you, I called it in on myself. I set my intention to break the contract, without even realizing what I was doing until it was too late. I triggered my own death."

I can't hear him talk about dying without full-body flinching.

And still, what?

Of course, I remember Clarke telling me about Jin's digitizing the contract, uploading it to their own version of the internet. So, she got her hands on it. She got him to call it in, to use the very magic I'd worried he might use against me, against himself.

And he came back from the dead, but...

The contract can't be unbroken.

I'm free.

Why do I feel like there's a pile of rocks sitting in my lungs right now?

"I'm still not sure how she did it. The coding, the magic itself, it's complicated spellcraft. The sort of thing a powerful witch might be able to accomplish, but not *Clarke*."

"You think she and Derek have a witch on their side? Why would any witch partner with them?"

"I don't really know what to think about anything anymore." Emyr takes a deep breath. "Maybe it's for the best. After everything, and now knowing you conspired with Derek, no one wants you near the Throne. I had to convince the Court not to stick you in the dungeon alongside him."

"Emyr, I—"

"I know." He nods, running his fingers through his curls and looking away from me again. "I know, you were only doing what you had to do."

"That's not what I was going to say. God, Emyr, I—I made my plans with Derek when I first got here. Okay? Before— before things changed between us. Before I realized who he is, who *you* are." I think back to Derek shoving me against the wall, his smell and his energy pushing in on me and drowning out my thoughts. "And I'm fairly certain he's been Influencing me this whole time."

Emyr glances over at me with his eyebrows raised but says nothing.

Nerves make my hands shake, desperation clawing at me. I need him to understand. Ever since I got back to Asalin, Emyr's been trying to convince me to give him a chance. But now he's given up on me, right at the moment when I need him not to. And it's all my fault. I'm going to be sick. "Look, I *love* you. I'm a disaster, and I'm going to keep being a disaster, probably, but I love you."

Breaking free of the contract is all I've wanted for years. Every night, I've dreamed of this moment. Finally having my autonomy, my freedom, to do whatever I want.

And it feels completely and totally hollow. Because this… this is not what I want.

Emyr swallows. "Maybe you do. But that doesn't change the fact that this isn't the life you want, is it?"

I want to argue. I *need* to argue, to tell him that he's wrong, but my tongue feels like it's made of cotton. I can't seem to make it work, can't seem to form words, can hardly seem to breathe through a mouthful of static.

"Your life is in the human world. Everything you love, everything you value, is out there."

"Not everything."

He sighs, shaking his head. "You asked me if I would choose you over the Throne. And I thought, for a moment, that I could. There was a part of me that wanted to. But this is my kingdom, Wyatt. These are my people. And this is bigger than the two of us."

"I never should have asked you to do that."

"But you did. And it's all right that you did, because it's how you feel. You don't want to be king. And I can't blame you. Especially now, knowing what's likely coming next."

I want to argue with him, but he isn't wrong. That isn't what I want. That's never been what I wanted, and that hasn't changed just because I've gone soft and caught feelings for him.

I continue to stare.

"You would be miserable. I thought we could work past it, but I realize now that this isn't your home. This isn't where you want to be. And I—" He sucks in a deep breath, looking down at his hands, curling them into fists. "I love *you* too much to trap you somewhere you don't want to be."

Something inside me breaks open. Tears sting my eyes, blurring my vision. I drag my knees against my chest, pressing my chin against them and wrapping my arms around my shins. For a long moment, we just watch each other. Finally, I mumble, "Will I ever see you again?"

"I don't know. It might—it might be too hard."

Shit. I reach up to swipe my hand against my face, rubbing away the tears that have managed to escape. "What about the bond? You said—you said you could feel me, every moment that I was away. You said you couldn't lose me again."

"It turns out I can survive more than I thought. I bested death, after all. I'll find a way to live through this."

I laugh, but it isn't really a laugh. To my own ears, I sound like a whining animal. "We're supposed to be together, aren't we? What about the bond?"

"You never did believe in the bond," he says quietly. "Fuck genetic compatibility, right? It doesn't have to mean anything."

I think of Paloma and Maritza, bound together even though they can't have children. Kadri and Leonidas, fated even though she never produced an heir. I think of the way Emyr looks at me, that hungry and wide-open look I'm not sure I'm ever going to see on his face again.

The fae have it wrong. I don't think this bond has anything to do with *biology*. And if I leave now, if I disappear from Asalin and never return, I'll probably never know what it really is.

"What happens next?" I ask, finally finished wiping my tears.

"I'll arrange for a flight to take you home tomorrow afternoon. I assume you want to return to Laredo with Briar?"

Briar.

Right. The door to Faery. All of that, and I still have to stand here and tell him about Briar and the changelings and the door to Faery standing wide open.

"Um…" I sniff, tilting my head up to consider the ceiling. "I guess. Sure. But, uh. We need to talk about—"

"Wyatt." Emyr's voice cracks around the syllables of my name. He's seemed so detached most of this conversation, holding me at arm's length. But for a moment, I can see underneath it. For a moment, he looks at me and he is a wide-open wound. "I need some space, okay?"

My heart, buried underneath an impossible weight and holding on to the last strands of hope in my body, finally crumbles. I'll tell him about the door. I'll make sure he knows. But I can't stay here another minute.

As I get up to leave, Boom rises to his feet and trots after me.

Emyr and I exchange one last look. For the first time, I can hear his words without them being spoken. We're both saying the same thing.

I love you. I'm sorry.

Outside, Briar is waiting for me. She takes one look at my face and flinches.

"I have to get out of here," I whisper. Behind me, Boom nips at my arm. I turn to look at him, something in me crumbling to dust. "But you have to stay."

He whines, snapping his jaws and shaking his head.

"I know." I pull him forward, leaning in to press my forehead against his. He licks and nibbles at my jawline. "You can't come with me, buddy. My world isn't meant for you."

How can it be my world if it isn't meant for Boom? If it isn't meant for Emyr?

"Take care of him," I whisper, scrubbing my fingernails into the fur on his neck.

Pulling back, I grab Briar's hand to drag her away.

Boom's pained howls follow us all the way back to the castle.

CHAPTER TWENTY-SEVEN

LIKE TOO MUCH AND NOTHING AT ALL

Before we're out of the woods, it starts to drizzle. When we step past the tree line and water starts misting both of our heads, Briar wraps her arms around me and kisses the top of my face. Once, twice, a third time. She nuzzles my temple, her warm fingers slipping past the neck of my hoodie and making circles into the skin of my shoulder blades.

"What do you need?"

"I'm just going to go back to the room." Probably take another depression nap. I can't handle any of this.

She sighs, nodding and squeezing my arms as she finally pulls back. "You want me to come with you?"

"No, it's okay." I'm going to have some kind of meltdown, I think, and I don't need to force Briar to take care of me during another one. "You should say your goodbyes. We're leaving tomorrow."

Leaving.

Everything hurts.

"Okay. I'll go check in on Lorena and Roman." Her full lower lip wiggles between the gap in her front teeth. "I love you."

"I love you, too."

I watch her head toward the village. Only when she's out of sight do I look away.

My eyes light on the carving of Vorgaine above the palace steps, half-shrouded in moss and ivy. Those eyes, a hundred of them, all seem to be locked right on me. As if this god, this ancient, dead god carved from stone, is looking directly at me.

If Faery is alive…

I don't finish that thought. I don't have time to think about that.

There's a petite Guard standing in front of the doors, slamming her fist into her palm as she gives a heated speech to three other officers. It's only when they leave, shuddering under the weight of her shards of amethyst energy, that I realize it's *Tessa*. She catches my eye and scowls, motioning me over to her.

I don't know what to do other than to walk up. "This is new."

"I look like a fucking nerd in this getup." She bristles, rolling her eyes and slumping against the stone railing. "How did your talk with Emyr go?"

The way she asks the question, I'm pretty sure she knows

about the contract. Emyr was right. Gossip does travel in Asalin.

"Not the way I hoped," is all I can answer, because I don't want to talk about it. Even if I tried, I'm not sure actual words would come out instead of whimpering. If I'm a feral dog, I'm officially a kicked one. "You gonna tell me what this is all about? Since when are you one of the Guard?"

"Oh, no. Not *one* of the Guard. The *Head* of the Guard." Tessa points to the white lines on her red coat, the ones that mark her rank. There are five of them.

I can only blink.

She continues. "Emyr's first order as king. Said they needed to bring in someone from the outside to take Derek's position, someone he knew wasn't in league with him and his followers. Because someone here *helped him and Clarke escape last night.*"

"*What?*" Something like cold dread erupts in me, steel marbles of fear spilling over the edge of the table where my sternum sits and landing on the floor of my gut.

"Yup. They weren't there this morning. We're putting together a search team to find them." She shakes her head. "And, uh, seriously, the dungeon could maybe use tighter security."

I would laugh if everything weren't terrible. "Right. Well, congratulations, I guess."

"Ha." She huffs, crossing her arms over her chest. Her translucent wings shimmy and shake at her back, flicking off droplets of rain. "Congratulations? Please. Do I *look* like I want to run this thing?"

"Why'd you say yes, then?" I ask the question around a yawn. Something about talking to Emyr has taken it out of me, leaving me depleted of all my energy. I think about the

days after the riot, not leaving my bed, sleeping constantly.
There is a part of me that wants to go take that nap and just
never wake up.

Small part of me.

Tessa shrugs one delicate shoulder. "Because he's right.
Someone from the outside does have to do it. And it gave
me the authority to issue *my* first order. Your witches will be
back in Asalin by morning."

That manages to perk me up, at least a little. "Jin and the
others?"

"Mmm-hmm. They've all been exonerated." Her green
eyes cut left and right, then she adds, "Whoever it was that
helped *them* escape, I'm sure their heart was in the right place.
Never should've been arrested to begin with, really."

"Right…" The kingdom is going to look very different
from here on out. Emyr on the Throne. Tessa heading up the
Guard. We've ushered in a new era.

It's just not one I'm going to be part of.

"So," I say, instead of cutting out my own heart the way I
sort of feel like doing. "You think you'll keep the job, then?"

"I don't know, Wyatt. I just—" She *sighs*, the sound rolling like a wave through her whole body. "Is this even a job
that should exist?"

"What do you mean?" I want to keep up with her, want
to be present. But everything feels simultaneously like too
much and nothing at all. Head full, but still somehow absolutely no thoughts.

"I mean…yeah, maybe I'm one of the good guys. But the
Guard has spent so long terrorizing people. Targeting people.
Lying and manipulating and twisting the system to their ad-

vantage. Maybe we don't need a good person taking control. Maybe we just don't need the Guard at all."

What would Asalin look like without the Guard? It's hard for me to imagine. My first thought is that there wouldn't be anyone to protect us.

My second is that the Guard has never protected me a day in my life.

When I don't say anything, Tessa pushes on. "And I love Emyr. I do. I think he's going to be great as king. But... I don't know. Don't you think the whole concept of a monarchy is a little outdated? I'm just thinking out loud. I don't know. We're changing the systems. And that's great. But maybe the systems don't need to be changed."

"Maybe we need to burn them to the ground."

I stare at her and she stares back, and after a long moment, she says quietly, "Yeah. Maybe so."

Someone calls her name, and she twists her head and nods.

"You gotta go," I say before she can tell me goodbye.

"Yeah. Duty calls." Another eye roll. "But hey, I'm gonna find you later. I wanna hear about what happened with Emyr, okay?"

I'm not going to agree to talk about it, because I don't know if that's an agreement I can keep. Instead, I grumble and wave her off, then enter the castle as she heads off to talk to one of her subordinates.

Things seem quiet inside. Too quiet for a kingdom that was just overhauled over the span of a few days. Too quiet for a kingdom whose most wanted prisoners are now on the loose.

Kadri is in the foyer, standing before the window overlooking the front lawns, leaning against her cane. Her energy is dragging, sweeping toward the ground. But when the front doors close behind me and her eyes shift in my direction, it snaps back to attention. Gray smoke furiously bubbles at her shoulders.

"You have a great deal of nerve being anywhere near me right now, Wyatt Croft."

"I never planned to hurt Emyr."

"Only to aid a traitor in stealing the Throne."

Right, well. She does have a point.

I'm going to forgive myself, I think. Eventually, someday, I'm going to have to learn how to slot the pieces of my heart back together and forgive myself for everything I've done. I'm going to have to let go of the anger I've been holding on to, the idea of the life I could've had that I destroyed. Twice. Because I have to. If I want to survive, I have to.

But Kadri is Emyr's *mother*. I don't expect her to show me that same grace.

After a pause, she asks, "Have you been to see Emyr?"

"Yeah."

"How does he seem?"

Heartbroken. Betrayed. Quietly furious. I shrug. "Okay, I guess."

She nods, her fingers gliding against the head of her cane, sharp eyes studying me still. Finally, she says, "It changes a person."

"What does?"

"Rising from the dead." Something like fear hides in the even timbre of her voice.

I remember, with a jolt, what Emyr said about his mother.

She was brought back to life with Healing magic. And now it's not working. It can't keep her here much longer.

She may simply slip away, unable to ever be revived again.

How long until Emyr slips away? How long can my magic, this magic I don't even understand, keep him here? How many years? How many days?

"One cannot undo death, not really. It is a specter that lingers forever once it touches a soul. Especially when one's death was not an accident."

I want to ask her if she really can't remember what happened the night she plummeted from the tower. When she lost her life. But I can't seem to make my mouth form the question.

"My son will never be the same again," Kadri tells me before turning and walking away, leaving me in the foyer with nothing but my racing thoughts and my grief.

CHAPTER TWENTY-EIGHT

THE FOOL

"Do you really have to go?" Jin whimpers the words.

I look up from packing my duffel bag, but quickly realize they're probably talking to Briar. Jin's sitting at the vanity in our room with Briar behind them, twisting little stems of baby's breath into their short, dark hair.

They landed in Asalin a few hours ago, and Briar took on the role of breaking the news about Clarke to them. They haven't left her side since. Right now, yellow and purple dance against each other until their edges turn into one vibrant shade of peach.

"I really do. But we'll keep in touch. And maybe I'll be back to visit."

Tears well in Jin's dark eyes, and they tilt their head forward, pressing it against the vanity top, big shoulders trembling. "I've had a very bad day. I wish you would stay."

Briar looks at me. I look back. What am I supposed to say? What's done is done.

"This is *your* fault," Jin mumbles, shooting me a glower that lacks any real heat. "You and Emyr need to figure your shit out."

"We've figured our shit out." I shrug. "Just because we love each other doesn't mean we fit. We need different things."

"And what you need is to run away again? *Really?*" They sniff. "At least neither of you is an attempted murderer. You just need to stop being such complete dipshits. No relationship is perfect."

"I think when people say that, they usually mean one person prefers Italian and the other would rather eat sushi. Not one person tried to coerce someone into an unwanted marriage and the other planned to help their archnemesis steal their crown."

Jin rolls their eyes, energy buzzing a little brighter as they sit up to argue with me. "First of all, what kind of person prefers Italian over sushi? Ew. Dump them. Second of all, that is not what people mean when they say that. And honestly, you both screwed up so fantastically that you might actually be perfect for each other."

I shrug. I don't know what to say. Briar and I are leaving for the airport in an hour. It feels like my future's been sealed. At least the next few hours of it.

Jin stares at themself in the mirror, watching Briar's hands work their way through their hair. "Really, everyone makes mistakes. That doesn't mean they're bad people."

I stare at them for a long moment. I don't ask if they think Clarke is a bad person for what she did. I'm worried I might not like the answer. Stockholm syndrome is a hell of a drug.

"Okay, all done," Briar says quietly, stepping back to observe her work on Jin's hair. She smiles, stroking her fingertips against their shoulders. "Can we go say goodbye to Auriga and Summanus before I have to leave?"

"For you, anything." Jin stands, leveling me with a hard look. "You *will* come back and visit, won't you?"

"Sure," I mumble, a halfhearted response, but before the two of them slip out the door, I add, "Hey, Jin?"

"Mmm?"

"You've heard the stories about what I did, right? The way my magic came off me? How it killed that fae the night of the riots and brought Emyr back?"

They nod.

"Do you have any idea how I did that?"

Jin frowns. "You don't have any control of your magic, Wyatt. It did what it needed to do, however it could do it."

"Well, do you…" I run my tongue against my fangs, twist my hands together in front of my belly. "Do you think, when I come back to visit, you could help me control it?"

To be able to do that on command. To wield that kind of power, and actually know what I'm doing the whole time. It terrifies and excites me.

They stare at me and don't say anything.

I continue. "I just don't, uh. I don't know anything about it. How it works. How I can do the things I do. How to, uh, *not* do some of the things I can do. And Lavender was going to teach me, before…" I don't finish that thought. We both know what happened, why Lavender never had a chance to teach me. "Do you think you could help me learn?"

"Of course." They rest one big palm against the doorway, eyes narrowing slightly. "But do you really not know where it comes from? Do you not know *why* you can do what you do?"

I blink. No. How would I? Everything there is to know about the witches has been hidden from me my entire life.

When I don't say anything, Jin continues. "Fae draw their power from the earth around them. Witches draw our power from what we *feel*. Every emotion in your body. Your magic is a manifestation of them. The fire burns out of control, the darkness drowns you, because you were never given the chance to learn how to channel those feelings. Your magic's just eating you up, breaking out in whatever way it can whenever you feel too much to keep it in any longer."

It's such an obvious thing and it still somehow manages to knock the wind out of me.

The memory of Briar's energy from the night Emyr died burns in my mind. The way her body pressed against mine and her energy crawled beneath my skin and latched on to me from the inside. It was only after that that I managed to bring him back. Magicked healing. Human love. And my desperately clinging to both of them, like a bridge between two worlds.

Briar once told me my darkness was a form of protection. I needed to protect the people I loved. And apparently I had the ability to do it. Because that darkness rose up and out of my body only when my people were in danger, only when I had to save them.

Of course, there's also the fire. The flames constantly burning beneath the surface of my skin, fueled by anger. There are things that don't need protecting, that *need* to be burned to the ground, and I'm more than happy to set them ablaze when the situation calls for it.

But isn't anger another part of love? Isn't it just the heart's way of letting you know a better world is possible?

"Wait!" I call out when Jin and Briar turn to leave again, apparently taking my silence as a dismissal. When Jin meets my eye for the second time, the words come tumbling out of me. "If our power comes from emotion, wouldn't that mean it's infinite?" A beat passes, heavy in the air between us. "Wouldn't that make us stronger than them?"

Jin tilts their head forward. "Why else would they hate us this much?"

And then the two of them are gone.

Alone in the big room, I'm not sure what to do with myself. There are too many thoughts competing for attention in my head, none of which I want to focus on.

I've written a letter for Emyr, explaining the truth about Briar's family and what happened with the door. It's the coward's way out and I know it. But he doesn't want to talk to me, doesn't want to see me again. And if he changes his mind about that, if he'd like to wring my neck once he finds out the truth, he knows where to find me.

Derek and Clarke are still out there somewhere. God only knows who the rest of their followers are, which fae in the Guard or the Committee ascribe to their screwed-up, genocide-happy beliefs. They aren't going to stop trying to go after Emyr *and* the witches.

And since the witches don't have any political power here,

it's gonna be all on him to make things right. Emyr's looking down a long, gruesome battle, and he's doing it all by himself with no idea who he can or can't trust.

I finish packing, shoving what's left of my things into the duffel bag.

My fingers ghost against my tarot deck. I haven't pulled in a few days. But I'm not sure I should now. No, I probably shouldn't. Do I really want to—

Oh, it would appear I'm already pulling the deck out of my bag.

I slide the cards free from their package. They're a beautiful set, solid matte black without illustrations, just the title and number of each card emblazoned with a gold stamp. The delicate weight of them is familiar on my fingertips. *Shuffle. Shuffle.*

My thoughts stay on Emyr, but they stay on *more* than Emyr. They stay on Asalin. On the other four fae kingdoms, too. The witches and fae living in less than harmony across the globe. The humans living in ignorance of their very existence. Faery, and what might be coming for us through that door.

All of that is weighing on me when I flip the card over.

I can't help but smirk.

The Fool.

New possibilities. Starting over. Naive optimism.

For once, I consciously agree to let love guide me. And I already know what I have to do.

My boots bang against the marble tile as I race through the hallway toward the Throne room, the sound echoing off the castle walls. I pass Roman, Lorena, and Solomon gathered together with Tessa, and my sister calls out to my back, but I ignore her.

By the time I reach the king's private wing at the center of the palace, Wade is leaving the bedroom. He frowns at me, blinking like he isn't sure he's really seeing me.

He looks rough. Dark circles under his eyes, hair disheveled and hanging limply around his neck. He swallows. "Thank you."

"For what?"

"For bringing him back." Are those tears in Wade's eyes? "If he'd died because I hesitated to turn Clarke in...if I'd lost him, I never would have forgiven myself." He sniffs. "I'm still not sure he's ever going to forgive me."

He doesn't wait for my answer, just heads off down the hall, heels clicking quietly beneath him.

I feel bad for the guy, I do. Guilt is a horrible thing to carry around.

But I also have more important things to deal with right now than Wade's feelings.

"You need better security," I inform Emyr's back when I step into his bedroom.

The king's suite is bigger than his old one, but nearly as bare. The biggest bed I've ever seen sits in the center, adorned with black silk sheets. There are two golden wardrobes and no windows. He's standing in front of one, and he turns his head over his shoulder to look at me when he hears my voice.

A beat passes before he looks back at his clothes. "There is spellwork in place. It prevents anyone with ill intent from entering."

"So, I really am pure of heart and dumb of ass, huh?"

He says nothing.

"Where did your parents go? You kick them out already?"

"My mother and father have retired to another suite, which should be of little concern to you."

I move over to his bed and sit down on the edge, watching his profile. "Hey, Emyr?"

"What, Wyatt?"

"Do you remember when you asked me if I would have brought you with me when I ran away?"

He pauses, for the briefest moment, before continuing his work. He doesn't look at me. "Yes."

"I would have." I lick my lower lip, grazing it with my teeth. "Oh, and, hey, Emyr?"

"What, Wyatt?" He sounds so tired.

"Do you really want to be king?"

"For crying out loud." He slams the wardrobe shut, reaches up to snatch a hand through his curls. "We can't do this again. You know I don't have a choice. I've let you go. Why do you insist on torturing me?"

"I've hardly begun torturing you," I answer with a huff. "And anyway, I didn't ask if you really *had* to be king. I asked if you really *wanted* to."

He grinds his molars together, facing me with a glower. "Someone has to do it."

"But do they, though?"

He blinks at me, the glare receding slowly, bleeding from the sharp lines of his face. "What—what do you mean?"

There is no eating an apple from a poisoned tree without getting sick.

"You want to reform this place. You want to make it *better* for *everyone*. And I know your heart is in the right place. But, Emyr…" I lick my lower lip, pushing myself to my feet to move up to him. "How do you reform something that's rotten from the foundation up? How do you fix a system using the same broken tools?"

He tilts his head down to watch my face as I creep closer. His golden energy washes out like a wave, licking at my skin. I can't help but sigh.

"What are you suggesting the alternative is?"

"Revolution, baby." I press my palm against his chest, leaning my head back to meet his eyes. "Sometimes things have to burn so new things can be built in their place."

"You and your fire metaphors," he mumbles.

"To be fair, it's not a metaphor if I intend to actually torch the place for good next time." It's a joke but it isn't, and neither of us laugh. My fingers make circles in the fabric of his shirt.

His gaze runs the length of my nose, over the new scars on my cheeks and jawline. "What might that look like?"

"Huh. I'm not sure yet. I am just one very small person with very few thoughts in my head. But no one does anything alone. You and me. Jin and the witches. Tessa and Wade. Briar. We can figure something out." I take a deep breath. "There is a world where you can have everything you want, Emyr. No more being split in half. We just have to fight for it."

"And we're fighting together?" I notice the tremble tucked at the back of his throat.

"We're fighting together. Fighting for a better future for witches, and fae, and humans. Fighting for them, and for us." I thump my hand against his chest. "Not as contractually bound fiancés. Not as two people backed into corners. But as…something."

"Something," Emyr repeats. His heart beats faster under my palm. His throat bobs.

I grin, flashing fangs. "Are you ready for a fight, Your Highness?"

"Please just kiss me."

"I was hoping you'd say that."

His mouth is warm and familiar, sugar and smoke and the quiet threat of fangs, and how did I ever think I could kiss him once and never again?

All around us, threads of black and gold entwine, filling the bedroom with light and darkness in equal measure.

It feels like a resurrection.

"Oh," I groan, pulling back just a fraction, our lips still dusting together. "One more thing. Briar is part witch, and she opened the door to Faery."

"WHAT?!"

★ ★ ★ ★ ★

ACKNOWLEDGMENTS

It would be a lie to begin this by thanking anyone other than M.J. Beasi. M.J. was the first person to love these characters and this story, the first person to demand I not give up on them or myself. Without their unwavering support through every step of this process, their fierce friendship, and their one-person mission to defeat my impostor syndrome in hand-to-hand combat, this book would not exist. I owe them so much more than I can repay.

I am forever grateful to Rena Rossner for reading this story in one of its earlier, messier forms and recognizing the heart of it. I cannot thank Rena enough for finding me a home at Inkyard Press. There, I've had the pleasure of working with Natashya Wilson, a dream of an editor. So much of what is right about this book is thanks to Natashya meeting eyes with the very soul of my work and sinking her claws in, dragging out its beating heart, and helping me get blood on the pages. It has been an honor to work with someone who truly understands the story I wanted to tell, sometimes better than I did myself. A huge thank-you to Bess Brasswell and the rest of the Inkyard team for always making me feel taken care of and valued, both as an author and as a human being. And infinite thanks to Ryan Garcia, whose artwork on the cover took this book to another level entirely. (Seriously, are y'all seeing this?)

Even if it looks like a battlefield half the time, I am so thankful for queer writer Twitter and the connections I've made there, the constant network of support I've found for my stories throughout the years. There are more names than I can list here, but y'all know who you are. And specifically, I want to shout-out Andrew Joseph White and Alice Scott for the LGBTWIP hashtag that brought so many people together. I am extra grateful to A.J. for offering early feedback on this manuscript that was both merciful and discerning.

Big thanks to the baristas both past and present at Starbucks 8804, who kept me in cold brew and listened to me ramble about magic and gay stuff. They were either genuinely interested or too polite to ask me to shut up. Either way, it was appreciated.

For my family, both blood and found, who have never once doubted me half as much as I've doubted myself. It is a humbling thing to be as loved as I am.

For Alina, my magic charger, who is always finding me right when I need them most.

For Erin, my safe place to land, who has taken my dreams and worked tirelessly to make them our reality.

For Fin, my heart made human, who inspires me every day to write toward a better tomorrow.

And finally, for every single reader fighting for that tomorrow alongside me. For everyone living in the margins who wants to burn it all down and build something new from the ash. This one's for us. Let's get to it.